MW01611566

RICK PARTLOW

EARTH AT WAR

1ST TO FIGHT

PRAMANTHA PUBLISHING
ST. JOHN'S

Cover art by: Tom Edwards (tomedwardsdesign.com)

Cover typography and interior formatting by: Steve Beaulieu (facebook.com/BeaulisticBookServices)

Editing by: Ellen Campbell (nosafewordsllc.com)

Published by Pramantha Publishing

This novel is a work of fiction. All of the characters, places, and events are fictitious. Any resemblance to actual persons living or dead, locales, businesses, or events is entirely coincidental.

Pramantha Publishing

PO Box 1613 ST JOHNS C

St. John's, NL

A1C 5P3

Canada

Library and Archives Canada Cataloguing in Publication

Partlow, Rick

1st to Fight / Rick Partlow ; illustrations by Tom Edwards; cover typography and interior formatting by Steve Beaulieu.

ISBN 978-1-988380-36-0

1ST TO FIGHT

1

I KEEP TRYING TO REMEMBER WHAT I WAS THINKING, strapped into a disintegrating totem pole thirty stories tall, about to ride it through the atmosphere and into orbit. The fact Daniel Gatlin had invited me, a science fiction author, onto the first privately-funded flight around the moon... Well, that was supposed to be the craziest part of that day.

But what was I thinking in that moment, right before the course of human history changed forever? I know I didn't expect any part of what actually happened. The confirmation, finally, that we weren't alone. The realization that the stars were far from peaceful. That the Tevynians wanted to conquer them all, and that it would fall to us to stop them.

Oh. I remember what I was thinking, now. As three times my normal body weight pressed me into the padded acceleration couch and a deafening roar penetrated the plastic and metal of my helmet, all I could think was that this was a huge mistake.

I almost gave into my Baptist upbringing and whispered a prayer as Cape Canaveral fell away beneath us, but I stood fast in the Jeffersonian Deism I'd adopted around the time of my divorce and took the beating of all those merciless gravities of thrust without so much as a whisper at my father's God.

A laugh pealed loud and merry above the roar of the rocket engines. I couldn't tell who over the helmet radio, but I suspected it was Gatlin. Oh well, who could blame him? This was his ticket; the rest of us were just along for the ride. Daniel Gatlin had lapped his competitors in the privatized space industry by sinking into his Gatlin Aerospace venture every penny generated from a life spent taking one business after another from start-up to IPO. I admired the hell out of his determination, but mostly I was just grateful he was taking me along on his trip around the Moon.

Like I said, I hadn't been the first choice. Gatlin had gone live two years ago with the announcement that he'd be personally commanding the *Selenium*'s first Lunar orbit mission and that he'd be taking along a poet to describe the "beauty of deep space travel." The only problem was, he hadn't been able to find a sufficiently famous poet who could pass the physical who wanted to get anywhere near his home-brew space program and when he'd switched from that idea to bringing along a science fiction writer, he'd run into a similar problem with the bigger names. Not that they didn't want to go, but they'd gone to seed. Maybe if he'd put his feelers out ten years ago, he could have had Card or Weir or someone really big, but people get old, and everyone Gatlin had read had fallen into old age and bad health.

Which left me, Andy Clanton, former Marine, still in my early forties, still fairly healthy, and writer of the best-selling science fiction trilogy that had been turned into a hit streaming series on PrimeFlix. Gatlin had never heard of me and he'd made it clear he had no interest in reading my books or watching the show, but he needed someone. At that point, he needed someone soon, while he still had time to get them through the training.

I was single, my son and ex-wife had very little interest in seeing me ever again, and my agent assured me this would guarantee a decade of New York Times best sellers, so I said, what the hell? What kid growing up didn't want to be an astronaut?

I began to change my mind when I first experienced freefall. I'd parachuted before, but there was a qualitative difference when the fall never ended, and being strapped into the confines of the crew capsule with four other people didn't help at all. They were faceless automatons inside their blue and grey pressure suits, their helmets hiding their visages from my position all the way aft in the capsule. I wasn't the lead dog and the view never changed; I couldn't even see the tiny portholes from where I was sitting, strapped in with my knees pulled back just to the point of discomfort.

All I could hear over the headphones was Julie trading cryptic technical messages with ground control. I rightly should have referred to her as Captain Nieves, since she was both the pilot and a Naval Reserve officer, and I was a Marine Reserve officer of considerably lower rank; but she insisted everyone call her Julie. Whatever I called her, I didn't want to interrupt what was probably very important pilot stuff so I stayed quiet until finally, Gatlin turned around in his seat, grinning behind the faceplate of his helmet. He was an odd-looking man, with eyes too close together and a nose that came to a point like a cartoon character's, but he was the closest thing real life had given us to Tony Stark, so I resolved to be respectful.

"We'll dock in about four more hours," he told me. Well, he could have been talking to the mission's medical officer, Dr. Patel, who was seated in front of me, but I was bored enough to assume it was me. "Can you believe it used to take two days for ships to dock with the ISS?"

"The Russians cut it to six hours in 2013," I said, then tried to shrug. It didn't work that well inside a pressure suit, strapped tightly into a seat barely large enough to fit me. "I'm grateful it doesn't take as long anymore, believe me. This is the experience of a lifetime and all that, but it's sort of like falling out of an airplane squeezed into a Smart Car with four of your closest friends. Wearing diapers."

My voice sounded weird trapped inside the helmet, muffled and distant. It was ironic; we were in the vastness of outer space, but everything was small and cramped and incredibly claustrophobic.

"You do know your space history, Mr. Clanton," Gatlin allowed, almost grudgingly. "From the descriptions I read of your television show, I would have thought your interests would be less...technical."

I didn't mean to laugh quite so sharply or bitterly at the remark, but the sound came out of its own accord, built up over years of acrimony and infighting.

"Sir, believe me, no one is more disappointed in the technical errors on the show than I am, but once you sign the contracts, the studio pretty much has you by the balls."

"Let's watch our language back there," Julie said archly and I felt a sudden rush of heat to my ears. I'd forgotten this would be streaming live to the whole world.

"Sorry," I said quickly.

"Oh, Jeez, Andy, I'm just yankin' your chain." She laughed, a loud and raucous sound for so small a woman.

"I'm a preacher's kid," I said defensively. "Old habits die hard."

"What would your pop say if he could see you now?"

Good question. Dad died three years ago, before I'd hit it big...well, as big as an indie writer is likely to hit it. He always thought I was wasting my time "writing that nonsense," and I should get a real job with a future. He'd always been disappointed I didn't follow in his footsteps and go to the seminary. She didn't need to hear that, though, and neither did the rest of the world. This was a high-tech book promotion, after all.

"He'd probably say I should stop running my mouth and enjoy the ride."

We were in the construction shack when we heard the news. Everyone on Earth probably remembers where they were when they heard it, but we were the only ones *off* Earth at the time, so none of us could ever forget. The shack wasn't anything to write home about, just a discarded fuel tank from an earlier NASA Orion shot Gatlin had bought on the cheap and converted to a cut-rate orbital station. It had served as quarters for the crews working on the *Selenium* these last eighteen months. There wasn't much left of it now but an empty, insulated shell and a pair of airlocks.

And space. Plenty of space. Julie and Dr. Patel started doing zero-g acrobatics almost immediately but I'd just been happy to have walls more than a few centimeters away from me. I let myself spin around in the empty open space at the center of the shack but didn't try anything tricky. This was being streamed as well; I could see the different views from the various cameras in one of the huge flat screen monitors affixed to the...wall? Bulkhead? Did they call it a bulkhead on a space station?

"Don't look stupid," my agent had said. Easier said than done.

Gatlin wasn't bothering with the first-timer playground shit; he'd been here before. He was anchored via a tether to the communications console beneath the monitors, and at first, I thought he was checking the external cameras to get a view of the

Selenium. I'd seen it already on our approach. For people who grew up on science fiction movies, it wasn't much, just a crew capsule a bit larger than the one we'd flown up on, mated to a booster rocket that was most of its mass. Still, it was the most impressive thing humans had put into space since Apollo, so who was I to complain? We'd be transferring to the ship in a few hours for the three-day round trip and I hoped there was a more dignified setup for using the bathroom than a damn diaper.

"Julie!" he snapped, not looking up from the video screen. "Get over here, now!"

That was uncharacteristic. Gatlin was consistently upbeat and polite, except for the occasional tweet when he was feeling political. He was a man who didn't have to be reminded the cameras were on him. I pushed away from the bulkhead and floated over just behind Julie, trying to ignore the flip-flop, "oh Jesus, I'm falling!" feeling in my gut.

"What is it, Mr. G?" Julie asked, grabbing the industrialist's shoulder to steady herself.

He didn't answer. He didn't have to. We could all see it on the screen, hear it over the speakers. It was a news report, from his network of choice but I doubt it would have made much difference for this report: it was straight from the White House, from the President himself. Gatlin wasn't even scowling, even though he and President Crenshaw had never gotten along that well.

"I liked him better before he got the bionic eye," Julie murmured. "He looks less piratical now."

Gatlin shushed her urgently.

"...need to reiterate," Crenshaw was saying, making a quelling motion, "there have been no threats, no signs of hostile intent, no communication at all. The..." He seemed to be struggling to find a word. "...the *object* simply appeared in cislunar space, that is, in an orbit around the Earth's Moon. There were telescopes pointed that direction and none of their observations spotted its approach. We have ascertained from telescopic views that it is not of natural origin."

The gathered media erupted at that until the Press Secretary quieted them.

"I am not going to speculate as to who built it or their possible intent," the President declared. "Not now nor in any follow-up questions. We have made attempts at communication and there's been no discernable reply. What we need to do now is to confer with the other nations of the world as to how we wish to proceed, how we wish to greet what may be the first visitors from another star." He gave the camera the earnest stare that got him elected. "This is perhaps the greatest opportunity humanity has ever been presented with. We are not going to act unilaterally. Thank you very much, and God bless America." A dramatic pause. "God bless us all."

"What. The. Fuck." The words slipped out before I could stop them, but no one complained, not even the publicity-conscious Gatlin.

"They showed it after the press conference," was all he said, fast-forwarding through the recording to a shot taken by one of the space telescopes and cleaned up with software enhancement. "This all happened shortly after we took off," he added.

The...thing, the object, was vaguely wedge-shaped and more than anything else it reminded me of the bad guy's star destroyers in the Star Wars movies, but not quite so bumpy and there was no water-navy-style bridge sticking out of the upper hull. It was smooth and shiny, reflective to the point of being blinding. There was no perspective to give it scale, but a graphic appeared to give us an idea of its size. The graphic was of the Burj Khalifa in Dubai, and this object dwarfed it, at least three times as long and maybe half as wide as its length at the base of the thing. At the base of the *starship*. The *alien* starship.

"Mother of God," Patel whispered from behind me. A Christian Indian, I presumed.

"Shame we didn't bring a physicist along," Julie said, still casually snarky despite everything. I wanted to be, wanted to be cool and funny and blasé, as if I'd expected this to happen, but this was...

"This changes everything," I said, a hack writer lacking the talent to think of anything more momentous. Suddenly our little trip around the Moon seemed pitiful.

"Do you think he meant it?" Julie wondered. I mirrored Gatlin's questioning look in response, and she clarified. "The President. Do you think we're really going to confer with all the other nations and decide what to do?"

As if in reply, two things happened almost simultaneously: the monitor showing the livestream from the station cameras went black and the Skype alert started to ring. Daniel Gatlin ran a hand through his salt-and-pepper beard and shared a rueful smile with us before he hit the touchscreen control to answer the call.

"I think we're about to find out."

The face on the screen was familiar. I'd seen it in press conferences and news reports as well as in countless memes on social media, but I wasn't laughing now.

"Mr. Gatlin." General Arlan Lee Smith, head of the US Space Force nodded politely. His south Texas accent and affable attitude had been fodder for comedians for the past two years, but everything I heard from my buddies still in the military was that he was competent and not at all a man to be taken lightly. "Congratulations on your successful launch. I trust you've heard the news, even up there?"

"What do you want from me, Arlan?" Gatlin demanded, not even bothering with curiosity or annoyance, just moving straight to anger. "Or should I ask, what does Crenshaw want from me?"

"An Orion capsule is launching from Vandenberg as we speak," Smith told him, seemingly unaffected by the multibillionaire's attitude. "It's going to dock with your construction shack, so you need to cut loose your re-entry module and make a space for them."

"Why the hell would I want to do that, Arlan? Won't I need the re-entry capsule to, you know, *re-enter*?"

"You'll be taking the Orion back down, Mr. Gatlin," Smith explained patiently, "while our crew takes possession of the *Selenium* and uses it to rendezvous with the alien spacecraft." He shrugged. "We'll re-launch the Orion if needed to retrieve our people."

"Do you have any concept of how much it cost to build the *Selenium*, General?" I thought I could actually see bits of Gatlin's teeth grinding off, so tightly were they clenched. "*My* money, my stockholders, my investors, *their* money?"

"Don't be naïve, Daniel," Smith snapped, finally losing patience with Gatlin's tantrum. "You'll be compensated, and not just monetarily." His smile was shrewd and not at all friendly, stretching his jowly face like the parting jaws of a snake. "Think of the technology sharing implications of this. *Someone* is going to be at the forefront of reverse engineering. Would you rather it be you, or your competitors?"

"So," I jumped in, just too much of a busybody to keep my damned mouth shut, "all that talk about international cooperation was so much bullshit?"

"On the contrary, Captain Clanton," Smith corrected me, probably trying to intimidate me with the idea he knew exactly who I was. And it worked. "We meant it... right up until the moment our intelligence sources told us the Russians were prepping a Soyuz for launch to do pretty much the same thing. Although I don't think they'll be as openminded about remuneration for your ship, Daniel."

"Since I doubt I have any real choice in the matter," Gatlin spat the words out, "what do you suggest I do about the Russians when they arrive?"

"They'll be three hours behind our Orion. If I were you, I'd hop into the capsule and be gone before they get there."

2

They fucked it up, of course. This is the government we're talking about.

We were all back in our suits, helmets on just as a precaution, when the Orion docked. Julie was talking them in over the tight-beam secure laser comms, on video with some bland-looking Space Force colonel named Michael Olivera. Listening to him drone on about approach vectors and riding the beam and the specs for the docking collar, I idly wondered if the Space Force had anyone on the payroll under the rank of colonel. I couldn't remember ever seeing anyone on the news who wasn't a colonel or a general.

What the hell did they call an E-1 in the Space Force anyway? Spaceman? No, that would be sexist. Maybe Spacer? No, that sounded like a part from an Ikea dresser. I should have known; I write science fiction, after all. I could ask Colonel Olivera once he got on board, but I didn't think I'd have time. Even talking to Julie on the comms, he sounded eager for us to be back on Earth.

I would have been angrier about the whole deal if it weren't for the aliens. Well, the ship anyway. There was no guarantee there were any aliens aboard. They might have sent robots. Hell, they might *be* robots, might be some big web of artificial intelligences looking to come make peace with our cell phones. Either way, being in space when the aliens came was going to sell a shitload more books than me circling the fucking moon. The next book I wrote that got optioned, PrimeFlix could kiss my ass, I was going straight to the damn House of Mouse.

"I really wanted to see the Moon close up," Dr. Patel lamented, less phlegmatic about the whole thing. His long, horsey face was even longer than usual and if we'd had gravity, I was sure his shoulders would have been slumped. "It would have made history, you know?"

"*This* is history, doc," I said, gesturing at the bulkhead to indicate what was happening. "Just being up here will get your name in the history books."

"Unless they kill us all," Julie pointed out. I assumed she'd muted Captain Cosmos of the Space Force, unless she just didn't care if he heard or not.

"If they wanted to kill us," Gatlin pointed out reasonably, "there are much more practical ways to go about it than flying their starship into Lunar orbit and shooting us with their death rays." He waved a hand in my direction. "All apologies to your wonderfully fanciful stories, Mr. Clanton."

"No, you're right, sir," I agreed readily. "Anyone who can get here from another star system could just set Ceres or Pallas heading straight for Earth and wipe us all out. There'd be nothing we could do about it at our current level of technology."

"Or they could infect us with a genetically engineered plague," Patel suggested, seeming quite cheerful about the proposition.

"Or that," I conceded. "If they're here, it's because they want to talk."

"Doesn't necessarily mean we'll like what they have to say," Julie murmured, then went back to guiding the Orion capsule in.

"There'll probably be a lot of people who won't like what they have to say," I ventured, leaning over her shoulder to see the latest from the news networks. Among the breaking stories scrolling across the bottom of the screen was the loss of the signal from *us*, which was the handiwork of the US government. "Starting with a bunch of churches, mosques, synagogues, temples, etc...."

"Oh, I don't know," Patel said. "The Catholic church has been fairly openminded about the possibility of intelligent aliens."

"It's easy to be openminded until you're staring a bug-eyed monster in the face."

"Orion, you're on the beam but you're coming in hot." Julie wasn't yelling, but in the few weeks I'd known her, I'd become used to her unflappable attitude, and she was...well, flapped. It caught my attention where volume might not have. "I repeat, you're coming in too hot, hit braking thrusters now."

I didn't know what to expect when the Orion mated with the shack's docking collar, but the resonant boom thundering through the hull of the construction shack was *not* it. There was yelling on the comm channel, yelling inside my helmet that I'm pretty sure was me, and those of us who hadn't anchored themselves to a handhold on the bulkhead were sent floating across the width of the station.

Luckily for my agent, we weren't livestreaming, because I was fairly certain I looked stupid tumbling head over heels backwards, arms windmilling until I fetched up against the opposite bulkhead hard enough to drive the air out of me. Julie was still cursing, but over her imaginative anatomical suggestions for the crew of the Orion, I could hear a persistent buzzing, and I saw an ominous red light flashing above the airlock.

"Keep your fucking helmets on," Julie said, as if any of us had other plans. "We're venting atmosphere; hull's breached."

Yeah, I could see bits of debris the construction crew had left behind on the last mission, food wrappers, a plastic spoon, a crumpled checklist spiraling toward the lock, toward what had to be a ruptured seam. Gatlin was moving with desperate urgency, ripping open a locker built into the bulkhead beside the airlock and pulling out something very much like a caulking gun. In retrospect, it probably *was* a caulking gun, because what he did with it was what I remembered my dad doing with a caulking gun under those mysterious circumstances where you use one of them. I, personally, have always been willing to hire someone to do that shit for me, so I had never actually owned one and sure wouldn't have known how to use one to seal a leak.

Whatever he was doing, I assumed it was enough, because Julie didn't offer to help him. She'd abandoned the one-sided yelling "conversation" with the Orion and pushed over to the airlock, grabbing the locking lever and setting a foot against a chock mounted on the bulkhead to give herself the fulcrum to yank upward then pull inward. My eyes went wide for a second and I opened my mouth to object, thinking she might be opening the hatch too soon, but I shut it just as quick, wishing I could kick myself. If there was a vacuum on the other side of the hatch, she wouldn't be able to open it all.

You could tell by the spacesuits these guys were government. Gatlin's suits were a cool, streamlined blue, the product of a professional fashion designer working with an engineer. The GI suits were bulky and clunky, and day-glow orange like they were about to go deer hunting in the Great Orbital Forest. The first one through was the Space Force colonel, Olivera, and he was shorter than I'd imagined, too narrow and wiry for his square-jawed face, like one of the Mercury 7 astronauts. Behind him was a woman, and by her wide eyes and look of total incomprehension, I judged she was a civilian, and one who'd never been to space before. The name tape across the right breast of her suit read "Shaddick, C." and I was guessing she was a research scientist of one type or another.

"Is everything okay?" she was asking on an open channel, the microsecond delay between the transmission in my earphones and her mouth moving in the clear faceplate of her helmet making it seem like a badly-dubbed foreign film. "Did we break it?"

"Inside please, Dr. Shaddick," Olivera snapped, guiding her out of the docking umbilical to make way for the next crewmember.

This guy...this guy I knew. And he wasn't Space Force and he wasn't a scientist.

"Jambo," I said, half in horror, half in disbelief.

"Hey Clanton," the bearded man grinned, squeezing his broad shoulders through the too-narrow passageway. "We run into each other in the strangest fuckin' places, don't we?"

James Bowie. Master Sergeant the last time I'd run into him in Venezuela, God alone knew what rank he was now. Special Operations Detachment Delta, or Combat Applications Group, or "the Unit," or whatever the hell name they called themselves this week didn't exactly advertise their ranks. Jambo was one hell of a soldier and not a bad guy; my horror came from the realization they'd brought a Delta operator along for a first-contact situation.

The last one through was a bureaucrat. There was no two ways about it, she just had that look. Too much confidence for someone in this situation was the first clue. The second was when she opened her mouth.

"Colonel Olivera," she said in a commanding tone, "we need these people off the station immediately."

Her face was pinched, not by nature but rather by the expression subletting it on a semi-permanent basis. That was how I knew she wasn't a politician: no one had ever gotten elected wearing that face.

"We're not going anywhere in your capsule, lady," Julie told her, head sticking through the docking umbilical, legs dangling out through the airlock. "Whoever the hell was driving this bitch shouldn't have been let out of command school without a refresher course in docking."

"It was piloted remotely," Colonel Olivera told her, sounding a bit put out, perhaps partly because he wished his commanders had let him fly the docking maneuver himself. "They did the best they could."

"Well, they fucked up." She pushed back out into the station and jerked a thumb towards the Orion. "When you hit the damn docking umbilical, you jammed the mechanism open. Your airlock won't be able to close without a repair."

"Colonel," the bureaucrat said, "can you check that?"

"No, I can't, Ms. Strawbridge," he said. "I'm a pilot, not an engineer or a technician, and you didn't seem inclined to bring one along with us, despite my recommendations."

"It doesn't matter," Strawbridge insisted, and I had the sense she'd be pouting with her hands on her hips if there'd been gravity. "They'll simply stay on board the station."

"Whoa, whoa, whoa!" Gatlin said, floating up to grab a handhold next to the lock. "There's no way in hell! How do you think we're going to survive in here until the damned airlock is repaired?"

"I told you the Soyuz capsule is heading this way..." Olivera began.

"Even assuming they'll help," Julie interrupted him, "which they have no reason to, by the way, where do you think we're going to ride? A Soyuz carries a maximum of eight crew. There's four of us. Do you want to assume they only brought four like you did—which was damned stupid, by the way? You're going to bet our lives on that without even *asking* the fucking Russians? 'Cause I'm not."

"Neither am I," Gatlin declared with a tone of finality. "And I very much doubt you're going to be able to access the *Selenium's* systems without my personal passcodes."

There was what must have been an epic staredown between the two of them, but I couldn't see shit because of the glare of the lights off their helmet faceplates. I assumed Gatlin had the better stare because Olivera finally sighed in surrender.

"Ms. Strawbridge," the Colonel said, "we need to make a call."

3

"My goodness," Patel said for probably the fiftieth time since we'd boarded the *Selenium*. "I wonder what they'll look like."

This time I decided to indulge him, mostly because the *Selenium* had proven to be a bit of a letdown. Oh, it was more comfortable than the Gatlin Aerospace Wyvern crew capsule we'd come up in, roomy enough to have its own little space-toilet, but all I cared about at the moment was getting to that alien ship.

"It's not robots," I told him, pushing against my safety restraints to try to get a glimpse through the tiny front view ports around Delia Strawbridge's fat head and bun hairdo. "I mean, not like Voyager or any of our automated probes."

"How can you be so sure?" Jambo asked me. Neither Strawbridge nor Olivera had much to say to any of us once we boarded the ship, and Shaddick had volunteered she was an expert in exobiology before Strawbridge stared her into silence, but Jambo had proven as garrulous as I remembered him and tickled pink just to be here.

"If they were robots," I reasoned, "they wouldn't bother with the theater of all this." I waved a hand at the image of the ship on the display above the pilot's console. "They'd just send something small, something that could make radio contact with us." I shook my head. "No, this thing, just appearing in space right next to us with no warning? Gotta be some sort of intelligence. Maybe a machine intelligence, but something that wants a conversation."

"You don't need to worry about the conversation," Strawbridge snapped, finally deigning to address any of us, "because you won't be part of it."

"You've been in contact with them," Gatlin said, "haven't you? It's the only thing that makes sense."

No response, though I noticed Strawbridge sharing an uncomfortable glance with Olivera.

"Of course they have," Julie agreed. She'd said about as much as the government types, just as annoyed to have been pushed out of the command chair by Olivera as he and Strawbridge were at the President's orders to take us along. "I bet the Russians and Chinese have, too."

"That what you think, Andy?" Jambo asked me. He had this look, a look you wouldn't notice if you hadn't lifted weights and played video games in the same FOB with the guy for months. He was telling me they were right without telling me.

"I think they told you the first one to reach them gets the goodies," I ventured. "They must have been watching us, they know we're fractured into power blocs. They wouldn't care who's the most technologically advanced because they'd be offering us stuff that would make what we have look like rocks and twigs. They want to see who has the old can do spirit."

Olivera's eyes flickered toward me, just an involuntary tick, but enough. The Colonel would have made a bad poker player.

"Oh Jesus," Gatlin moaned, rubbing a hand across his face. "And no one back in Washington or Moscow or Beijing ever wondered why aliens would be so interested in who was the most ruthless and efficient?"

"Don't you guys ever *read* any of my books?" I asked, shaking my head in wonder. "Because the ones that start like this never end well."

"What would you suggest we do?" Olivera asked me. Strawbridge tried to shush him, but he waved her off. "Oh, please, who's he going to tell that won't find out soon anyway?" Back to me, his pale face reddening around the edges. "When the aliens pop into existence out of nowhere, out of hyperspace or whatever you call it in your novels, and tell you to drop by for a chat, what do you do? Ignore them? Count on international cooperation?"

"I write science fiction," I said, sniffing at the thought, "not fantasy."

Jambo sniggered. "If the Russkis needed us, that'd be different. They'd be fallin' all over themselves to get a place at the table. But they knew they could here have it all to themselves."

"That's why we couldn't wait for an engineer, or a physicist," Olivera confirmed. "We went with what we had or could get in an hour, because the Soyuz capsule was already being prepped for launch. As it was, that Orion skipped nearly all the normal safety protocols to get it into orbit first."

"I think you're right, Mr. Clanton."

It took me a second to realize who had spoken because she was strapped into a seat behind me and to my left, and because she hadn't said a word since being dressed down by Strawbridge. Dr. Shaddick was somewhere in her forties if I was any judge, with shoulder length brown hair and the sort of nearly-green shade to her face I used to see shipboard when I was in the Corps. Spacesick this time instead of seasick, though.

"I'm right about so much," I told her. "Could you be more specific?"

"They won't have sent robots," she clarified. "I think they're biological. Sentient machines wouldn't even bother doing the research and investing the resources it must have taken to develop a method of faster than light travel. Time would mean nothing to a computer intelligence because it couldn't die, and it wouldn't need to worry about the resources needed to send a ship on a slower than light voyage to the stars."

I frowned. She was right, and it bothered me because I hadn't thought of it first.

"I'd guess they're very much like us," she went on, winding up for a classroom lecture. "Probably evolved on a terrestrial world, likely with an oxygen-nitrogen atmosphere."

I felt the need to show off. "You're thinking that because they were able to figure out our language," I said. "Because they understood we used modulated sounds to communicate."

"Check out the brain on Andy," Jambo murmured. His words were a bit distorted in a very familiar way and my eyes went wide.

"Jambo, did you seriously manage to sneak a chew into *space*?"

"It helps to keep me calm." He smiled around a disgusting mouthful of chewing tobacco.

"You better get rid of that shit before you put your helmet back on, soldier," Julie warned him. "And by the way, we did our last boost five hours ago. Shouldn't we be flipping around and starting our deceleration burn by now?"

I tried to get a look over Olivera's shoulder at the Lidar readings, still couldn't see past Strawbridge.

"We've been assured it won't be necessary," Olivera told her. I got the impression from his tone exactly how much he thought of the assurance, but the Colonel was a good little spaceman and followed orders.

"Assured by who..." I started to ask, then trailed off, realizing the only possible answer. I began to entertain the possibility we were all going to die, not from any malevolence but just on the chance the ETs might not know little details about the human body, like how many gees we could take without being squashed flat.

The alien ship was growing alarmingly large in the view screen hooked to the external cameras, and I wondered how much the view was magnified. I really wished I had a better seat; this felt too much like watching the whole thing on TV.

"I think we should hit the braking boost...," Julie said, tensing against her restraints as if she were about to launch herself at the controls. Colonel Olivera wasn't paying attention to either her suggestion or her behavior; his eyes were fixed either on the ports or the instrument panels.

"We *are* decelerating," Olivera declared, wonder in his voice. "At something like fifty gravities."

The velocity readout on the overhead screen confirmed his words, counting down like the bomb timer in an action movie and even a dumb Marine like me knew it was entirely impossible.

"I don't feel a damned thing!" Julie exclaimed.

I didn't waste time on words, just hit the quick release for my safety harness and kicked forward, beating Gatlin to the move by barely a second. We both ignored the outraged squawking from Strawbridge and Olivera, hanging above them, oriented the other way over their acceleration couches to get a better view out the ports.

The ship was so close it seemed unreal, a mountain of metal hanging from nothing, outshining the Moon with silvery glory. The metal was smooth even up close, with no visible break or striation, though it seemed to be covered in gently curved, elongated ovoid bumps over the entire surface.

"I don't see any visible effects of whatever they're doing to us," I said, able to tell by our approach that we were still decelerating. "But I guess I wouldn't."

"I wonder if it's electromagnetic or gravitational," Gatlin mused, fingers stroking the window as if he could reach out and touch the starship.

"You can ask them when we get there," I said, nodding toward what seemed to be the bow of the ship, though that could have been my earthbound prejudice—the narrower end, anyway. A whole section of the hull was sliding aside, and my mind boggled when I realized how huge the opening had to be given the size of the ship.

"Neither of you is asking them anything," Strawbridge reminded us. You could see her irritation level rising like the damage meter on a video game boss. "All four of you are staying in this ship."

"Yes, Mother," Julie said, *sotto voce.*

I ignored them both; the opening in the side of the alien ship was dark and yawning and getting closer. I'd felt fear many times in my life: the first time I'd been shot at, when my son had trouble breathing just after birth, when my wife had taken him and left during my fourth deployment and I'd come home to an empty house, when the Osprey I was flying in had been hit by antiaircraft fire. All of them had their own, unique quality, a special taste and smell to the moment. This one was a giant, empty pit in the stomach, the sensation you get when you're driving in your car and you know you're going to be in an accident but there's nowhere to go and nothing to do and all that's left is gritting your teeth and waiting for the impact.

We were inside. The transition had been quick, so abrupt I nearly blinked and missed it. The darkness was gone— there was a gentle light that seemed to be off in the distance yet from everywhere at once. No one made a sound, as if all seven of us were holding our breath. Around the *Selenium* was some sort of... catwalk? Sort of? A spiderweb collection of structures that seemed like they should be familiar, as if I should be able to guess their purpose but I couldn't quite do it.

"Can you tell if there's atmosphere out there?" Dr. Patel asked.

"Sorry," Gatlin said with a chuckle. "I didn't put exterior atmosphere sensors on my interplanetary spaceship."

"So, we thinking Klingons or Vulcans?" Jambo asked, fishing a spacesick bag out of a dispenser on the back of the pilot's acceleration couch and spitting his chew into it, then sealing it and tossing it in a receptacle.

"I'm afraid there won't be any humans with funny looking bumps on their heads, Mr. Bowie," Dr. Shaddick told him, almost giggling with excitement. She'd been waiting for this her whole life. "I'd be willing to bet they have aural and optical senses, but I'd be shocked if their brains were even located in the same place as ours, much less their equivalent of eyes and ears. Despite what the science fiction Mr. Clanton writes might tell you, the existence of an alien species that evolved independently of ours in another star system and still came out as similar to us as the Klingons or Vulcans would be almost incontrovertible evidence of an intelligent creator."

Through the viewport, I saw part of the spiderweb structure beginning to stretch toward us, the gaps between the threads gelling into a solid surface and the pit inside my stomach grew just a little deeper.

"I think we're about to find out."

There was the slightest of vibrations, a kiss from a feather, and the *Selenium* was motionless.

"There is an Earthlike atmosphere outside your vessel." I spun around instinctively, expecting one of them to be standing behind me. The voice hadn't come from the speakers on the comm panel, it had seemed to come from just over my shoulder. "Your environmental suits will not be necessary."

"Shit," Jambo drawled, eyes darting from one bulkhead to another, the fingers of his right hand twitching as if searching for a gun. "Hope y'all don't mind if I keep mine on anyway."

"If they wanted us dead," Olivera pointed out, "there are easier ways."

"Sure," he acknowledged, holding onto his helmet like a life preserver, "but maybe not as funny."

Somebody knocked on our airlock. All eyes went to Strawbridge and Olivera except their own, which each went to the other because no one wanted to make *that* call. I sighed and pushed across the cockpit to the airlock, spinning the locking wheel counterclockwise.

"I, for one," I threw over my shoulder, "welcome our new alien overlords..."

The inner lock open with a slight squeak and I thought I heard Olivera start to object when I went to the outer hatch. I yanked down the lever to unlock it and pulled it inward.

I would have lost the bet. It was a robot at the door.

"Oh shit," Jambo muttered from behind me. "A toaster."

Well, not quite, but I've got to admit, it was the first thing that came to my mind, too. The thing was vaguely humanoid, at least to the extent of having a dome-shaped silver head I could look at when it talked, its eyes glowing blue in a way that I totally did not find creepy. At least they weren't red.

The humanoid resemblance ended about waist level, which made sense. Why saddle a perfectly functional robot with legs and make it walk like a human when you're on a spaceship with no gravity? Its base was some sort of rounded pedestal and a pale wash of what could have been steam puffed out of a port in its side, and I thought it might have been steadying itself in front of the airlock.

"Um, hello," I said. "Thanks for having us over."

"I'm Delia Strawbridge," the government rep finally kicked

her brain and mouth into gear, pushing past me and nearly running into the robot before she stopped herself. "I represent the government of the United States of America, the largest and the most powerful of the nation states on the planet Earth, and I bring greetings from the President."

"We know who the United States is," the robot informed her, its voice the same one which had assured us the air was breathable. "You need to accompany me to the bridge." The blue-tinged eyes, not metal or plastic and definitely not biological either, looked through the hatchway at the gathered crew. "All of you."

4

"There's gravity," Olivera was murmuring as we walked. "How the hell is there gravity? It's impossible."

I had been just as shocked as anyone when I went through the hatch and found myself being pulled down to the web with gradually increasing force, but by the time we'd passed out of the docking area and into the main part of their ship, I'd forgotten it among all the other unlikely things. Olivera didn't seem to be able to move past it.

"This is all impossible," I reminded him. "Faster than light travel, aliens, floating robots. Just roll with it."

The robot bothered me more than anything. I'd assumed it was just maneuvering through the microgravity with on board maneuvering jets, but it was still floating while the rest of us clomped along, looking stupid in our space suits.

Hell, even the corridor seemed impossible. Not that they had corridors—form follows function, after all—but I could have sworn we were walking nearly straight up at some points but the gravity stayed constant-down was under our feet and I was never sure if it was just my imagination.

The corridors were three meters across and empty. Not a hide nor a hair, not so much as another robot. Was the ship a living thing? Maybe the robot was built just for us...

No, then there wouldn't be corridors.

No one else seemed to want to talk to the thing, like they were embarrassed at the idea, but someone had to ask the question.

"Are you all robots?" I blurted. "I mean, is the ship like, an artificial intelligence?"

Strawbridge shot me a glare, as if I were somehow breaking diplomatic protocol, like bringing up politics or religion at Thanksgiving dinner.

"If we were all computer intelligences," the robot pointed out with frustrating logic, "why would I be taking you to the bridge? An AI would have no sense of personal space nor any need to bring you to meet it face to face, as it would have no face. I am simply here to soften the transition for your first meeting with the Helta."

"The Helta?" Strawbridge interjected. "Is that what you're called?"

"I am called a robot," the machine corrected her. "But yes, the Helta are the race who wish to speak with you."

"And they're worried enough about how ugly they'd look to us that they sent a robot to run interference," Jambo muttered. "What are we talking here? Wormfaces with tentacles for arms?"

"Through here," the robot said, ignoring the question. It motioned with black fingers on a silvery hand at a closed hatch to the left side of the corridor, broad and sturdy-looking, like something meant to keep out vacuum in an emergency.

"Whatever it is," Shaddick said, her voice trembling a little with what I took for excitement rather than fear, "you can bet it will not only be stranger than we've imagined but stranger than we *can* imagine."

The hatch slid aside. Shaddick's breath caught in her throat. Patel gasped, and Julie swore softly, and whatever smartass response that had been about to tumble out of me from acerbic instinct died aborning. In the end, it was Jambo who spoke the first words from a human being to an alien species.

"You have got," he uttered with appropriate gravitas for the historical event, "to be shitting me."

They were koala bears.

Oh, I know, they weren't *really* koala bears. Koala bears aren't five feet tall with opposable thumbs, and they don't wear uniforms reminiscent of a Napoleonic-era Prussian infantry soldier. Okay, that's not totally accurate either, but the knee-high black boots and the white pants and shirt with a short blue jacket sure brought it to mind. And once I had the image of koala bears wearing Prussian uniforms in my head, it just wasn't coming out anytime soon.

I was so mesmerized by the sight of them, it took a moment for the rest of the picture to come into focus. The compartment the robot had called the bridge didn't resemble the fictional Enterprise or any of the real US Navy vessels I'd served on. I'd visited the Hayden Planetarium in New York once, and the vessel's control room was about as large as the main auditorium, a sphere with a squared-off deck but lacking the tilted seats. The surface of the sphere was a featureless slate grey, but as we neared the center of the room it gradually darkened into an image of space, of the Moon, startlingly close.

It might have been designed to impress us, but my eyes were on the Helta stepping forward to meet us. I had this one pegged as a male, though I couldn't have explained why, since there were no obvious differences between any of the half a dozen of them on the bridge besides their height, and this one happened to be the tallest.

"I am Joon-Pah," the Helta said, and I nearly jumped at the

words. The fact he knew English wasn't surprising since the robot had already spoken to us, but I just didn't expect a thing that looked like a were koala to have the vocal cords to handle it. "I am the appointed master of this ship, and I greet you in the name of the people of Helta and the Alliance of Free Worlds."

"There's an Alliance of Free Worlds?" I asked, feeling like a kid on Christmas morning finding out Santa is real after all. "You mean like a Federation of Planets?"

"Shut up, Clanton," Strawbridge snapped, finally coming into her own now that there was someone to be a diplomat to, even if that someone looked like a furry at a science fiction convention. "Captain Joon-Pah, my name is Delia Strawbridge and I am here as a representative of the President of the United States to bring greetings to you from the people of Earth—"

"I'm sorry, Dr. Shaddick interrupted, exasperation in her voice, "but this is just fucking impossible." She pointed at Joon-Pah and I cringed, imagining all the human cultures who didn't like people pointing at them and then transferring that feeling into an alien with a hyperdrive and artificial gravity. "Just look at them! This isn't parallel evolution or form following function! There is no way something like this could have evolved naturally even on Earth, much less on some random alien planet!"

"Dr. Shaddick," Strawbridge hissed. "Control yourself for God's sake." She turned back to the alien. "I am so sorry, Captain Joon-Pah. Let me assure you—"

"She is correct," Joon-Pah acknowledged, and Strawbridge's jaw dropped. "We did not evolve naturally, and the story behind how we came to be is one you will need to hear. But it is not as important as the reason for which we're here." The guy was an alien and even if he'd been a real koala, I had no idea how to read the emotions of a koala, either, but I got the impression he was scared, or perhaps uncomfortable with what he was saying. "We are, by nature, a peaceful people who seek to avoid conflict at all costs, yet we find ourselves in a brutal war with an implacable foe. And we are losing, badly."

"You're at war?" I asked, the words nearly catching in my throat. "With who?"

The Heltan's eyes were dark and liquid, and they fixed on me with what I'd taken before for fear or reluctance.

"Why, with you."

The image of the moon had been replaced by one of Earth, but not the Earth we knew. I wouldn't have been able to tell that from the picture of the world from orbit, but the view dove and soared, a magic carpet ride taking us all the way from high orbit down into the atmosphere and through mountain passes, scraping the tops of redwoods impossibly high before hugging the dunes in desolate deserts.

There were no cities in this version of Earth, just wilderness, broken here and there by the occasional village where men and women dressed in skins tended fires or knapped flint. It was a world of at least ten thousand years ago, maybe even earlier, and I was too astonished to remember to ask how they'd obtained the footage or, assuming it was just some sort of simulation, where they'd gotten the information they needed to make it.

"This is the story," Joon-Pah intoned, his voice as sonorous as if he was sitting at one of those stone-age campfires, "of all life in the known galaxy, and it all begins below us, on the world you call Earth, a hundred thousand years ago. Back then, there was but one technological civilization in all the galaxy, a race we call the Elders, for lack of a better term. They had existed for millions of years, and in all that time, they searched diligently for other sentient races to share the universe with, and yet had found none, had found nothing but primitive, one-celled life. Until they came across Earth. Until they found a treasure trove of complex life forms. And you."

The video showed the primitive humans again, focusing on them, bringing their filthy, hairy, fur-clad shapes into sharp relief, but somehow managing to show the glint of intelligence in their eyes.

"It was then that the Elders knew their purpose, knew what they must do. They were powerful beings with technology that makes even ours seem childlike and impotent. They began to transform the moribund planets of the galaxy into living worlds using their own mighty powers...and using the life they'd found on Earth."

The image shot out across the water and over to another continent, where it found some species of bear I didn't recognize, though it wasn't actually a koala. Maybe it was a sun bear like they have in India, but I couldn't be sure. There was a whole family of them, a female and three cubs wandering through some forest, and then a beam of light hit them and they were gone. Others, a lone male, then two juveniles kicked out by their mother but still traveling together, vanished as well.

What came next was definitely computer animation, though of a quality that would have put the special effects on my streaming show to shame. The bears were brought to some sort of futuristic laboratory, where machines probed at them and took fluid samples, though no image of the Elders was shown. I wondered if it was because they didn't actually know what the Elders looked like or if there was some sort of religious reason, like Muslims forbid images of Mohammed.

The bears were being genetically altered, I inferred. The samples were put in some sort of device that glowed and shook and did all sorts of weird shit, and then were implanted back into one of the bears and it changed—shown in time lapse—and then the whole thing was done again. It sped up and finally, what came out was something that looked like the Helta.

The next shot was of a family of Helta living in a wattle hut in a forest clearing, on a world very Earthlike but subtly different, things like a different shade to the sky.

"And it was not just us," Joon-Pah said. None of the rest on the bridge had spoken as of yet. I couldn't tell if it was out of discipline, deference to Joon-Pah's leadership or fear of us. "Many other species were altered as well, brought to sentience by the Elders and deposited on their newly-habitable worlds along with other, simpler life engineered to survive in their new environments."

A panning shot across multiple continents this time, and this time other animals were taken for experimentation: wolves, ravens, mountain lions, hyenas, and even out into the ocean for dolphins, killer whales, octopi...

"That's fucking nuts," I blurted, ignoring what had to be a half a dozen dirty looks aimed my way. "You're saying these Elders terraformed planets and then took some of the most complex predators on Earth and mutated them into sentience so they could populate the galaxy?"

"I am saying exactly that, Mr. Clanton," Joon-Pah agreed. "And had they ended their efforts there, this galaxy would be a far more peaceful place. But in their *wisdom*...." Again, I wasn't certain, but I thought I detected a bitterness behind the word. "... they decided to transplant one more species, one which needed no mutation to reach sentience."

The image rushed back across the planet to those Stone-Age tribesmen in their huts, making knives from flint.

"Us," Michael Olivera said.

I realized he'd been silent since we'd reached the bridge. He looked like a cow smacked between the eyes with a mallet just before it got its throat slit at the slaughterhouse.

"Quite." Joon-Pah, slashed a hand across what had to have been some sort of haptic hologram and the projected image faded back into the Earth-Moon system. "Understand, we knew none of this for tens of thousands of years. The Helta developed our own civilization, our own sciences, and as we did, we discovered the truth about our origins. We knew almost immediately our world had been designed and, for many thousands of years, we worshipped the designers as our creators, what you would call our gods. This gave us a great incentive to perfect space travel, a way to go and meet our gods, to prove our worthiness. And in our haste to meet our creators, we discovered the principles of hyper-dimensional physics and developed a method of accessing and traversing another state of reality."

"You made a hyperdrive," I said, grinning broadly. "You actually made a damned hyperdrive."

The curves of the Heltan's mouth seemed naturally to be smiling, but the smile grew broader at my words.

"That is probably as close as we can come to describing it in terms that aren't pure math," Joon-Pah said. "Call it a hyperdrive then. And we discovered our neighbors, the Vironians, the Skrith, the Chamblisi... and," he finished, his mouth flattening out, "the Tevynians."

The image in the central projection changed again. The face was a human male, pale-skinned, with a long, straight nose and ice blue eyes, red-blond hair swept back into something resembling a mane. There was something fierce and feral in those eyes, in the cut of his jaw, and the clothes he wore seemed to be some sort of uniform, though in a colorful, checkered pattern that would have put my grandfather's worst golf pants to shame.

"Jesus Christ," Olivera murmured, and I thought it was a curse until I saw him crossing himself.

"We were naïve," Joon-Pah confessed. "We shared freely with our new friends, gave them our technology and asked next to nothing in return. We thought we were emulating our gods. And it seemed, at first, that we'd done the right thing. Genetic testing showed us that all our legends were truth, that all the races of the galaxy shared the same DNA as ours, that all life came from a single source and we were all one family under the skin.

"Most of our newly-discovered neighbors willingly became our allies and we developed a brisk trade. Except the Tevynians. They behaved in a friendly manner at first, until they were able to get their hands on one of our starships. Then they began to loot and pillage and hijack whatever was within their reach. They were a nuisance at first, an irritant costing us a few ships here, a few lives there..."

Joon-Pah tossed his head in what I thought was a gesture of negation.

"We were fools. Had we banded together immediately against them, we might have had the chance to put a stop to their depredations before it was too late, before they were too strong. Now..." The Heltan trailed off.

"What?" Olivera prompted. I think it was a testament to how stunned Strawbridge was by all this that she wasn't still trying to play diplomat.

"They have kidnapped our engineers, seized one of our colony systems where we construct starships, and built themselves a fleet. Their technology lacks the sophistication of ours, but they make up for it with numbers, for they breed like rats, fast enough to overcome their woeful attempts at medical science. And in battle, they show no care for their own lives, throwing themselves into hopeless situations, determined simply to kill more of us than we do of them."

"Yeah, that sounds like humans," Jambo agreed.

"What they're doing makes no sense from any rational point of view," Joon-Pah said, his teeth bared in an expression I took for anger or frustration. "They have the hyperdrive, they have fusion power, or at least they have of it what they can steal from us. They even have our engineers and machinery to build more. With that, they could go anywhere, mine what they need from asteroids and comets, build space stations to house however many people they want. But they don't think that way. They weren't a truly technological civilization before we found them and they lack the history to handle this sort of power peacefully."

The Heltan's eyes turned soft and more liquid, if that was possible, and his shoulders sagged.

"And we lack the history to have any experience at open warfare. Despite their primitive nature, or perhaps because of it, every effort we have made to fight them, either singly or with the rest of the Alliance, has ended in disaster." Joon-Pah went to one of the couches the crew used for chairs, leaning against the back of it in obvious exhaustion.

"I must be honest with you and your government. The rest of the Alliance..." He closed his eyes for a moment, as if forcing back pain. "Even many of my own people oppose our coming here. When we discovered the location of Earth a few years ago, found the origins of our own peoples and the Tevynians, there was much sentiment to put this whole system under quarantine forever. But I see no other option. Our backs, as your saying goes, are against a wall."

There was an empty feeling in the pit of my stomach. I knew what was coming. I'd read books about what was coming. Hell, I'd *written* books about what was coming, and it never ended well.

Joon-Pah fixed his gaze on Strawbridge, raising his right hand with the palm-down in a gesture that probably had some significance in his culture.

"I am here to offer you, your United States specifically and whatever allies you choose, an exchange. A deal, I think you would call it. We will give you what we have, fusion generators, hyperdrives, all of our technology and the training to build it yourselves, in exchange for your aid in this war."

"Holy shit." Julie breathed the words like a prayer.

Gatlin had not said a word. I'd glanced over at him a few times, expecting him to say something. He was famous for having an opinion and not being afraid to share it, but he'd kept silent this whole time, his eyes as wide as a child on Christmas morning, drinking everything in. I couldn't read his thoughts, couldn't put myself in his head. If I could, I'd have been the billionaire and he'd have been the moderately successful science fiction writer.

He wanted to say something now, though. I could see the muscles in his jaw working, like he was barely able to keep his mouth shut. I figured he wanted badly to yell at Strawbridge to take the deal, visions of starships and asteroid mining dancing in his head, but he knew pressuring Strawbridge or Olivera would do no good, he'd have to save his pitch for the President.

"I—I'm afraid I can't make this decision on my own," Strawbridge stuttered, her voice raspy, as if her mouth was dry. "I'll have to consult with the President, and he may require a Congressional authorization..."

The sound wasn't quite like anything I'd ever heard in any of the various and sundry countries I'd visited in my misspent youth, but there's something about an alarm that must be universal. The howling klaxon echoed off the bridge bulkheads and the Heltan crew who had been silent and respectfully still while Joon-Pah spoke to us were suddenly strapping themselves into their seats, grumbling at each other in a language of gutturals and modulated hoots and honks.

Joon-Pah bared his teeth and lurched to a central acceleration couch, fingers dancing over controls there. The image in the center display zoomed in beyond the moon to a position somewhere past the Lagrangian Points. A rainbow ring, its very existence impossible in the vacuum of space and through it, was a hole into...somewhere else. I blinked and looked again, but there was nothing inside the hole. Not blackness, not an absence of light, just nothing, as if my eye couldn't focus on it. Instead, I focused on the spaceship coming through the hole. It was as large as the one we were inside now and of similar design.

"Tell me you were expecting friends," I said to Joon-Pah.

"They followed us," the bearlike alien said, and his English was good enough to convey the despair. "It's the Tevynians." Joon-Pah was trembling, his breath coming heavy and fast. "They'll kill us all."

5

"WE NEED TO GET BACK TO OUR SHIP AND GET OUT OF HERE," Colonel Olivera insisted, sweeping around the compartment until he found the exit, as if he'd lost his bearings in the few minutes we'd been there.

"They will destroy you the second you're outside our defense shield," Joon-Pah snapped. He rounded on one of the stations along the bulkhead and snarled something at the crewmember sitting there. He—or possibly she—waved through a haptic hologram with his hand and the alarm ceased. "Our only hope is to distract them long enough to force them to chase us from this system. And hope we can draw them away from here before they destroy us."

"And then what?" Strawbridge asked, her voice a subdued squeak.

"You brought this thing here," Olivera yelled, his face flush with rage. "Can't you fight it?"

Joon-Pah stared back at him for a moment before he barked an order to one of his crew. The view in the holographic display was moving, moving fast toward the Tevynian ship, and I put out a hand instinctively, trying to brace myself against something. All that was available was the back of Joon-Pah's chair, but I grabbed it anyway. It didn't do a damned thing for my inner ear, but it did settle the panic building in my chest just a little.

"Are we accelerating?" Julie asked, staring at the display.

"At the equivalent of nearly one hundred gravities," Joon-Pah replied between orders to the crew in his native language.

"Why the hell aren't we being squished into a thin, fine paste against the back wall, then?"

"They control gravity," I reminded her.

My voice was calm and I wondered why. But then I remembered sounding calm when I was giving orders to my platoon during firefights down in Caracas, when streams of lead were raining from the balconies on both sides of the road, when my stomach was turning cartwheels and panic was gnawing its way out of my chest like a living thing.

"We do have gravity plates," Joon-Pah said, "but the reason you don't feel acceleration is because our drives use a method of manipulating spacetime, the equivalent of what you might think of as a boat propeller. The drive field also serves as our defense shield, and it's also what we use to open the wormhole into hyperspace."

His words had a strange emphasis I hadn't noticed before, as if he were having to hunt for each one, and I figured it was because he was even more scared than I was. He knew what was coming.

Something flared from the nose of the Tevynian ship, a pale blue streak of lightning that should have been just as impossible to see in space as that damned rainbow ring, and yet there it was. The blue glow enveloped the view in the projection and the deck shuddered beneath us. Patel and Shaddick both shrieked, Patel falling to his knees, palms flat on the ground as if this were an earthquake.

"What the fuck?" I exploded, anger displacing fear at the wrongness of it. "That was some kind of energy beam! How the hell could I see it with no atmosphere? And why did the damned ship move when it hit us? Was that some kind of gravity weapon?"

"Is this really important right now?" Olivera snapped. "Don't we have other things to think about?"

"The weapon is a particle accelerator," Joon-Pah answered. "Or rather, an *anti*-particle accelerator. The glow is Cherenkov radiation, and the ship moved because the energy from the shot caused our drive field to fluctuate, and to shrink. A few more and it will disappear altogether, and we'll be defenseless."

"And don't you have the same kind of gun?" Olivera asked him, desperation in his voice.

"We do. And we're firing...." Joon-Pah made a gesture at one of the crew to his right. "Now."

Blue lightning lashed out from somewhere above the camera view and a hemisphere of azure fire enveloped the nose of the monolithic Tevynian vessel for just a moment. There were shouts in the Helta language from the bridge crew, but they stopped after an announcement from the crew who'd fired the weapon, the one I was dubbing the Weapons Officer in my head.

"Glancing blow," Joon-Pah told us. "They were ready for the shot. We're breaking off and trying to lead them out to safe jump distance."

"One shot?" Jambo asked, looking from the view on the screen, which was veering away from the Tevynian vessel. "You're only firing one shot?"

"You don't understand. They'll sail straight into the guns, take any damage in order to kill us..."

"The fuck?" Jambo looked as if he wanted to slam a fist into the Heltan's face, and maybe he did. "Do you guys not have any kind of tactics or battle plans or *anything*?"

Joon-Pah stared at him blankly, the way those new Japanese robot receptionists at my agent's office did when I told them dirty jokes.

"I know the words," Joon-Pah said, "but we do not have your history of warfare, not in space, not anywhere. What would you have us do?"

"You got physicists, right?" I asked him. "Drive technicians, people who understand how things work?"

Joon-Pah made that tossing-head gesture again, then gabbled something at a crewmember to the left. The ship lurched and I had to grab at the back of the chair to keep from pitching over.

"Goddamnit!" Julie yelled.

"What do you have in mind, Clanton?" Olivera wanted to know.

"This is our ship's hyperdimensional specialist," Joon-Pah said, gesturing at the...male? Maybe? Whatever, the Helta was a head shorter than me and a bit paunchy. He looked like something I'd won at the state fair for my girlfriend when I was fourteen. "Whatever you intend to do, it had best be quick. That last shot severely attenuated our drive field. One more hit and we're dead."

"What happens if you touch one drive field to another?" I asked, looking at the...engineer? Yeah, I was gonna call him an engineer. "Rammed it straight on?"

A cross-chatter between the two and neither seemed happy.

"Head on, it would cause both fields to collapse, violently, and possibly kill us all." More gabble from the engineer. "If we were able to skim the edge of their field, however, experiments have shown it would send both ships heading away from each other at relativistic speeds, with little damage to either." He cocked his head toward me. "But what would be the point of that?"

"Can you hit it with enough accuracy to control which way both ships ricochet?"

Olivera's head snapped around, realization in his eyes and a smile spreading across his face.

"Mr. Clanton," he said, "that is fucking brilliant." He jabbed a finger at Joon-Pah. "Have them turn this Goddamned ship around. Now."

The Heltan didn't argue. I didn't think about it at the time, didn't consider the implications until much later, but it was obvious to everyone that Joon-Pah didn't *want* to be in charge, and Olivera did. Joon-Pah relayed the order to his helm officer and I think had to say it again—the helm officer stared at him for a moment, perhaps wondering if his captain had gone insane. But the ship was turning and, as she did, a slight, distant rumble shook the superstructure.

"Near miss," Joon-Pah explained. I don't know how he had learned English, whether by old-fashioned memorization and practice or some high-tech computer reading it into his brain like something from my books, but his command of tone and inflection was getting better just from his short interaction with us, and the clipped tension of the words spoke volumes. "They won't miss again at this range."

"Do you people not have any concept of evasive maneuvering?" Olivera demanded. "You know, moving your ship in irregular, hard-to-predict patterns to make it harder for the bad guys to hit you? Can we not even *try* that?"

I'd begun this with sort of a jaded view of the Space Force in general and Olivera in particular, but I have to admit, the man was growing on me.

"Fuck it, let me do it," Julie said, tapping the helm officer on the shoulder. "I can't read these Yogi-bear hieroglyphics you got going on, but I've been watching Boo-boo here pilot and it doesn't look that damned hard."

"Julie," Gatlin said, the word trailing off at the end uncertainly. "Now isn't the time—"

"Oh, for God's sake," the pilot sighed. "Here, let me show you."

She leaned over the helm officer's shoulder and ran three fingers through the haptic hologram and I paid attention to the details of it for the first time since we'd been there. There was a small, three-dimensional model of the ship on the helm display, with lines running along each axis. Julie stroked the lines at the port axis with two fingers. The view in the central display changed as the ship rotated to port and Julie barked a laugh, then made an orchestra-conductor motion through the hologram. The image spun like a kaleidoscope and even though we felt none of it, the view was enough to spur a twinge of motion sickness.

The Tevynian ship fired on us, but the pale blue tendril went wide and we felt not even a shiver. Joon-Pah gestured at the helm officer and the Heltan cut loose his seat restraints and vacated the position. A self-satisfied smirk crossed Julie's face as she slid into the chair.

"What about the intercept vector?" Olivera asked. "Can your engineer figure it out?"

"He has," Joon-Pah said, still watching the display, one of the muscles beneath the light fuzz on his cheek twitching when he saw the display spin the opposite direction, the image of the moon swinging through it as if it were a pendulum. "It is doable, though extremely risky. One degree off and both ships will be destroyed. But what course do you wish the ships to be launched on after collision?"

"Ours needs to go out in the clear, somewhere outside lunar orbit. Theirs..." Olivera grinned, the face of a stalking wolf. "Somewhere a lot closer."

The engineer exchanged a long string of gabble with Joon-Pah, and his translation to Olivera and Julie was nearly as incomprehensible as the Heltan language, involving degrees and speeds and vectors and lots of math I didn't have the education to understand. I'd been intent on serving as a Marine infantry officer and a degree in history had seemed the best way to go at the time...

Even if I'd taken any high-level calculus courses, the way the Earth, moon and the enemy ship were twirling in a giant tornado of light thirty feet high at the center of the room would have been way too distracting for me to figure out any more than the fact they were talking about the ship's course.

This was, I decided, just a bit too much. I'd started the day on a once-in-a-million-lifetimes trip around the moon and now I was on an alien ship with a crew full of were-koalas, getting shot at by humans from another planet. I mean, I *write* this stuff and it was still more than I could have imagined. My stomach was clenching and I was starting to hyperventilate every time a blue flash went across the holographic image. I didn't know how Julie was doing it, but then fighter pilots have always seemed like a different species to me.

"Man, I hate this shit," Jambo said, distracting me from the virtual rollercoaster above us.

"What?" I asked. He seemed steady enough to me, but his fists were clenching and unclenching reflexively and his eyes kept darting back and forth between Julie and the display. "You mean the part where we're on an alien ship in the middle of some kind of half-assed interstellar war or the part where all we get to do is watch someone else try to keep the Earth from getting blown up."

"Yeah, that part," he agreed, the corner of his mouth turning up. "And I don't even have a chew. Damned space suits." He looked down and to my left and I realized I'd forgotten about Patel.

He was still crouched on the floor, eyes wide, staring up at the holographic lightshow, teeth clenched.

"Are you okay, Dr. Patel?" I asked him.

Shaddick didn't seem too happy about the situation either, but at least she was still on her feet. Maybe about to cry, but at least standing. Strawbridge was pale, her hands shaking, but keeping it together, if only just. Gatlin...he still watched everything with a keen eye, not showing the least bit of fear.

"Oh, I'll be fine," Patel assured me, the quaver in his voice belying the reassurance of the words. "It's all just a bit much to take in, you know?"

"Oh, I know," I said, offering a hand and pulling him to his feet.

"Okay, I got the coordinates set," Julie said, shooting a dirty look at the helm officer when he tried to lean over her shoulder and check. "Boosting now. Everyone hold on to something...I don't know what the physical effects of this are going to be."

"Oh, goodness," Patel murmured. "I should have stayed on the floor."

"The deck," I corrected automatically and Jambo laughed, clapping me on the shoulder.

"Still a Marine, huh, Andy?"

"There are spare acceleration couches against the far bulkhead," Joon-Pah told us. He touched a control on the arm of his command chair and half a dozen of the seats folded out of the bare bulkhead.

Jambo and I ushered the others toward them, though Daniel Gatlin shrugged his arm away from my guiding hand and fell back into one of his own accord, immediately pulling the restraint webbing around him. The stuff was weird, not polymer or canvas, more like silk straight out of a worm's ass, except it wasn't sticky. When I tried to figure out a way to buckle it around Patel, it seemed to understand and fastened itself to another strand of the stuff on the other side of the chair.

Jambo had Dr. Shaddick and Ms. Strawbridge secured, so I grabbed one of the seats myself. Just sitting down was a huge relief, as if the effort to keep myself upright in the face of all this had been an emotional drain. The restraints folded me into their spiderweb embrace and I watched the screen, hoping to hell they all knew what they were doing.

"This was your idea, you know," Jambo reminded me. "What do you think this is, Pirates of the Caribbean or something? Ramming speed in outer space?"

I glanced over at him, ready to be pissed off, but he was grinning, treating it all like a joke the way he had when we'd been pinned down by mortar fire in Venezuela, my platoon and his half-team of operators trying to hide in the wreckage of a *panaderia*. A flight of V22s had saved our asses that day, but there wasn't any cavalry to hope for this time.

"Hey, Army boy," I reminded him, "I'm just a jarhead sci-fi writer. It's their fault for listening to me."

The enemy ship filed the display, larger with every second and then shrinking slightly and expanding again, like the cameras were having trouble zooming out fast enough to keep up with the intercept speed. I couldn't see anything around it, not the Moon or the Earth or even much of the blackness of space. Just the smooth, shining silver surface, some material we probably hadn't even imagined yet, strong enough for the hull of a starship.

A fucking starship. I'm on a starship. If I die now, I can say I was on a starship.

Well, *I* wouldn't be saying it, because I'd be dead. But people would say it *about* me. If there was anyone left alive to say it.

"Field intersect in three," Julie droned, in full pilot mode, that tone they used even when enemy SAMs were closing and they were making their last transmission back to the carrier. "Two...now."

The Tevynian ship was a silver blur in the display, too close to focus on, and then something happened. When I was a kid, my friends and I used to shoot rubber bands at each other when we thought the teacher wasn't watching. Sometimes, when I'd really want to get some range on the shot, I'd pull the rubber band back really far, so far it thinned out to half its normal width and I just knew it was about to snap. And a few times it had, the shorter end flopping onto the floor, the longer one smacking me in the face causing much more pain than it had been worth.

In that instant, I felt just like the rubber band. The pain wasn't physical, at least I don't think it was. Mental, psychosomatic, those don't seem to adequately explain the gut-punch feeling. It was almost psychic, spiritual even, and though it only endured for a fraction of a second, in that eyeblink of time I was in agony before it faded away as it had never been.

I heard someone scream and opened my eyes, not remembering that I'd closed them. The display was black, and I thought for a moment that the cameras were gone, burned away or shattered or something, until I saw a glimpse of stars and realized we were out in space, far from Earth or Lunar orbit.

"How fast are we going?" I asked. My throat was dry for some reason. I don't know who I was asking, since Julie wouldn't be able to read the instruments to tell me, but Joon-Pah answered.

"Twenty-three percent of the speed of light," he said.

"Holy mother of God," Gatlin breathed. "And in less than a second..."

"Turn us around, Nieves," Olivera ordered Julie. "Get us headed back to orbit."

"Yeah, getting there," she confirmed, the scowl on her face showing exactly how much she enjoyed him ordering her around.

"What about the enemy?" Olivera asked Joon-Pah. "Did we see what happened to them?"

"Yes. The ship's telescopes picked it up just as we began to accelerate." The Heltan tapped at something beside his left hand and the view on the display rolled back like a video reversing.

It stopped on the out of focus lines of the Tevynian ship, and then it began to roll forward, a frame at a time, super-slow-mo. The monolith of silver metal streaked across the far-off blue sphere of the Earth, boosting impossibly fast, maybe thousands of gravities of acceleration but they wouldn't be feeling it because it was a gravitational slingshot. Right up till they slammed into the surface of the Moon. I'm sure they felt that. Briefly.

The spear of energy rising up from the blank white of the Moon would have made the Tsar Bomba fusion explosion seem tiny by comparison, stretching dozens of miles out above the Lunar surface before it expanded into a half-dome of light hundreds of miles across.

"Beautiful," Olivera said, laughing softly. "Well done, Nieves."

"I aim to please," Julie said with the sort of smug self-satisfaction I expected from a fighter jock.

"Fuck me," Jambo breathed, eyes still locked on the explosion. "No one's gonna miss that. Cat's out of the bag now."

He was right about that. A blast that big would be seen by half the world and on the internet in seconds.

"Everyone already knew about the aliens," Strawbridge protested, a weak objection in a tiny voice.

"Yeah," I agreed, sinking back in the seat, both with a profound relief we weren't going to die and an the understanding that nothing would ever be the same. "And now they're going to know about the war." I caught her eye, offering sympathy. "I hope you're good at your job, ma'am. Something tells me we're going to be needing shitloads of diplomacy."

6

"Well, this is a huge fucking mess and there ain't no two ways about it."

I had my differences with the President, but one thing I always appreciated about him was his way of cutting through the bullshit and getting to the point. I never expected to be witness to it in person, and particularly not seated at the long, narrow table of the infamous White House situation room, flanked by generals and cabinet-level secretaries and watched over by steely-eyed Secret Service agents.

They'd replaced some of the flat screens with holographic projectors a couple years ago, which I'd been all agog over when I'd first seen footage of it. It didn't seem so damn impressive now that I'd seen the inside of an alien starship. The ship, which we'd learned was called *Truthseeker*, floated in one of the projection tanks, silhouetted against the familiar blues and greens of Earth. I wondered if one of our geosynchronous birds had taken the shot or if we'd launched a special satellite just to observe the ship.

President Crenshaw ran a hand through his short-cut brown hair and eyed his National Security Advisor balefully.

"Tommy, you really think we should do this? Get ourselves involved in an alien war, for God's sake? It sounds insane."

"I don't know that we have any choice, sir." Thomas Caldwell was a squat, broad-bodied troll of a man with a boxer's nose and the square jaw of a cartoon superhero. He'd been a Marine colonel before he'd gotten into the political end of things, so I had a soft spot for him. "The Helta are here and..." He frowned across the table at Delia Strawbridge, who looked very different in a business suit instead of a space suit. "Is it Helta? Heltans?

"As near as we can tell, sir," she said, "one is a Heltan, more than one are Helta."

Caldwell nodded curtly.

"The Helta are here, asking for help," he continued, "and if we tell them no, the Europeans, or the Chinese, or the Russians will tell them yes and we'll find ourselves a third-world country in a matter of months." He grimaced. "Or part of someone else's empire, more likely."

"That is alarmist nonsense!" Kristy DuPont exploded, apparently unable to contain herself despite the scowl her interruption earned from the President. The Secretary of State didn't bother to apologize, half-rising from her seat, leaning over the table, her white Dior jacket bunching up at the shoulders. "We should consult with the UN, build a consensus to deal with these aliens! My God, isn't the very existence of aliens, the fact they've come to us, a signal that we should put aside our petty differences and come together as one species to step into a new universe in peace? The Helta's enemies are humans, surely they would negotiate with other humans! We should offer to act as go-betweens..."

"And maybe that will be possible, Kristy," Crenshaw cut her off, impatience evident. "But what is *not* possible is for us to ignore human nature. You've seen up close how belligerent China has become, particularly in the wake of their economic downturn and the Korean reunification. They'd do anything to regain their status, both economically and politically, but they don't have the capital to do it. Do you think for one second Chairman Xiang wouldn't throw a quarter of a billion Chinese soldiers into a fire in another star system in exchange for total domination of Earth?"

"We can deal with Xiang if we have a united front!" DuPont insisted, but Caldwell's laugh drowned her out, the barking of a pit bull.

"Sure, we'll deal with the Chinese after they're armed with alien death rays. How would we do that, Kristy? Sanctions? When he's about to get fusion reactors and automated fabrication plants that can make whatever he wants out of raw materials? Nukes? Because if Xiang has force fields and lasers, I don't know nukes even *could* deter him, if we were desperate enough to go that route."

"I'm afraid Tommy's right," Crenshaw told her. "Perhaps we can attempt negotiation with these Tavvy...Tevvy..." It was his turn to appeal to Strawbridge and I could tell by the wrinkling of the muscles beside her eyes that the woman was trying hard not to roll them in frustration.

"Tevynians, sir."

"With them, yes," Crenshaw nodded. "But that is *after* we make the agreement with the Helta. We can survive without their technology, but we *can't* and *won't* survive if the Chinese or, God forbid, the Russians get their hands on it." He sucked in a breath, settling back in his chair, his one natural eye thoughtful. "The thing that concerns me is whether we can believe the Helta. All we have is their word that *any* of this is true."

"Sir, if I may," Colonel Olivera broke in. At Crenshaw's nod he went on. "We don't have to take their word for all of it. We have independent confirmation of what happened with both ships. Now, anything's possible and we could entertain some idea where the second ship was remotely piloted, but the Helta couldn't have known that Mr. Clanton here...." He inclined his head toward me and I felt my ears get hot as I flushed at the attention. "...would come up with the idea of striking one of their drive fields with another. It would have taken some mighty fancy last-minute footwork to fake that. And to what end?" Olivera had seemed a bit cowed by the presence of the Commander in Chief and all the brass at first, but he was warming up now, doing that whole hard-charging colonel-in-a-briefing thing. "If they wanted harm us, they could have just destroyed us. They could send an asteroid from the belt hurtling into the planet and there isn't a damned thing we could do about it. If they wanted something we had, they could take it."

"Except our willing help," DuPont reminded him, her nose wrinkling, either at the idea of getting involved with the Helta or of talking to the Space Force colonel.

Caldwell addressed her as if she were some particularly rare strain of idiot, a sentiment with which I could sympathize.

"Our willing help?" he repeated. "Do you think they're vampires and can't set foot on the planet unless we invite them in?"

I couldn't help it, I laughed. I tried to turn it into a cough, but it was enough to get Crenshaw's attention. I tried not to cower beneath it. He was just a fucking Navy Squidward when it came right down to it.

"What about you, Mr. Clanton?" the President of the United States asked me.

The fucking President of the fucking United fucking States! Holy shit!

And then,

Why am I more nervous about talking to the President than I was to meet aliens?

"Pardon me, sir," I said, managing not to squeak. "But what about me what?"

Crenshaw grinned through his close-cropped beard.

"You're a science fiction writer," he reminded me. "I've watched your show," he added and I resisted the urge to tell him how sorry I was. "You and others like you have imagined these sorts of scenarios for decades now...over a century. Do you think the aliens are telling the truth?"

I very nearly blurted out the first thing that came into my head, the way I usually did, but I forced myself to shut up and consider the question carefully. This was, quite literally, the fate of the world we were talking about.

"Mr. President," I said, "the aliens are either telling us the whole truth or it's the most elaborate con in the history of the world. There's no way anything like the Helta evolved naturally, and unless we're just totally wrong about everything when it comes to how evolution works, their genes came from Earth. That means for this to be some kind of con, whoever was running it had to have come to Earth and gotten DNA and then created enough of these bear-things to crew a starship, and God alone knows how long that would take or to what end they'd do it. Like Colonel Olivera says, if they mean us harm, there isn't a damn thing we could do to stop them."

Crenshaw turned to Dr. Shaddick, who, if anything, seemed more nervous than I was to be here. It was chilly in the Situation Room, but she was already sweating through her makeup.

"And we're sure," he asked her, "that these things actually do have DNA from Earth?"

"They have DNA, period, sir," Shaddick told him. "DNA evolved on Earth. For it to be *anywhere* else means it had to have come from here."

"I thought there were some theories about comets seeding the universe or something?" Crenshaw said, forehead wrinkling in thought. "Carrying DNA all over the galaxy?"

"The panspermia hypothesis," I supplied. "But the idea was

that the comets or space dust or whatever carried RNA. DNA evolved from RNA on Earth, wherever the RNA came from."

Shaddick looked at me wide-eyed, obviously shocked I knew about it. I shrugged.

"I write *science* fiction. I don't just pull everything out of my ass, I do *some* research." I actually did a shitload of research, not that you could tell it from the TV show. "Anyway, Mr. President," I went on, "since the Helta had to have come from Earth originally, or their genes did, I'm inclined to believe the rest of their story. But that's all academic at this point." At his questioning look, I expanded. "They have star travel, they have fusion power, they have artificial gravity, they have force fields. That one ship could destroy our whole civilization, pretty much end all life on Earth. While I believe what they've told us, what I don't know and am not willing to guess at is if they're telling the truth about how altruistic they are, particularly towards people who look *just* like the ones trying to kill them."

I shook my head, the strength of my conviction leaving me in a bleak sigh.

"If they're being honest about their intentions, about who the good guys and the bad guys are in this, then we need to help them, because these Tevynians *will* get around to coming here and taking us on eventually. And if they're not being honest... Well, we have to at least pretend to go along with them until we get enough of their technology to keep them from destroying us."

"Good point, Mr. Clanton. Okay, for the sake of argument, say we accept their deal. Kristy, what's the fallout likely to be?"

DuPont looked like she'd rather chew nails than consider us accepting the deal, but she was a professional, even if she was a State Department mealy-mouth just like the ones I'd hated with a passion when I'd been active duty.

"China will squawk and scream and threaten," she said, "but I don't think Xiang would be willing to risk outright military action, particularly once we have the Heltan technology. Most likely, he'll bide his time, try to get his spies in our manufacturing centers and get his hands on whatever of the technology he can the old-fashioned way."

I found myself nodding, and so was the President. The Chinese had built their economy on industrial espionage for decades, and there was no reason to think they'd give it up now.

"This is going to divide Europe, politically," she warned, her fingertips tapping the surface of the table in a nervous tic. "If I had to bet, I'd say Britain will throw in with us and provide troops in exchange for a share of the goods. Davidson has proven a bit of a hawk in Venezuela." She shrugged. "It's not exactly Europe, but we can probably count on Australia as well. But Germany and France." More tapping. "They'll be reluctant. They have serious internal issues, socially and economically. I'm not sure how much they could offer even if they were of a mind."

"Is there anyone else we can count on?" Crenshaw wondered.

"Poland," she declared without hesitation. "They've been trying to work their way closer to us, putting troops into the peacekeeping force. They aren't exactly cutting edge, but they won't need to be, just willing. Japan is already worried about China, so I'm sure they'll take advantage of the opportunity to bolster their economy and their military."

"No one else?" Caldwell asked, sounding surprised.

"Well, Israel, of course, though I'm nearly as worried about industrial espionage with them as I am with China. Various small countries who might contribute personnel, eventually, but no one who I would consider a key ally." She closed her eyes for a moment, as if gathering her thoughts before she went on. "The biggest threat isn't going to be China, though. It's going to be Russia."

Nods all around at that, but the first one who spoke, to my

surprise, was Jambo. He'd sat at a corner of the table, silent as a churchmouse, probably feeling as out of place as I was.

"We beat them to the *Selenium*," he said. "And we beat them to the alien ship. They're gonna take this shit personally."

A dozen pairs of eyes turned towards Jambo and the big man seemed to shrink a bit under the attention.

"It's always personal with the Russians," he insisted. "They won't let it go, and even if you bring them into this at some point, they'll still hold a grudge."

"Mr. Bowie is correct," DuPont acknowledged. She frowned, squinting at Jambo. "Is it Sergeant Bowie? Captain Bowie? Major?"

"Mister is fine," Jambo told her, enigmatic as always. Unless of course he was a Warrant now, in which case, technically, he would be Mister.

"Whether we go through with this or not," DuPont said, "the Russians will hold it against us."

"You bet your ass they will," Caldwell agreed. "Which is why we should shut them out of it. We try to let them in as junior partners or some such shit, it'll bite us in the ass."

"Then I need the two of you," Crenshaw said, pointing at DuPont then Caldwell, "to work up a tactful way of presenting the idea to Congress, because we're going to need to get a declaration of war *plus* a treaty with the Helta."

"We're going to need a lot more information to present if we're going to pull that off, sir," DuPont warned him. "I'm talking holographic video, statistics, names and maps and whatever they can get us. Strawbridge, that's your responsibility."

"Yes, ma'am. I already explained that to Joon-Pah and he promised to transmit something to me within the next couple days."

"I'll have Nathan schedule an emergency meeting with the Speaker, plus the chairs of the Intelligence and Defense committees later today," Crenshaw said, almost as if he were making a note to himself.

I figured he meant Nathan Fulton, his Chief of Staff, but the inside-baseball stuff was making me feel out of my depth again.

"Which brings me to how we're going to incorporate the technology the Helta have promised us," Crenshaw continued. "That's where you come in, Daniel."

Daniel Gatlin's suit was worth more than the advance I'd received for my last book, and of all of us, he looked the most at home in the White House. I knew he'd entertained running for the office, but decided he could accomplish more for the country and the world with the power of his industrial dynasty behind him. I wondered if this business would change that sentiment, eventually.

"Gatlin Aerospace will be in charge of integrating the new propulsion systems into existing airframes for space use," Gatlin said, sounding more as if he were dictating the terms instead of merely sharing them with the others at the table. "Other technologies will be parsed out to a few subsidiaries and a handpicked list of firms I feel we can trust, with priority given to the fusion power generators the Helta have already agreed to help us build, and to the new weapons systems we can implement using their power storage technology."

"This is something else we're going to have to push through Congress," the President said, sighing as if he found the task daunting. "It'll go against policy, just handing all this over to prechosen companies rather than opening it up for competition, but this technology is beyond sensitive and we have to be able to control its dissemination, at least at first." He shrugged. "As time goes on, we'll begin releasing some of it to open source, beginning with those technologies that have peaceful applications, such as to agriculture or medicine."

He nodded toward Dr. Shaddick and Dr. Patel, who had

taken seats about as far from him as they could, probably hoping he wouldn't notice them.

"You two are going to be on the task force to adapt Heltan medical and biotechnology for human use, by the way." He grinned. "So, don't make any other plans for the next three or four years, assuming I win reelection."

His eyes flickered toward me and Juliet Nieves. She was sprawled in her chair like she owned the place, and I envied her nonchalance.

"You two either. As of today, you're both being reactivated from the Reserves for the duration."

Julie grinned like she'd been expecting it, but my reaction was a bit less matter-of-fact. Memories of Caracas streets blocked off by barricades of burning tires, of the man next to me pitching backwards, his blood splashing my face before the crack of the sniper's round reached my ears streamed though my mind. I shook the ghosts of wars past out of my head in time to catch President Crenshaw's next words.

"Captain Nieves, you'll be training on the new dual-environment fighters and shuttles Gatlin Aerospace will be building, so your actual job description won't be changing much, just the source of your direct deposits."

"And their size," she murmured with a veteran's skepticism.

"What about me, sir?" I asked. "What am I going to be doing?"

Jambo laughed softly and I glanced over at him, wondering if he, like Gatlin, had been in on the planning for this meeting before the rest of us.

"Funny you should ask that, Andy..."

7

Have you ever run downhill so fast it seemed your legs were moving on their own and you didn't dare stop or even try to slow down because you knew you'd fall and tumble so hard, you'd break your neck?

Every day of the last two months had felt like that, and every day seemed to go by faster than the last, and somewhere at the bottom was a hard ending, but I couldn't stop. Movement was life.

The morning sun was painfully bright, yet the chill in the air was a slap in the face. I could see my breath puff on the exhale as each three-meter stride slammed the armored soles of the exoskeleton's boots into the brittle, frozen earth. It was spring in western Idaho, but you couldn't have proved it by me. There was still snow at the tops of the mountains in the distance, still a shining haze of frost on the grassy hillsides, and every morning when the Army driver picked me and Jambo up from base housing in a beat-up, old, camo-painted CUCV with no working heater, and took us out to the proving grounds, I had to huddle inside a field jacket with polypropylene snivel gear under my combat utilities. Luckily, the armor was well insulated, though I was sure I was going to regret that come summer.

It had taken some getting used to, running in the stuff. There was the tiniest bit of lag between the twitch of my muscles against the five hundred pounds of Kevlar and ceramic armor, servomotors and battery pack and the actual movement of the exoskeleton. It wasn't much, just enough to make me question my balance and nearly go face first into the rocky ground over and over for the first week trying to use it.

Carrying the machine gun felt even stranger. It was a standard M240B 7.62mm light machine gun, though the enclosed double drum feed system was new, as was the sight. Heads-Up Display sights had been tried with infantry weapons before, of course, but they'd run headlong into the dual roadblocks of reliable power sources and a nasty tendency to break down in real-world conditions. We had the power source licked, thanks to our Helta friends, and we were going to find out the hard way if the shit still had a tendency to break in the field.

For now, the targeting reticle was being projected onto the lens of the goggles I wore under my helmet, but the plan was to work the HUD into the full-face visor of the final production model...the one that would go into space. That model probably wouldn't have MILES gear and a machine gun equipped with a blank adapter either, but we were still in the early stages. So early, there was only the two sets of the shit. And the other one was out there somewhere in the hills, hunting for me.

I followed the old creek bed between the hills, my steps carrying me at a speed of somewhere around twenty miles an hour despite requiring no more effort than a light jog. For the test, I had a hundred-pound ruck and the machine gun with a 200-round drum full of blanks and a spare in a special harness, ready to switch out. I didn't have a great deal of confidence in the weapon's ability to burn through that many blanks without jamming, but one problem at a time.

The pressing problem at the moment was James Bowie and how much fun he seemed to be having killing me each and every single day. Simulated, of course. I'd expected it at first. Even with the new technology and the exoskeletons, tactics were tactics and combat skills translated to any format, and Jambo had more experience in combat in any one deployment than I had my entire military career. But it was becoming a matter of pride: he was Army and I was a Marine and damn it, I had to hold up my end for the Corps.

I tried to think while I ran. I couldn't really crawl into a hole and hide, not in this stuff. Maybe once we started screwing around with the thermal insulation and camouflage, we could design one of these suits to actually blend into the surroundings instead of standing out like a bonfire, but for right now, I had to run.

Jambo was a consummate professional in the art of violence, but even he began to show some tendencies over time. Every day so far, he'd circled wide and worked his way to the center in a shrinking spiral. I'd tried to slip in behind him, tried slicing across the center of the Area of Operations, even tried running a circle in the opposite direction and nothing worked because he was just a more natural shooter than I was, especially on the run.

I slowed to a trot, my eyes going to a jagged outcropping of rock a bit over a mile away, on the edge of our training area...or, if I was being honest, maybe just a couple hundred meters outside our mapped training area. Maybe I should try getting to the high ground and making him come to me.

It's for the test, I told myself. That was why we were out here, right? To test the suits, figure out tactics, probe their operational limits. That was what Dr. Henckel kept telling me back in the lab, anyway.

I ran the mile faster than I'd ever managed it during a Marine Physical Fitness Test and could have done it even quicker if I hadn't had to keep my eyes open for rocks and chuckholes. The armor wasn't loud, but the servomotors had a tell-tale hum that increased in volume the faster I moved, and the reinforced boots thumped into the hard-pack ground with a Samba beat and the whole thing began to remind me of the last time I'd been dancing at D-Edge in Sao Palo. The beat slowed as I approached the narrow, winding path up the rise, eyeing it with the sort of calculation I would have used for a free climb.

Going uphill in the exoskeleton was tricky, not because of the effort involved of course, but because of the balance. It might have felt like I was jogging in shorts and a tank top, but in reality, I was carrying about half my weight on my back and it was very possible for me to tip over backwards and wind up stuck there like a turtle in the sun. I had to lean into the climb and the damned backpack rose up so high behind my back that I couldn't tilt my head back far enough to see anything except the ground in front of my nose.

It would have been a great opportunity for Jambo to snipe me from long distance and laugh his ass off when the laser hit my MILES receiver and tripped the shutoff for my suit. I would have been frozen in place, bent over at the waist, looking like I was about to take a dump. Bastard would probably have taken a picture of me, too, even though he wouldn't be able to post it online until all this was declassified. Hell, there was probably some top-secret, tier-one operators' Facebook page where he could put it up and let SEAL Team 6 and the Nightstalkers laugh at me.

Yeah, I was rambling, but what else was there to do when you're shuffling up a hill like an arthritic armadillo? If Jambo was watching, he must have been laughing too hard to get a clean shot, because I made it to the top of the hill without dying. I wasn't out of breath, of course, because my muscles weren't doing the work, but I was sweating despite the chill morning breeze.

The hill was rocky and barren and way too slick, and I moved cautiously toward the edge in a sort of skating motion, careful to keep my center of gravity over my feet. I wasn't exactly scared of heights, just terrified of looking like an idiot, and tumbling off the side of the hill to my death was perhaps as stupid a death as I could currently imagine.

It was beautiful up here, despite my worries about embarrassment and death by misadventure. It reminded me a bit of my adopted home outside Vegas, though the rocks were a different color and it probably got colder here in summer than it did in Vegas in winter. But the skies were just as blue and the land just as open and *Goddammit, there's Jambo.*

He was skirting the creek that traced the southern edge of the training area, about a mile away at a guess. I raised the machine gun until the reticle projected in my goggles settled on him and the built-in rangefinder told me I'd overestimated the distance. It was one point two kilometers, which worked out to about three quarters of a mile.

I should really learn to start thinking in metric. Once we're out there, everything's going to be in metric.

But damn it, why? We'd won the space race and now we were going to the stars! It wasn't like the Helta used meters and kilograms and all that shit. We should have made them convert to inches and miles and pounds and to hell with the rest of the world.

But the military was in charge and they already used metric, so that battle was lost. The thought pissed me off enough I thought about trying the shot at three quarters of a mile. Theoretically, the targeting computer should be able to correct for drop and windage...

Or fuck, you know what? A MILES laser doesn't even have *drop or windage, so I'm going to just shoot him.*

Yeah, it was cheating, sort of. But as my old platoon sergeant, Gunny Swoboda used to say, "if you ain't cheatin', you ain't tryin'."

I settled the aiming reticle on the tiny, fast-moving stick-figure of James Bowie, led him by a few degrees and held down the trigger. There was no recoil, of course, not with blanks, but the M240B chattered hoarsely and a fountain of brass cartridge casings spilled from the right hand side of the weapon, tinkling on the bare rock at my feet. I knew I'd missed—Jambo kept moving, faster if anything, trying to make it to the cover of a lonely stand of skinny trees, which wouldn't have saved him from 30-caliber bullets but would be quite effective against the laser designator. I would have cried foul, but living in my glass house, I refrained from throwing stones.

Instead, I just threw more lasers, sawing back and forth with the machine gun and watching that damn reticle pass over Jambo like twenty times and wondering how many shots it was going to take to bring the son of a bitch down.

Then he stopped, joints freezing up, and the momentum he'd built up from the run sent him pitching forward, landing on the ground face first.

"Shit!" I squawked, lowering the machine gun and keying my radio with desperate haste. "Jambo, you there? Are you okay, man?"

Nothing for a few seconds. I tried to watch for movement, touching a switch to toggle the zoom feature of the goggles, but of course, he wouldn't be moving whether he was conscious or no, not with six hundred pounds weighing him down and the joints of his armor frozen.

"Yeah, I'm good," he replied, finally. His tone was flat, and I wasn't sure if he was pissed off or embarrassed. "The chest armor kept my face from getting busted open. But I ain't going anywhere until you get your ass down here and use the admin key to unfreeze my fucking suit, so if you don't mind?"

"I'm on my way," I promised, feeling much more gratified than I should have to finally get a kill on Jambo.

This was a kid's game. I was playing fucking Cowboys and Indians with a Delta operator wearing a high-tech set of superhero armor and getting paid for it. A little. I wasn't sure if that was the most awesome statement about my life ever, or the most pitiful. What was it Allie had said about me when she'd left? Something about me being an overgrown adolescent, among other, more serious accusations?

I hesitated at the top of the steep trail down the hillside, trying to figure out how the hell I was going to traverse it without tumbling to the bottom and breaking this incredibly expensive armor as well as, possibly, my neck. Simply walking down would require me to lean backwards so far, I likely wouldn't be able to see my feet, which wasn't going to work. Or, I could walk backwards, leaning forward, but I still wouldn't able to see where my feet were going.

Damn it, Clanton, you moron. You forgot the first rule of climbing: have a plan to get down before you climb up.

I scanned right of the path and saw a section of the cliff outcropping where part of the face had collapsed in on itself, leaving behind a series of steps spaced at about ten or twelve feet, one below the other, terminating in a pile of rubble near the bottom.

I could jump. Theoretically, the armor could take it, could absorb the shock. It seemed incredibly reckless and dangerous and a horrible way to treat expensive, experimental equipment, and the only argument I could make for it was *fuck it, why not?* So, obviously, I did it.

It had been my experience in a life full of doing stupid and reckless things that the best way to approach them was to run into them head-first and at full speed, since hesitation was usually worse than recklessness. I jumped from the edge of the cliff, yelling—because yelling seemed to be the thing to do when you jumped off a cliff, but it turned into a pained grunt when the soles of my boots smacked into the first of the steps. I was stumbling forward, about to lose my balance, and I was forced to turn it into a leap, bringing my legs up and leaning in, trying not to go head over heels.

On the second jump, I didn't have my breath back yet, so I didn't try to yell, just sort of wheezed. Cold wind slapped at me and the twelve feet seemed like thirty or forty, and when I hit again, I bit my lip and tasted coppery blood in my mouth and still couldn't stop. Stopping would mean falling, and jumping was better than falling.

The third jump was easier, the drop not quite as far, the landing not quite as rough, and the rock platform was a bit flatter and much broader, enough that I was able to scrape my soles against the dirt-covered rock and stop myself. One last hop, only about six feet, and I'd be back on the ground *and* have some valuable data for Dr. Henckel when we got back to the lab. The exoskeleton had held up fine and I hadn't broken any bones.

I stepped down and absorbed the impact on bent knees...and then something went "crump" and I smelled acrid fumes coming from the battery pack on my back. I tried to straighten up, but the armor was frozen in place and lights were flashing red all across the system display ocular.

"Oh, shit," I muttered. I keyed my mic, hoping at least the radio was still working. I guess it must have been hooked up to a separate battery system than the suit servos, because it crackled to life. "Jambo," I transmitted, "I got a problem here. Another blown battery pack."

"Oh, Jesus tapdancing Christ," he moaned, the sound filled

with static. "I know this shit is alien and all, but can't they make one of the things that lasts more than four operational hours without blowing up?"

"We better call in the chopper to pull us both out of here," I said.

"Great. I'll just lay here on my belly like a drowned rat until then."

"Jambo," I said, settling against the restraints holding me inside the exoskeleton and trying not to let my leg muscles cramp up from the bent over position, "if you knew what position I was in, you'd be thanking your sweet and fluffy Lord you were on your belly. These assclowns really need to work out some sort of quick release to let a guy get out of this shit on his own before it goes into mass production."

"Yeah, I'll make that suggestion," he said, laughing humorlessly. "Right after I tell them to go fuck themselves."

"I don't know why the hell you guys insisted we go to Medical," Jambo said, a bit too loud and plaintive, still pissed off from the morning's fiasco. "Neither of us got hurt, unless you count butthurt, which, if you do, Andy here might have sprained his ass."

The Medical Building was all we called it. Nothing here had an official designator and nothing was named after some dead guy from World War Two, because nothing here was official. The buildings had been in place but they were cleaned up—barely, and repurposed. I don't know what the Medical Building had once been, but it was cement block covered by cracked and crumbling stucco, three stories tall and featureless but for the American flag flying outside.

Inside was a different story. The walls had all been lined with white plastic, the floors tiled, and I'd seen at least four isolation labs since I'd been here, one of them fitted with some sort of ceiling to floor transparent tanks filled with pink liquid. I'd half-expected to see disembodied brains floating in them, but as far as I could tell, they were all empty except for the pink soup.

I couldn't have told you the name of any of the technicians or doctors who worked in the place except for Doc Reed and his staff in the first-story Wellness Lab. Yeah, I know, but that's what they insisted on calling it. Jambo and I reported there on arrival, when it seemed like we'd been the only people on the base, and the Doc had given us the once-over, right down to MRIs and CAT scans. Since then, we hadn't been back, splitting our time between the Armor Lab and the training grounds, except for the few hours a night they left us to sleep. I suppose the furnished house they'd loaned me to stay in was nice, but I couldn't have described an inch of it to anyone besides the bedroom and the shower. I certainly hadn't cooked a single meal there, though I could have written a research paper on the chicken-fried steak they served in the chow hall.

We'd stepped through the doors into the Wellness Lab expecting to see Doc Reese, his salt-and-pepper hair tied in a ponytail and bouncing on the back of his lab coat, or maybe Nurse Glenda with her bleached-blond perm. Instead, we nearly ran straight into Colonel Olivera and Julie Nieves.

"Holy shit," I said, my mood brightening immediately, at the presence of Julie if not Olivera, "what the hell are you guys doing here?"

Olivera looked very much like the last time I'd seen him, down to the mottled grey Space Force utility fatigues, but now Julie was dressed in the same uniform, her hair a touch shorter, a subtle difference in her appearance that I couldn't quite put a finger on, something less sloppy and civilian. She was wearing the full bird on her collar, what would have been a captain's rank in the Navy but a colonel if she was in the Space Force, as the tab on her chest advertised, and I belatedly realized that I myself was only a newly-minted Marine Corps major and should perhaps have greeted both officers with a bit less informality.

"Hey Andy," Julie said casually, not taking offense. "Yeah, I don't know why we're here either. I was testing shuttles at Edwards when Mike came to pick me up in a V22 and brought me here."

It took me a moment to process that when she said "Mike," she was referring to Colonel Olivera, then another second to remember the two of them were the same rank.

"Well, spill it, sir," Jambo said to Olivera, as at ease with the senior officer as he had been with the generals and admirals I'd seen him around since I'd been reactivated. "What's the secret? Have we all been exposed to some alien herpes or something?"

"I'd tell you if I knew, Mr. Bowie," Olivera said.

I looked around the Wellness Lab's waiting room and saw no one, not even the dull-looking, pinch-faced tech who hadn't said a word to us the first time we'd visited.

"That's just strange," I opined, spreading my hands. "Why would they want us four in particular here?"

"How did you sprain your ass?" Julie asked me, frowning. "What sort of alien probing do you two have going on at this bumfuck base anyway?"

"I spent an hour and a half stuck in my exoskeleton, bent over when the damn battery pack exploded this morning." I didn't try to keep the disgruntled tone out of my voice. "I hope your shuttles are coming along better than our powered armor."

"Powered armor?" She cocked an eyebrow. "Are we talking battle suits like Starship Troopers?" She made a face. "The book, of course, not the abomination of a movie."

"The less said about the movie, the better," I agreed. "But no, it's not Starship Troopers, it's the same Goddamned exoskeleton

DARPA has been working on for the last thirty years." I shrugged. "They actually have the setup working pretty well, as long as you plug it into the wall, or a diesel generator. But with the new battery packs the Helta helped us design, they're actually practical now, along with a bunch of other stuff we've just been waiting for a way to power."

"They *would* be anyway," Jambo interjected, rolling his eyes, "if the damned things stopped burning out. The techs keep saying it's just a matter of a few adjustments, but I'll believe it when I see it. I'm not sure I trust this alien shit yet."

"Well, I hope I can change your mind about that, Mr. Bowie."

I recognized the voice, though it had been months since I heard it. Jack Patel wasn't in uniform, nor was he in a lab coat, just a black polo shirt and khakis, but he'd been drafted into this as well. I figured they probably hadn't wanted anyone who'd been on the alien ship free to talk to conspiracy-theory podcasts or scandal websites. They'd shanghaied those of us who still had military commitments and bribed the rest with high-dollar, important-sounding jobs, and Dr. Patel was one of the latter.

"Hey Doc," I said, shaking his hand. "Have you been hauled out here with the rest of us suspects, or are you the detective who's about to tell us why you've brought us here today and announce the real killer?"

Patel stared blankly, like I'd just asked him what color Tuesday was, and I sighed.

"Never mind, I guess you're not a fan of old murder mysteries. Do you know why we're here?"

"Of course!" He grinned, snapping back to his perpetual good mood. He waved behind him at an assistant I hadn't noticed before, a very serious young woman carrying a locked plastic case in her left hand with a holstered SIG on the opposite hip. "Open it up, would you, Ms. Gennaro?"

She set the case down on a low table across from the ratty

couch in the waiting room, then tapped a code into the lock. It popped open with a curious pneumatic hiss, revealing a row of opaque plastic vials and an injector gun. I regarded Patel with narrow, suspicious eyes.

"Are we getting vaccinated against some mutated bug from the Helta?" I demanded. "Because I've been worried about that. If they were engineered from Earth life, we *could* catch their diseases..."

"Something much better than that," Patel assured me, fitting one of the vials into the gun. "Although I guess that's coming, eventually. But for right now, you get to be the Guinea pigs for the very first piece of medical technology the Helta have shared with us." He raised the injector gun like a pistol at high ready. "So, who wants to be first?"

"Back up a second," I told him, holding up a hand. "Guinea pigs for *what*?"

"It is *so* cool," Patel enthused. "It's a tailored bacterium, biological nanotechnology, really, designed to retelomerize your cells and gradually rejuvenate them." He shrugged. "Theoretically."

"Retelo...what?" Julie asked. "What the hell are you saying?"

I felt the hairs stand up on the back of my neck.

"Oh, shit," I murmured. "I think I know."

"You know what a telomere is, right?" Patel asked us, then frowned as he saw that at least a couple of us didn't. "Okay, well, a telomere is a region of repetitive nucleotide sequences at each end of a chromosome, which protects the end of the chromosome from deterioration or from fusion with neighboring chromosomes, you see..."

"In fucking English, Doc," Jambo interrupted, sounding as if his patience was beginning to wear thin.

"A telomere is the shit in your chromosomes that makes your cells regenerate," I said, deciding an interpreter was needed. "You know your whole body replaces its cells regularly, right? Well, as you get older, your telomere chains get shorter, and you can't replace your cells anymore. That's why we age." I swallowed the lump in my throat, unwilling to say the next part, but knowing they needed to hear it. "If the Helta have a way to renew the telomere chains..."

"No shit," Jambo breathed, his eyes going wide.

Julie's mouth dropped open, but I thought from the expression on Olivera's face that he at least had suspected what we were talking about.

"If this works," Patel said, his smile growing even wider, "we're looking at a very extended lifespan."

"And the Helta already have this?" I asked him.

"Oh my, yes," he said, nodding so hard I thought he might pull a muscle. "Joon-Pah is nearly two hundred of our years old, and he's considered barely middle-aged. His medical staff told me the oldest recorded Heltan back on their homeworld is over three hundred, which is when they developed the treatment in the first place, and that guy looks as young as Joon-Pah."

And who the hell knows how young a fucking koala bear looks?

"So, if we take this shit," Jambo said, nodding toward the injector, "we're gonna be immortal?"

"Not exactly immortal," Patel corrected him. "You can still die from disease or, of course, violence or accident. But this *should* greatly expand your natural lifespan. Probably not indefinitely, but certainly by at least a century, probably more."

"Well, hell!" Jambo said, yanking up his right sleeve. "Put that shit right here, Doc!"

"Jambo," I began, "are you sure..."

But Patel had already pressed the injector against the big man's arm and thumbed the trigger. The device hissed with an almost sinister sibilance and the deed was done.

"So, when will I know if it works?"

Patel regarded the big man with a critical eye.

"If you have any degenerative conditions," Patel said, "you can expect tissue regrowth in a few weeks. You're still in your forties, and I don't see any gray hair yet, so you may not notice any blatantly obvious external signs for quite a while." He grinned. "But in ten years, when you still look basically the same as you do now, you'll know for sure it worked."

Jambo scowled, obviously a bit disappointed and pulled his sleeve back down.

"Who's next?" Patel asked, extracting the expended cylinder and grabbing another.

"Is this a directive from higher up, Dr. Patel?" Olivera asked, looking at the injector gun the way a Marine drill instructor might look at an unmade bunk.

Patel chewed on his lip as if considering how to answer that. "Let me put it this way, Colonel. At this point, it is being strongly encouraged. But, everyone included in the crew will have to receive all injections deemed necessary by the President's Leadership Council."

"Mission?" Julie repeated, raising an eyebrow. "What mission? What crew?"

"Oh, goodness," Patel said with a nervous chuckle, "look at me, I've said too much. Sorry, my bad, really not supposed to talk about it."

"Well, fuck me," Olivera sighed, unzipping his fatigue jacket and pulling it off, then pulling back his T-shirt's sleeve. He stopped Patel with a glare before being injected. "If this works and doesn't kill us all, I need to know my wife and kids will have a chance to get it, too."

"Assuming everything goes well," Patel assured him, "and we have every reason to believe it will, this will be a standard medical treatment available to the entire population within the next five years. And, of course, the families of service members will have priority."

Olivera grunted his skeptical reluctance, but offered his arm. Julie said nothing, but took off her jacket and let the researcher give her the injection. She looked good, I thought, and wasn't much older than me, and I had to remind myself she was a superior officer and I was back in the Corps.

Then every eye turned my way and Patel held up the last vial of serum, teeth bared in a smile.

"Hey look," I protested, raising my hands palms out, "I don't mind a little gray. I think it'd make me look more distinguished, you know?"

"Think of the mission, Andy," Jambo urged me. He shrugged. "Whatever it is."

"I don't want to be on any mission!" I insisted. My voice was getting a bit shrill and I reined myself in a little. "I'm really happy just helping to develop the Infantry Weapons System, honest."

"Come on, Marine!" Julie slapped me on the shoulder. "You wanna live forever?"

"Kind of," I admitted.

"Well, here's your chance then!" She shot me a smile and something about it woke up the stupid-ass college kid who would do anything to impress a girl. "Bare that arm, boy!"

I moaned, knowing it was a lost cause, and pulled up my sleeve.

"It's not the first time the government's stuck it to me," I said, wincing as the shot went into my arm, feeling like something solid had been stuck into my muscle. "Although usually, they pick a lower target."

8

"LADIES AND GENTLEMEN OF THE FIRST EXTRAPLANETARY Detachment of the 75th Ranger Battalion, I am Major Andrew Clanton." I touched an armored glove to an armored chest, my voice amplified by the external speakers of the sealed helmet. "And this is Master Sergeant James Bowie." Jambo offered a casual wave with his left hand, the other holding an oversized rifle across his chest. "We are your Chief Training Officer and NCO, and we are going to oversee your familiarization with the M-2034A2 Mobile Infantry Combat Exoskeleton."

"The 'MICE?'" someone blurted from near the rear of the gaggle of Rangers. They were all wearing helmets as well, but their visors were up. In the last couple of months, Jambo and I had found it took some getting used to before people were comfortable with a closed visor.

We'd found that out when I began hyperventilating the first time I tried to use the new armor with the visor down.

"We are *not* calling it the MICE," Jambo declared, "no matter what acronym the Ordnance pukes laid on it. We helped develop this shit and we get to name it, that's the deal."

The woman up front grinned at that. She was tall and statuesque even without the armor. With it, she was...well, she was taller and more statuesque and wearing damned expensive armor. Her hair was cut short and tightly curled and her eyes were dark and piercing and didn't seem to miss a thing. We hadn't been introduced, but I'd read her file. Lt. Colonel Daniela "Dani" Brooks, newly-christened commander of the detachment, a force of 300 Rangers, which was significantly smaller than a battalion, more along the order of two companies. She'd seen actual combat in a cross-border incident with the joint US-Mexican task force against the Sinaloa Cartel as a company commander, which was a plus, but I had my doubts about her. I planned on keeping them to myself, since that was none of my damned business.

"So, what's the name?" she asked me, seemingly amused by the exchange.

I hesitated. Jambo and I had gone back and forth on this for weeks, vetoing each other's kookier and more esoteric ideas until we'd both been ready to just give in and let the Ordnance guys have their way and maybe try to convince everyone it was pronounced "Mike" instead of mice."

But a lot of googling and drinking had led to something that was a bit more distinctive if not quite as catchy as we'd been going for.

"We call it the Svalinn," I told her.

"The what?" the man beside her wondered, face screwed up in consternation.

He was older than me, older than her, with a head shaved against the disloyal desertion of his hair and lines etched into a mask carved from a granite cliff. Sgt. Major Jeffrey Devries, veteran of Venezuela, the Cartel Wars and Syria before that. Bronze Star, three purple hearts. Him, I had no doubts about.

"Svalinn," I repeated. "It's from Norse legend..." I began to explain, but Col. Brooks interrupted me.

"It's the shield of the gods," she explained. "It stands between the Earth and the Sun and keeps us from burning up."

I raised an eyebrow. "Wow," I said, impressed. "It took us hours playing around on the internet to find that one."

"It was well worth the effort," she assured me.

"It's better than MICE, anyway," Sgt. Major Devries murmured.

The three hundred Rangers had gathered here in the live fire range at what I had found out was originally an Idaho National Guard training area. They looked damned impressive in the Svalinn armor, each of them carrying the same weapon as Jambo and I. We didn't go out in the armor without the weapon. It was doctrine and we followed it because we'd written it.

"We are here at Staging Base Alpha," I told the Rangers, "not just to get you used to the new armor, but also to familiarize you to what is going to be the standard weapon for the Extraplanetary Detachment, the M900EMA1 Kinetic Energy Weapon." I held up the heavy, fat-barreled weapon one-handed. "This is an electromagnetic weapon that fires 4mm depleted uranium darts at 3,000 meters per second from a double drum of two hundred rounds."

It was a damned sight more high-tech than the light machine guns Jambo and I had carried around the first couple months, but then, so was the armor. I was frankly amazed at how quickly they'd perfected the stuff and rushed it into production. Maybe "perfected" wasn't the right word. They'd made it usable, which would have to be enough for now. The weapon, though...*that* made me salivate, after seeing what it could do to the frontal armor on an M1A main battle tank.

"The armor and this rifle wouldn't have been possible just a few months ago," I explained. "They both depend on the high-temperature superconductors and the new energy cells the Helta taught us how to make. The energy cells are incredible pieces of technology, but they are not infinite. Your weapons have fresh energy cells built into each drum of ammo and your armor will need to be recharged after seventy hours of normal use."

"We're Space Rangers," one of troops piped up from a couple ranks back. "Why aren't we using lasers? Can't the aliens build us laser guns?"

I winced at the question, wondering whether any of these guys had actually read my books, and was about to go into a long-winded explanation when someone else did it for me.

"That would be a damned good way to get yourself killed in a firefight in about two seconds." The kid was three ranks back and I could barely make out his earnest, chiseled features, but the handy-dandy Identification Friend or Foe display projected into a corner of my helmet's visor told me he was Corporal Randolph Quinn, a team leader in Second squad, First platoon, Delta Company.

"You're one hundred percent right, Corporal Quinn," I told him. "Care to explain to all these people why that is?"

The kid's face reddened. He was about twenty-one if I judged right, and probably not used to being the center of attention.

"Um, sir," he stammered, "it's because of the thermal signature. I mean, we didn't have starships or any of that shit, sir, and we already had thermal sights built into our optics. If you tried to use a laser in a gunfight, it would be like shining a damned spotlight. Everyone within a klick would know right where you were."

"Exactly right, Corporal Quinn." I grinned, though he couldn't see it. "I bet you've read my books."

"No, sir," he admitted. "But I watch the show..."

"Of course you do," I muttered, frowning. "Jambo, take the

whole bunch down to the static range and we can start running them through familiarization fire one at a time."

I hung back as Jambo set off, our squad of half-trained trainers following, most of the Detachment in tow. Lt. Colonel Brooks stayed behind as well, staring at me as though she could see right through the reflective visor. I popped it up politely and was immediately hit by the oppressive late summer heat. I'd gotten used to my own personal air conditioning.

"Did you have any more questions, ma'am?" I wondered.

"Just one, Major Clanton," she said. "I've read your file, of course. I assume you've read mine." I didn't answer and she smiled thinly and went on. "I've also skimmed a few of your books. You're old-fashioned in many ways, particularly for a science fiction writer. I wonder if you have a problem with women serving in the infantry?"

"I might have once, ma'am," I admitted. "Most women can't match most men for upper body strength, and I've always been of the opinion that they didn't belong in the infantry for practical reasons. But those don't matter anymore, do they?"

To illustrate my point, I bent down and picked up a case of ammo from a stack on the ground in front of me. The metal cannister held a thousand of the depleted uranium darts and probably weighed one hundred pounds, but I lifted it one-handed using the Svalinn armor and tossed it to her with a casual, underhand throw. She caught it just as easily, her arm barely giving an inch in the exoskeletal armor and she nodded understanding.

"Happy to see it doesn't bother you," she said, setting the cannister back on the ground. She was still smiling, but the expression had taken on a hard edge. "I'm used to working with assholes, but that doesn't mean I enjoy it."

Ooh. Put me in my place, didn't she?

"I'll tell you what I don't like and can't abide though, Colonel," I said, determined for some stubborn reason not to be one-upped. At her cocked eyebrow, I went on. "I can't abide this Space Ranger shit." I shook my head, pursing my lips in distaste. "We've all stepped straight into every space opera novel I ever read as a kid, and by God, it should be the Space Navy and the Space *Marines*, not this namby-pamby, bureaucratic-sounding Space Force shit, and definitely not the damn Space Rangers. What's the damn unit motto gonna be? To infinity and beyond?"

That got her. She laughed, an honest laugh this time, and the hardness left her eyes.

"Major," she said, "only a jarhead could take Space Marines seriously."

It had taken some doing and a lot of ear-chewing for the tech types to understand the importance of making the Svalinn armor capable of firing from the prone position. I'd actually had to call Olivera and have him call the fucking *President* to force the modification down their throat.

It's impractical, they'd whined. *It decreases the functionality of armor in the neck and arm joints...*

I'd yelled at Theo Blackwell, the General Dynamics rep, that the increased protection on the neck and arm joints wasn't going to do a damned bit of good if all the Rangers were standing out in the open getting hit square in the chest because they couldn't assume the prone firing position. Then I'd yelled the same thing at Olivera before realizing he outranked me and apologizing. And of course, the whole time, Jambo had been yelling at *me*, as if it were my fault, and letting me stick my neck out with the brass, just the way good NCOs have since Alexander the Great.

But it was a testament to my own personal abrasiveness that the Rangers getting their first live range time with the M900s were lying in the prone with the stock tucked into their shoulder, the same way infantry has been shooting their rifles since the cartridge was developed.

"I'm sure all of you boys and girls know how to shoot," Jambo was saying, transmitting over their helmet frequencies at the same time as he was amplifying it through his Svalinn's external speakers. He was also calling two captains and two master sergeants "boys and girls," but I wasn't going to be the one who broke Jambo of a career's worth of bad habits. "But let me be the first to assure you, the M900 is *not* like any of the rifles you've fired in your whole damned life. It has a variable rate of fire, for one thing. Check out that little switch on the side. That's the manual control, just in case something goes wrong with the contact link between the rifle's pistol grip, your gloves and your helmet's Heads-Up Display."

"Master Sergeant Bowie," one of the company commanders had rolled onto his side and raised his hand like he was in elementary school asking the teacher if he could go to the bathroom. I knew who he was without checking the IFF transponder. The two company commanders were Jeremy Spires and Alicia Freeman, and this guy didn't look like an Alicia.

"Sir?" Jambo said curtly. He did not, I knew, like being interrupted.

"Why did they go for something as complicated as a contact link through the gloves? Why not just link the weapons optics and controls to the helmet wirelessly?"

"For the same reason we built and tested this armor, sir," Jambo told him, thumping his chest with his fist, producing a hollow thump, "instead of just putting an M900 on a remotely piloted drone and calling it a day. Our friends the Helta may not be much for soldiers, but they're very, very bright when it comes to gadgets, and one of the first things they did when they thought there might be the possibility of going to war with the Tevynians was to develop jamming systems that could shut down any and all wireless control systems." He smiled thinly.

"And because the Helta suck at war, the Tevynians promptly *stole* those jamming systems and kidnapped Helta technicians and forced them to mass-produce them. Now, every Tevynian battle group, every fighter, every infantry company they put in the field has a full suite of signal jammers to make sure no one can use remotely piloted armed drones against them."

The woman next to Spires, the aforementioned Captain Freeman motioned at Jambo, then used the same hand to swipe a strand of blond hair out of her eyes.

"Why not just use autonomous armed drones, then?" she wondered.

Jambo shot me a sour look and I rubbed my thumb and fingers together at him, letting him know I hadn't forgotten our bet. I'd *told* him one of the Rangers would ask it.

"Couple reasons," he said, showing admirable patience, particularly for a Delta operator who'd never had to defer to any officer outside his chain of command for most of his career. "One, autonomous systems are susceptible to hacking, and it would be damned inconvenient for all our armed drones to start attacking us in the field because the Tevynians figured out a way to fuck up their target designation systems.

"And two, the Helta have...." He made a face, partly because this was hard to explain and partly, I knew, because he found the whole thing ridiculous. "They have what you might call a religious problem with letting robots kill people. I don't know where it comes from. Hell, to be honest, *they* don't know where it comes from, but they are just dead set against artificial intelligence in general and armed robots in particular. They *have* robots, but they can't think like a human, or a Heltan, and they're not much more sophisticated than one of the automated receptionists you can find in the high-end boutiques in Europe and Japan."

"And it's a damned good thing they don't have AI," I put in. I was standing behind the firing line, flanked by Colonel Brooks and Sgt. Major Devries, watching the show, and the two captains twisted around to look back at me. "Because if they did," I finished, "then the Tevynians would have them by now, and we'd be fighting them. So Thank God for small favors."

"Anyway," Jambo went on, his voice rising, letting them know he didn't want to be interrupted again, "getting back to the M900. You can adjust the rate of fire with the knob on the gun or using the eye-controlled HUD in your helmet, and we're going to practice both. The thing to remember is, the faster you fire, the slower the muzzle velocity is going to be. If you're going up against armor or troops behind thick cover, set the gun for single shot and you'll get the full 3,000 meters per second. If you've got multiple targets in the open, lightly armored, set it for the maximum rate of fire, six hundred rounds a minute, and you'll empty that two hundred round drum in twenty seconds, but the slugs will only be traveling about 1,000 meters per second. Everyone clear on that?"

There were nods all around and Jambo grunted in satisfaction.

"All right then, the next thing to keep in mind about the M900 is there *is* no windage or elevation. This damn slug is going fast enough when it clears the barrel that it ain't gonna have any bullet drop before it hits the fuckin' horizon. Windage...well, maybe if we're in a hurricane, but nothing you're going to have to worry about."

He lifted his rifle and held it out for all the platoon and the officers and senior NCOs to see. He tapped his finger against the armored cylinder riding atop the receiver.

"This is your optics. As I said, it's hooked up to your helmet HUD via the link through your gloves, but if you have to, you can use the optics with your eye the way God intended. Normally,

I'm a big proponent of having physical backup sights on a rifle just in case the electronics goes all to shit, but in this case, the rifle, your armor, just about everything is powered and if the electronics go to shit, you're going to be running around in your skivvies anyway."

He cocked his eyebrow at them.

"Now, if the brass decides to send good old Master Sergeant Bowie into combat in one of these here Svalinns, I am definitely going to bring a regular bullet-shooting gunpowder pistol as a backup, because I might be naked, but I ain't ever gonna be unarmed." He slapped a palm against the SIG holstered at his chest, looking distinctly out of place on the high-tech armor. "Word to the wise."

He hefted the rifle.

"Side note here, you ain't gonna be firing this thing unless you're in armor. It weighs a shit-ton and kicks like a son of a bitch. You won't notice it in the Svalinn suits, but if the power goes out, don't bother trying to salvage the rifle. And the last thing we're going to talk about before the live fire is, make sure you know your fucking backstop. It's important with a regular weapon and it's a million times more important with these fuckers. If this slug misses, it's gonna keep on going for a couple kilometers until it hits something and likely fucks it up. If it hits something flimsy, it's going to fuck it up and keep going until it hits something harder." He looked around. "Hoo-ah?"

"Hoo-ah," they responded. It was an Army thing. Marines said "ooh-rah," but mostly as a sign of enthusiasm or a battle cry. The fucking Army used it as a catch-all response to "do you understand type questions."

"Okay, then. Everyone, take up your firing positions!"

At a normal live fire range, there'd be a range control tower with a loudspeaker to give orders, but the armor's communications gear made that unnecessary. Jambo could handle it, and I was his backup.

"There's no need to chamber a round with these weapons. They strip the rounds from the drum magazine magnetically when you pull the trigger. Center the aiming reticle in your helmet's HUD on your target. Be sure you're firing at the target in *your* lane."

The targets were decades-old, junked Bradley armored personnel carriers filled with sand just to make sure the rounds stopped right there. They were five hundred meters out, far enough to keep it from being a point-blank shot but close enough no one should be able to miss with the helmet targeting systems.

"If anyone is having trouble achieving a target lock with the reticle, put your weapon down and raise your hand."

One person did. It was inevitable. Someone always did. Jambo rolled his eyes and went to advise the private in question quietly, going so far as to put the man's hands in the right position on the stock before he walked back to just behind the firing line.

"With your right thumb, switch the safety off. Your weapons should already be set to semiautomatic. If they are not, you will see the notification in your HUD."

Jambo had the rangemaster voice down pat, bringing back fond memories of Parris Island.

"Are we ready on the left?" He peered down the line of shooters to his left. "The left is ready! Are we ready on the right?" His head swung around the other direction. "The right is ready! Shooters, the range is hot! Commence semiautomatic fire!"

It took a moment. Everyone wanted to make sure they didn't screw up the very first firing of the M900, not knowing that Jambo and I had taken that honor ourselves weeks ago. The first round came from a private, of course. The discharge of the M900 was a sound like nothing else, a whining snap combined with the crack of the round burning an ionized hole through the atmosphere and the thunder of the air filling the evacuated hole. It was as close as I would ever come to hearing the sound of a real blaster from a science fiction movie and I was sure it would never get old.

"Solid hit there, Private Meinke," Jambo said.

It was. I'd zoomed in on the old Bradley with the helmet's optics and the puff of smoke coming off its turret armor was clearly visible.

As if Jambo's words had been a signal, the rest of the platoon opened fire and the unique sound of the individual KE guns somehow blended into the rolling crackle of every firing line at every range I'd ever visited in all my years in the Marines. The impacts were distant, metallic bangs, nothing I could have heard singly, but together a handbell choir practicing, the next valley over.

I checked the IFF screen and found Corporal Quinn at the left end of the formation. The gravel crunched under the soles of my boots as I strode down behind his position and crouched. His form was excellent for someone using both the armor and the rifle for the first time, and every round he fired was hitting the retired Bradley, center mass.

"Cease fire, cease fire, cease fire!" Jambo bellowed. "Shooters, safeties on! Now, using your manual switches, adjust your rifle's rate of fire to maximum ROF."

This was going to be fun. It was riding my first bike, kissing my first girl, and jumping out of an airplane for the first time all rolled into one, and now that I'd had my chance, it was nearly as fun to watch someone else. Quinn examined the rifle controls carefully for a moment before turning the knob to the far right, then settled the buttstock against his armored shoulder again.

"Pull the rifle in tight," I advised on the general communications net. "That muzzle's going to try to climb on you and if you let it climb too high, you're going to send rounds downrange about five kilometers."

"Shooters!" Jambo called again after giving them about ten seconds to manipulate the controls. "Are we ready on the right? The right is ready. Are we ready on the left? The left is ready. Shooters, the range is hot! Safeties off and commence firing!"

If the M900 fired on single shot was a sci-fi movie blaster, the weapon on full auto was a summer thunderstorm captured in a bottle. The noise from the line of shooters was incredible, deafening even through the sound baffles of the Svalinn's helmet, and the effects on the targets was nothing short of devastating. Quinn's Bradley was being ripped apart like someone had taken a can opener to it, steel armor peeling away in sheets from the turret, sand drifting out of holes the size of a man's head. The kid fired in controlled bursts, which was more restraint than I'd been able to show when they'd given me the chance, but he still emptied the drum in a matter of seconds.

He found the ejection control and popped the drum free, then switched on his safety and rolled off the weapon, grinning like a teenager who'd just lost his virginity.

"Sir," he said to me, "I will go anywhere you want and fight whatever space monsters you throw me at, as long as I can have this gun."

"Corporal Quinn, you are a man after my own heart." I grinned, the expression feeling lopsided on my face. "Welcome to the fucking Space Rangers."

9

The last time I'd seen Joon-Pah, he had been surrounded by his crew inside an alien starship, and his own strange appearance had blended in with all the rest of the strangeness. Sitting at the table of the White House Situation Room though, he very much looked like a man-sized koala bear stuffed into human clothes, and I couldn't stop staring at him until Jambo nudged me with an elbow.

"At least now I don't feel like the most out of place guy in this room," he told me, grinning.

"You never were as long as I was here," I assured him.

At least we didn't have half the brass in DC in this meeting the way they were at the last one. Olivera and Julie were there, the first time I'd seen them in the five months since our "only-the-good-die-young" injections. None of us had died, or grown a third eye or mutated into an alien monster yet, so I was still hopeful it had worked.

Gatlin was present, looking a bit haggard and overworked, and I wondered if he'd taken the anti-aging shot and would start looking younger in a few months, once his skin cells had replaced themselves with less decrepit copies. He'd said hello to me and Jambo but had otherwise been engaged in a long, technical and nearly incomprehensible conversation with Joon-Pah about gravimetic force vectors, whatever the hell those were.

Delia Strawbridge had shown up and greeted us all with a perfunctory nod, her eyes locked on a tablet. She kept tapping it with a stylus and making troubled faces at whatever it was showing her. If they'd invited Shaddick and Patel, it would have been a *Selenium* reunion, but I guess those two had more important things to do than meet with the President.

The only one here who wasn't on the original crew was Colonel Brooks, who'd flown in with Jambo and me from Idaho. She hadn't been any happier with the interruption in training than we had, but I suppose if you can't trust your subordinates to handle things while you're gone, you should have picked better ones in the first place.

We all sprang to our feet when he entered the room, the Secret Service agents with him staring long and hard at Joon-Pah like they expected a chest-burster to pop out of him and go lay eggs inside Crenshaw. Which, I guess, you know, wasn't entirely unjustified as paranoia went, given that the President of the United States was in the same room with an alien.

With the President was the National Security Advisor Thomas Caldwell, who I'd expected, and the Honorable Sonia Harrell, the Speaker of the House, who I had not. I tried not to glare at the tall, bleached-blond woman with Face by Botox as we all seated ourselves again.

"Speaker Harrell wished to be part of our briefing today," President Crenshaw explained, the strain in his smile showing he'd never quite mastered the art of political bullshit despite his current lofty position.

"If I'm supposed to keep approving these ridiculous budgets," Harrell interjected in the snide, condescending New York City accent that always made me want to jam icepicks in my ear, "then I need to be briefed straight from the horse's mouth." She made a face with collagen-injected lips. "By all rights, Mister Joon-Pah here *should* be testifying before Congress—"

"I'm sure *Captain* Joon-Pah has better things to do with his time than putting on a dog and pony show here in DC," Crenshaw said. "His people and the crews from Gatlin Aerospace have been working around the clock trying to complete the defenses—"

"This nation's political process doesn't stop just because aliens invade, Mr. President. And I might add that the way you've kept all this away from our long-time allies is simply shameful—"

"It isn't me that's keeping the Germans from stepping up and taking a role in this," Crenshaw said, obviously losing patience with the opposition leader. "It's their own political divisions. They were given the same chance as Britain and Australia and Japan—"

"And the brinksmanship you've been engaging in with China and Russia..."

I rubbed fingers against my temples and wished I was back in my Svalinn with a KE gun in my hand.

"We're here for a briefing," Crenshaw reminded the Speaker, stopping her intended diatribe. "Mr. Gatlin, the Speaker would like to know what progress your people have made with the orbital defense platforms and the dual-environment fighters Congress approved."

"Things are going remarkably fast, sir," Gatlin said, then added, perhaps a bit reluctantly, "Madame Speaker. The engineering crews Joon-Pah loaned us have been invaluable and we're already processing ore from the automated Lunar mines in the orbital smelting facility. The first defense platform should be operational within six months, maximum, the next three months after that." He shrugged. "You have to understand, these are fairly straightforward structures, launching platforms for anti-ship missiles with fusion warheads and remotely-controlled railgun mounts. The fighters are going to be a longer-term project, I'm afraid." He spread his hands apologetically.

"It's the materials, you understand. Orbital platforms can be made from raw nickel iron because we don't have to fly them anywhere, but building a fighter that can fly in space *and* the atmosphere requires synthetics we haven't even developed yet, carbon nanotube production on an industrial scale..."

"We are helping as best we can in this," Joon-Pah said, and I swear to God I saw Harrel's eyes bug out when he spoke, like she thought he'd been a movie prop or something until then. "However, building the production facilities for mass fabrication of the material will take nearly a year, and there is nothing we can do to advance this significantly."

"Until then," Gatlin declared, "all we have are the two armed shuttles we were able to put together from the spare parts the Helta had on the *Truthseeker*. Those are fully adapted for human pilots and crew and can be configured to carry either fifty Rangers in full armor or a load of cargo. Those should be enough for the mission."

Again with people talking about *the mission.* I'd heard the words over and over the last few months, but no one could or would share any details. I was getting a bit pissed off. Operational security is a fine thing, but I'd say the guys training your front-line troops need to fucking know.

"I'm still not comfortable with the accelerated pilot training and the shortened safety testing," Julie said, scowling, unfazed by Harrel's presence. "We're talking about flying these things in space under conditions we can't even begin to imagine."

"My own people have gone over the craft from top to bottom," Joon-Pah assured her. "And we will have time for full flight tests en route. But we don't know how long it will take the Tevynians to figure out where this system is. The ship chasing us wasn't able to report back, but they must have a general idea what sector it was investigating. It could be a matter of months, or even weeks."

"I'm afraid there's no time for the usual military safety protocols, Captain Nieves," Crenshaw told her. "Captain Joon-Pah is right. This mission has to proceed on schedule." He speared Colonel Brooks with a look. "Colonel, are your Rangers ready for this?"

"Hoo-ah, sir!" Brooks responded, a bit stiffly. This was her first meeting with the President...her first time in DC, in fact, and I knew she wasn't used to the politics. "They've all been checked out with the new armor and weapons and they're ready to kick some ass!"

Jesus. Fucking Rangers. Bunch of hard-charging yahoos.

"And what say you to that, Major Clanton?" Crenshaw asked me. "Master Sergeant Bowie?"

"This stuff is nearly as new to us as it is to them, Mr. President," I admitted. "But everything we've figured out to do with the Svalinn armor, Colonel Brooks' Rangers can do it to the letter and by the book."

"Of course," Jambo put in, "Andy and I wrote the book, so..."

Crenshaw chuckled at that, though Harrel's expression looked skeptical. Well, what expression could get through the frozen features.

"Sir," I said, less reticent this time to speak up, half because the newness of it had worn off and half because I hated Harrel and wanted to piss her off by ignoring her, "I know everything has been hush-hush and need to know, but can I ask what the mission is that everyone keeps talking about?"

Crenshaw turned to Caldwell.

"Tommy?"

"Right," Caldwell sighed. "I suppose it couldn't hurt." He looked around at Brooks, Jambo and me, confirming what I'd guessed about who had been kept in the dark. Before Caldwell had the chance to spill the beans, Botox Queen opened her mouth again.

"Would someone care to explain to me why a hack science fiction writer is in this room and taking part in a top-secret briefing?" She smiled at me with as much insincerity as a politician could muster. "No offense, Mr. Clanton."

"That's *Major* Clanton, Madame Speaker," I reminded her with as much disdain as I could put into the words without being charged with insubordination.

"Major Clanton was part of the initial contact with the Helta," Crenshaw reminded her. "He was on Mr. Gatlin's translunar ship."

"And it's bad enough we've given Daniel Gatlin's company a monopoly on the new technology the Helta have provided," Harrel snapped, glaring at the man. Gatlin stroked his beard, clearly amused by the rant. "Why haven't we thanked *Major* Clanton for his assistance, made him sign an NDA and then deposited him back on the set of his TV show in Hollywood?"

"It's filmed in Canada," I corrected her. "As I'm sure Captain Joon-Pah will corroborate, all alien planets look like Canada."

"Excuse me interrupting," Jambo said, in a tone that made it clear he wasn't the least bit sorry, "but Andy here is one of two people, myself being the other, who tested every bit of equipment the new Ranger units are going to be using. He basically invented the tactics for the things. If we're going operational with this unit, he needs to be involved."

My ears were warm and I hoped to God my face wasn't as red as it felt. For Jambo, that was basically a declaration of undying love.

Joon-Pah made a sound like a cat coughing up a hairball and

everyone stared at him. I decided it had to be his equivalent of clearing his throat, or maybe his imitation of us doing it.

"Major Clanton was instrumental in coming up with a tactic to defeat the Tevynian ship," he said. "Something none of the Helta would have thought of."

"And something *I* wouldn't have thought of, either," Olivera admitted, "because I had no concept of the technologies we were dealing with. Clanton and science fiction writers like him have been imagining this sort of thing for decades. He may not know the physics, but he can visualize the concepts."

"We're living in a science fiction world now," Julia put in. "Who better to advise us?"

"In the country of the blind," Crenshaw said with a piratical smile, "the one-eyed man is king." He nodded to Caldwell. "Proceed, Tom."

Harrel looked as if she'd bitten down on something sour, which wasn't too different from the way she always looked, but she said nothing.

"The First Extraplanetary Detachment," Caldwell said, "is being deployed for a scouting mission in the *Truthseeker*, accompanied by the refitted shuttles and commanded by Space Force Colonel Olivera. While production of the new weapons and aerospacecraft continues back here, along with training of the new troops, the detachment is going to one of the Helta's core systems on a mission to secure some starships of our own."

My heart was thumping wildly, a fire raging in my imagination, the sort of feeling I'd had when I was eight years old and reading the Robert Heinlein juveniles or watching the old Star Trek movies. *Starships of our own.* We were going to have fucking starships. While I was still alive to see it. It was enough to make me forget the war we were going to have to fight to get the stuff.

"If all goes well, and the arrangements I set in place before I left to seek you out come to fruition," Joon-Pah said, "there should be no fewer than two and perhaps as many as three cruisers of the same class as the *Truthseeker* in the construction and repair docks in the Heshib systems asteroid belt, ready for us to commandeer."

"Once we have the starships back in orbit," Gatlin added, "we can begin refitting them with the new weapons systems we've added to the *Truthseeker*."

"New weapons systems?" I repeated, intensely curious. What weapons systems could we come up with that were better than a fusion-powered particle accelerator?

"Yeah," Olivera said, grinning. "That's actually based on your little billiard ball strategy. Apparently, there are all sorts of things you can do with the drive field on one of these ships."

"And me and Jam...Master Sergeant Bowie are going to continue training the troops back here?" I said. It was disappointing, but it made sense. The training had to be done if we were going to have enough troops to deploy on two or three starships of our own.

"I have another idea about that," Olivera said, regarding the two of us thoughtfully. "Sergeant Bowie was pulled away from his own CAG team to train the new detachment, so I think it's only fair to put him in charge of the Special Operations team on this mission. They'll be equipped with the new Svalinn armor and KE guns, plus a few other goodies we've developed. And I think you, Major Clanton," he jabbed a finger at me, "should accompany the mission attached to the special operations team as a technical advisor."

"How 'bout that, bro?" Jambo enthused, slapping me on the shoulder. "You're gonna be the first jarhead to go the stars!"

My head swam, my thoughts a rush of adrenaline and wonder and sheer, fucking terror.

I'm going to the stars, the eight-year-old kid screamed at me, the sort of scream I would have made at the top of the first big dive on a rollercoaster.

But the part of me that had survived combat, seen friends die, witnessed enough horror and death to drive me into a bottle for the better part of five years countered the child with sober, adult cynicism.

And the stars are at war.

10

I'd gotten my cell phone back when we left the Situation Room and I tossed it in my hand a few times, seeing a million possibilities. The base in Idaho had full-spectrum communications jammers to keep anyone from doing anything stupid like sending their geotagged selfie taken in a Svalinn suit, but we were in DC and the skies were wide open.

Jambo and the others joined me on the front steps of the White House, waiting for our limo. I squinted in the bright, late summer sunlight, sweating already. DC in August was a humid, bug-infested nightmare. Beyond the fence and lines of security police, protestors chanted and waved signs for the media drones. The protests had been going on since the day the Helta showed up, dwindled to almost nothing, but experiencing a resurgence every time some new tidbit of information was released. I wasn't sure what, exactly, this group's problem was, whether it was denying aliens existed, insisting it was all a hoax, protesting the US getting involved militarily, protesting the UN not being involved or maybe a bunch of furries complaining they should be included in negotiations since the Helta were obviously their brethren.

"We have to be ready to ship out in three weeks," Olivera told us, slipping on his cover.

It's a damned hat. Why can't the military just call things what they are instead of inventing new shit for us to remember?

"We'll be leaving from out there," Julie added, careful not to mention the name of the base or where we were leaving *for*. "Our rides will be ready to go and can take off from basically anywhere."

"Your special operations team will be there when you get back," Olivera said to Jambo. "I know it's going to be an accelerated training course with the armor and weapons, but you can continue their training en route."

"Are you two heading back with us?" Brooks asked, gesturing toward Olivera and Julie.

"Negative," Olivera told her. "We have some last-minute checks to finish." He checked the time on his smart watch and scowled. "In fact, we have a helicopter to catch. Glad I didn't bring any luggage."

"Our flight leaves in the morning," Brooks said, grinning, "and I fully intend to take advantage of the expense account room service in our hotel." She sighed. "And maybe I can video chat with my family before I go to bed. I haven't seen any of them in months. I think my kids have forgotten I exist."

"My daughter is in Honolulu with my ex-husband," Julie lamented. "It's six hours earlier there so we talk on the phone about as often as you see your family live and in person, Dani."

"Here's our car," Olivera told Julie, nodding at a driverless Honda pulling up to the curb. It was a government vehicle, of course. They didn't let any cab, driverless or not, inside the White House gates. "Safe flight to you three."

I shuddered, knowing it was ironic for a science fiction writer to be a Luddite and not caring. I would *never*, not if I lived to be four hundred, which I just might, get used to driverless cars. The two of them slid into the back seat as if it was the most natural thing in the world, chatting as the car pulled away and blended into the traffic.

Brooks was frowning at the line of limos, cars and buses waiting to pull up to the pickup area.

"Where the hell is our limo?" she muttered. She waved at us, heading back up the steps. "You two hang out here, I'm going to go see if they have the driver's contact number."

"If we're gonna be a while," Jambo told me, "I gotta hit the latrine." He grinned at me. "That's the 'head' for you jarhead types...and our president."

"I'll wait here," I said, "in case the limo arrives."

Once he'd disappeared, I pulled my phone out and scrolled through the numbers, knowing it was there but forgetting what I stored it under. A for Allie? No, nothing. C for Clanton? Not for a while now, but no, not there, either. J for her maiden name Jackson? No. F for her new husband's name, Franklin? Again, no.

Ah, there it was under B. For bitch.

I touched the screen and called my ex-wife.

It rang a good nine times and I was confident it was going to go straight to voicemail. I hung up before it did. I didn't really want to hear her voice, particularly not being artificially cheerful. I scrolled down to Z for Zach.

It rang fifteen times, and when it was picked up, I actually felt a little lightheaded.

"Zack?" I said, hope welling up in my chest.

She killed it, of course.

"You know you're not supposed to call him directly," Allie said, a primary school teacher scolding a student. "You're supposed to go through me."

"I've *tried* to go through you," I shot back, not bothering with pleasantries either. "You refuse to answer my calls and you won't let him talk to me. Despite the fact that you're legally *required* to by our custody agreement."

"Then you should speak to my lawyer, not call his cell directly." Her voice was flat and unapologetic, she wouldn't even consider the idea she was in the wrong.

"No," I snapped, "my *lawyer* will call your lawyer and then you're going to wind up back in court. Don't tell me you don't think I can afford a lawyer, Allie. You know exactly how much money I'm making and we both know how much I'm paying in child support. I may not be a real estate mogul like Paul, but I can tie you up in court if that's the way you want this to go. All I want is what the courts ruled I could have: an opportunity to talk to my son at least once a week. Now are you going to give me that opportunity?"

"This isn't a good time, Andy," she said, the hardass act finally cracking around the edges. "Zack and Paul are *just* starting to bond. It's taken a long time and I don't want to confuse things right now."

And I could believe that the quaver of emotion in her voice was real or not at my own discretion. She had proven how good an actor she was when she kept reassuring me over video calls that everything was fine and the only reason Zack was never around when I got time at the comm center was because he was so busy with sports. Then I'd come home from Venezuela to an empty house.

Not that I hadn't deserved it.

"It may not be a good time, but it's the only time I've got," I told her. "Jesus, you've seen the news. You know what's going on. You know where I was when all this started. This may be the only chance I have to talk to him for months."

And I was probably saying more than I was allowed to, but I was past caring. I was going not just off the planet but out of the fucking star system. I wanted the chance to tell my son goodbye.

"He's starting to call Paul 'dad,'" she blurted. "I don't want to let his alcoholic absentee father fuck up his one chance to have a stable family."

"Goddammit, Allie, you know that's bullshit," I growled. "I haven't had a drink in three years. I had PTSD and I was self-medicating and yeah, I was in a bad place and needed help. And I got it, but God knows it wasn't from you." I snapped my mouth shut on the next word, knowing I was letting her get under my skin. Again. "It doesn't matter. All that was between us, and it's over. I want to talk to Zack. I don't care who else you're telling him to call 'dad,' I am still his father."

She hesitated and I actually thought she might give in and make this easy. I must have forgotten who I was talking to.

"It's not a good time," she repeated, her tone a slamming door. "And I can't trust you."

"Allie—" I began, but there was no arguing with a closed door.

"You'd better go ahead and call your lawyer," she said, "because you're not talking to Zack."

The phone went dead. I cursed loud enough to turn a few heads on the curb around me and pressed my lips together hard to contain the litany of invective trying to get out, restrained myself from smashing the phone on the concrete, mindful for the first time in months of the uniform I was wearing.

I should have known better. I should have realized how it would go and just done what she said and called my lawyer first. But the God's honest truth was, Paul Franklin *was* a real estate mogul and he could afford better lawyers than I could, even with the TV deal. They'd tie this up in the courts for weeks just because they could, and by the time it actually got to a judge and the decision was made, I'd be too far away for it to matter. She'd win the way she'd always did, because she was the only one playing.

"Bro, are you sleepwalking or something?"

My head snapped around at Jambo's voice and I tucked the phone against my leg, hiding it out of instinct, though I didn't know why I should. He knew about the dissolution of my marriage. He'd even admitted to me once, after way too little sleep on way too long a training op, that he'd been married once, though he wouldn't say more than that.

"What?" I asked him, blinking in confusion.

"The fucking limo, man," he said, pointing in front of me. "It's right there."

I turned back toward the road and sure enough, there was a long, black car with a real, human driver waiting patiently in the left hand seat.

"Oh, sorry," I told him. "I was thinking about something. Should I run in and get Colonel Brooks?"

"Colonel Brooks is here, too," she announced over my other shoulder. "Good Lord, you *are* a bit out of it, aren't you, Clanton?"

She seemed amused by it rather than suspicious, so I just laughed and passed it off.

It was exactly the second limo I'd ever ridden in, so I couldn't say with any sort of certainty if it was high-end, but it was nicer than my Ford. I sank back into the seat and tried to think. The last time I'd talked to Zack, he'd gone on and on about a new fantasy MMORPG called Abysmal, how he'd made some new friends on the message forums dedicated to it on Threadit. I snuck a look at Jambo and Brooks, who were engaged in a discussion of the relative merits of .45ACP vs. 9mm for personal defense, just to make sure they weren't paying attention, then pulled up the search engine on my phone and found the message forum for Abysmal.

The limo ride back to the hotel took nearly forty minutes in DC traffic, and it almost wasn't long enough. There were *three* message forums for Abysmal on Threadit alone and I had no fucking clue what Zack's screen name would be.

Unless it was ZackClanton32.

Damn, someone has to have a talk with that kid about OpSec.

I'd found the screen name, and it was fairly obvious it was him. His manner of speaking, his word choices, the many times he'd referred to being born on a military base in California and now living in Austin, they all confirmed it was the right Zack Clanton.

At least he still uses my last name.

Registering for a log-in took another five minutes, and by the time I'd been authorized to post in the forum, the limo was stopping in front of the Hilton and someone was opening my door for me.

"You're lucky you have your own room, Colonel," Jambo told her as we escaped the brief taste of summer in DC into the blissful climate control of the lobby. "I hate to speak ill of an officer, but my boy Major Clanton here snores like a wounded rhino."

"I'd advise some tactical earplugs," Brooks told him. She tipped her head at the hotel's restaurant. "Did you boys want to grab some lunch?"

"Why don't you go ahead, Jambo?" I said. "I got a headache. Think I'm gonna go up to the room and catch a nap."

Jambo squinted at me the same way I saw him look at a guerilla leader who'd promised his people would be in place to support our attack right on time, *no problemo.*

"You sure you're okay, Andy?"

"Oh, yeah," I insisted, already pressing the button to call the elevator. "It's just the heat. And the time change. A couple hours of shut-eye and I'll be raring to go."

"All right," he relented with a shrug. "Pop a couple Vitamin I. There's a bottle on my nightstand."

"Will do." Then the elevator door opened with a chime.

I waited until I was free of Jambo's inquisitive stare before I tapped my phone screen to life again. I had to go through three different menus to find the private message function on Threadit, but finally, the dialogue box opened and my thumbs froze on the keyboard.

What the hell was I going to say?

Zack, this is your father. I've been trying to call but your mother always says you're not available...

No. Damn. Didn't want to play him against her. Playing games was her thing, not mine. I backspaced out of the last sentence.

I've been trying to call, but haven't been able to catch you. I remembered you said you liked this game, so I checked since I don't have your personal number. Here's mine. I tapped in my cell number. *I'm working with the military again, so your best bet will be to message me. I may be getting deployed very far away soon, so please get in touch with me as soon as you can.*

Love,

Dad

My thumb hovered over the button and I chewed on my lip, still not sure if I was doing the right thing. It was a violation of security, I was fairly sure, though I hadn't asked anyone. It was definitely a violation of our custody agreement, though that hadn't stopped Allie at any point.

"Fuck it." I hit the button, then turned the screen off and slipped it into my pocket.

An older lady riding beside me in the elevator raised an eyebrow and I blushed.

"Sorry, ma'am," I said.

"That's all right, son," she said with a knowing smile. "My

late husband was a Marine and he couldn't string five words together unless one of them was 'fuck,' so I'm used to it."

I laughed politely.

"I'm sorry he's gone, ma'am."

"Me too, every day," she said, eyes clouding with old memories. "He died in Afghanistan. A long time ago, now, but I miss him every day." She smiled wistfully. "At least my son had the brains to join the Space Force. Even with all this nonsense about these aliens, I'm pretty sure he'll never face anything more deadly than a paper cut."

I tried not to let the wince make it to my face.

"Yes, ma'am," was all I trusted myself to say. "I'm sure he'll be fine."

I got out on the twelfth floor and fumbled for my room key, wondering what the hell I was actually going to do. I didn't need a nap, I needed a drink.

I thought of my son and took a nap.

11

"You payin' attention to this shit, man?" Jambo asked, sprawled out on a couch in the break room of the Staging Base Alpha Training Headquarters, which was a very elaborate and fancy name for an ancient office building with half a dozen offices that we hardly ever used except when the time came to file reports on the official servers, which were isolated, even from the Space Force net.

I'd been using my personal tablet to tap into the heavily-censored entertainment net, trying to see if Zack had messaged me back. It was a forlorn hope at this point, I knew. We were scheduled to ship out in two days and the whole base was a buzz of activity, cargo trucks and power-loaders and heavy-lift helicopters heading in and out at all hours and a damned space shuttle pulled into a special, oversized hangar they'd constructed for it a couple months ago.

And it all left damned little for us to do except try to familiarize the Special Ops team with the suits and weapons in the time we had left. Even that had been put on hold for the moment. The live fire ranges were shut down because of all the air traffic and, more importantly, the repair shops and the techs were all shipping out to the *Truthseeker* and no one wanted to break a suit and have it left behind.

So the Delta boys were doing what operators do best when there's no real work to be done: shamming. And this was the best place to sham, far from the prying eyes of any officers. Except me. I was technically an officer, but I was outside their chain of command and might as well be a civilian as far as most of them were concerned. They were a bunch of odd ducks, all twelve of them, all ragged denim and ancient, faded T-shirts and scraggly hair, and every single one of them carried a gun everywhere but the shower. Maybe. I'd heard at least one conversation about "shower guns," but they might have been just yanking my chain.

Even here in the break room, absorbed in hand-held games and virtual reality goggles, sprawled over couches or hunched over folding tables, Glocks or SIGs or HKs stuck out of shoulder or belt holsters, and those were just the guns I could *see*.

"Paying attention to what?" I asked Jambo, tossing an empty Diet Coke can into the recycling bin.

I grabbed another from the fridge and frowned at it. I still needed to figure out a way to smuggle a few cases onto the ship. There was no way I was going to be able to live without caffeine for however long it would take to complete this mission, and I just can't stand coffee. God knows, I've tried. In the military, coffee is nearly as ubiquitous as divorce and every bit as bitter.

"The fucking news, bro," Jambo said as if I'd asked a dumb question. He had an hourly update running on the TV, though God knows why. All the talking heads were computer generated now, not like when I was a kid and we had real people to spout bullshit at us on the news.

I pulled the tab on my drink and sat down next to him while he rewound the segment he'd just watched. It was CSNC news, which I guess was a pretty balanced report, mostly, but I don't know why the hell they thought some old, bald dude was more convincing than a good-looking woman. I mean, they were both CGI saying the same shit...

"Russian President Anatoly Popov addressed a special session of the UN Security Council this morning, reiterating his contention that the United States' treaty with the Helta is tantamount to a declaration of war."

Popov was a fat fuck, and that's about the kindest thing I could say about him. He'd taken over after Putin died, but his attempt at imitating Putin's strongman routine seemed less an homage and more a satire. Every time he tried to sound commanding, he came off like a cartoon character, with his shock of white hair standing up like a rooster's comb, and yet this was the asshole who controlled a third of the world's nuclear weapons.

"The United States has no right to involve the people of this world in an alien war!" He pounded the podium in rage and I remembered old video clips of Khrushchev slamming his shoe on the table of the General Assembly in the 1960s. "A decision which affects every nation on this planet should be decided on by the UN, not by a single nation for the selfish purpose of enriching their coffers and leaving the rest of us to accept our fate! The people of the Russian Federation demand that the United States submit this matter for an immediate vote of the full United Nations General Assembly and pledge to abide by its decision! We further demand that if the General Assembly does vote to allow this alliance to occur, that all military duties be shared by the members of the Security Council. We will not allow the United States to lead us to destruction in an attempt to aggrandize themselves!"

The bald old man replaced the fat old man, though his expression was just as serious.

"Russia's representative to the UN immediately introduced

such a measure to the full General Assembly, with the majority of the nations condemning the alliance between the United States and her allies and the alien Helta, but the United States vetoed it. President Crenshaw conducted a news conference shortly after to give a response to the vote."

"This charade is about one thing," Crenshaw said, joined *en media res*, "and that is President Popov's greed. He doesn't care about the fate of the world, he cares about Russia not having access to weapons technology. And I am not of a mind to provide weapons to a man who has already invaded his neighbors. I don't think the people of the Ukraine would appreciate us aiding in the absorption of their independent nation by Russia.

"The fact is, the Tevynians know about Earth, know our location, and they have the ability to reach us. We can turn down alliance with the Helta and throw ourselves on the mercy of a military force that has so far shown it has none, or take this opportunity to be able to defend ourselves. I would prefer that everyone in the world understood this was the wisest choice, but I will not sit back and wait for them to acquire both the brains and the courage to make the decision, not when it's my family, my nation, my world hanging in the balance."

"Ooh," one of the Delta weapons' specialists said through a mouthful of crackers, "good line. Give that fucking speechwriter a raise."

"As for President Popov's contention that we are hoarding the Helta technology for ourselves," Crenshaw continued, "I wish to assure him that we will be disseminating the technological advances they've shared with us as soon as we can separate those which have weapons potential from those which are purely beneficial. But everyone needs to bear in mind that our main goal is to defend our world against not just a possible but a *probable* attack from an aggressive and imperialist government. It won't do a bit of good to provide cheap transportation and power to the nations of the world a few months faster if we are subsequently taken over and subjugated by the Tevynians."

The singularly unattractive announcer simulacrum reappeared, with a shot of black-clad marchers clogging a city street somewhere that might have been Portland or Seattle, waving signs that said shit like "No alien wars!" and "Get the US out of the UniverSe," which at least had the benefit of being imaginative. The marches and signs and yelling were a constant background noise and no one paid attention to them anymore, besides the media and the political hacks.

"Protests continue in many major cities as—"

Jambo hit the pause button, looking as if he wanted to throw the remote control at the screen.

"I knew the fucking Russians were going to cause trouble. You'd think Popov would be happy we're so focused on the Tevynian threat that we didn't do a damned thing about the Ukraine, that everyone is too distracted to even care, but he just keeps pushing this thing."

"I think it's 3-D chess," the guy eating the crackers opined. He'd said his name was Gus, but he'd never bothered with a rank, or a last name. "I think he's pushing this shit in public *because* it's distracting the press and the rest of the world. He knows he ain't getting those alien weapons, so he's gonna grab as much territory as he can with both hands while no one's looking. He probably thinks by the time we have the guns and the time to confront him, his people will be so dug in, it'll be impossible to push them out."

"You're giving him too much credit," a tall, rangy redhead piped up, without looking away from his handheld video game. Everyone called him Ginger, which I assumed was a nickname. "He isn't smart enough to think that strategically. "He's saying this shit because he believes it, and if the boys and girls in DC aren't taking his talk about this being a declaration of war seriously, then they damn well should be."

"What do you think, Andy?" Jambo asked me. "You think Popov is for real or is it all just bullshit?"

I thought about it for a second. I hadn't had a lot of time to follow the news the last few months, but I knew things were tense. There'd been riots everywhere, from Rio to Riyadh and Beijing to Boston, and cities were still burning in some places. Governments had gone under in the Middle East and Africa and a dozen border wars had gone hot, including Pakistan and India, though they hadn't gone nuclear. Yet.

China had been curiously quiet, and most people were of the opinion that Crenshaw had negotiated a deal with them to keep a lid on at least one of our biggest worries.

"I don't know," I admitted. "I mean, I think even Popov—"

A notification chime drew my attention and it was all I could do not to gape like an idiot when I saw the message icon blinking at me on the Threadit screen.

"Just a second," I told Jambo, stepping out into the hallway outside the breakroom.

Out in the offices, Space Force enlisted men were packing away equipment for the shuttles, but none of them so much as glanced my way. I touched the message box with a trembling finger and read the response.

Dad, I've really missed you. I keep asking mom to let me call you, but she won't let me and she's put a block on my phone. I want to see you before you leave. Where are you? Zack.

I was breathing hard, about to hyperventilate. I felt more nervous then when my V22 was going down outside Maracaibo. He'd answered me. He wanted to see me.

Holy shit. I hit reply, hoping maybe I could catch him before he signed off.

I'm in western Idaho, but I won't be here long. I don't think I can get to Austin before I have to leave.

I shouldn't have told him that. I knew it, knew I could face a court-martial for giving away our location. This was stupid. There was no chance I could see him, but maybe I could figure out a way to get ahold of him for at least a video chat before I left. Maybe on a third-party app that could get around the block on his phone...

The message icon lit up again.

I am at Uncle George's house in Bend for two weeks before school starts. Could you come to Bend in time?

Mountain Home, Idaho to Bend, Oregon. I cursed, not remembering the distance if I ever knew it, and checked it on the tablet's mapping software. Under six hours if I drove. If I could get ahold of a car. Where the hell was I going to get a car?

Fuck it.

I made my decision. My fingers flew over the keyboard, the thoughts cohering on the tablet screen.

I can be there this evening. Seven o'clock. What's the address?

A pause, not overly long, not any longer than before, yet it seemed to take years and I wondered if he'd backed out, decided it was a bad idea, decided he believed what his mother had been telling him. The chime surprised me, though it shouldn't have, and I nearly dropped the tablet.

There's a convenience store just a couple blocks from Uncle George's house. I walk down there all the time to buy candy bars. I'll drop an address pin in this post. Meet me there at 8PM. Love you, Dad. Can't wait to see you.

I could barely see the screen. There was something in my eye and I had to wipe my sleeve across my face before I typed a reply. *I'll be there. Love you, too.*

I waited another two or three minutes just in case there was another massage. When none came, I turned the tablet off, folded it up and stuffed it into my pocket. It was one of the general-issue folding tabs from the break room, cheap and ubiquitous, but I didn't want anyone stumbling on the search history for this one, at least not for the next couple days.

I sucked in a breath and tried to think, but raw emotion surged in my chest and it was everything I could do to keep from sobbing. I hadn't seen Zack in person in nearly a year, and I'd begun to think I never would. The last time we'd been in the same room, he'd been quiet, reticent, only willing to talk about online gaming and the latest virtual reality headsets. He was thirteen, smack in the demographic for my show, but said he'd never watched it. He hadn't been willing to talk about his friends, school, or even sports beyond a noncommittal one or two sentences of "they're all right" or something like that.

I thought I'd made peace with it, accepted I'd made mistakes, not the least of which was marrying Allie in the first place. It had seemed the thing to do. You graduated college, you got your commission, you bought a new car and you married your girlfriend. The fact you'd be spending the next year or so in one training school or another, moving from one base to another while your wife was alone, having to deal with her own career along with the hassles of setting up your new life together by herself wasn't something anyone thought about.

I'd been assigned to a stateside base, which had seemed lucky, and we'd thought everything would be fine. Then Venezuela had happened and the vicious cycle began. After the first combat tour, Allie had been so grateful I survived and I'd been so happy to be back, we decided to have a kid. And the shakes, and the flinching at loud noises and bright lights, and the constant paranoia? No big deal. It would go away over time, we were sure. And we were right, it did.

Then the next tour came and I'd had to leave Allie alone, still working, this time with a three-month-old to take care of on top of that. He'd been over a year old when I came back and still it had seemed magical, not dying, not getting wounded or maimed despite the other men and women dropping all around me, having Zack toddle up to me at the welcome home ceremony. I'd missed his first steps, but I was back now. And the shakes were back, too, and the paranoia. When I'd driven past the grocery store because I didn't like the looks of one of the vehicles parked outside, Allie had said she understood, that she realized it would take some time for me to get readjusted. When I started to wake up screaming, I went to see a Marine doctor and they'd prescribed sleep medication. It worked so much better when I took it with a shot of vodka.

I volunteered for the third tour, and then the fourth one after that, because the death and the blood and the fear all seemed easier to deal with when I was somewhere I could shoot back at them, where they were real things and not just in my head. We'd joked how we had it so much better than the previous generation who'd done all their fighting in Muslim countries where alcohol was forbidden. Passing around a bottle of rum at night in the little adobe hut at our firebase was a good way to take the edge off, even if it was technically against regulations. And if I hit the bottle a little too hard when I was home between deployments, and didn't spend much time at home with my family, well, none of those civilians understood me.

I guess I hadn't blamed Allie for leaving me. I'd probably been expecting it. I *did* blame her for not having the guts to wait and tell me to my face instead of just taking off and letting me find out when she didn't answer her phone or come to pick me up at the airport and I had to take a cab home to find the house deserted. I did blame her for trying everything she could to keep Zack away from me even when I got off active duty and got cleaned up. She had every right to be angry with me for neglecting our marriage, but no right at all to involve Zack in our problems.

I guess I'd thought, deep down, that I'd have time to make

things right with Zack when he got older and more independent from his mother. Now, I was heading into space and God knew whether there would be another chance. I couldn't blow this one, whether it got me in trouble or not.

The motor pool. It would be almost abandoned with everyone getting ready to leave. Maybe I knew where to get a car, after all.

12

THE SUN WAS KISSING THE PEAKS OF THE CASCADES WHEN I pulled into Bend. I hadn't been there since the year after Allie and I got married and I'd forgotten how beautiful the place was. The mountains were bare of snow at this time of year, but I could picture them with their white winter caps. The river was the main attraction in the summer, and there were probably still kids bungee-jumping off of the main bridge even this late in the day.

School started in a couple weeks and the last of the summer tourist traffic should have been packing the roads, but I cruised right into town with only a couple slow-downs and one long stop for pedestrians. I guess tourism had taken a hit with the whole alien thing going on. I wondered how many people would lose their businesses because of all this, how many would suffer in the short term. In the long term, it might even out with cheap power and improved medical care and incredible new technologies, but for now, a lot of innocent people were going to be hurting. I wondered how many wouldn't take kindly to a government vehicle driving through.

The car I'd borrowed—well, technically stolen, though I

intended to bring it back—was unmarked and unobtrusive, just a normal four-door sedan in all its beige blandness, though it had US government plates. I was lucky to have found the keys for it in an unlocked cabinet, because the only other choice was that damned camo-colored CUCV and I didn't have any faith in its ability to get me all the way to Bend without breaking down.

The sedan was the same model I'd driven doing recruiter duty as a reserve officer, no frills, not so much as a connection to let me play music from my phone, so I had to let the mapping software guide me through the phone's external speaker, which felt incredibly old-fashioned and damned inconvenient.

The navigation app took me through the historic downtown area and out into what had been an upscale neighborhood ten years ago. Back then, Bend hadn't *had* anything that could be called a bad part of town. There were good neighborhoods and there were awesome neighborhoods, or so Allie had told me more than once. She'd wanted us to move there once I got out of the Marines, and her older brother, George, had been all for it.

But everything changes, and Bend had changed as well. It was still a beautiful city and the crime was low, but parts of the city now had shuttered and abandoned businesses that no one could afford to tear down and rebuild. Like the convenience store my navigation program led me to.

I pulled to the side of the road and double-checked the address. No, this was it. The store, which had also been a gas station, had been shut down for a while, judging from the buildup of mold and dirt on the plywood across the windows and the graffiti scrawled on the faded block walls. There were no other businesses on the street except a small coffee shop that was closed now, if it was still in operation at all. The rest of the block was high fences across backyards and only a couple of pedestrians in sight.

A couple of cars cruised past, one of the drivers looking

annoyed as he pulled around me. I cursed softly and turned into the store's parking lot. The gas pumps were empty shells, stripped of their electronics, and I parked beside them, totally confused.

How long had it been since Zack had been here? Did he not know it was closed down? Something felt wrong. I pulled out the folding tablet I'd taken with me and tied into the free city WiFi, checking to make sure Zack hadn't left another message. Relief surged in my chest when I saw he had.

Dad, I asked Uncle George and the store is shut down. I'm going to sneak out anyway and meet you there at eight.

I checked the time. He'd sent the message an hour ago and it was already a couple minutes past eight. I wanted to send a reply and tell him not to come here, but it wouldn't have done any good now. He'd already be on his way. I sighed and stepped out of the car, pacing across the parking lot, watching for him.

I hadn't taken the time to change out of my field utility fatigues before I left, and I felt very much a sore thumb standing alone in front of the shuttered business in camouflage and combat boots. I was just screaming for some local cop to stop and check on the strange guy in camo hanging out where he had no business being. If the base had reported the car as stolen, all it would take was law enforcement running the tag number and I'd be sitting in a Bend holding cell when the shuttles left for the *Truthseeker*.

I rubbed the back of my head as I looked up and down the sidewalk. No one.

Damn it. Where *was* he?

I was so absorbed watching for Zack that I almost didn't notice the panel van when it pulled up. The gentle squeak of brakes alerted me and the first thing that struck me was how old the thing was, probably a 2020 model, the white paint faded and peeling, the headlights clouded with the cataracts of age. It was the sort of van you expected to hear about in a police BOLO. I was relieved that it wasn't the cops, but then I thought it might belong to whoever owned the closed-up gas station and I began trying to come up with a good excuse why I was here.

I could tell them I was lost, that I had come to town to talk to someone I was recruiting for the Marines. That sounded reasonable, particularly since all the services were recruiting fairly heavily right now. The address the guy gave me must have been off by a number or I typed it in wrong, that was the story. He has to live around here somewhere and I texted him and I was just waiting for a reply.

Yeah, that sounded good. It helped being a writer, or as my dad had liked to call it, a "professional liar."

The driver's side door was facing me and it creaked open and I almost went into my pre-packaged spiel before I got a good look at the guy and hesitated. He didn't look like a gas station owner. In fact, he didn't look like anyone who belonged in Bend, Oregon at all. He had a face like a topographical map of New Jersey, worn and eroded and lopsided, and a shock of white hair offset a wild salt-and-pepper mane. He was thick through the torso beneath a loose, untucked polo shirt, not a bodybuilder but someone you could tell was solid and strong and you didn't want to fuck with.

He was someone who wouldn't have seemed out of place prowling downtown Caracas with an AK47, and I had a strange feeling I might have seen him there, but it was probably just a flashback. I didn't get them nearly as often since the therapy, but they did happen. This was probably just some local dude, maybe the owner's son-in-law or brother-in-law.

Keep your cool, Andy.

I waited for the ugly dude to say something, but he just stared at me for a long, disconcerting second, and I wondered if maybe I'd miscalculated and this parking lot was some sort of local hook-up spot. Then the cargo doors in the side of the van popped open and three of Ugly Dude's relatives and closest friends piled out. There were differences, one a few inches shorter, one a few inches taller, one who was battling male pattern hair loss with a horrible combover and another who'd surrendered and shaved his head. But they all shared the same general look, thick in the arms and heavy in the chest and gut, wearing what might have been called business casual if you stole laptops off the back of a cargo truck for a living.

They were muscle, plain and simple, and I had a thundering revelation that I had royally fucked up.

"Mr. Clanton," the driver finally spoke, "if you would just—"

I moved. One of the things I had the luxury for now that I made my own hours was regular martial arts classes. The school I attended was nominally Krav Maga, but in fact, the owner and head trainer had been a professional MMA fighter and we learned and trained with techniques from boxing, wrestling, Muay Thai, Brazilian Ju Jitsu and just about anything else he felt might be useful on the street. But the most useful things Danny Ross taught us were tactics and strategies, not techniques.

And one thing he'd stressed was, if you think someone is going to attack you, don't just stand there and wait for it, move. Do something. And the best time to do it was when they started talking. Talking was a mental shift, and moving back to action took a second longer.

I used the second to make a break for my car. I'd thought about running across the street and trying to climb the fence into someone's backyard, but if these guys had guns, I'd be involving some innocent family in whatever the hell I was messed up with. If I got in the car, got the doors locked, it would take them several seconds to bust out my window, maybe enough time to get the car started and get the hell out of here. Unless they had guns, in which case I was dead either way so why not give it a try?

I felt metal, hooked my fingers under the door handle before he hit me. He was the thinnest of the bunch and also the fastest, and he slammed chest-first into me and drove my right shoulder into the side of the car. Pain flared in my shoulder joint, and the breath went out of me in a gush, and then he was yanking me away from the vehicle. I still had my fingers locked on the handle and as I was pulled away, I pulled the door open before my hand was yanked off of it.

This was one of the situations I'd learned to counter from Danny. I spun into the pull and wrapped my arm around both of his. He smelled of cheap cologne and Russian cigarettes and I planted a fist into his floating ribs. He grunted in not nearly enough pain for my tastes, and since I knew how much it hurt to get punched there, I judged he was too used to pain and had been hurt before and wasn't scared of it, which made him a very dangerous opponent.

He was slipping his arms free of my grasp and I let him, helping along with a push-kick to the hip, sending him stumbling back toward the others. I dove toward the open door of the car and I *almost* made it.

How do I describe what it feels like to get hit with a Taser?

You know how sometimes you wake up in the middle of the night with a Charlie Horse cramp in your calf? And how it seems to hurt worse than anything until you stretch it out and work the muscle loose, but then it's gone and you sometimes wonder if it even happened? Well, imagine that except in *every muscle in your fucking body* until the asshole pulling the trigger decides you've had enough.

I didn't remember falling, but I was on the pavement, gasping for breath, the leads from the Taser still sticking out of my shirt and I thought about trying to pull them out, but the guy with the bad combover hit the trigger again and I seized up, teeth grinding together until he let off it again. When my vision cleared, I was staring into the barrel of a well-worn

Glock 9mm, probably as old as the van, held in the hand of the driver.

"What I was trying to say," he rumbled in a voice deep and tinged with an unmistakable accent, "was that if you would just relax and come with us, we could avoid any unpleasantness."

"My bad," I said in a hoarse rasp.

He turned to the skinny one, gesturing back at me. "Pick him up."

Skinny was none too gentle about it, and I was sure he would have welcomed an excuse to pay me back for the punch in the ribs, and probably would do it later with or without one.

"My son," I said, forcing the words out past pain and my better judgment. "What did you do with my son?"

The driver laughed, though I couldn't tell if it was from mockery or sympathy.

"Your son is in Texas, Mr. Clanton. He was never here."

Oh. Oh, shit.

I was such a sucker. Zack had never messaged me.

Skinny was hauling me toward the van when the van decided it didn't want to wait and started coming towards us. My brain wasn't working at one hundred percent, so it took me a moment to understand the crashing and screeching meant something had run into the van and pushed its rear end off the curb and toward us.

Old, faded white Detroit metal slammed into Skinny and brushed me against the right arm hard enough to spend me spinning away, tumbling onto my ass on the pavement again, which was getting old. The van skidded to a halt, its passenger's side rear quarter panel caved in.

And out in the street, its front end caved in and steam pouring from its busted radiator, was that ancient, camo-painted CUCV. Jambo stepped out, still dressed in the same blue jeans and flannel shirt he'd been wearing when I left him in the breakroom, but the look on his face and the SIG 9mm in his hand were much more reminiscent of earlier days, when I'd seen him stalking the shadows, hunting for Communist counterinsurgents on the streets of Caracas.

The driver was off-balance, stunned and staggered by the collision, but he still had his old Glock in his hand and Jambo wasn't about to give him the chance to use it. The SIG barked twice, then again, the Mozambique Drill, two rounds to center mass and a third to the head. Blood and other things I'd hoped to never see again sprayed from the back of the driver's skull and he fell forward, the old gun slipping out of his finger and clattering to the pavement.

There were three left, and a brief conviction I should help spurred me to roll onto my knees and try to rise, but I might as well not have bothered. The others did have guns, though they'd apparently decided they didn't need them to take me. Jambo was another story, and they were drawing the weapons from concealed holsters, but the time that took was an eternity when their opponent's gun was in his hand.

He didn't perform the same drill for each of them, since it likely would have taken too much time. It was just like he'd told me when my platoon had shared a barracks with his team and they had tried to teach us a few things that would keep us alive. One round for each, he'd said, then repeat as needed.

People who are shot with a handgun or even a rifle don't behave in real life the way they do in the movies. They don't fly backwards and they don't die immediately unless the dramatic situation requires them to linger. They might not even notice they've been shot if their adrenaline is pumping, at least not until their blood pressure drops to the point where they can't remain conscious. The only sure way to put someone down with one shot was a CNS hit, Central Nervous System, right in the brain or the spinal column, which was a risky shot for most people. Not for Jambo.

I would have shot them center mass if it had been me, but he took three straight headshots and the first two went down like marionettes with their strings cut. The third decided discretion was the better part of valor and tried to run, tried to put the van between him and Jambo. I made a grab for the driver's Glock, but Jambo plopped himself down to the prone and fired beneath the panel van.

The last of the four, Combover, screamed as the bullets shattered his ankles, went down hard on his face, unable to arrest his fall. I grabbed the driver's gun, the smooth, worn polymer of the grip feeling alien in my hand. Combover had dropped his pistol, something polymer and ceramic and made in the Czech Republic, and he was desperately stretching his fingers toward it, knowing what was coming.

I thought Jambo might try to take him alive, which was, I suppose, naïve of me. He walked up behind the man and put a 9mm slug through his combover, permanently ending the man's futile attempt to combat the ravages of time.

I forced myself to look away from the blood and carnage, bringing the Glock to low ready and checking up and down the street. There was screaming from somewhere close, and a few shouts, and I was sure I would hear police sirens all too soon. And how the hell was I going to explain this?

"Get in the car," Jambo told me, reloading his SIG, slipping the partially-empty mag into a pocket of his jeans. "*Your* car," he amended. "The CUCV is toast."

"Shouldn't we wait for the police?"

He gave me a look just like the one my DI in boot had given me when I'd asked her when I'd be allowed to use my cell phone. Then he reached into the passenger's door of the CUCV and came out with a thermite grenade, pulled the pin and tossed it into the driver's side foot well.

"No."

I suppose that answered the question. I jumped into the sedan and dumped the Glock in the center console to free a hand to start the car and close the door all at once. White smoke was already pouring out of the cab of the antique GMC sport utility by the time Jambo slid into the passenger's seat and buckled his seat belt with leisurely unconcern.

"Don't speed," he reminded me as I pulled away. "Take the first left here. Then again. Now right."

A column of smoke was still visible above the houses and trees behind us, and I could definitely hear sirens in the distance.

"The cops are going to trace this back to Alpha at some point," I reminded him. "Someone saw this car drive up that road. They'll find a traffic cam that has the plate eventually."

"They will," he agreed. "And by the time they do, we'll be in another fucking star system. Now tell me why."

I didn't try to stall and ask what he meant.

"They hacked my son's account on a gaming forum." The whole thing sounded so incredibly stupid when I said it out loud. I tried to concentrate on driving casually and keeping my eyes on the road and the mirror. A Ford SUV burned past in the opposite direction, lights flashing, siren blaring and I studiously ignored it. "My ex won't let me see him and I didn't have time to get a lawyer before we shipped out. I just wanted a chance to talk to him before..."

"And they suckered you." He took a package of chewing tobacco out of his shirt pocket and stuffed some into his mouth.

"Zack has an uncle out here." I shrugged, feeling like a huge idiot. "He comes out sometimes before school starts. It made sense."

"Why didn't you tell me?" Something about the plaintive

tone made me glance over at him. The big man with the bushy beard, the operator who'd killed more people than cancer, who'd just executed four gunmen right in front of me, sounded as if I had hurt his feelings.

"I didn't want to put you in a place where you'd have to break regs to help me." And I'd been afraid he'd say no, but I wasn't going to admit that.

"You should've trusted me." He folded his arms in a sullen pout for a solid thirty seconds before professionalism won the battle over petulance. "You know who they were, right?"

"Russians," I said, nodding. "I smelled the cigarette smoke on them. Same shitty Russian cigarettes the Venezuelan soldiers used to smoke. FSB, I'm guessing? But why me?"

"You were on the news. They knew you went to the *Truthseeker*, knew you hadn't been seen in public since then. Hell, they might have caught you coming out of the White House. They probably figured you'd be easier to subvert since you were Shanghaied into this whole thing, and because of your family situation."

"Sure," I granted, still confused. "But what the hell did they think snatching me would accomplish? It's not like I could give them the plans to the Svalinn suit or explain the tech specs of the Helta battery packs."

"No, but there's one thing you *could* have given them," Jambo said, the words drawn out as if he was piecing it together as he spoke. "Access." His eyes fixed on mine, alight with terrible certainty. "Access to Alpha."

"Shit." I felt around for my phone, remembered it was in my back pocket. "Can you call them?"

He already had his phone out, tapping in a number then putting it on speaker.

"We're sorry," a sincere baritone announced, "but the number you've dialed is busy. Please try again."

"The fucking base commander's office is busy?" he snapped, hanging up. "Since when?"

Another number, but the same announcement, then a third.

"Oh, man," he said, half a moan, hand covering his eyes for a moment. "They've initiated a comms blackout for the launch. They must have done it after I left."

"There's got to be an emergency line," I protested, shifting in my seat, looking around as if the answer to the problem was somewhere in this beat-up old sedan. "They wouldn't just cut off all contact."

"Of course, there's an emergency line, but it's accessible only through scrambled sat phones." He scowled at me. "And you know what I forgot to go grab before I went off to rescue my friend from doing something monumentally stupid? My fucking official scrambled satellite phone that was locked in a fucking secure room guarded 24-7 and under video surveillance."

"But you had time to grab a thermite grenade?" I countered, staring at him wide-eyed.

"That was just laying around," he said, dismissing it with a wave.

"Look, what about calling another base?" I suggested. "Or just the fucking White House?"

"It won't do me any good to spill my guts to some useless motherfucker on another base who doesn't have the authorization to get a call in to Alpha. The place is beyond top-secret, Andy. The shit Gatlin rolls out for press conferences at his lab in Tennessee is for show, the shit at Alpha is for go.

"And just calling the White House won't do a damn bit of good until and unless I could get them to transfer me, some schmo calling on a private cell number, to someone in the Joint Chiefs."

"How about—" I was in the middle of a suggestion but he motioned me to silence, and his forehead wrinkled in concentration as the road passed beneath the tires with a rhythmic bumping. He tapped something else into his phone and hit send.

"I sent an email to Tommy Caldwell," he told me.

"National Security Advisor Caldwell?" I said, eyes wide. "You have his email?"

"I knew him back when," he said, shrugging. "Not well enough for him to swap phone numbers with me, but he emailed me an advance copy of his book a couple years ago. God knows how long it'll take for him to see it. Which leaves us only one option."

"What?"

He gestured at the road ahead.

"Drive like hell."

13

"Sir, you don't have authorization to enter at this time."

The gate guard was Army because it seemed like everyone on the Goddamned base was Army except me, and an E6, which meant he had enough rank and enough time as an NCO not to be intimidated by a major, particularly one in the wrong service.

And, okay, it *was* two in the morning and the base *was* sealed tighter than a drum because of the spaceships landing and launching, but Jesus, it wasn't like people didn't know who Jambo and I were.

"Fine," Jambo said, speaking across the car and out my window at the guard. "Then get General Jessup on the horn and *get* us authorized, because this is a fucking emergency, Sergeant!"

He shoved his ID at the man and the guard seemed hesitant for the first time. I knew why. Jambo's ID didn't say "Delta Force" on it, obviously, but it was an active ID and the guy using it was bearded, with hair longer than regulation, and dressed in civvies and there weren't too many people outside CAG who could get away with that. A CID warrant officer working undercover, maybe, but those wouldn't show you their ID.

"Um, I can't, Master Sergeant," the guard said, showing Jambo quite a bit more deference than he'd shown me. "General Jessup was called to DC. Let me try to see if I can wake up the XO."

That would be Colonel Shockley. I'd met him a grand total of once and couldn't have picked him out of a lineup with a gun to my head.

"Great," Jambo sighed. He tapped the dashboard of the sedan, full of spastic energy now that we were here.

I envied him, wishing I was full of any sort of energy. I was wiped out after driving nearly twelve straight hours, with a fucking fistfight, a gun battle and getting tased sandwiched in. Plus, we'd stopped a grand total of once for gas on the way back, which was awesome mileage for the hybrid sedan, but it meant I had to pee like a Russian racehorse in heat. More than anything, I just wanted to be out of the fucking car.

And we weren't even at the *real* entrance yet, the fortified one where they'd stop us and search the car and run our biometrics. This was just the road gate, four *miles* from that one because everything in Idaho was like fifty miles from everything else.

I put my head back against the headrest and might have dozed off, because the next thing I knew, the guard was knocking on my window again.

"The duty officer wouldn't wake up the Colonel," he said, "but he did call down to the training center and someone who called themselves Ginger vouched for you, so you can head up the road to the internal security entrance."

"And then we'll be someone else's problem," I added for him after the window was shut.

The security floodlights at the front gate faded into blackness quickly and only the mottled glow of the sedan's headlights preceded us down the rough, pitted road. A pair of glowing eyes regarded us from somewhere off the road near the trees, probably a coyote. I'd heard them yipping and howling at night all the time. There was no moon for them to howl at tonight, though, just total blackness. Someone had told me wolves were moving into this part of Idaho, and when they did, it would be bad news for the coyotes. Predators don't like competition.

The street gate had been well lit and obvious, but the actual main entrance was dark and shadowy, nearly invisible until we'd almost reached it. They didn't need lights. The guards here had night vision and crew-served weapons and they saw us long before we saw them. I slowed down to about ten miles an hour and coasted up to the solid metal gate, acutely aware of the Browning 50-cal staring me in the face from the right side of the road, behind a reinforced concrete bunker.

"Just stay cool," Jambo told me. "These guys should have their shit squared away."

They had it squared away enough for the MP who approached the driver's side of the car to be carrying an HK M27 carbine at low ready, his night vision goggles giving him a bug-eyed appearance. I rolled down my window and kept my hands on the wheel.

"Thumbprint," the MP sergeant demanded curtly, holding up a small reader connected to the security system back inside the hardened guard shack.

I pressed my left thumb to the scanner and when the light went green, the MP pulled it away and glanced down at the screen, the barrel of his rifle raising slightly lest either of us get any ideas while his eyes were turned away. The corners of his mouth turned down, but at least he lowered the rifle and seemed to relax just a bit when he glanced back up.

"Major Clanton," he said, nodding. "You're cleared for entry, but you should have returned before the base was sealed. Did you have orders authorizing your absence from the base during the lockdown?"

"We were investigating a possible security breach," Jambo said. The MP's eyes narrowed and he circled around to the passenger's side and let Jambo identify himself.

"Master Sergeant Bowie," the MP read off the ID, then paused as he reached the Delta operator's authorizations. "Oh, yes, sir. I see you're cleared for access at any time." He frowned again. "But sir, it says here you left in an issue CUCV. Where is it now?"

"Had some overheating issues." Damn, the guy didn't even miss a beat. Wish I could think on my feet like that. "Look, Sergeant, we need to speak to Colonel Shockley. It's pretty much life or death that we get the base on alert and get all available forces ready to move. Can you get his office on the horn and...?"

"Sergeant McCrae!" The yell had come from the guard shack, from a young Spec 4. I couldn't see much of his face with his night vision goggles on, but his voice had the tinge of desperation. "The radar is showing multiple airborne targets inbound!"

"Oh, shit," Jambo said mildly. "Too late."

"Open the gate!" the MP guard, Sgt. McCrae yelled, then waved me forward. "Get that thing inside!"

The heavy metal leaves of the gate seemed to crawl away from each other and I stuck my head out the window and craned it around, searching for the threat in the pitch blackness. I heard it before I saw it, a chorus of distant, shrilling whines barely audible over the grind and scrape of the opening gate.

"What the fuck?" I said, looking over at Jambo, eyes wide. "They don't have jet fighters, do they?"

"Too small for manned fighters," the MP Spec 4 said, still half in and half out of the guard shack door as his sergeant passed by to check his readings. "Gotta be unmanned drones."

"Inside!" the sergeant yelled at me, sticking his head out and snarling in impatience. "Hurry!"

He didn't have to tell me. I'd just been waiting for the gate to open wide enough and I wasn't sure it was yet, but I didn't give a shit about the paint job on the government sedan so I jammed the accelerator to the floor and barreled through. Something smacked against the side-view mirror on the passenger's side and it folded in, but I didn't slow down.

The spiteful chatter of M27s drowned out the car's engine as the gate guards opened fire behind us, seeing something with night vision that I couldn't. The sedan leapt away from the gate before it could close again and the rifle fire faded to a background mutter, but a deeper, angry thudding still reached us, vibrating the car windows. That was the 50-cal taking its turn, still speaking with ultimate authority over a century after the round had been developed by God's own prophet, John Moses Browning himself.

"Don't they have signal jammers out at the fence line?" I asked Jambo, fishtailing as I fought to keep the sedan on the road.

"They do," he replied, still calm, his SIG in his hand, pointed out the window. "And I assume the Russians know that, too. I'd imagine these drones are autonomous."

Something exploded at the gate, nearly a mile back now, and a flare of light brightened the darkness just for a heartbeat. A curse died on my lips stillborn when I nearly ran straight into a column of Striker armored vehicles rumbling down the road in the opposite direction and taking up most of it.

I jerked the wheel to the right and hit the dirt and grass field beside it going at least sixty miles an hour. The steering wheel did its best to bury itself in my chest and my foot slipped off the accelerator as the ruts and holes in the terrain pounded the chassis of the sedan and threatened to rattle the car to pieces before I could bring it to a safe stop. The sedan bounced on its suspension and I fought to regain my breath, hands trembling as I steered it back toward the road. The Strikers were still passing, a dozen of them hell bent for leather to intercept the threat at the front gate. I couldn't see them very well with just the headlights for illumination, but I thought I caught a glimpse of a SAM battery mounted on the back of at least one of them.

"Get us back on the road," Jambo told me, urgency just barely edging into his tone. "This is a feint."

"How can you be so sure?" I asked, trying to keep the adrenaline trembles out of my voice as I steered back onto the blacktop.

There were lights up ahead, the first sign of the facility, telling me we were about three miles from the headquarters building.

"Because they wouldn't launch the drones this far ahead of a ground attack if they were hitting the front gate," he said. "They're drawing away our infantry reaction force."

"Well, shouldn't we, like, *tell* somebody?" I tried not to shriek the words, but it wasn't easy, not with the fucking Russians attacking.

"That's where we're going, Andy. Cell phone ain't working, ain't got no satellite phone or radio, and I don't think those boys in the Striker would turn around on our say-so, not with drones shooting missiles at them."

"The Strikers are all heading that way," I protested, jerking a thumb behind us. "And the Rangers are on the *Truthseeker* with their armor! All we got is the one shuttle waiting to take us up with the rest of the gear and I don't even think it's armed yet! Who are we gonna warn?"

"Not everybody's upstairs," Jambo told me, grinning tightly. "There's still us."

"Boss!" the Delta op I knew only as Gus yelled as he clomped out of the armory in full Svalinn armor, an M900 cradled in the crook of his arm. "What the hell's going on? Should we head for the gate?"

I took a second to grab the Glock I'd taken from the Russians out of the center console of the sedan before I ran after Jambo, leaving the car in the middle of the street outside the fortified building.

"Negative," Jambo said, his tone shifting from calm and laid back to commanding as if he'd changed gears in the car. "It's a red herring. If I had to guess, I'd bet on the approach up the river valley from the training ground. Nice and flat, and once the Strikers are all the way out at the gate and decisively engaged with the drones, even if they set off the perimeter alarms, there'll be no one to stop them."

Ginger came out behind Gus, still trying to get his helmet sealed, and a short, painfully skinny older man I'd heard the others call Pops followed him, looking bigger than he ever had before bulked up inside the powered exoskeleton. Jambo eeled past him, waving for me to follow and I nearly ran into another Delta operator in full armor, then four more after that one, all with their visors down.

"Make a hole, make it wide!" I barked in decades-old habit and they moved just as instinctively to let me through.

Jambo already had both our suits unlocked from their charging cradles and was unstrapping the chest plate on his, the helmet laying on the floor at his feet. I jammed the Glock into the thigh pocket of my utilities and let automatic reflexes take over, honed by hours of drills putting on and taking off the armor. We'd been the ones to teach the drills to the Rangers, so we had to know them first, and Jambo insisted we know them better, which I had, in fact resented at the time. I hadn't argued though, because one of the first things you learn as a brand-new second lieutenant is that you *never* argue with your senior NCO.

This wasn't the first time I'd discovered the wisdom of the lesson, but it certainly was the most dramatic. I had my armor on before Jambo, though I'd been forced to remove my right thigh covering to get the damned Glock out of my pocket before I sealed up again. I sealed the helmet and the HUD flickered to life, showing me the IFF transponders of all twelve of the Delta team...and another five avatars, somewhere off to the east, near the landing field.

"They're going for the shuttle," I told Jambo, and the others, since I had the general net open. "It's packed with Svalinns, M900s, heavy weapons, and it's already crammed with Helta tech. And all we got guarding it is a leftover Ranger fire team."

I was moving while I spoke, grabbing my M900 out of the open rack on the wall, left unlocked by the first Delta ops to hit the armory. I checked it automatically, linking the weapons sight to my helmet, then finding a loaded drum and slapping it home before I jammed two others into the pouches on my harness.

"Good thinking," Jambo said, tilting up his visor so he could look me in the eye. "That's where we need to be. You know how fast these things can run, Andy. You're on point."

Joy.

I paused before I left the armory, grabbing that stupid Glock off the ground and sliding it into one of the empty pouches affixed to my chest plate. I don't know why I bothered, maybe just because it bothered me to leave a loaded weapon behind.

I *did* know how fast these things were, though, and they were faster now than the early prototypes we'd tested, despite carrying twice as much armor. It was pitch-black past the armory, most of the buildings totally shut down, even to the external lighting due to the base lockdown, but for me, it might as well have been mid-day. I'd used night vision gear almost constantly in the Marines, but it was nothing like this shit. Night vision goggles had been improved a lot in the last few years, but the image on the issue gear like the MPs had been wearing was flat and monochrome. The computer processors the Helta had given us took light-intensifying filters, infrared filters, thermal imaging, sonic echo detectors and some sort of miniature Lidar and put it all together into a seamless, three-dimensional, full-color picture, then overlaid the mapping program on top of it and the IFF transponders on top of *that*.

I jogged, then trotted, then ran, then outright sprinted and hoped the Delta boys could keep up. Pavement concussed under the hammer-blows of my boots as I followed the roads, knowing it would be faster going than trying to cut cross-country.

"Ranger security team," Jambo broadcast, including me in on the transmission. "This is Master Sergeant Bowie, do you copy?"

"Roger that, Master Sergeant," a familiar voice returned almost immediately. "This is Corporal Quinn. We're pulling security for the shuttle. Do you want us to go help at the front gate? No one's gotten ahold of us, but I heard the alarm..."

"Stay there," Jambo interrupted him. "We're coming to you. Do you know the location on the shuttle flight crew?"

"They were racking out in the guest officers' quarters, Master Sergeant. As far as I know, they're still there, unless someone stuffed them in a shelter."

"Send one of your privates to go hunt them up and tell them to get that damned thing ready to fly. We're pretty sure it's the primary target and we can't let the Russians have it."

"The Russians?" Quinn repeated. "The Russians are attacking us?"

"It's a working theory. If you capture any of them alive, you can check for passports."

I was trying to concentrate on running, but I had a thought. The armor the Training Command wore, unlike the stuff we issued to the Rangers, had secure log-ins with base security. I wasn't sure Jambo remembered it, since the computer stuff wasn't his strong suit, so I risked a flicker of my eyes toward the communications display, focusing on the correct menus until the screen read my eye movement and connected to the security system.

A dozen alarm codes streamed down the right-hand side of the display, all of them connected with the attack on the front gate, the lack of radio communications in the whole area and thermal readings indicating multiple explosions in that direction. But down at the bottom of the list, neglected and nearly unnoticed, was a single report of a faulty perimeter sensor out in the proving grounds, exactly where Jambo had said the attack would come from.

I checked the time stamp. The alert had come through a full ten minutes after the drones had hit the front gate. Enough time to draw the Strikers out and make sure they were decisively engaged before anyone noticed the force sneaking in the back door.

I nearly slammed into the side of a parked HEMMT cargo truck and cursed, putting my full attention back to navigating the streets. Off to my left, lit up like a golden sunrise, a coyote watched, curiosity glowing in its eyes.

"Jambo," I called, my voice the slightest bit breathy from the exertion. My own biological muscles might not have been moving the mass of metal, but my arms and legs were still in motion, and pretty damned fast motion at that. "They breached the proving ground eight minutes ago. Aircraft, do you think?"

"Aircraft would set off the perimeter radar. Even nap-of-the-earth would kick up too many alarms. They used airborne drones for a distraction, so the main attack is on the ground."

It wasn't fair. He didn't sound out of breath at all, and we both ran the same number of miles a week for the last three months.

"Four-wheel-drives coming up the trails from the river," Gus interjected, his tone as calculating and cerebral as always, like he was playing chess with Pops instead of running at thirty miles an hour down the main street. "Let's say twenty miles an hour in the slow sections. If they go straight for the landing field and the shuttle, they should be there within eight to ten minutes."

"What's our ETA, Andy?" Jambo asked me. I felt a vague irritation that he would make me do math in my head when I was trying to blaze a trail for us, but that was Jambo, always testing and pushing even in combat.

I checked the map overlay, estimated the distance on the route I was taking, then worked out the time and somehow didn't trip over a garbage can that had rolled out into the road in the alley between two buildings.

"Eight minutes," I decided. It was actually eight minutes and something, but I didn't have a calculator, so a rough estimate was as good as he was going to get.

"Andy."

"Yes?"

"Go faster."

14

I HADN'T ACTUALLY SEEN THE SHUTTLE BEFORE. ALL THE work to assemble them had been done out at Edwards Air Force Base and they'd flown in and loaded up and shipped out the first one while I was on my quixotic quest to Oregon. So, the view from the hilltop beside the old basketball courts was the first time I caught sight of the thing.

I don't know what I expected. Maybe something akin to the old space shuttle SSTO orbiter except with rocket engines. It wasn't that. The design was reminiscent of a hammerhead shark, if you took out the tail fins and replaced them with reaction drives. I say reaction drives instead of rockets because calling them rockets would have been a disservice, a crude estimation of something decades or even centuries farther advanced than what I'd ridden into orbit with Daniel Gatlin.

And the thing was huge. Easily a hundred yards long, maybe one-twenty, and at least fifty yards across at the widest spot on the fuselage, not counting the stubby, swept back wings. It was a jack of all trades, cargo ship, orbital transport, troop lander and dual-environment fighter all wrapped into one.

The Ranger team was clustered near the nose of the thing, and I was so happy to see the shuttle and the Rangers, I almost didn't notice the thermal signatures burning in across the plains to the north.

"Time for sight-seeing later, bro. You're on point, show the boys how it's done."

My breath was coming short now, and it had nothing to do with running all the way here at thirty-five miles an hour. I hadn't been in real combat since Venezuela, not counting watching Jambo execute the Russian muscle at the gas station. And he was putting me on point. Oh, it made sense. I knew more about the suit than anyone except him, and he was the team leader and had to sit back and manage the team.

"Quinn," he said, "stay up with the shuttle. If the flight crew doesn't get on board, you're the last line of defense. Don't let these fuckers get to it."

I think Quinn responded, but I didn't hear him. I couldn't hear anything but my own breath inside the helmet, the pulse in my ears, the pounding of my boots on the dirt. I raised the M900 to shoulder level and the targeting reticle flickered to life in my HUD, jerking fitfully with each galloping stride until the targeting computer realized what I was trying to aim at and synched the servos in my arms with the motion of my legs. The range to the lead vehicle in the column was nearly a mile, and even the computer simulation couldn't give me a good rendition of the vehicles, just a red and white mass of engine heat on thermal, but there wasn't any award for coming back with unfired ordnance, so I squeezed the trigger.

To be more accurate, I *touched* the trigger. It was electronic rather than physical and had no pull, no break, no reset. The slug had next to no drop at this range, either, not at the muzzle velocity the electromagnetic coils imparted to it.

I hit the target. At least I thought I did. I was fairly sure from the spray of white on the thermal imaging display, the characteristic sign of the depleted uranium slug penetrating vehicle armor and heating the powdered metal to a plasma. But the vehicle kept moving and I cursed, figuring I'd missed anything vital. I fired again, but the enemy wasn't stupid and they'd realized with the first shot they were being attacked.

I knew what the white-hot flare from the top of the vehicle was before the helmet computer helpfully warned me of the incoming missile and reassured me it would take care of things. The bangs from my backpack shouldn't have surprised me, but I flinched anyway, despite the dozens of times I'd heard and felt the countermeasures launch in training. They were grenade launchers, or perhaps light mortars if you wanted to get technical, but the rounds they kicked free had their own small rocket motors as well, taking the 40mm warheads in a lazy arc directly into the path of the oncoming missiles.

The warheads burst in clouds of electrostatic chaff a half-second before the small thermite charge backing the chaff exploded in fireworks sprays of white light. It was the trifecta of countermeasures. The chaff would fool radar, the thermite would distract heatseekers and the smoke would block a laser designator. I'd seen it work in training against real missiles with dummy warheads and I was one hundred percent confident in it. The gritted teeth and the effort it took to keep from closing my eyes was just nerves.

The missiles corkscrewed out of control and plowed into the ground a couple hundred yards away from me, throwing up clouds of dirt and smoke. I'd been moving forward the whole time it took for the exchange of fire, and so had they. I could see them now, the front vehicles in the column.

I'd been thinking about what sort of vehicles they might have while I ran, about whether they'd risked a trans-polar flight of supply planes to drop actual Russian military APCs and tanks or if they would rig up something with civilian vehicles, up-armored cargo trucks with missile launchers and crew-served weapons mounted. I hadn't expected Brads.

The M2 Bradley Fighting Vehicle had been the main Army APC for decades before time and the shifting battlefields had left it on the scrapheap. The Russians had rescued it from that scrapheap, perhaps quite literally. I didn't know where they'd procured them, but a company-sized column of the old battlewagons was coming straight up the valley, and one had just demonstrated to me that their TOW missile launchers still worked, and I wasn't about to doubt their 25mm chain guns did as well.

I switched the KE gun's cyclic rate with the helmet menu, brought it tight against my shoulder and held down the trigger. My upper body tried to twist away from the recoil of the M900, but I held firm and thirty of the darts sought out the juncture of the gun turret and the chassis of the lead Bradley. A halo of burning gas formed a glowing ring around the turret and while the Brad didn't stop, it did drift off to the right in an aimless arc until it nosed into a ditch and stuck there, its treads digging in deeper with every turn.

"Alpha Team," Jambo ordered, "spread out echelon left and swing in on them before they get up the hill. Andy, I'm covering your right flank."

The team stretched into a wide line keyed on Jambo, angled forward and to the left of the Bradleys' approach, and I took my place just to his left, still eating up ground. The line accordioned in and out with the terrain and I lagged behind, leaping over ruts and rocks, then surged ahead when the ground was clear. Five hundred yards separated us from the Brads and I wondered if they were having trouble seeing us, or perhaps simply trouble believing what they saw. I wouldn't have blamed them. Thirteen man-sized figures glowing bright on thermal from our battery packs, running at twenty miles an hour wasn't something they'd expect.

They were quick learners. The Brads peeled out of their column and split out wide to meet our charge, their chain guns barking and spitting flame. I winced at the reports rolling over the plain of the river valley, not knowing for sure how my chest armor would stand up to a 25mm round and definitely not wanting to find out. I mean, we'd done ballistics tests and theoretically, the chest plates could keep the round from penetrating, but the pure concussion of the hit might be enough to kill the wearer outright. Or might not.

The others were firing, and I didn't want to feel left out. It was easier now that they were close enough to make out the details of the APCs. I targeted the left-hand tracks of a Brad no one else seemed to be shooting at and squeezed off thirty more rounds. Depleted uranium tore through the treads and the entire track came apart at the joint, spilling off the rollers and forcing the APC to a grinding halt. The turret still worked, though, and it swung toward me, the 25mm already chuffing big, slow chunks of metal in my general direction before they'd even figured out where I was.

I'd done a lot of training in the suit, but the instincts learned in the Marines were older and ingrained deeper into my subconscious. I threw myself forward into the prone...and slid about ten meters on my belly before a large rock stopped me abruptly. I whispered thanks to a God I hadn't talked to in years for the blessings of groin armor. He might not have been listening, but it's best to be polite.

The impact of the rock against my forearms was hard enough to bruise even through the armor, but the servomotors keeping my fingers closed on the M900's grip weren't impressed by personal suffering and did their job. I didn't thank God for them, though, since I figured they were working for the government and just doing their job. I did mine, propping the barrel of the KE rifle on the offending rock and settling the aiming reticle on the turret of the immobilized Bradley. One shot for maximum penetration, aimed for the base of the chain gun. I touched the trigger pad and the M900 kicked against my shoulder, bucking harder than it had when I was standing.

The barrel of the Bushmaster 25mm cannon separated at the base with a spark of metal on metal and pinwheeled through the air, landing a good twenty yards away in a puff of dust.

Damn good shooting. What I wouldn't have given for one of these things back in the day...

"On your feet, Andy!" Jambo nagged in my ear like my mother trying to get me ready for school in the morning. "We've got the rear platoon splitting off to the left, and if they can't steal the shuttle, they'll probably just blow the fucker up."

I'm glad he could keep track of what was happening, because the threat display in my HUD looked like a first-person shooter in tournament mode. Blue icons were mixing with the red ones the helmet computer had determined had to be enemy because I kept shooting at them, and streaks and clouds and plumes of white and yellow and red kept erupting on the thermal imaging. I assumed that signified gunfire and explosions and missile launches, but there were eighteen of us, counting the Rangers, and fourteen Brads...well, less than that operational now that we'd been shooting at them for a while, but at least nine were still moving, and I thought two of the one not currently in motion were at least still firing.

I pushed myself up to my feet, the motion smoother and easier than it had been since I'd hit my forties, and tried to figure out what the hell was going on. I could see the ones Jambo had been talking about, the last four in the column, where the command group would have been if this had been an Army company from the 1990s. They'd let the rest of the vehicles keep us occupied while they slipped up a draw to the east and tried to make it up the hill and get control of the shuttle.

To what end?

Did they just want to blow it up and deny it to us, or did they bring their own flight crew with the idea of stealing it? Did they really think they could get it airborne?

They wouldn't have tried this shit if they didn't believe they could pull it off.

Or would they? They'd wanted *me*, wanted me to get them into the base, and I had to assume it was to get on board the shuttle and try to figure out its systems and fly it out of here. Without me, without the opportunity to get access to the ship, were they still going with plan A or was this a desperate attempt to salvage something from the operation? It wasn't just an idle debate in one of the tiny, unoccupied corners of my mind as I ran to cut off the flanking force. If they'd given up on trying to steal it, then they were here to destroy it, and they'd know they needed something more potent than a TOW missile. If they hadn't given up on it, then they didn't have enough troops...

"Major Clanton!" It was Quinn. "Master Sergeant Bowie! I'm seeing something on thermal coming in from the air!"

"Jambo!" I yelled, grunts punctuating the words as I took steps two meters long. "What was that you said about them not sending in more planes?"

"They aren't planes, sir," Quinn told me, and I realized I'd transmitted on the open channel. "Too small, not hot enough. They're not even hot enough for drones."

I slowed just a half-step, chancing a look upward, trying to find something man-made in the sea of stars. With the light-intensifying night vision filters in the visor, the view of the stars was even more distracting than usual out here in the mountains. Instead of thousands of stars, there were tens of thousands, most of which I wouldn't have been able to see with the naked eye.

And somewhere up among them, I saw the heat sources Quinn had spotted, blurry with distance but coming in fast, too fast to be paratroopers, and if the thermal image was of humans, then they were stretched out horizontally, like...

Oh, shit.

"They're gliders!" I said and very nearly went tumbling head over heels when the toe of my boot struck a rock. I extended my other leg out far in front of me and landed with my knee touching my chest like I was posing for a superhero comic book cover. It nearly knocked the wind out of me despite the armor but I still wished someone had taken a video of it. "They're sending in commandos on gliders!"

"Quinn," Jambo said, still collected and steady despite the firefight in which he was embroiled and the shit-show this was all turning into, "we'll take the APCs, but your Rangers are going to have to handle the dismounts."

"Roger that, Master Sergeant."

The kid sounded confident, which might be because he was well-trained and just that good, or might be because he was a kid who'd likely never heard a shot fired in anger. I'd been pretty confident, too, before they sent my ass to South America. He'd get the chance to find out. I wasn't sure if I'd be around to see it, though, because I was running headlong toward four Bradley Infantry Fighting Vehicles, and one of them had just launched a TOW missile from only three hundred meters away.

This close, the grenade launchers didn't have a chance to even activate and I gave in to my gut feeling and ran even faster. TOW stood for Tube-launched, Optically-tracked, Wire-guided, and if these were original equipment, that meant the Russians firing them would have to look them in on me with their eye in the scope. And if I was moving too fast to follow, they were fucking out of luck.

The Svalinn would do thirty-five on the flats, and I was going downhill. Too fast to even try to shoot, so I gave up on it and ran straight in. My legs were cramping up and I hoped I didn't tear a muscle moving this fast but I didn't dare slow down. The missile zipped past me close enough that I actually saw the guide wire playing out across the distance to the lead Bradley, and a second later, the crump of an explosion two hundred yards behind me told the tale of its fate.

A second Bradley targeted me with its chain gun, the rounds chewing up dirt only meters away to my left. He was trying to lead me like a duck hunter with a shotgun, and I was running right into this firing arc, too fast to stop, too fast to even turn without totally wiping out. Something impacted my hip with the force of a sledgehammer, and suddenly, I was flying through the air, spinning out of control.

15

My suit reacted before I could, the safety protocols taking over just the way I had totally forgotten that we'd encouraged General Dynamics to design them, and the Svalinn's joints all locked into place, my arms and legs going stiff and pressing together in the fraction of a second before I hit the ground, even holding my rifle straight up and down in front of my chest like I was on a parade ground.

The hit from the 25mm hadn't registered on the pain meters yet, still concealed by shock, but hitting the ground hurt like a son of a bitch. The armor was padded, and the reinforcement of the joint locks kept me from breaking anything, but it didn't stop my brain from sloshing around in my skull. The only thing that kept me from turning into a vegetable with multiple brain bleeds was the spin. I didn't hit the ground flat, didn't lose all my momentum in one, devastating impact. Instead, I rolled, shoulders thudding into the soft soil on the hillside, sending up showers of loose dirt, then hips catching as I lost momentum, then my back finally hitting as I came to a stop and the suit unlocked. I almost screamed when my arms and legs moved again, my whole body feeling like one giant bruise and a white-hot dagger sticking into my left hip where the round had caught me.

Yellow warnings were flashing desperately for attention in my helmet HUD, trying to tell me how badly the Svalinn was damaged, maybe trying to tell me how badly *I* was damaged, but there just wasn't time to deal with it now. I was maybe seventy yards from the nearest of the Brads, and I still had my gun in my hand, and everything else could wait. I shook off the haze clouding my thoughts, not able to formulate anything resembling a coherent plan but at least knowing I still had my gun...as long as it had survived the fall.

A quick look told me it had, but the drum was gone, accidentally ejected and laying somewhere back along the nearly fifty yards I'd rolled after taking the hit. Fortunately, I'd practiced reloading so often I didn't need to look, and it didn't even seem to matter that my fingers were numb. The exoskeleton's servos forced my hand to go where I told it to go, slave-masters driving my body on despite its reluctance to comply. The new drum slid home and I stumbled to my feet, my hip rebelling, my breath coming in agonized gasps.

A 25mm Bushmaster was depressing its barrel as far down as it would go, maybe a second left before it shot me in the face and ended this wonderful second phase of my military career. I fired the M900 from the hip on full auto. It wasn't as fun as it sounded, given the condition of my hip and shoulders. The weapon nearly tore itself out of my exoskeleton-enhanced grip, but the armor-piercing darts punched their way through the turret and the Bushmaster's barrel lurched downward, blown off its mounts. I slewed the KE gun down, taking out the tracks on that side as well and disabling the vehicle.

The first Brad in the line was still moving, trying to complete its mission, but another burst at max ROF shredded the vehicle's right-hand treads. It spun to the left with one last, futile gunning of the engine by the driver, blocking the path of the rest of the four-vehicle column. We were only five hundred yards or so from the shuttle, too damned close, but there was no clear shot up the hill for their missiles, even if the TOWs could take it out.

The rear Bradley revved its diesel, trying to skirt the rest of the APCs, trying to get around and make its way to its target. I took a deliberate, plodding step toward it, only on my feet because the suit wouldn't let me fall. The helmet's sensors warned me before I noticed, my human senses clouded by what I dimly realized was a mild concussion, but I didn't comprehend what they were trying to tell me until the bullets began smacking into my left arm.

I'd been shot before, over a decade ago, and back then a SAPI plate had saved my life, but I'd damn sure known I'd taken a hit. It had felt like a major leaguer had taken a full-power swing with a baseball bat into my chest. This time was different, a visitor gently knocking on the door, reminding me they were here. Only these visitors were Russian troops. Spetsnaz, I guessed, since they cared enough to send the very best, two squads of them spewing out of the open hatches of the immobilized Brads.

The camo utilities and body armor they wore were very familiar. I'd seen it in Venezuela, seen it in Syria, seen it on the news in the Ukraine. It was state of the art before the aliens had landed, and sturdy enough to stop 5.56mm military rounds. It wasn't much against depleted uranium darts traveling at over 4,000 feet per second and cycling at six hundred rounds per minute. I swung the M900 right to left, spraying a hundred rounds across the mass of troops rushing at me. They still didn't know what they were dealing with and I almost felt bad for them, despite the 5.45mm rounds bouncing off my chest armor. My shots didn't bounce off.

I hadn't seen the effects of the KE gun against live targets, though the ballistic gelatin tests had given us some indication how devastating it would be. Someone had proposed live pigs, or possibly goats, but the DoD had vetoed it, not wanting to arouse any animal rights protests, so these Spetsnaz troops got the honors. The rounds tore through their body armor as if it wasn't there, putting neat little holes through it and passing right on to hit the troops behind them before they spent themselves. I couldn't see what they did to the insides of the men they passed through, but I imagined what the temporary wound cavity would be from something traveling that fast and the effects would be if it hit a bone on the way through and I wasn't surprised at the bodies spinning away and tumbling to the ground.

A red flashing in my HUD warned me the drum was empty, but not enough of them were down. They'd been too close and there were too many, a good twenty men, and my spray-and-pray burst had taken out only half of them. I would have thought the others would be running like hell, but maybe I shouldn't have assumed that. They were on US soil with no other sure way out than our shuttle and I was just one guy standing in their way. They swarmed me like mosquitoes at a bayou picnic, trying to take advantage of the lull in the shooting.

I wasn't a hundred percent sure there were absolutely no weak spots in my armor where one of them might stick the barrel of a rifle and get lucky, and I knew the visor of my helmet could take maybe one or two hits before it shattered. Lacking a bayonet, I waded into the Russians swinging my M900 like a baseball bat. It was a damned heavy weapon and when it struck, it broke bones. Spetsnaz soldiers were thrown to one side or the other, clutching at shattered arms or legs, or, in one case, limp as a dishrag with his head lolling on a broken neck.

That was enough for them. There were three of them still standing and they finally decided they weren't going to take me down by themselves. They ducked around the end of one of the Brads and headed up the hill. Two of the Brads were trying to join them. I stopped moving long enough to finally swap out my empty drum for my last full one and nearly didn't start again. Pain washed over me like the evening tide coming in, and I would have dropped the reload if not for the suit. I gasped and wanted to just stop right there and curl up in a ball.

Hadn't I done enough? How many people had I already killed tonight? Couldn't the Rangers hold them off?

Not while they're trying to hold off the glider troops, moron.

Damn my conscience. I didn't want to hear it right now. I shoved the full drum home and put one foot in front of the other, wanting to scream with each step. Two Brads left mobile. Had to take them out. Couldn't think about the pain, the exhaustion, the emotional shock. If I just took those two out, I could rest. Rest would be nice. Maybe a long stay in a hospital might be fun. Traction. Could use some traction.

Right now, had to shoot some fuckers. The Brads were revving their engines, trying to make it up this hill. I had to take out those engines. The engines were bad for the environment or something. But I was facing their metal asses and the engines were in front. I could have tried to run up in front of them, but it seemed like a lot of effort. Instead, I set the M900 for single shot, brought it to my shoulder and set the reticle on the hot blob of white that was a diesel engine represented in my HUD by thermal imaging.

I fired three times, I think. It might have been more. The rounds punched through the rear armor at 10,000 feet per second and right on into the engine, probably going through the driver on the way. Whether it hit him or not, smoke began pouring from under the engine hatch at the front of the Bradley and the APC ground to a halt. It actually began rolling back down the hill and I shuffled to the side so as not to get run down by it.

That would have been an embarrassing way to die, getting backed over by an armored vehicle like some stray dog in a downtown driveway. Allie would have loved that. I giggled, realizing somewhere deep inside my addled brain that I was slipping into shock.

No time for shock, no time for concussions, no time for contusions and abrasions and maybe a cracked hipbone. Just one Bradley to take out now.

I was distracted when something flashed by overhead, a hang glider, then another, then a third tumbled out of the sky, ripped apart by a burst of KE darts, and I might have heard a scream as the airborne trooper fell with it. I sniffed with disdain. Seemed a waste of expensive depleted uranium. This all seemed like a waste.

I was forgetting something. Oh, right, the Bradley.

Just get it done, Allie said to me in that nasal tone she used when she was pissed at me. *You keep putting it off and it just gets harder the longer you wait.*

"Yes, ma'am," I mumbled aloud.

Something was nagging at me, though. If they couldn't take over the shuttle, how had they intended on destroying it? It was huge and well-armored and they couldn't be sure a TOW missile or two would do the job. If it was me, I would have rigged up one of these Bradley Infantry Fighting Vehicles like a big-ass IED, an Improvised Explosive Device, maybe with artillery shells or C4 if they had it, just packed inside the troop compartment ceiling to floor.

Too bad for them they hadn't thought of that.

I shook my head. I kept letting my thoughts drift. Somewhere behind me, Jambo and the others were still fighting the other Brads, while up ahead, Quinn and his team of Rangers was shooting down glider troops and I was standing here woolgathering. While I'd been lost in a haze, the APC had rolled up another hundred and fifty yards. I swore, bringing the KE rifle to my shoulder, intent on using the same kill shot as I had with the other vehicle, right through the troop compartment and into the engine.

I pressed the trigger pad three times as fast as I could and then, as near as I could tell, the old Bradley exploded like an atomic bomb.

The world swam in front of my face and I didn't want to breathe because it would hurt too much. I sure as hell didn't want to move, but I tried anyway and the suit obeyed, trying to get me upright, but something hard and unyielding and heavy was on top of me and I couldn't quite move it. What the hell was it? Why couldn't I see anything?

Shit. I couldn't see anything because my HUD wasn't working and my visor was spider-webbed with cracks. I managed to get my left hand around whatever was pinning me down and yanked up my visor.

"Oh," I said aloud, "*that's* what it is."

The rear hatch of the Bradley was sitting on top of my chest. Most of the engine block and the forward driver's compartment was fiercely burning, the only light shining in the darkness now that my night vision gear was gone. The rest of the Bradley, as near as I could tell, was somewhere in orbit. I guess the Russians were just as smart as I thought I was, which was depressing. And painful.

"Jesus Christ, Andy, how the hell do you get yourself in situations like this?"

The weight of the hatch lifted off of me, but it still blocked my view until the massive piece of metal spun away and crashed down the hill. A suit of Svalinn armor stood above me, its visor dark and reflecting the flickering light of the burning pieces of

Bradley fighting vehicle. An armored gauntlet pulled the visor up and Jambo stared down at me in bemusement.

"Oh, you know," I said, trying my best to answer his question. "my ex-wife would say it's because I hang out with the wrong crowd. People like you are a bad influence." I squeezed my eyes shut against a flare of pain in my hip. "You got any morphine, dude? I could really use some morphine. And a fuckin' hospital."

"Well, I'll tell you what," he said, grabbing my hand and dragging me to my feet. "You got two choices."

While he spoke, I was staring up the hill to where the shuttle waited...with its belly ramp open, light streaming out from it.

"You can stay here and let the local hospital check you out, but the shuttle is leaving now. The word came down once I called in the report about the attack. Everyone is boarding immediately and we're taking off. So, you'll be stuck here for the duration." He grinned, still holding my hand in his tight grip. "Or." He nodded toward the shuttle. "You can suck it up for a little while longer, get your ass on that bird and go on the biggest adventure humanity has ever experienced."

I looked from him to the shuttle, then back to him.

"Well, when you put it like that...," I said, then gripped his hand tighter and nodded. "I hope you guys have a good time and I'll see you when you get back."

Jambo rolled his eyes.

"Stop fucking around and get on the plane, Clanton."

"You know, you really should start calling me Major Clanton."

I hobbled along beside him, passing the lifeless bodies of the rest of the Russian assault team, stepping over the fluttering remains of shattered and shredded hang-gliders.

"I'm gonna start calling you a major pain in the ass."

The ramp to the cargo bay of the shuttle was a gate to another world, one so much more advanced than this one, one I'd only dreamed of and written about in fairy tales. Quinn and his Ranger fire team were already strapped into racks especially built for the Svalinn armor, not much seats as metal gurneys designed to secure the armor for transport, and us with it. The Delta team joined them and I saw that all of them had made it, though Pops had a huge crater at the center of his chest plate, probably from a 25mm round. Relief took some of the weight off my chest, but I thought about the MPs at the front gate and how I was going to feel if any of them had been killed...

"This is my fault," I said quietly as Jambo helped me get strapped in. "I should stay behind and tell the base commander."

"Be a boy scout later, Andy," he said, tightening the strap across my chest for emphasis. "Right now, I just want to get into space, where it's safe."

A crew chief for the shuttle was circulating through the cargo bay, checking the straps on the supplies, and once he saw Jambo trying to belt himself in, the man hurried over and helped him. He looked sort of like a crew chief on a helicopter except that his helmet was fitted with a visor and sealed into a pressure suit. Once he'd seen to Jambo, he briefly checked on each of us, cinching my chest strap even tighter before jogging back toward the front.

He'd barely disappeared into the cockpit when the turbines began spinning up, going from a high-pitched whine to a roar vibrating through the fuselage. I hadn't even noticed the belly ramp closing until it shut completely with one last grinding thump, a sound reminiscent of a coffin lid closing.

The gentle vibration of the turbines climbed in pitch and ferocity until the deck shifted beneath us and the force of the belly jets pushed me down into my suit and the rack beneath it. This might have been, I decided with the sort of clinical detachment I adapted when I was scared shitless, the largest VTOL aircraft every built by humans. *Partly* built by humans. The

Helta had provided the engine, the reactor, the weapons and the material for the airframe.

But we helped! Said the eight-year-olds handing tools to their father as he repaired the car.

The shuttle's vectored thrust nozzles began to angle backwards and the acceleration shifted from upward to forward. For the second time in my life, I left the planet. But this time, I was going a lot farther than the Moon.

16

"Well, you were right," Jack Patel said, his grin as cheerful as if he was about to tell me I'd won the lottery. "You do have a cracked hipbone and a mild concussion."

Jack, I'd discovered, wasn't his real first name. He had a long, extremely Indian first name that his western friends found hard to pronounce, so at some point in elementary school, he'd become "Jack." Which sounded exactly as easygoing and chill as the Patel I knew. He seemed like he was in absolute heaven in the sickbay of the *Truthseeker*. Well, I called it a sickbay, anyway. I think the official nomenclature was the medical lab and, in truth, it did seem fancy enough for the name.

I was lying on a white table that looked exactly like cheap plastic but felt as comfortable as the bed in the Hilton in DC. It had no obvious sensors on the surface, yet the holographic display floating in the air above it showed my entire body stripped of flesh, the internal organs in living color, the heart and lungs pulsing with life, the bones a harsh white. A red halo surrounded my left hip, though I couldn't quite make out the crack.

"This shit is amazing, Doc," I told him, shaking my head. I hadn't even had to take off my utility fatigues.

"Isn't it?" he enthused. "I swear, Andy, I've come up with two dozen new medical treatments just from having access to this place. It's the most incredible opportunity of my career. If I have enough time, I think I can put together a nanite injection that can remove cancers from anyone, no matter what stage of the disease they're in."

"You do that," I told him, "and it won't matter what the Russians or the Germans or the protestors say, we're golden." I waved at the 3D image of my body and the arm in the display waved back. "But what are you going to be able to do for me with all this fancy gear?"

"For the concussion?" He shrugged. "Nothing, really. I mean, if it were more serious, a major brain bleed, I could stop it easily enough. Wouldn't even have to open you up, just a nanotube running in through your eye socket to the bleed."

My lips peeled back from my teeth in a scowl of pure horror and he laughed at the expression.

"You'd be sedated at the time. But it's not really necessary. If there were serious brain damage, or repeated trauma to the brain requiring treatment, I think I know how to program this thing to encourage the repair of brain tissue, but I haven't tested it and I am sure you'd rather I didn't use your brain for the first experiments."

"You know me so well," I said, swallowing hard at the thought. "What about my hip though?"

"Ah. Well, I can take care of that right now, but you're going to have to take your pants off."

I glanced around the sickbay. We weren't in a private compartment or anything. The Helta didn't go much for that, I'd seen on the way in from the docking bay. Some parts of the ship had been temporarily modified to suit the humans who'd be making at least this one trip with her, but all the public sections of the ship were wide open spaces without so much as a divider. I'd heard from Julie that even the barracks and bathrooms were communal, though I had yet to see that for myself.

Helta techs were at various stations around the lab, absorbed in tasks I couldn't interpret on machinery I couldn't understand, while Ranger medics and human medical staff watched them and made notes on tablets. None of them seemed to be paying attention to me, so I sighed and took off my pants.

It didn't hurt, exactly. Patel had given me an injection just above my beltline right after I'd arrived, deposited by Jambo before he went back to see to his team's lodging for the voyage, and the pain had lost its intensity, fading into the other bruises and cuts I'd accumulated. You'd think I would have gotten used to being naked in front of doctors after the time I'd spent in the Corps, but I still felt self-conscious at his clinical gaze.

Patel whistled softly to himself, touching a series of haptic controls in the holographic display. In response, a section of the bulkhead slid aside and a segmented polymer arm snaked out into his hand as if it knew he'd been looking for it.

"Lay back," he told me with a shooing motion. "Relax. Close your eyes if you like."

"That sounds ominous," I said, but complied.

"There may be a little pressure."

Oh, shit. Whenever a doctor said that, it meant you were going to hurt like hell. Something cold and metallic pressed against my hip and I gritted my teeth, prepared for the pain. It wasn't as bad as I thought. Patel was jamming the end of the segmented arm hard into my skin, and my hip felt as if it was heating up under the thing, but the discomfort was dull and distant. The heat got worse and I almost cringed in anticipation, but it never crossed the threshold from uncomfortable to agonizing and I tried to control my breathing and relax.

"How long is this gonna take?" I asked, eyes still closed.

"Just another moment," Patel said, his tone distracted. "And... there we go."

The pressure fell away and I opened my eyes. There was a pinprick-sized hole in the skin over my hip, blackened and just barely visible, but no other external effects. In the hologram, though, the halo had turned from red to blue, which I thought must be better. These were aliens, though. Maybe red meant not that bad and blue meant "sorry, buddy, you're going to die now."

"Oh, yeah," Patel said, nodding as he stepped closer to the projection, peering at my hipbone. "Beautiful. It's like it's been in a cast for weeks. Not quite fully healed, but certainly stable enough to use."

"You mean it's fixed already?" I asked, amazed. I'd had broken bones before and none of them had a recovery period that was what I would call fast or fun.

"Fused with a medical laser," he confirmed, sounding very satisfied with himself. "I'd send you a bill, but you won't make that much money in your whole life."

"Way to hurt a guy," I said, pulling my underwear and trousers back on, then slipping into my boots. "Is there anything I need to do? Antibiotics? Painkillers?"

"Infection won't be a problem. That shot I gave you when you came in was a combination local anesthetic, antibiotic and Tetanus booster. As for painkillers?" He sniffed with disdain. "Maybe it you're a wimp. It's not going to hurt any worse than it does now." He waved at me with both hands. "Go. Find your compartment and get settled in. Get a shower. You stink."

"Thanks, Doc," I said, laughing. "You've got a hell of a bedside manner."

Finding my way to the human quarters from the sickbay

wasn't as easy as it sounded. The ship was organized horizontally, which made sense. They had artificial gravity and didn't have to worry about acceleration from a reaction drive, so they could have arranged it however they wanted, but they'd chose to orient everything to an x-axis in line with the direction of travel and a y-axis perpendicular to it. Since the ship was freaking huge, this meant every level was just as freaking huge.

And God alone knew what alien thought processes had gone into the floor plan for the place. The sickbay was near the center of the ship and so was the bridge, which both made sense in a way, since they were in a highly-shielded section of the vessel. But the food stores and the fabrication shop were also on the same level, which didn't.

I wandered through the fabrication section, the boxy machines inactive and un-crewed at the moment with nothing to make or repair. They'd been busy as hell when the ship first arrived in the system. I'd seen the footage of humans and Helta working round-the-clock shifts using raw materials brought up from Earth and later, the automated mines on the Lunar surface to fabricate the parts for our battery packs and KE guns and a thousand other things. Eventually, they'd been used to fabricate parts for our own fabricators, which were now running back in Daniel Gatlin's shops on Earth.

Gatlin had confided to me that the technology would revolutionize the global economy in a matter of years. Not decades, but years. And that wasn't counting the fusion reactors, the medical technology, the batteries, the high-temperature superconductors, and a half a dozen other things I was probably forgetting. In ten years, our whole society would be unrecognizable. If we survived. That was the trick, the surviving part. Even if the Tevynians didn't come for us, how much would it take for the Russians to lose their shit and launch a nuclear strike?

I found myself wishing the ship had elevators. Starships in

my books had elevators, starships in the movies and on TV had elevators, and the really freaky alien spaceships had gravity chutes and teleporters and cool stuff like that, but we got the aliens who liked to walk. I mean, walkways that took you at a ninety-degree angle to the decks were kind of cool and played hell with my inner ear, but I was still walking, and my hip was still sore.

And I got lost. Twice. And somehow, I had the bad luck to get lost when there were no humans around at all. The Helta looked up from their tasks and regarded me with what passed for polite curiosity among the alien bear people when I tried to ask them which way to the crew quarters. One of them pulled out something that looked like a cross between a tablet and a scratching post for a miniature cat and did something to it and it spoke to me in oddly-accented English.

"I do not speak your language. Please ask the translator any questions you may have."

I tried to smile, but managed more an exasperated baring of teeth.

"How do I get to my quarters?" I enunciated carefully, not knowing how sensitive the thing was.

"I apologize," the translator said, "but I am unable to parse your accent. Please try again."

Accent? I was born in Florida and live in Vegas, I didn't have any accent!

"I said," I repeated, trying to make my voice flat and Californian, "how do I get to the human living quarters?"

"You seem to be asking for the life support control station. Is this correct?"

"No, that's not correct." *Damn, my hip hurts...*

I grabbed the translator out of the Helta's hand and held it like a microphone on karaoke night at the bar.

"Do you know where the humans are staying?"

"Humans are located on Earth," the machine said helpfully, "as well as Tevynia and a handful of colony worlds that..."

I shoved it back at the Helta and walked away. It was only a starship larger than anything humans had ever built. I'd just wander around until I ran into another American, or collapsed of dehydration.

Luckily, another American found me. It was Corporal Quinn, and I spotted him running down a perpendicular corridor as I was about to head up it, and my inner ear rebelled at the sight of him trotting down the side of a wall.

"Hey, Major Clanton!" he yelled.

Then I saw the frown cross his face, the same one I got whenever I came to a junction in the gravity-skewed corridors and my personal sense of up and down was insulted. He shook his shoulders as if he was trying to get rid of the disorientation, then took the last few steps past the curve to where I stood next to something that might have been a giant, cybernetic mushroom or the Helta equivalent of an espresso machine or anything in between.

"Quinn," I said, wanting to hug him, "I have never been so glad to see a familiar face. For the love of God, tell me you know how to get to the crew quarters."

"It's back up this way," he said, pointing to the way he'd come. "About half a mile through life support, then up another deck and on your right. But you're not going there."

"And why would I not go there?" I asked him. "I'm tired, I just had my hipbone fused with a laser and I've been told I stink and need a shower."

Quinn took a whiff and his nose wrinkled.

"They were telling you the truth, sir," he agreed. "But you're still not going there. Colonel Brooks sent me to find you. She said Colonel Olivera has been trying to reach you but you're not answering your comms." He tapped the tiny, flesh-colored bud barely visible in his right ear. It was, I knew from previous briefings, connected to something similar to a cell phone or small tablet attached to his belt, except that this model worked via radio waves, WiFi or satellite signal, whichever was available.

"I'm not answering it because I don't have one yet," I said. "Since I came here directly from a battle and went to the battle directly from a borrowed car, and I think even my damned cell phone is still sitting in that car." I squeezed my eyes shut for a moment in frustration. "And dammit, I didn't even remember to put my cell service on hold while I was gone. If one of those damn Space Force clerks finds my phone and starts streaming porn—"

"Colonel Olivera wants you on the bridge, sir," Quinn interrupted. "He said to drop whatever you're doing and get up there immediately."

"Shit." I didn't want to sound like a whiner, but I did. "I was just up on that level! In the sickbay, getting my broken hip fused. Couldn't someone have checked?"

"Sorry, sir," Quinn said. "I'm just following orders."

"Yeah, yeah. Unless you brought a wheelchair with you, you can call and tell them I'm on my way." I turned around and began walking back the way I'd come. "Limping," I added over my shoulder.

The Helta I'd passed stared at me as I passed them coming back the same direction and I wondered if they thought all humans were this peculiar or if they'd just pegged me as the weird one. I was beyond caring. The local anesthetic had worn off and beyond the dull ache in my hip, my shoulders, neck and lower back were one giant mass of bruised muscle, and I wondered just what the hell was so important that Olivera thought it couldn't wait.

The bridge had changed quite a bit from my last visit, more

than any of the rest of the ship I'd seen so far. Duty stations had been added to let human crewmembers stand watches alongside their Helta counterparts, to learn on the job for when we had our own ship, and most of the holographic displays had English readouts beside the Helta language. Julie was at the helm, with a Helta driver on one side of her and another human trainee on the other, because the Helta trusted her abilities now more than they did their own. Joon-Pah was still at the captain's station in the center of the compartment, but Olivera had a chair at his right shoulder, a back seat driver.

"Clanton!" Olivera said, rising from his chair as I got to the bridge. "You got here just in time."

"What's up, sir?" I asked him. "Sorry I don't have comms yet, there wasn't time before we had to leave on short notice."

"Yes, I heard what happened." Olivera hopped out of his chair with enthusiasm in his step. "That's why I called you here. You kept us from possible disaster and I thought, given your background, you might like to be on the bridge for this historic occasion." He grinned like a kid at Christmas. "We're about to jump into hyperspace, for the first time in human history."

Unless you count the Tevynians. I didn't say it, though. He was obviously psyched for this, and who was I to harsh his buzz?

"Is there someplace I could sit down?" I asked him.

"No need to strap in for this one, Andy," Julie answered for him, twisting around in her seat, favoring me with a smile. "We'll either make the jump or we won't, no turbulence involved."

"There is nothing to threaten us in hyperspace," Joon-Pah expanded. "Or, rather, whatever else is in hyperspace is impossibly isolated from us."

They'd all misunderstood, but I didn't try to correct them. Olivera obviously thought he was offering me a rare honor, and even though I'd been played for a fool by the Russians and would have probably fucked up the whole mission without Jambo, I wasn't going to ruin the whole thing for him by acting like a wimp.

"All stations," Olivera said, hands on his hips, consciously melodramatic, "are we go to depart Earth orbit?"

"Engineering is a go." The squat, troll-like Space Force officer was Captain Cochrane, a PhD in physics qualifying him to train under the Helta hyperdimensional specialist. I hadn't met him, but Olivera had given me a rundown on the crew after we'd received our Ponce de Leon shots.

"Tactical is a go," Major Baldwin reported. She was new to the Space Force, transferred over from the Navy due to her combat experience. She was a soft-spoken, petite woman and I never would have guessed she was the only Naval officer to ever sink a Russian destroyer in battle.

"Docking bay is a go." Major Franich. Yet another Navy transfer and I wondered if they were going to have so many Navy officers, why didn't they just make it the Space Navy instead of keeping it under the aegis of the Space Force? But he'd been the CAG on an aircraft carrier during the Venezuelan War, which made him, in my opinion, overqualified to wrangle a pair of shuttles.

"Life support is a go." Captain Bennett was the only one on the bridge below the rank of O-4. She'd been a civilian NASA employee before the Helta had shown up, and the Space Force had brought her over to learn how to keep us alive in space.

"Helm is a go," Julie confirmed. "We are ready to break orbit, sir."

Julie was a Lt. Colonel now instead of a Captain, because, well...Space Force. Air Force ranks, which came from Army ranks, instead of Navy ranks, and yes, I know I was entirely too bitter about there not being a Space Navy and Space Marines. Damn Army.

"Take us out of orbit, Colonel Nieves," Olivera said.

I felt nothing, of course, which seemed anticlimactic. My grand total of two trips into orbit had made me an expert on what space travel should feel like, and I wanted acceleration pressing me into my seat. The view in the holographic display was spectacular, real enough I could almost have believed I was looking out a window instead of sitting close to the center of the ship watching a feed from the external cameras. But without acceleration, it was like watching a rollercoaster ride on television instead of being in the car on the track.

This particular track led us away from Earth with the ease of leaving the rollercoaster station, skipping the multiple gravities a rocket would have required, skipping the orbital transfers for raw power, punishing spacetime for trying to stop us instead of us for defying gravity.

"How far away from Earth do we have to be to jump?" I wondered, my curiosity overwhelming the aches and pains trying to distract me.

"Just beyond Lunar orbit is good," Julie told me, her voice a bit distracted, most of her attention on manipulating the helm controls, setting the ship's course. "We're going a bit farther just for safety reasons, since this is a government operation."

"You're lucky they aren't making us all wear reflective belts," I reminded her, which drew sharp, snorting laughs from all the military veterans, though Captain Bennett looked clueless.

Joon-Pah also seemed confused and cocked his head sideways toward me.

"Are these reflective belts a defense against laser weapons?"

Julie laughed so hard I thought she was going to take the ship right into the Moon and make another huge crater beside the one the Tevynian ship had left.

While Olivera endeavored to explain to the Heltan about the military's obsession with making men in a combat zone wear reflective belts when they were doing PT for fear of traffic casualties, the *Truthseeker*, as a poet might say, slipped the surly bonds of Earth. The stars didn't twinkle outside the atmosphere, I noticed. With no air to distort them, they were preternatural in their clarity, too beautiful to be real, an ocean of them with not a single patch of blackness bare of the distant glow of alien stars.

I was hypnotized by them, lost in the depths of interstellar space, and I wasn't aware of the passage of time until I heard Julie's voice again.

"We'll be clear to jump in five minutes," she announced.

I blinked, wondering if I'd simply been woolgathering for that long or if the ship was even faster than I'd imagined.

"How do you navigate in hyperspace?" I asked, the question like bread scattered on the waters, waiting for whoever might be able to answer it.

"They explained all that to us in training," Julie said. "Turns out there are these gravimetic lines of force running between all mass everywhere, and when it's something as big as a star or even a planet, the slope is sort of downhill, to force an analogy that's way too broad to be meaningful except as an illustration. In practice, what it means is that there's a sort of roadway system all throughout the universe, and the closer shit is together, the more roads there are to choose from. So, from here, it's a matter of putting ourselves in the right spot to hit a major road to another star system." She smirked as she glanced back at me. "Then, when the interstellar roadways intersect, we take a left turn at Alpha Centauri."

I grinned back at her. Julie was a smartass and I could always appreciate a good smartass.

"You need a road map for that kind of thing?" I wondered. "I'd hate to have been the first guy to start jumping around without one."

"The first Helta to take a starship into hyperspace didn't return," Joon-Pah said. His English was getting better and I could hear the obvious pride in his voice. "Neither did the second, nor the third. And yet, we persevered."

"Must have all been male pilots," Julie murmured. "Too stubborn to stop and ask for directions."

Even Olivera couldn't contain a snort of laughter at that one, though I felt a little bad for Joon-Pah.

"We are at the on-ramp for the great interstate in the sky," Julie said. "Sublight drives to full stop. Request permission to make the translation to hyperspace, sir." Her eyes narrowed as she awarded Olivera a glare. "And don't you dare say 'make it so,' Colonel."

"Damn," Olivera said, and I wasn't sure if his disappointment was feigned or he'd actually been about to say it. "Very well, Helm. Jump at your discretion."

"I could do some melodramatic countdown," Julie said, "but there's no real reason for it, so...." She put her fingertips against four glowing orange circles hanging in the holographic control board and stroked them downward. "Jumping now."

The view in the main screen shifted, the stars seeming to rotate counterclockwise, slowly at first and then twisting into a kaleidoscope of color, coalescing into a rainbow ring around a hole into nothing. Not blackness, just...nothing. An absence so complete I couldn't even look at it straight on, just get a sense of it out of the corner of my eye. The absence swallowed us up and reality seemed to shift, stretching me out and spinning me around and sending my stomach outward through my mouth, then everything snapped back to normal and the view on the holographic display went to a simulated image of the exterior of the ship.

I stumbled back a step, though the experience hadn't been a physical one.

"We're in," Julie announced. "We are in hyperspace. Twenty hours until our first navigation check at Alpha Centauri A."

A cheer went up among the human bridge crew, which

seemed to bemuse the Helta. I suppose it would be like people cheering when their plane took off from the airport to them.

"You're part of history now," Olivera told me, his smile stretching wide. "Twice over."

I was. But all I could wonder standing on that bridge, heading for another star system, was if my son would ever hear about it.

17

I SHOVED THE PILLOW OVER MY HEAD, BUT THE KNOCKING persisted.

"I don't *want* to go to school, Mom," I moaned, so wonderfully comfortable under the almost unbearably soft blanket.

"Get your ass out of the rack, Andy," Jambo replied, his voice was so clear on the compartment's intercom, he could have been standing right at my bedside, "beforeI use my master code on the door and drag you into the hallway naked."

"Yeah, yeah," I said, loud enough to be heard through the closed hatch. "Gimme a minute."

I made a face he couldn't see and swung my legs out of the bunk, sitting up in the darkness for a moment to get oriented, then touching the glowplate on the bulkhead next to me. Soft light filled the compartment, the lines familiar to me, if roomier than I'd ever had on a cruise in the Med. We'd built the crew quarters. The Helta didn't have the concept of private rooms, instead sleeping communally on what I'd first thought of as a big trampoline. That was something that obviously wasn't going to translate for humans, but thankfully, our specs and their construction bots made short work of turning some spare storage into crew compartments.

I performed a short self-diagnostic before I stood, preferring not to find out the hard way that one of the gigantic bruises I'd collected in the fight yesterday was making my leg muscles cramp up. Nothing seemed to be malfunctioning, and I actually felt better than I'd thought I would.

Maybe that youth drug is kicking in. I feel better than I have since I was in college.

I'd gone to bed in a T-shirt and shorts after an incredibly welcome shower—and the heads on this ship were also built to human specs because the Helta version of bathrooms and showers didn't even merit consideration for human use, but I'd left a fresh set of utilities hanging off the edge of my locker, waiting for me. It was a damn good thing our personal effects had been pre-loaded on the shuttles and taken to the *Truthseeker* ahead of schedule, or I'd have been bumming spare uniforms from the Rangers.

I was no stranger to dressing quickly, and I even took the extra minute to brush my teeth, ignoring the continued knocking on the hatch. Jambo had been leaning on the hatch and, when I opened it, he nearly fell inside.

"Jesus Christ, Andy, what took you so long?" he demanded. "We're not going on a date, you didn't have to pick out your best dress."

"A couple things, Jambo," I said, arching an eyebrow. "First of all, this..." I pointed at the hatch, "is a hatch, not a door. And this is a bulkhead, not a wall. And that is a passage, not a hallway."

"And this is a Space Force," he countered, grinning lopsidedly, "not a Space Navy, so I don't have to use that squidward lingo. You're in the Army now, jarhead."

I pointed to the USMC tape across the chest of my utility blouse.

"This says otherwise, and as long as I'm along, we have at least one Space Marine. Anyway, what time is it, and how long was I sleeping and why the hell did you drag me out of bed?"

I wondered how Olivera would react if he heard the two of us jabbering back and forth like this. Technically, I outranked Jambo, but also technically, I was an advisor attached to his Delta Force team, which meant I was under his command, even though I wasn't *in* his chain of command and I was commissioned in an entirely different branch of service. It was all so muddy and complicated that it was easier just to forget our ranks. It was certainly easier for Jambo, since he was used to dealing with the murky rank structure in Delta.

"It's 0715 Greenwich Mean Time," he answered seriatim. "Which is our ship time, just so you know. You slept for almost nine hours, which should be enough even for a washed-up Marine reserve officer, and I am waking your ass up because we're about to come out of hyperspace for our first navigation check and Colonel Olivera wants a stand-to." He jerked a thumb behind him. "We need to haul our sorry butts to the armory and get geared up. They gotta make sure your new helmet is working right, anyway."

"What about breakfast?" I wondered, pushing the door shut before I followed him down the passage. It was well lit and stretched another fifty meters behind me and thirty ahead to a T intersection. "Do we get breakfast or is that another cultural difference we have to deal with?"

"The Helta only eat one large meal a day, in fact," Jambo informed me, "and snack a lot. But us humans will be eating chow on our own, since our table manners disgust the fuzzy-wuzzies, apparently. And breakfast is delayed until we jump back into hyperspace on the other side of Centauri B." He shrugged and fished a protein bar out of his thigh pocket, tossing it back to me. "But I brought you something to tide you over, since I know what a bitch you are when you're hungry."

I nodded thanks and began tearing into the bar, the stale chocolate and peanut butter taste barely registering in my mouth. I just wanted something in my stomach before I got all cranky.

The armory, it turned out, was nearly a half a mile from our quarters and I was just about convinced I was *never* going to find anything on this ship without being led around like a ten-year-old kid. Infuriatingly, everyone else seemed to be navigating it okay, because we passed by and were passed by a handful of Rangers along the way. I knew some of them enough to be nodding acquaintances. Thank God we didn't have to salute on board ship or my arm would have been worn out by the time we got where we were going.

I don't know what the armory had been before the modifications to the *Truthseeker*, but now it was one of the most fortified sections of the ship. The hatches into the section could all be sealed at need against pressure and radiation, and Jambo had assured me the three-inch-thick emergency seals were good against small arms fire as well, though he didn't explain how he'd tested them out.

I'd seen a few Helta along the way, moving from quarters to duty station or the other way around, but there were none of the aliens in the armory, by their choice rather than ours. It was just humans, mostly Rangers, besides Jambo's team, except for a squad of MPs who'd come along with the ridiculous title of "ship's security." As if a company of Rangers and a Delta team couldn't provide more security than a dozen Army cops.

They were in line at one of the stations when we arrived, though, being handed out standard non-powered armor and M27 carbines by an officious armory clerk who sounded like every other armory clerk I'd encountered in every facet of the military. His general air was that the weapons were his and he was just loaning them to us, and we'd damned well better bring them back in good working order and cleaner than we'd been issued them.

Jambo butted ahead of a squad of Rangers, ignoring the dirty look the E5 in charge of them gave us, and leaned up against a waist-high counter across from the skeletal, ashy E6 clerk. Row upon row of Svalinn exoskeletons were lined up behind him, accessible through a single entrance into the armory storage area, forbidden fruit hanging just out of our reach.

"Hey Jonesy," Jambo said to the man, "Major Clanton here needs some comms. We had to leave in a hurry and his set was left behind in Idaho."

"Shit, Jambo," the supply sergeant said, making a face at him. "You think I'm a damn Wal-Mart or something? A fucking officer should know how to keep track of his equipment, all due respect, sir."

"Oh, yeah," I said, nodding. "I can just feel all the respect oozing out of you." Okay, I might let Jambo get away with ignoring my rank because we were old friends, but some fucking Army supply geek? Oh, hell no. "Listen Sergeant Jones, I've had a shitty couple of days and been forced to kill way more Russians than I ever expected to. Let's leave aside the fact I outrank you, and the further fact that I am authorized by Colonel Olivera to requisition whatever I damn well please without so much as a by-your-leave. No, let's just concentrate on the most salient information here." I cocked my head to the side. "Sorry, do you know what 'salient' means? In this case, it means important, as in could end your fucking career level of important. If I can't get what I need from you, I'll just head down and find Colonel Brooks and let her know the reason. You know how many *thousands* of Rangers would have killed their mother for this mission? You know how easy it would be to get you transferred to a supply depot in fucking Alaska? To make sure you never leave the atmosphere again?"

"Sorry, sir," Jonesy said, eyes going wide, as if he hadn't expected a textbook officer tirade from a Marine major. "I honestly didn't mean no disrespect, it's just that we're in a fucking spaceship, you know? All we got is all we got, and there won't be any replacements for it until we get back to Earth."

"And because you explained that to me so carefully and respectfully, I will make sure to take extra-special good care of this particular set of comms that you're about to issue me," I promised him. I put a hand out, waggling my fingers expectantly.

"Yes, sir," he said, sliding open a drawer in a heavy, metal storage unit attached to the bulkhead. He pulled out a plastic case and handed it over to me, but held onto it when I tried to grab it. "Gonna have to sign for it first, sir," he added, raising an eyebrow.

"Of course." It wouldn't be a government operation if I didn't have to sign for it. I took the stylus and signed the tablet he offered me. "You do much reading, Sergeant Jones?"

"I think I read a book once," Jonesy said, taking the tablet and making his own mark while I pulled out the communications unit, sticking the earpiece in and hooking the case with the transceiver onto my uniform belt.

"How'd you like to be in one?" I offered, my smile malevolent, with instincts not as old as the military ones but just as ingrained after the last ten years as a writer.

"Hey, that would be damned cool," Jonesy enthused, grinning. "Think they'll put me in your show?"

"I can make some calls," I offered. "They're always on the lookout for interesting new characters." *To get killed off in the first ten minutes to establish a threat.*

"Awesome man...I mean, sir. Let me go grab your armor."

Jambo was laughing softly as Jonesy went off to free our Svalinn gear from the racks.

"Damn, Andy, that was impressive," he murmured, low

enough that the supply sergeant couldn't hear him. "You chewed his ass then turned him into a fan all in about ten seconds. Didn't think you still had it in you."

"Attention!" The order came from one of the Rangers, a junior NCO, and all the rest of the command present locked up immediately.

I turned and saw Lt. Col. Brooks entering the compartment with her officer corps in tow. Technically, I suppose I should have come to attention as well, but none of the rat-bastards had locked up when I came in, so I didn't feel too guilty.

"As you were," Brooks said immediately, waving the courtesy off. "Everyone get back to work, we're pressed for time."

"Good...morning? I think? Colonel," I said, nodding to her. "Is it morning? Do we have morning on the ship?"

"Beats the hell out of me, Andy," she admitted. "But it feels like zero-dark-thirty up in here, with everyone busting their asses to get geared up and then waiting around and doing nothing."

"We all had our share of that, ma'am," Jambo said, stepping past the desk and strapping into his Svalinn. "But at least this time, we got some reason for being worried."

"Not so much worried as cautious, Master Sergeant," Colonel Olivera said from behind us.

I hadn't seen Olivera walk in just behind Brooks, and maybe he'd intended it that way to keep from having the same sort of fuss made for him. Julie was with him and both of them looked a bit haggard. I had the sense that they'd been on duty since we'd left Earth orbit and still hadn't had a chance to sleep.

"You two here to get strapped, sir?" I asked him. I'd been heading back to put on my gear, but I paused to nod to Julie.

"Policy," he confirmed, half his mouth turning up as if he'd tried to smile but was too tired for it. "My policy, so I'd damned well better follow it. All detachment personnel are to be armed whenever the ship drops out of hyperspace, just in case."

"Why not just go armed all the time?" I asked him. "And maybe have the Rangers rotate platoons in and out of their exoskeletons for a reaction force?"

Olivera sighed, exasperation rich in the sound.

"And I would love to do just that," he assured me. "But as much as the Helta need our help, we still need theirs to get our own ships. And Joon-pah has shared with me just how uncomfortable it makes his people to be around weapons."

"You're shitting me," Jambo said, stopping mid-motion strapping on his chest armor. "They're fighting a fucking *war*, and they're uncomfortable with us carrying guns?"

"That was basically my response as well, Master Sergeant," Olivera agreed. He motioned at Jonesy with an impatient get over here gesture. "Sidearms and gun belts, Sergeant. One for me, one for Colonel Nieves, quick as you can." Jonesy, to his credit, didn't try to give Olivera the same ration of shit he'd given me, just went about his business. Olivera turned back to Jambo and I. "Anyway, I tried reasoning with him and he said he could put aside his own feelings, but he was worried about his bridge crew being distracted and since, God forbid that the furry bear people who are going to give us a starship should be nervous when our lives are in their hands, I am going to bend over backwards to keep the captain happy."

"You sound a bit on edge, sir," I said, tightening the armor plates on my right arm. "We have something specific to be worried about at Alpha Centauri?"

"Should be nothing there at all," he said, taking a holstered SIG from Jonesy. "The place has a couple habitable planets and we may want to try putting bases there at some point, but for right now, there's not as much as a vertebrate in the whole system." He shrugged. "But yeah, I'm worried. We have one ship, a company of Rangers and two armed shuttles, and that's it. If we run into any serious resistance out here, anything like what the

Helta have been going up against, we're pretty much fucked." He checked his watch and swore softly. "I have to get back to the bridge." He eyed Brooks and Jambo. "And you all have to get locked into the shuttles before we jump."

"Aww," I complained, "I was hoping for a seat on the bridge again."

"Not this time. But you can watch from the shuttle's remote feed." He waved on his way out. "Hell, you'll probably have as good a view as I will."

"We're going to be in a new star system," Julie said, sounding much more excited than Olivera about the whole business. She was practically giggling as she headed out the hatch. "And there I was thinking that flying a ship around the Moon would be the coolest thing that ever happened in my life. That was just a trip around the block by comparison."

"Is it bad that I don't feel at all guilty about pulling rank and getting a seat in the cockpit?" I asked Brooks.

Well, "seat" probably wasn't the right word. Both of us were in full Svalinn armor, which pretty much precluded sitting, but we were squeezed into Shuttle Alpha's cockpit along with the flight crew. I don't know if Captain Holden, the pilot, was crazy about Brooks and me looking over her shoulder, and if it had been me, she might have risked telling off a technically superior officer here in an advisory capacity. But Brooks was Authority with a capital A, and not even a Space Force zoomie was going to question her right to be there.

"Not bad at all," Brooks assured me, her arms folded across the chest of her armor, her M900 slung at her back. "You know as well as I do all the times having rank just means getting blamed for shit other people did. You have to grab all the good you can."

Her visor was up and unsealed and I could see the grin on sturdy, hard-jawed face. "Besides, you know. First time in another star system and all that. I wasn't going to miss it, even if I had to bribe the pilot."

"I accept bribes, by the way," Elizabeth Holden told us. "Also, we're coming up on jump in thirty seconds. Might want to watch the show."

She motioned at the viewscreen, which was tied into the feed from the *Truthseeker's* external cameras. I was a bit disappointed when I'd first seen the specs and saw that the shuttles weren't going to have actual windows. I mean, it made sense from a structural integrity standpoint for the viewscreen to be purely electronic, but even the space shuttle had windows.

"Ten seconds," Holden droned. She was one of those pilots who liked to make announcements. I'd run into them before on transport birds and I couldn't stand them. "Five...four...three... two...one."

There was the same feeling I'd had before, but attenuated somehow, as if leaving hyperspace wasn't as spiritually traumatic as entering, or maybe I was just getting used to it. The screen flickered to life and the twin suns of Alpha Centauri A and B were off the port bow.

"Holy shit," I said, unable to hold the words in. I turned to Holden. "Can we see any of the planets from here?"

"Don't ask me," Holden said with a shrug. "This is just a feed from the bridge."

I scowled, stewing for a second before I remembered that my comms unit could link into the bridge's command channel. I accessed it from the touch pad on my left forearm and brought up the image from the security feed into my HUD display. Olivera and Julie and the rest of the bridge crew looked different somehow viewed from the high angle, like actors in a play.

"Sensors?" Olivera asked. I knew he was tense because he'd

told me, but I couldn't detect a bit of it in his voice. He had the fighter pilot cool down pat.

"Nothing, as far as I can tell," Major Baldwin said. She glanced over at the Helta officer beside her. "Klohn-Gro, you see anything?"

I expected the Helta to speak through Joon-Pah or an electronic translator, but apparently, the Helta bridge crew had been learning English over the last few months, even if the random workers I'd run into yesterday hadn't.

"The sensors detect no habitation," the Helta said, and if his accent was stilted and poorly pronounced, it was still a damn sight better than my Helta. "I would like to take a closer reading of the third planet."

Baldwin looked back over her shoulder at Olivera.

"We got time for that, boss?"

"How long for a fly-by, Nieves?" Olivera asked the Helm officer.

"Just close enough for a good sensor sweep?" Julie asked, shrugging. "We're already in the correct orbital plane, and this exit point isn't that far away. Maybe an extra two hours in real-space, unless you want to try a micro-jump."

"Are we sure we can do those?" Olivera sounded skeptical.

"They are certainly possible," Joon-Pah said. "Navigationally, they are simpler than a jump between star systems. Though I admit concern for the stress on the superstructure of two jumps in such quick succession. There is a certain resonance established in the cellular frequencies of all matter during a jump. You may have felt this."

I sure did. Thanks for warning us beforehand, Fozzie.

"It is mostly harmless to living organisms, but with repetitive exposure, it can weaken the molecular bonding we use to seal the seams of our ship. Most ships of the Alliance adhere to a policy of one jump per system for this reason."

"We'll try to keep it to a minimum," Olivera promised. "But I'd like to test the procedures, just to give my people an idea of what to expect. Nieves, jump us as close as you can to planet three." He squinted at Joon-Pah. "Does it have a name?"

"No one has claimed it. It was considered too close to your system for any Alliance power to colonize. I suppose it is up to your people to name it."

"Let's take a look at it first. Nieves, plot the jump. Baldwin, sound the warning."

For some reason, knowing the resonance was real made it worse. Reality winked at me, my stomach lurched and the screen blanked out for just a few seconds before the stars reappeared. And for a just a moment, I thought we'd somehow returned to Earth. The third planet out from Alpha Centauri A could have been her twin, blue and green and sparkling like a gem in the sky.

"Good God," I murmured. "Where do I sign up to emigrate?"

Olivera glanced around, eyes sharpening enough for me to catch it even in the security camera view.

"Clanton, if that's you, I'd like to remind you when you use your issue comm unit to spy on the bridge, you should mute your audio input." I winced, my ears warming with embarrassment when I saw Julie laughing. "I agree with you, though," he said, nodding toward the screen. "It's beautiful. You ever been down there, Joon-Pah?"

"I'm a ship's captain," the alien replied. "I do not, generally, go on expeditions to uncharted worlds."

"Captain Kirk would be so ashamed," Nieves lamented.

"Here's your closer look, Baldwin," Olivera told the Tactical officer. "See anything worth the trip?"

"Running orange slice scans of the planet," Baldwin said, fingers playing the haptic hologram like harp strings. "And it's got some pretty polar ice caps, maybe a mini-ice age going on. Five major continents and a whole bunch of islands, looks like a few active volcanos, two moons, each a bit smaller than Luna..." She'd been leaning over, squinting at the readout, but she straightened suddenly, twisting around in her seat. "We got a satellite in orbit around one of the moons, sir."

"Shit." Olivera jumped out of his seat, leaning across her control station and staring into the sensor readouts. "Joon-Pah, tell me this is one of yours."

The alien captain made a slashing motion in the air, his shoulders hunched over as if he was getting ready for a fight.

"No. I mean, yes, the technology is ours, but the Helta would never take such a risk so close to your system. It would have been like leaving a beacon for the Tevynians. But the Tevynians have stolen our technology, kidnapped our engineers and scientists. This is one of theirs, and this is so very, very unfortunate."

"It can't transmit through hyperspace from here, can it?" I asked, ignoring the fact that I was sticking my nose in all the way from the shuttle.

"No, it's too small. They'd need a transmitter far enough from the gravitational pull of the moon to open a stable wormhole, and that's not something we'd miss. It would have to be the size of a starship."

"Then they must come through here on regular patrols and download the surveillance data," Olivera decided. "It's definitely seen us by now."

"I can target it with the particle cannon," Baldwin offered. "Take it out in a couple minutes."

"Opinions?" Olivera said, looking around. "That means you, too, Brooks, Clanton, Bowie."

"If we take it out, they'll still know we were here," I pointed out.

"Agreed," Brooks put in. "And they'll know we know they've been here. We gain nothing."

"Worst case scenario," Jambo cut in, "they come back here

before we do, find out a Helta ship has been in the area. What do they do?"

"The ship would transmit to their homeworld and ask for guidance," Joon-Pah replied. "Given what I have seen from our previous history with them, they would probably be told to wait there for reinforcements."

"And if they come back and find it destroyed, the same thing happens," Olivera assumed. "Okay, so worst-case scenario is, we find them waiting for us when we come back."

"Better to let them think we don't know they'll be here," Brooks suggested.

"Agreed." Olivera motioned to Nieves. "Take us out of here, Julie."

I cut the feed from the bridge and shared an "oh, shit" look with Brooks.

"What do you think happens when we come back through here and there's a shitload of enemy ships?" I asked her.

"Let's just hope we have some more ships of our own when it happens," she said. "Or this is going to be the shortest war ever."

18

"I AM," I SAID EARNESTLY TO JAMBO, "BEGINNING TO HATE this fucking shuttle."

"Amen, brother," he agreed, resting his helmet back against the upright rack the Svalinn armor was strapped into. "At least it's for real this time."

I nodded, though he couldn't see it. We'd been confined to the shuttle for every single emergence from hyperspace and God*damn*, there had been so many jumps in the last ten days. *Or was it twelve?* Every time we hit a transitory system, we'd come out for a nav check. This one was different, though. We all knew it, and the darkness in the shuttle was only a symptom, not the cause.

The interior of the aerospacecraft was cloaked in shadow, the lights dimmed in the cargo and passenger compartments to keep the cockpit as free of distractions as possible for the pilots, or so I had been told. Personally, I thought it had more to do with tradition. Combat runs in V22s or Blackhawks were always blacked out, which meant nothing in space...but our pilots and, more importantly, our crew chiefs had been brought over from the Air

Force and the SOCOM Air Wing, the Nightstalkers, and old habits die hard.

I think the Delta boys preferred it that way and not just out of tradition. I know I did. Darkness carried with it a privacy, the chance to be alone inside your head and not worry whether someone else might see the fear in your eyes.

"Yeah," I said, mostly to myself, not caring whether Jambo heard or not. "It's for real this time."

I closed my eyes and tried to play the details from Olivera's briefing back in my memory. It was harder than it used to be. Once upon a time, I would have taken notes on every point, then expanded them for my platoon and spat them back out again in front of the men and, in the process, memorized every radio call-sign and every map point. But this was the new, high-tech Space Force and everything was forwarded as a PowerPoint on our tablets and I didn't have a platoon, or anything to do except keep my head on a swivel and try to be helpful.

I'd still tried to be a good little Marine and pay attention in the briefing, despite Jambo's constant sotto voce commentary.

"Why do we have to do this in person?" he'd muttered to me while Olivera delivered his opening remarks to the two hundred humans and Helta gathered in the ship's largest conference room. "This is the 21st Century...we could all be in our own compartments watching it on a video screen or a tablet."

"Maybe he was worried people would get distracted by something," I'd suggested, glaring at him. "Like someone talking in their ear during the briefing, for example."

"This is the star system we know as Kepler 62," Olivera said, getting to the meat of the matter. He pointed to a sun-like star hanging at the center of the projection near the front of the room. "It's about 1200 light years from Earth and it'll be our next stop in exactly forty-six hours and twenty-three minutes."

"And thirteen seconds," Julie Nieves added from where she leaned against the hologram projector beside him.

"Holy shit," Pops said, a few chairs over from me, not even trying to keep quiet about it. "We traveled *twelve hundred light years* in less than two weeks? How fucking fast is this thing?"

Olivera scowled, looking as if he wanted to chew the Delta Force weapons specialist out for talking out of turn, but Julie answered it for him.

"Time and distance aren't a factor in hyperspace." She grinned briefly and I'd thought, not for the first time, just how cute she looked when she smiled. "The Helta don't actually call it hyperspace, by the way, in case you were wondering. But it's as good a name as any. What matters in hyperspace is the strength of the gravimetic attraction between the transit nodes, the star systems we're flying between. And that doesn't always mean how massive the stars are or how close they are, though don't ask me why. What it boils down to is, it takes longer to fly the four and a half light years from Earth to Alpha Centauri than it does to fly the ten and a half light years from Earth to Epsilon Eridani."

"Sail," I'd insisted, arms folded across my chest, jaw set. "The term should be 'sail,' not 'fly,' dammit."

"Oh, give it a rest for Christ's sake," Jambo said, rolling his eyes.

Joon-Pah was standing off to the side, almost unnoticed, which is quite the accomplishment for a bearlike humanoid, but he stepped forward at a gesture from Olivera.

"The system you call Kepler 62," he said, his soft voice being amplified by some unseen microphone, "we know as Waypoint. It is one of our key industrial centers, and one of our largest colonies, with two habitable planets. More importantly for our needs, it is the location of one of our largest shipyards, where our commercial ships are retrofitted into military vessels for the conflict. The...faction of my government which supports this effort to bring the people of Earth into our conflict has many supporters in the Waypoint system, and one of them is the administrator of the shipyards in the system's asteroid belt. We have exchanged numerous communications and he has assured me that he will have at least three starships in the same class as the *Truthseeker* in the dock and ready for us to commandeer when we arrive."

"This should *not* be a combat operation," Olivera had stressed. "The ships will be empty and the Helta will recognize this ship as one of their own, with clearance to be there. But as always, we will treat it as a threat situation until we confirm it is not. Both shuttles will be loaded and ready to launch and the ship will go in weapons armed. Do walk-throughs of all emergency scenarios with your units. If there are any further developments, I'll send out a fragmentary order to your comms."

There'd been no frag-o's, so I assumed everything had stayed the same. I remembered what the old saying was about assuming, but I chose to be optimistic.

"Jumping in thirty seconds," the announcement came from Captain Holden, the pilot, Our Lady of Countdowns.

"Whaddya think we'll name the ships?" Jambo asked. "You think there's already an approved list somewhere, written up by some subcommittee or presidential advisory board?"

"Probably," I agreed. "Something suitably inoffensive and noble-sounding, like the *Friendship of the International Community* or something."

"Ten seconds."

"Our pilot has seen too many fucking movies," Jambo opined. "We really don't do that shit."

"The sad thing is," I said, "people like her are probably going to make it catch on and everybody is going to start doing countdowns."

"...two, one, jumping now!"

Twisting, roiling, wrenching and more than anything now that I knew to expect it, a painful vibration, the resonance Joon-Pah had talked about. It was like being at a heavy metal concert and standing right in front of the speaker, except the speaker was the universe and God was playing the tune.

I shook off the lingering haze and linked into the bridge security feed again, determined to keep my mouth shut this time. We'd come out of hyperspace deep in the black, in the system's asteroid belt, Kepler 62 a glaring flashlight among the firefly swarm of stars and asteroids. The spacedocks were glowing spiderwebs in the darkness, lit up from without and within, the interior lights glinting through thick windows while floodlights shone bright white on the half-assembled skeletons of starships.

Before anyone on the bridge said a word, I knew something was wrong.

"There's only one ship in the dock," I told Jambo.

Not that I was suddenly a starship expert, but it was hard to miss something as big as a Helta cruiser, and there was only one of them visible on the whole stretch of outer space scaffolding that was the Waypoint Shipyard. It wasn't surrounded by the spiderweb structure like the ships still under construction, instead, it was nestled into some sort of pressurized docking port that led into the interior of the dock.

"We've detected multiple explosions in orbit around the habitable," Baldwin reported, talking over the confused chatter in English and Helta. "Also getting thermal flares from the planet's moon and from the deuterium mines in the atmosphere of the gas giant." She spun her chair around toward Olivera. "Sir, I think there's some sort of battle going on."

There were at least a couple good things about having Space Force in charge of the mission instead of a Space Navy. Olivera didn't sound any alarm klaxons or yell at the crew to get to their battle stations. Everyone already *was* where they needed to be if we got into any fighting.

"We're picking up a repeating transmission from in-system," Joon-Pah said, interpreting the gabble from the Helta communications officer. "I'm setting the computer to translate."

A portion of the main screen lit up with a Helta dressed in what I'd come to understand was the standard uniform of the Alliance forces, the Napoleonic drummer boy outfit, except this one was charred on the left sleeve and the thin fuzz on the face of the Helta officer was burned away, leaving a weeping open wound. More evidence of carnage was visible behind the wounded alien, tendrils of smoke churning toward the air filtration vent on the bridge of their ship, nearly identical to the *Truthseeker* except for the blackened scars burned into the bulkhead.

"This is Gara-Shan, Captain of the *Illuminator*," the ship's computer translated the message into English for us. Somehow, it still managed to convey the weariness and pain the Helta's inflection. "Any Alliance ships, this is the Helta vessel *Illuminator*. I am invoking our treaty and calling for aid. The Waypoint system has come under attack by Tevynian forces and we are being overrun. We only had three functioning cruisers in-system, and two of them were out at the shipyards in the asteroid belt, and only enough crew on hand for one of those to take flight. The *Destiny* was destroyed early in the battle and the *Illuminator* has taken heavy damage. Our main drives are down. I don't know how much longer we can hold out, but we will keep firing at the Helta ships, trying to keep their attention on us so the civilians can continue their evacuation."

Gara-Shan reached off camera for a control and the image switched to something I thought must have been recorded earlier. The green and blue arc of the Helta planet filled most of the screen, a placid background for something far less pleasant. A thread of iridescent lightning streamed from the surface, though the atmosphere, the beam disappearing as the atmosphere thinned out, but its effects clear when it struck what I assumed was a Tevynian ship in high orbit. A sphere of destruction expanded outward from the wedge of silvery metal and burning gas spewed like a giant maneuvering thruster from the port bow, sending it skewing off to starboard.

Into the gap left by the wounded Tevynian cruiser, a swarm of huge, spherical spacecraft blasted out of the atmosphere, wildebeests fleeing a lion. I tried to count them but they kept coming, ten, twenty, fifty, a hundred maybe, boosting out of orbit on glaring white drive flares, a dozen times brighter than one of our shuttles. The lead ships were almost to the orbit of the planet's moon when they made the jump into hyperspace.

I hadn't seen it from the outside before and I nearly gasped. Space itself seemed to split apart like a weak seam on a pair of pants, beginning like the slit pupil of a cat, then expanding into a circle, ringed by a shifting, glimmering rainbow. Where the inside of the hole should have been, the camera glitched, fuzz and distortion filling the screen until the spherical ship was through and the hole repaired itself.

Before the next opening wormhole could disrupt the picture, the image switched back to the Helta captain.

"Tens of thousands have made it off-planet, mostly from the areas around the spaceport, but there aren't enough ships in the whole Alliance to evacuate the whole population. If you can hear this message, we need military support..."

"Captain!" a voice yelled from behind the Helta. The officer turned and the image faded in a burst of multicolored lights.

I winced, knowing I'd probably just witnessed the deaths of everyone on the ship.

"It just keeps repeating," Joon-Pah said. The computer wasn't translating for him and his own ability at English, while much improved, lacked the proper inflection to convey his mood, but I could still sense his fear and agitation. "I believe Gara-Shan recorded it onto an emergency beacon and launched it, because the sensors do not detect her anywhere in-system." He paused. "We are, however, detecting numerous unregistered ships similar to Helta design all over this system."

"Are you getting any other transmissions?" Olivera asked him. "From the habitable or any of the outer space facilities?"

"There seems to be widespread jamming of all transmissions from our world Fairhome, as well as the mining facilities at the gas giant. This would be in accord with Tevynian methods of operation when invading a system."

"We're too late," I said to Jambo, making sure I muted my mic. "The enemy got here first."

"Oh, that's unfortunate," he said mildly. I figured he'd want to hear what was going on, so I tapped the control on my forearm and shared the feed with him and the rest of the Delta team.

"There's still one cruiser at the shipyards," Olivera said, pointing at the familiar delta shape nestled against the structures there.

"There may also be unmounted hyperdrives here and here," Joon-Pah told him, pointing to two of the skeletal superstructures one level in towards the center from the completed cruiser. "If we can procure those, you could, with our help, build your own ships."

"He seems awfully damned calm for someone who's watching one of their largest colonies get conquered," Pops said from the rack on the other side of me.

"I don't know," Jambo said. "Maybe God could tell you what a man-bear-alien is feeling, but I don't have a fucking clue."

I ignored them, trying to see what everyone else was seeing on the Tactical board, but the view from the security camera was off-center from the display and I could only make out green and yellow lights. I had no idea what they signified and might not have been able to figure them out even if I'd been standing on the bridge instead of snooping on it from afar.

"If we can get a crew on the other ship," Julie suggested, "maybe we can do something to help fight off the Tevynians and save your colony."

"They have at least six cruisers in the system," Joon-Pah said, waving a hand at the tactical display. "And even if we could win against that many ships, they've already begun landing soldiers on the surface. You do not have enough troops to drive them out or kill them all. If they repeat their behavior from other incidents such as this, they'll either strip the world of all that's useful, then leave, or they'll occupy it and wait for reinforcements. They do not intend to slaughter our people, though they do force our engineers and technicians to work for them. The best way we can help the people of the colony is to start winning. Then the Tevynians may draw back to their own systems."

"I don't like it," Olivera declared, his anger and frustration much easier to read than whatever was going through Joon-Pah's mind. "If it was my world, I'd be heading down there right now. But it's your people and your decision. And if we're not going to dig in and fight for Fairhome, we need to get to that ship."

"Great minds think alike," Baldwin said. "You see those bug-eyed insect-looking things attached to the construction scaffolding beside the Helta cruiser?"

I squinted at the image in my HUD and then remembered I could see the view directly and pulled up the feed from the shuttle's main screen instead. It took me a second to force both feeds into different spots in my helmet HUD since the suit had this quaint idea that I should be able to actually see out of my helmet visor, but I finally spotted what Baldwin was talking about. The things didn't look so much like insects to me as they did seed pods, but I could definitely tell they didn't belong on the scaffolding.

"From what the computer is telling me," Baldwin went on, "those are boarding pods, used mostly by the Tevynians. They're already on the ship, trying to take it for themselves."

"This just gets better and better," I said and tried not to turn it into a moan. No use sounding like a whiner. I craned my head around to look at Jambo. "Three guesses what the next order's going to be and the first two don't count."

"Okay," Olivera said, and his voice sounded louder and crisper in my headphones than it had in the security feed, "all personnel, listen up. The Tevynians have beat us to the punch and are trying to take this system, and the only remaining cruiser. We have to take the ship from them before they can get it operational. Captain Holden, Captain Chambers, you will launch at my command and dock your shuttles as close as you can to the Helta cruiser without taking enemy fire. Colonel Brooks, you and your Rangers are going to board that ship and eliminate any Tevynian troops you find on board. Master Sergeant Bowie, your Delta team will accompany our flight crew into the ship, following the Rangers. Keep them alive and get them to the bridge. That is our number one priority. You got me?"

"Yes, sir," Brooks and Jambo said in broken chorus.

"Good luck and get it done. Shuttles Alpha and Bravo, you are cleared to launch."

"Launching in ten seconds," Holden announced and I rolled my eyes.

"You know, you're right," Jambo told me. "This shit is going to spread. We need to nip this in the bud now, before it's too late."

"I'll get right on that," I promised.

"Launching!"

Sound and vibration filled my head and acceleration pushed me back into the lining of my suit and back into the tilted bracket holding the suit in place and back toward the tail of the bird as I felt thrust again for the first time in two weeks.

"You okay?" Jambo asked me, his voice strained from the boost.

Was I okay? Everything was going to shit and I was being sent to go kill the bad guys and blow some shit up.

"Feels like old times."

19

"It's just like the simulations," Jambo was droning in everyone's ear as we headed down. "Remember your training and you'll be fine."

We were in free fall and I was *not* fine. I was trapped in a closed helmet and needed badly to puke but I kept my mouth shut for multiple reasons.

"Flight crew," Jambo went on, "you guys stay on our six. That means stay behind us, let us go first."

"We know what it means," one of them said a bit petulantly. I couldn't tell who it was, but since the highest-ranking member of the auxiliary flight crew was a Space Force Captain, I didn't think Jambo was too impressed. "We're in the military, too."

"Oh, I know you are," Jambo said, his tone rich with amusement if you knew him well enough to recognize it. "So be good little Spacemen and Spacewomen and stay the fuck behind us."

I hadn't wanted to do it, not in free fall when I was already having inner ear issues, but I couldn't help myself. I touched the control pad on my left forearm and tied into the shuttle's exterior cameras, just unable to deal with dropping blind. The other shuttle had launched first, taking Colonel Brooks and most of her Ranger company in ahead of us, and their drives were a sunburst glow hanging in space off our starboard bow. It only looked a couple miles away, but I knew things seemed closer with no atmosphere to distort the incoming light, and it could have been twenty miles away, or fifty.

Probably fifty, given we needed to stay clear of their exhaust. They didn't have the space warping field the *Truthseeker* used for sublight travel, just old-fashioned reaction drives, but ones that made ours look like Twelfth-Century fireworks by comparison. Julie had tried to explain it to me, but all I got out of it was that there was some sort of compact nuclear reactor involved and the reaction mass was metallic hydrogen but it could use any sort of metal in a pinch, which was damned good since we didn't know how to mass-produce metallic hydrogen yet.

If the shuttle appeared close, the shipyard drydock seemed like I could reach out and touch it. What had appeared to be smooth, featureless spider silk from a distance clarified with proximity to something rough and intricately detailed, dotted with construction machinery, airlocks, observation windows and tiny, cylindrical transfer pods with manipulator arms protruding from their noses like the claws on a crab. And as we descended ever closer, details kept emerging and my sense of the scale kept changing. Everything was so much larger than I had first thought, the windows not as tall as a man but instead taller than a ten-story building, the cylindrical pods not one person affairs but huge, nearly as big as one of our shuttles. And the spiderweb scaffolding stretching across the perimeter of the shipyard wasn't the fifty or a hundred yards I'd supposed; it was nearly a kilometer wide.

And the Tevynian boarding pods docked in a staggered line along the edge of the Helta drydock's auxiliary airlocks were so much larger than I'd thought, each about as big as our shuttle, big enough for the lot of them to carry a hundred troops or more. My stomach churned, and it wasn't just the microgravity.

Shuttle Alpha swung its nose around toward us and gave a short, braking burst, then rode what momentum was left from their acceleration in to one of the unoccupied docking collars along the surface of what was oriented as the top of the structure. Maneuvering thrusters flared at Alpha's nose and the aerospacecraft's nose lowered, bringing it horizontal over the airlock before the pilot gave one last, insistent braking thrust with the belly jets, mating them gently to the lock.

Then the camera view swung wildly and a giant banged a hammer against the hull as our own steering jets fired, flipping us end for end just before our own drives began decelerating. I was pressed into my seat with what felt like a couple gravities of thrust, and the image in the HUD of my helmet shifted to a view of the *Truthseeker*. The starship had reoriented itself, the nose pointing inward toward the Helta habitable. I wondered if the Tevynians had spotted us from there, or if perhaps, the ones inside the docked Helta ship had seen us and called the others. And if they did know we were here, I wondered how long we'd have.

"Ranger one here," Brooks reported, her voice tinny and distorted in my headphones. Probably interference from the metal in the lock, I guessed. Our radios were improved with Helta technology, but they were still using microwave communications and physics was physics. "We're through the airlock. No enemy troops in sight, no Helta. There's gravity inside, so be prepared. We'll set up a perimeter and wait for you to dock."

"Roger that," Jambo replied. "Leave a light on for us."

The deceleration burn cut off, the steady roar replaced with staccato bang of the maneuvering thrusters and I tried not to hyperventilate.

You fought a shitload of Russians just a couple weeks ago.

You'll be fine. You can do this. That was the little angel in Marine combat utilities on my shoulder, still toting an old M16A5 with a bayonet mounted under the barrel.

The devil was on the other shoulder, wearing a torn T-shirt and cargo shorts, one hand with a jack-and-Coke on the rocks, the other with a Glock, eyes haunted with survivor's guilt.

You were using science fiction tech and fighting Russians limited to the obsolete military surplus gear they could scrounge up on US soil. These motherfuckers fly between stars and they're going to kill you.

I wanted to tell the little devil to just go fuck off, but he wouldn't go away, mostly because he was a part of me. The worst part.

"The Tevynians won't have exoskeletons," I said out loud, as if I was reminding the Delta team of our opposition. I was really talking to myself, trying to argue my way into confidence. "Joon-Pah said their native technology was behind ours before the Helta found them. The Tevynians think of the Helta as the gold standard for tech, so they're basically just repurposing what they can steal from them. Our most likely opposition will be light infantry in unpowered armor, carrying energy weapons."

"Right," Jambo said. "Don't get cocky though, they're absolute fanatics. Think jihadis but with lasers." The communications icon next to Jambo's IFF avatar changed colors and I knew he'd switched to a private channel with me. "You doing okay, Andy?"

"Oh, yeah, just great," I said. "Nothing about a quart of vodka wouldn't cure."

"That's not who you are.," he said, almost snapping at me. I blinked. Jambo just didn't *get* angry. Not even when I'd run off and he'd had to rescue me from an FSB snatch-n-grab team. "You don't need that shit to deal. Just key on my movement, stay in the center with me, okay? We'll be fine. The Rangers are doing the heavy lifting, anyway."

His last couple sentences had drifted back into laid back, unflappable Jambo territory and my breathing slowed down to normal.

Then the belly jets kicked in and slammed against the deck beneath us until metal ground on metal with a painful, wailing shriek and gravity returned abruptly.

"We're down," Holden told us, as redundant as usual. "Gisecki, cycle the lock."

"Everybody up!" Jambo yelled, hitting the quick release for his restraints and hopping to his feet. "Rangers, you're at the lock first! Link up with your company on the other side! Pops, you're point for our team, and Ginger's on drag, riding herd on the flight crew. Flight personnel, keep your helmets sealed until we have control of that ship. We don't know how easy it would be for the bad guys to flush the atmosphere so we need to make sure they're all clear before we take the chance." He looked around. "Any questions?"

"Yeah," one of the Delta boys muttered, the deep, gravelly voice telling me it was the one they called Dog. "How do I get out of this chickenshit outfit?"

Even Jambo had to laugh at the classical reference.

"Stay tight, keep your fields of fire clear and don't wander in front of anyone's gun barrel. Good luck."

The shuttle's crew chief waved us an all-clear and motioned toward the airlock set in the deck of the shuttle just aft of the passenger compartment. One of the Ranger squad leaders jumped through the hatch, disdaining the ladder built into the lock, counting on her Svalinn suit to absorb the shock of the landing. And Rangers being Rangers, of course all the others had to do the same thing. When Delta's turn came, they made a point of descending the ladder as carefully as possible, just to prove they weren't douchebag kids like the Rangers.

I was a Marine, *and* I knew what the exoskeletons could do. I jumped. The inner lock was a ring of green, barely visible as I zipped through, then darkness enveloped me for a single heartbeat before my boots struck deck plating hard enough to send a vibration ringing through it. I didn't take time to look around, just moved out of the way of the lock and found the nearest bulkhead to huddle against, my M900 pointed outward.

The corridor was broad, maybe thirty yards across, the bulkhead against the inner side of it a dull orange with writings in Helta etched in white across its surface, broken up here and there by flat, two-dimensional video screens. The screens were all frozen on some sort of logo I thought might have been the Helta flag or coat of arms or something, with more alien writing scrolling up and down the sides. I had no idea what it said, and wasn't going to spend enough time staring at it for the helmet computer to translate for me.

All my staring was in the other direction, out the huge, impossibly clear window stretching from deck to overhead, or ceiling to floor as the Rangers and Space Force crew would say. Through the transparent material, which I assumed wasn't glass, the vast, menacing bulk of the Helta starship hung in black nothingness, distant sunlight glinting off its polished, silvery surface. The enemy was somewhere inside her, but from without, she seemed dead and deserted, a haunted house in space.

I tore my gaze away from the stunning view and checked behind me, saw the last of the flight crew climbing down, with Ginger in his Svalinn clambering out of the lock last.

"We're all in," Jambo reported.

"Fourth Platoon," Brooks ordered, the transmission sent on the general band so all of us could hear it, "I want you to stay here and guard the shuttles and the approaches into the Helta starship. We don't know that the enemy isn't behind us somewhere."

"Yes, ma'am," the Fourth Platoon leader responded, not seeming very enthusiastic about the idea. Fourth had been in Shuttle Bravo with us, and I wondered if just being on the wrong bird had doomed him to rear guard duty.

"Rangers moving out," Brooks announced. "We can see the maintenance lock from up here."

We'd been briefed on this part. Oh, we hadn't known there'd be opposition, but Joon-Pah had shown us the layout of the drydocks and given us the clearance codes to get through the locks just in case the particular Helta in charge when we arrived weren't favorably disposed to letting us take their ship.

With three fourths of a company of armored Rangers ahead of me, I couldn't even see the maintenance lock until the Army grunts had moved around the curve in the hull and into the lock. It was recessed into the outer hull of the drydock, an armored, shielded collar half in and half out of the skin of the facility, enveloping the hull of the Helta star cruiser all around what seemed to be some sort of cargo lock, the hatch large enough to let a tractor-trailer through it, the lock deep enough for three platoons of Rangers.

I wasn't the commander, but I would have been a bit more hesitant to squeeze my whole force into the lock at once. All it would have taken was one Tevynian at the right control board to power up the ship and separate from the dock and the whole bunch of them would have been floating free in space.

"Hold up here," Jambo ordered his team and the flight crew, and I wasn't sure if he was reading my mind or I'd been reading his.

I guessed Brooks was transmitting orders to her troops from the hand gestures she was making, but I wasn't tuned into her net. I got the gist of it when I saw one of the squads from Brooks' platoons move to the control panel for the lock's massive hatch, most of the Rangers deploying around it to pull security while two went to work on the code input. The interior of the lock and the control panels mounted there were familiar to me after a couple weeks on the *Truthseeker*, but might have anyway. For all that the Helta were bear people in strange, gaudy clothes, they had more in common with humans than they had any right to. Or maybe there was a pragmatism to it, form following function, but I thought I could have worked out which controls did what even without the briefing we'd been given.

The airlock hatch slid aside and the squad Brooks had detailed to breach it squeezed through before the opening was a meter wide. The nine Rangers were lost in a cluster of red and blue cargo loading equipment, disappearing between twenty-foot-tall bulbous, bulky, machines with claws and forks and sleds and a few things I couldn't identify on first view. Stacks of oblong cargo containers were piled high on sleds, heavy machine parts were clenched in padded claws and the loading equipment was scattered randomly in the broad lane of the cargo loading passage leading to the ship's hold, some of them jammed against the bulkhead, some rammed into each other, as if the workers had jumped off while the machines were running.

The light in the passage was dim, the shadows deep, and as I edged closer to the lock, passing through the lines of Delta operators and the perimeter they formed, I saw the reason for it. The light panels were in the overhead, fifty feet off the deck, and some of them had been charred black, whatever technology they used to produce illumination burned out by energy weapons. As my eyes adjusted to the lower light, I saw more blast marks on the bulkheads, charred black scars across the red and blue of the loaders.

"They put up a fight here," I said, holding my rifle at low

ready, expecting the enemy to swarm out from between the machines.

"We have bodies," Brooks said on the general net, for us and for the relay from the shuttle to the *Truthseeker*. "Helta bodies, sixteen that we can see just out in the entrance corridor. Looks like energy weapons. At least some of them were armed, so I'd guess they made a stand here."

"Any sign of the Tevynians?" Olivera asked from back on the ship.

"Nothing yet. I'm going to push in, move to contact."

"Roger that. Be careful."

"Go ahead and move into the lock," Jambo ordered. "Ginger, keep the flight crew on this side until we sweep through into the ship."

This was the part of military operations I hated, sitting around, waiting for the guys in front of you to move out. It was worse when it was a mechanized convoy and you were stuck in a HMMWV with no air conditioning, sweating your ass off in full body armor while the guys a mile ahead of you at the front of the line rumbled out at five miles an hour. Every local who passed by was giving you the stinkeye and every bit of trash was an IED.

I felt too close to the Rangers platoon ahead of us, too packed together, and I could hear my DI in boot yelling at me from Parris Island, "One fucking grenade would take out the whole bunch of you!" But Gunny Wolczk wasn't here and I badly wanted out of the lock, so I edged ahead of Jambo, toward the front of the team and toyed with the idea of taking advantage of my unattached position to squeeze through the Rangers as well.

But Jambo would have yelled at me and it was embarrassing to have an NCO yell at me when I was a major, so I waited. I knew the suit, knew the comms setup and could have linked to the helmet camera from the Ranger on point, but I didn't need that kind of distraction when I was down here on the ground with a rifle in my hand, so I just waited like the rest of the grunts.

A yard at a time, a step at a time, I moved past the lock and between the machinery. The bodies were sprawled between the machines, not dressed in the uniforms Joon-Pah and his crew wore but in some kind of light body armor. Whatever it was made of, it hadn't been enough. The energy weapons the Tevynians were using had ripped through it, blowing fist-sized holes through chests and stomachs, melting helmet visors and turning the heads inside into puddles of charred and congealed blood. I swallowed bile and gave silent thanks for the filters in my helmet keeping out the smell. The smell is always the worst part about dead bodies, especially ones that were burned. It was sickly sweet, nauseatingly appetizing, like roast pork. After Venezuela, I'd almost become a vegetarian.

Blood had pooled around the bodies and I wished I could have kept from stepping in it, but the suits weren't great for seeing your feet while you walked. I couldn't feel the wet stickiness, couldn't feel the slight adhesion to the deck, but I knew it was there and it nagged at the edges of my psyche, trying to force my eyes back down to the bodies. I ignored the pull and kept my attention on the bulkheads, the hatches there, watching the Rangers try each of them using the universal entrance codes Joon-Pah had provided. One would key the lock and their battle buddy would dart through with their rifle at their shoulder, checking the interior then dashing back out.

I had to give them credit, the Rangers worked like fingers of the same hand, moving in tandem and continuously advancing until we reached the hold. The compartment was cavernous, at least five hundred yards from stem to stern, two hundred across and fifty tall, the center stacked high with storage containers, nearly reaching to the distant overhead, held in place by what looked like magnetic locks. The oblong ovals were clustered in neat rows, leaving aisles between them broad enough for the loading machines lining the perimeter to travel between them and shift the cargo.

The Rangers split by platoons and Brooks sent one to either end of the compartment and a third straight up the center. The Delta team followed the center group, keeping the flight crew we shepherded at the middle of our defenses. I kept my eyes and suit sensors up on the catwalks ringing the upper levels of the storage bay, watching for enemy troops left behind in ambush, but there was nothing. The lack of opposition was maddening. We knew they were on board, knew they'd had a head start on us. If Jambo or Brooks had led their troops, they would have left a rear guard along their avenue of ingress and kept watch for anyone trying to take them from the rear.

But they're used to fighting the Helta, I reminded myself. *And the Helta don't know how to fight. Maybe it's made them sloppy.*

Whatever the reason, there were no enemy in the hold and we moved on, heading for the central transport core, the cockeyed gravity tunnels leading through the rest of the ship. And stopped.

"Master Sergeant Bowie," Colonel Brooks called to us over the comms, "Major Clanton. You'd better come up here. We have survivors."

20

There were six of them, all in the typical Helta Navy uniforms and they were scared shitless. I couldn't speak Helta, didn't know their body language as well as I would have liked, but the uncontrollable shivering, the way they flinched away from us was universal. We were faceless, hulking suits of armor carrying strange weapons, silent and menacing.

They huddled together inside a storage compartment, flanked by pressurized bottles of something I couldn't identify. Even the translation software in my helmet only told me the markings were some sort of alphanumeric inventory designator.

"Has anyone tried talking to them?" I asked Brooks.

"Not yet," she said. "And no one has lifted our visors, either."

I got what she meant. In the reflected light from the overheads, they wouldn't be able to see through our helmet visors. And we looked exactly like the Tevynians who had just come through here trying to kill them.

"Let's keep it that way," I suggested.

I don't know how I'd become the Helta liaison all of a sudden, except maybe that Jambo and I had more experience interacting with them than any of the Rangers. I pulled up the menu on my control pad and instructed my external helmet speakers to translate to Helta from English.

"We're friends," I said. A half a second later, the words came out of the speakers in Helta, the voice sounding natural rather than automated. "We won't hurt you. Which way did the Tevynians go?"

One of them stepped forward, his hands shaking, lips pulled away from his teeth in an instinctive fear reaction.

"I'm Brannas-Fel," he said. "We are with the engineering crew." Well, he said the words and then a few seconds later, I heard them in English, which made for a weird badly-dubbed foreign movie vibe. "We hid in here while the security force tried to hold them off at the airlock."

"Did you see which way they went?" Jambo asked. "Do you have any way of finding out where on the ship they are now?"

"I think I can find out," Brannas-Fel told us. "I need to access a data terminal."

"Over here," Brooks said, motioning across the passage to one of the computer input terminals. They were in every corridor, not so much to access the ship's computer, although they did allow it in an emergency if there was some problem with the remote tablets, but more to act as display boards for alerts.

The Helta engineer seemed hesitant to leave the shelter of the storage closet and he stuck his head out and checked up and down the passage to satisfy himself we had both approaches covered before he darted across to the terminal. The others stayed in the compartment, staring at us with wide eyes, apparently still unconvinced of our good intentions.

Brannas-Fel was scrolling through menus, touching a control here and there until he came to something I couldn't read or identify except that it had some sort of thermal readout.

"They shut down the internal security cameras," he said. "They know enough about our systems to do that. But they left the medical scanners up, the ones we use to monitor crew health. It's not as exact, but I can tell which parts of the ship are still occupied." He scrolled through more of the screens, from one compartment to another. "There are a few other Helta hiding on board still, but not many left alive. The Tevynians have a different thermal signature than us, so they're easy to spot." He pointed a long-nailed finger at the screen. "There's a large group at the bridge, and a smaller one in Engineering. They haven't bothered with the auxiliary control room, so they've probably locked the controls out from there."

"You seeing this, *Truthseeker*?" Jambo asked.

"Yeah, we're getting it," Olivera replied. "Colonel Brooks, take that ship and do it fast. I think they've seen us. One of the Tevynian ships is heading this way from Fairhome. We have maybe three hours, four at the most until they get to firing range."

"Roger that, sir," she said. "Master Sergeant, recommendations?"

"There're more troops on the bridge, ma'am," Jambo said, his tone clinical. "Plus, I wouldn't want to let a bunch of Rangers loose on shit we shouldn't be blowing up, so my team will take the Helta engineers with us and take Engineering. You should take the flight crew with you to the bridge and clean out the resistance there and get the ship moving. Hoo-ah?"

"Hoo-ah, Master Sergeant." Jambo's utterance of the Army catch-all phrase had been ironic. Colonel Brooke's was not. "You sure you don't want to take one of our platoons with you?"

"Drop us a squad to pull rear security," he said. "Gimme Second squad, First Platoon, if you don't mind."

That was Quinn's squad, which I suppose meant he'd been as impressed by the guy as I was.

"Sgt. Masterson," Brooks said, "your squad is detached to Master Sgt. Bowie and the Delta team, hoo-ah?"

"Hoo-ah, ma'am," the squad leader replied. "Let's go get 'em, Master Sergeant!"

I wasn't paying attention to the exchange, though. I was watching Brannas-Fel watching the readout on the screen. He'd scrolled through the compartments to one that looked suspiciously like the one we were in now, and he was staring intently at the thermal readings from us. His eyes were growing wider, his lips peeling away from his teeth and his shoulders were shaking.

"Brannas-Fel," I said, and his eyes darted my way, the thicker hair on the back of his head bristling like a cat about to pounce. "We aren't Helta, but we are your allies. My name is Andy Clanton. Joon-Pah sent us."

"Captain Joon-Pah?" The name seemed to shake him out of his trance. "So you are from the Source?"

"We call it Earth," I said, "but yes. Don't be afraid of us. We're here to fight the Tevynians. We're on your side." I motioned down the passageway. "And if you can guide us to Engineering, we're going to take this ship back."

The Rangers were already heading off down the corridor at the double time, trailed by the flight crew. The squad Brooks had left with us stared at Jambo and me, waiting for some guidance.

"All right, Andy Clanton," Brannas-Fel acceded. "It's this way." He nodded towards a T intersection ahead. "Follow me."

This ship, whatever its name might be, was almost an identical twin to the *Truthseeker*, if the *Truthseeker* had been empty and haunted. And littered at odd intervals with dead bodies. Joon-Pah had seemed pretty sure the Tevynians wouldn't slaughter his people on Fairhome, but they didn't seem to have any problems killing the crew of this ship. Some of the dead Helta crew we encountered had weapons, but most did not.

The first body we came across holding a pistol, Jambo had gestured to Brannas-Fel, then to the handgun.

"You should take that," he suggested.

"I'm am engineer," the Helta objected, backing away from the body and the gun it held as if he were afraid that he could catch an infectious disease from it. "I do not use weapons."

"Well, the fucking Tevynians do!" Jambo said. "Would you rather go down without a fight?"

"I'm an engineer," Brannas-Fel repeated as if that explained everything.

Jambo uttered a disgusted curse that I hoped wouldn't translate and moved on.

Engineering was near the rear of the ship, or at least as far to the rear as the crew could travel. A starship wasn't like a seagoing vessel. The reactor was sealed behind radiation shielding and so was the hyperdrive, so there was no easy accesses to either, no crews swarming around them with wrenches like the diesel engine on a destroyer. I'd toured the engineering compartment on the *Truthseeker* and it was more like a physics laboratory, the only physical components available for the crew to service having more to do with power channeling. Power trunks ran up and down the compartment like stalactites and stalagmites in a cavern, superconductive fibers braided into them in a crystalline lattice. The power trunks could be fixed or replaced if they blew out, which could happen when the defense shields were overloaded, but if any significant component of the hyperdrive or the sublight drives or the reactor went down, well...you were just fucked until you found a drydock.

Which was, perhaps, why Jambo hadn't wanted the Rangers near Engineering.

"It's down this ramp," Brannas-Fel told us, gesturing at the juncture of another of the gravitationally-twisted passages that led down to another level.

The top of the ramp was dim and shadowy, which meant at least some of the light panels had been destroyed. The Helta had stationed troops here as well, and there'd been a firefight. Moving closer, I saw two corpses and, shockingly, they weren't Helta.

"Check this out," Pops said, calling to Jambo while I knelt over the bodies. "Yogi and Boo-boo actually nailed a couple of them."

The man's sarcastic tone wasn't unwarranted. We'd seen a lot of dead Helta and, until now, no Tevynian casualties. These were wearing the same sort of grey-hued light body armor the Helta security forces had worn, carrying identical laser rifles. Their helmets were slightly different, designed for heads a different shape than the ursine Helta, but also stylized similar to the images of the Tevynians we'd seen in the briefings by Joon-Pah. The metal was shaped into a swept back mane at the crest, the visors narrow and opaque. Both of them were males and both had been shot square in the chest and I applauded the marksmanship of the Helta who'd done it. Most of them, it seemed, hadn't possessed the intestinal fortitude to stand against the enemy and shoot accurately.

I shifted my rifle to my side and worked at the fastenings of the helmet of one of the Tevynians, feeling ghoulish but needing to see it myself before I really believed. I twisted the helmet off, feeling the neck give easier than a living man's would have and pushing down the nausea rising in my throat.

The face was human. Not just humanoid, not just a close resemblance, not a near cousin descended from the same genetic material. Human. The features were long and slender, the hair red-gold and swept back into a mane with some sort of gel, meant to resemble a lion or a wild boar. Handlebar mustaches drooped from a pouting upper lip and the eyes now open forever were ice blue. Tattoos in blue ink wrapped around the man's neck and up to his face, twisting into runes up his chin and alongside his eyes.

He looked tantalizingly familiar—not this *particular* Tevynian but the look of him. I'd seen his like somewhere before and I couldn't remember where. I pulled the rifle from his hands and looked it over. It was bulky and awkward, not really built for human fingers, with the isotope batteries built into the bulbous rear stock, lacking any sort of pad or shoulder notch to maintain a good firing position for a human, while the emitter was a solid crystal, grown, I'd been told, in orbital processing facilities using the Helta manipulation of gravity as a tool.

Unwilling to leave the energy weapon behind to be used against us, I pulled it off the corpse and slung it over my back, barely feeling it against the power of the exoskeletal muscles. Jambo grabbed the other after making one last argument with Brannas-Fel to try to get him or one of his engineering crew to accept a weapon.

"Okay," Jambo said, speaking loud enough in my ear that I wanted to wince at the possibility we'd be overheard. Old habits die hard. Inside our helmets, he was nearly inaudible to anyone outside. "Once we head down this ramp, someone is going to see us. The only easy day was yesterday and it ends once we're down there. Sgt. Masterson, detail two of your Rangers to stay up here and keep an eye on the Helta engineering crew. Ginger, give me one of your micro-drones."

The Delta operator had to ask Pops for help, since the drone was stuffed into a side pocket on his backpack, but eventually, he put the tiny quadcopter drone in Jambo's outstretched hand.

"Everyone hook into the visual."

Jambo touched a control on his forearm pad and the drone hummed to life, then darted downward into the gravity ramp.

And thumped to the floor almost immediately, the feed going dark.

"Damn," Jambo sighed. "What the hell?"

"Is that a radio-controlled device?" Brannas-Fel asked. "Because there's a dampening field on the corridors leading to the Engineering room to keep all electromagnetic interference away from the instruments there."

"Of course, there is," I muttered in disgust. "We have starships and powered armor, but we have to fight like it's fucking World War One."

"We'll figure out a workaround for their ECM eventually," Jambo said, "but that's a later thing. This is a now thing." He turned, his visor scanning all of us, then shrugged expressively, an exaggerated motion in the Svalinn armor. "So, who wants to go in first?"

"I'll do it," I said, the words seeming to burst out of me like an alien life form hiding there between movies to kill me off when the actor playing me decided he didn't like the script of the sequel. I wanted to shout down the idiot who had said it, then realized the idiot was me. And that I was right. "You and I are the ones with the most time in the suits," I argued. "And you can't walk point because you're in charge." I grinned, though it felt more like a rictus. "I, on the other hand, am in charge of Jack and shit, and Jack just left town."

"Jesus, Andy, you sure about this?" Jambo hadn't bothered to change his comms to private, but I suppose all the Delta boys knew enough about me and my background to figure why he'd asked the question. "I mean, this is our first dust-up with these guys. We don't know what they're capable of."

"Just follow me in on a tight wedge," I told him. "I'm going to make a beeline straight across the compartment and draw their attention towards me. And try not to hit anything important, after all the shit you gave the Rangers."

"All right," Jambo acceded. "But you're not going alone. Quinn!"

"Yes, Master Sergeant?" the Ranger corporal asked, stepping out of the loose perimeter his squad had formed to our rear.

"You and Major Clanton are taking point. Follow his lead and do what he says and otherwise, just keep him from getting killed."

"Roger that." Quinn's visor scanned back and forth for a second before he found me. We all looked alike suited up.

"Stack up, boys," Jambo ordered. "Sgt. Masterson, the rest of your people are in behind ours and don't shoot anything in front of our firing arc. I'm not looking for Blue-on-Blue fire here."

"I'm against it as well, if my opinion means anything," I added, staring down the maw of the gravity ramp and letting my mouth run the way it always does when I'm nervous. "Blue has always been my favorite color."

"Andy." This time, Jambo was on the private net and his voice wasn't his no-nonsense Combat-Mode Jambo, it was more the guy who I'd come to know as a friend these last few months. "You don't have to do this."

"You know I do, bud," I said, though whether I was trying to convince him or myself, I wasn't sure. "You guys ready?"

"We're set," Jambo declared. He was, I thought, the recruiting poster for the Space Force, his rifle held at low ready, his armor half in shadow from the gravity ramp, half in the light of the corridor.

"This would make a hell of a book," I said, "if I ever get the chance to write it."

"It's not your genre, Andy," Jambo said, and I could hear his grin even if I couldn't see it. "It's not science fiction anymore, it's current events."

The team formed into a tight wedge and I, Andrew Jackson Clanton Jr., preacher's kid, Marine, failed husband, failed father, recovering alcoholic, hack science fiction writer, and possibly the luckiest man on the face of the Earth, was going to lead a hardass group of Delta Force operators and Space Rangers into the engine room of an alien starship.

"Ooh-rah," I murmured, then started running.

21

I WASN'T WORRIED ABOUT MINES OR BOOBY-TRAPS. THE Tevynians wouldn't booby-trap their only way in or out of Engineering, and they probably didn't even know we were here if they'd shut down the security scanners. If they expected anything, it would be more Helta, poorly organized, lightly equipped, bad at fighting. Or at least that thought was what kept me running.

The deck sloped down at a ninety-degree angle, but the second I stepped on it, it was straight up and down and the deck behind me was the one cockeyed from reality and *God, I hate that shit! Why can't they just use elevators?*

My footsteps echoed in chorus with Quinn's in the hollow emptiness of the gravity ramp, but he hung off my left shoulder, just out of my peripheral vision, and all I saw was darkness. My helmet's vision enhancements penetrated the gloom and still showed me nothing, the bulkheads blocking any thermal readings from inside the compartment ahead, the corridor itself featureless and empty. I could understand not having a sentry actually in the hallway—hell, I wouldn't want to be standing on the edge of the gravity shift, either. But there was definitely going to be at least two or three of them after I hit the next right-angle shift, and even if they didn't expect me, they'd burn me down the second I came out of the junction, and I could only shoot at one of them at a time...with the rifle, anyway.

The grenade launchers mounted on either side of the suit's backpack power unit were built for open spaces, needing a three-meter vertical clearance to launch safely, but they also had this handy little programmable detonation feature. I'd read about them when I was researching the *United the Stars* series and shamelessly stole the idea, and I'd assumed Jambo would already know about them, but he had never heard of them. It had taken ten emails and a half a dozen phone calls to get them into production, which wasn't a bad average for the military procurement system.

"Grenades," I told Quinn, hoping my helmet's laser line-of-sight communications would work where the radios wouldn't.

"In here?" His tone was incredulous. He knew the limitations of the weapon as well as I did.

"Program for independent detonation just the other side of the junction and follow my lead."

I toggled the menu for the targeting reticle over to the grenade launchers while I ran, which was worse than trying to walk and chew gum, but we'd practiced it and I was, ironically given the company I kept, better at it than any of the Rangers except Quinn. The warheads were a special blend designed post-Helta and issued specifically for this mission and although I hadn't had any hand in designing them, they sure as hell sounded like something I would have written into my books. A kilogram of a new chemical formula the Helta had provided, something we were calling HyPex, short for hyper-explosive, ten times more energetic than C4, surrounded by adjustable baffles of the same sort of alloy the Helta used for spaceship hulls, packed in with sintered metallic hydrogen. I told the baffles which way I wanted the blast to hit, which was, in this case, in a 180-degree half-sphere in front of me, and they would arrange themselves in mid-flight. The warhead would burst when and where I told it to, and all that energy would turn the metallic hydrogen into a plasma. And you did not want to be standing where that plasma came through.

Twenty meters to the junction. This wouldn't work until we were right on top of it, and even if it did, the disorientation passing through the junction was going to be a problem. Hopefully, Quinn could pull it off if I couldn't.

Ten meters. I was nowhere near a full sprint for the suit, just a steady gallop, but the junction was rushing up at me and I had to time this just right.

Five meters. I couldn't do the math in my head, so I guessed. This was close enough.

"Now!"

I threw myself forward into a head-first dive, sliding through the junction on my belly, gravity shifting ninety degrees suddenly and violently, wrenching at the muscles of my back. I pushed the pain into a compartment and triggered the grenade launchers. The discharge pushed back on my shoulders and I turned the push into a scramble up to my feet.

I had about a half a second to process what I was seeing. My mind worked back to front in reverse order of importance to my survival, which I found intensely annoying, so the first thing I noticed was the cluster of figures standing at a control station surrounding the base of the largest power trunk. They had some sort of computer equipment in latching cases with them, laid out open on the deck, with cables hooked up to data ports in the slanted surface of the control panels, though I had no clue what any of it was for. They were wearing body armor but they had their helmets off and two of them were women, their hair long and twisted into braids.

There were four or five of the technicians, but if they had rifles, they weren't carrying them at the moment, so the worst they could do to me was delete my Facebook account. They'd brought a reinforced infantry squad to guard the techs, which was much more of an immediate problem. Six of them were arrayed in a half-circle perimeter around the central power trunk, though from their stance and the way the emitters of their lasers were pointing down at the deck, I don't think they expected company.

The last four were the problem. They'd been assigned to guard the entrance, and they were taking their job seriously, weapons held at the ready, the crystalline emitters somehow much more intimidating than a conventional barrel. Though nowhere near as intimidating as the four grenades exploding right in their faces.

It felt strange not to duck. It was one of the first things they taught you on the grenade range in Boot: once you pull the pin, Mr. Grenade is not your friend. But the baffles focused the explosives away from me and the armor protected from fragments and I stood there like a big idiot and watched the grenades blow up.

It reminded me of the Fourth of July fireworks shows in Tampa when I was a kid, starbursts of pure white at the heart of the blasts, with spears of plasma stabbing outward, the sun rays crossing each other, leaving not a centimeter of space for anything to live. One second the four enemy troops stood ready, unmoving, statues guarding a mountain pass. The next, all four of the proud, broad-shouldered soldiers were the walking dead, still on their feet only by the grace of inertia, sliced to pieces by the plasma warheads.

Their corpses hadn't even begun to fall before the rest of the Tevynians opened up on us. We'd had to set the warheads blind, not knowing where the enemy troops would be, and we'd both set the proximity fuses too shallow. The grenades had killed the shit out of the sentries at the door, but the other six were fifty yards away, halfway across the compartment, and the concussion might have knocked them back on their heels, but it sure as hell didn't kill them.

The lasers fired in the infrared range, so theoretically, they should have been invisible, and if we'd been in a vacuum, maybe they would have been, but not here. They ripped apart the air, the high-energy bursts ionizing tunnels of atmospheric gases, blasting streams of plasma and filling the whole compartment with static electricity. It probably would have been much more impressive if they'd been aiming, but they fired in a panic at the explosions and came closer to hitting each other than they did Quinn or me.

I was aiming. If I could have set the M900 for full auto and buzz-sawed back and forth, I could have taken the whole lot of them out in a second, but we kind of needed the ship intact, so I put a single round into the closest of the Tevynians at low velocity. The slug didn't flash or crackle or create its own lightning, but it punched through the Tevynian armor like it wasn't there and the enemy soldier pitched forward.

There were a lot of things I could have done right then, and maybe some of them would have been smarter than what I did. I could have just gone down to the prone—the rest of the team was coming in behind me and I just had to buy a couple of seconds. Or I could have charged straight in and counted on their own confusion to keep them from hitting me. Instead, I headed left and I *think* I yelled at Quinn to go right. I don't honestly remember saying it, but he went the opposite direction and I had to assume it was because I told him to.

Another of the Tevynian soldiers went down, tumbling to the side, I guessed from Quinn's shots because I was too busy running to get an accurate bead on any of them and I didn't want to risk hitting the Ranger. Lasers sliced into the bulkheads, sending flashes of molten and sublimated metal flaring in gouts of fire only a meter behind me, and if I could have run faster, I would have, but then I would have overshot the eight foot tall spindle of superconductive cable mounted near the starboard bulkhead, replacement parts for the power trunks. They had them on the *Truthseeker* and I'd figured without even looking they'd have them here, too.

I threw the Svalinn into a slide like I was stealing third base back in Little League, digging the fingers of my left hand into the slick, synthetic floor plating to try to stop before I passed out the other side of the spindle. Laser pulses hit the superconductive cable and coruscated down the length of it, sending heat and static electricity pouring into the insulated deck and throwing up billows of smoke and steam as fireproof material tried very hard to burn.

Finally coming to a halt, I threw myself out onto my left shoulder just far enough past the spindle for my rifle's barrel to clear it, dropped the reticle onto one of the Tevynian soldiers who was rushing straight for my position and touched the trigger pad. I hadn't felt the kick of the first shot, too numbed by the adrenaline, but I felt this one, especially from the prone. It wasn't quite as bad as firing a full-power shot at the Brads back in Idaho, but the M900 let me know it was there. The Tevynian had no doubts, not once the depleted uranium slug ripped through his sternum and took a few inches of breastbone out the back of his spine.

One of the women at the control console cried out and threw her hands across her face a half-second too late to stop the blood spatter. I had a preternaturally clear view of the blood hitting her across the cheek, her neck, the horror in her eyes so much like the horror I'd seen in the eyes of people on the streets of Caracas. She *was* human. I mean, I'd known they looked just like us, but I'd thought they might have been changed, mutated by whoever had taken the Helta and fucked with their genes, maybe turned the humans into something more aggressive and evil. I should have known better. Humans didn't need mutation to be evil.

I rolled off my shot and a lightning bolt of ionized air crackled into the floor where my head had been only a heartbeat before, and I could feel the heat from the laser cooking the deck plate even through the heavy armor, the feeling of stepping out of a transport bird into the heat of a summer afternoon in Kuwait.

It had been less than ten seconds and I'd killed six people, but someone was hosing laser fire into my position, charring the bulkheads on either side of the spindle and turning the bundles of superconductive wire into the white-hot coils of a Van Der Graff generator and I was going to have to chance jumping out into the oncoming fire because the only reason to pin me down was to have another of their soldiers flank me and *where the hell is Jambo?*

The laser had stopped firing and it took me nearly a full second to notice, for the charge crackling through the cables to dissipate and the smoke and flames pouring off the bulkheads to die away. All I could hear was the rasp of my own breathing inside the helmet, hard enough that the interior of the visor fogged up faster than the internal cooling fan could clear it off.

"Clear," Jambo said, his tone flat and clinical. It warmed up to something more human with the next words. "You okay back there, Andy?"

It took me a couple of seconds to work up the nerve to step out from behind cover. The Tevynians were dead, all of them, men and women, soldiers and technicians. I hadn't heard the shots from the KE guns over the thunderclaps of the laser rifles, but they'd done their job just as well for the lack of attention. It all looked too antiseptic. Their armor had contained much of the carnage, the insults to human anatomy that the weapons of war inflicted. No intestines spilled out, no stink of voided wastes penetrated the filters of my helmet, just pools of blood spilled in silence.

The technicians had tried to run, but there'd been nowhere to go. They faced away from the shots that had killed them, all but one tall, statuesque woman who seemed proud even in death, her green eyes fixed and staring her defiance to gods only she could see.

Why? Why the fuck had I let them pull me back into this? Had I forgotten what it was like?

I'd heard it said that when parents decided to have a second child, it was after enough time had passed that they'd forgotten the lost sleep and the screaming and the puking and the dirty diapers and only recalled the good parts, the fond memories. I think that must have been true of war, as well. It had been too long and I'd forgotten the sights and sounds and smells of death, the fear and the horror and the waste, and only recalled the camaraderie and the jokes and the glory of surviving the unsurvivable.

"Andy?" Jambo repeated, and I thought it must have been his Svalinn suit clomping across the compartment toward me. "Are you all right?"

"Yeah," I said, my voice dry, my mouth filled with cotton. I took a sip of water from the nipple positioned next to my chin. "Yeah, I'm okay." I switched to the general net. "Quinn, you good?"

"Yeah, right here, sir." A Svalinn suit raised its hand, the words somehow disconnected from the motion. We were robots, faceless automatons, killing machines.

"Pops, go get those Helta engineers in here," Jambo said. "Have 'em make sure nothing got too banged up for this ship to fly. We need to get the hell out of here."

"I'll do it," I volunteered.

I left them there and strode across the compartment, past the Tevynians I'd killed with the grenades, trying not to look at the bodies on my way out of the hatchway. The gravity ramp wrenched at my stomach and this time I had to clamp my jaws shut to keep from puking. The Rangers waited at the juncture, alert and spastic, ready to fire at any shadow, while the Helta huddled against the bulkhead, looking very much like they would have rather been anywhere else in the universe.

"It's clear down there," I reported. "Take the engineers in to check out the equipment.

I settled back onto my heels and popped up my visor, taking a breath of the ship's air. It was recycled and had the antiseptic scent of the unnatural, but it was better than the smell of my own sweat. The engineers alerted at the sight of my face like squirrels spotting a circling hawk and it took Brannas-Fel a long moment to reassure them before they were willing to accompany the Rangers down into the compartment.

Brannas-Fel hung back, hesitating beside me as the others headed into the gravity ramp.

"Is it true?" he asked, and this time the clicks and gutturals of his own language were loud and clear before my headphones translated it for me. "Are you really here to help us?"

"We're not Tevynians," I told him. "We're from Earth, what you call the Source. Joon-Pah came to us asking for help fighting this war and we came here to get a ship so we could protect our world from your enemies." I sighed. "Well, we'd hoped we would get three ships, but we didn't expect the system to be under attack."

"There are hyperdrives," he told me. "In the next construction spar over from this ship, I saw three hyperdrive units latched to one of the dock tenders. They were intended to be installed in ships under construction here at the shipyards but they hadn't been delivered yet. If you can get to the tender, you could bring it into our hangar bay."

"Thanks," I said, nodding to him.

"If you can actually help us fight these monsters," he told me before he headed down into the gravity ramp, "that will be thanks enough."

"Colonel Brooks?" I called. No response. I tried to find her on IFF and saw that she and her people were still heading for the bridge. Shit. She would be too busy to deal with this.

I sucked in a breath, realizing what I had to do and wondering why the hell I kept doing it.

"Colonel Olivera?" I tried.

"I read you, Clanton. What's your situation?"

"We have the engine room secure." I told him. "Colonel Brooks is still en route to the bridge. But I found something out from one of the Helta engineers. I think I know where we can pick up some extra hyperdrives and it's not far away."

"We aren't going to have time to wait for Brooks," Olivera warned. "Those Tevynian ships will be in firing range in less than two hours."

"Yeah, well, lucky for you," I said, trying not to sound as bitter as I felt, "you still got us."

22

"You really volunteered us for this shit?" Jambo asked again.

I was running too fast to look over at him, and even if I hadn't been, I couldn't have seen his face through the visor, but I could picture it from his tone. Scowling, with an eyebrow arched in disbelief.

"I really did," I said. The words weren't quite gasped, but we were sprinting at over twenty-five miles an hour through the Helta ship and between the motion and the multiple adrenaline dumps I'd experienced, my breath was coming in ragged heaves. "Will you stop asking me that? What? You scared?"

"You're Goddamned right I'm scared. I'm in space, motherfucker! I'm fighting aliens in space, and the only reason I ain't petrified is that it's just so Goddamned cool. But what's with you volunteering for everything all of a sudden? I seem to recall you wasn't all that happy to be going on the trip in the first place."

I didn't answer him right away. It felt wrong to be running through an unsecured ship, no security, no tactical formation, but we just didn't have the time. We'd barely had time to convince Brannas-Fel to come along and find him a space suit and *then* convince him to ride on the shoulders of one of Masterson's Rangers, which was why we were only running at twenty-five miles an hour, letting our slowest member keep up. We needed the Helta to fly the tender because sure as hell none of us could do it. Even if we had one of the flight crew with us, they might not have been able to figure out the controls in time.

I double-checked my comms were set for a private line to Jambo before I went on.

"I fucked up," I told him. "I got suckered by the Russians and could have totally blown this whole mission. You saved my ass and you risked your career to do it. I figured I at least owe it to you to act like I belong out here."

There was nothing but the echoes of our boots pounding on the deck, the bulkheads and hatchways and displays blurring on either side of us.

"You don't owe me nothing, Andy," Jambo said. "You're my friend. That's what friends do."

I didn't know what to say to that, so I took the safe way out and said nothing.

If there were any other surviving Helta crew between us and the cargo lock, they stayed in hiding. Nothing moved on the path we retraced and all the bodies stayed dead. I toyed with the idea of stopping to pick up one of those cool laser rifles, but refrained. It was new and shiny, but it wasn't hooked into my helmet sighting system and I wasn't sure it could do anything my KE rifle couldn't except draw a shitload of return fire. Besides, Quinn was along for the op and I remembered his answer to one of the Rangers asking why we didn't have lasers, and he was still right.

"Left here," I told Jambo when we passed through the construction lock connecting the cruiser to the drydock.

"Don't you mean hard a'port, jarhead?" he asked, galloping

past me and curving to the left, slicing the pie as he took the corner.

I stayed a couple yards to his right and checked our six as I followed, catching a glimpse back down the formation. The rest of the team and the Ranger squad attached to it had fallen into a loose, staggered column, stretching back over a hundred yards. And yes, I still thought in yards and feet, despite the efforts of Jambo and Colonel Brooks to get me to use the metric system. Fuck it. I'd been drafted into this and if they wanted Andy Clanton, itinerant SF writer as their Space Marine, they were going to get my civilian yardstick and my nautical terms right along with me. The Helta sure didn't use meters, anyway and it didn't matter whether I converted their quatloos or whatever they called them into yards or furlongs.

The passageway off to the left had an air of disuse to it, jammed with equipment and storage bins and racks of unused space suits and helmets in a peculiar shade of mauve. The Helta had some funky fashion sense. We had to slow down for the clutter and it gnawed at my nerves, a ticking clock inside my head. My eyes kept going to the curved, ceiling to floor windows, and every glint of the system's primary off the construction arms and the machinery hanging off of them teased me with visions of incoming enemy ships. If the Tevynians got here before we had the hyperdrives on board the ship, we'd be stuck in open space in an unarmed tender with a hotshot Helta engineer for a pilot.

I kept expecting the stacks of gear and goods to thin out, to let us speed up again, but they didn't, and we crawled along at what would have been a personal-best five-k run pace for me back when I was a young lieutenant but felt painfully slow in the Svalinn armor. And the clock kept ticking, kilometer after kilometer. Ten minutes. Twenty. A half an hour...

"There's the tender," I told Jambo, jabbing a finger at the window, my voice wavering in relief.

It wasn't anything to write home about, all of it open to space, just a tiny cockpit at the front with room in the compartment behind it for twenty or thirty workers in spacesuits to strap into standing braces against the boost from the small drive bell at the rear. The hull was skeletal, mostly a support for the material handling arms, all of them full with the hyperdrives. Now those... they captured my attention. They were twisted nautilus shells, their lines shedding my eyes, more alien than anything I'd seen from the Helta, just *wrong* on an instinctive level. I almost stopped right there to stare at them, as ridiculous and suicidal as it would have been.

"Shit," I murmured aloud, not intending to.

"Weird lookin' things, ain't they?" Jambo agreed.

"The Helta didn't make those," I declared, still running, trying to pay enough attention to the path in front of me to avoid barreling into another rack of pressure suits.

"What the hell do you mean?"

"I don't know," I admitted. "But look at everything else about them, their tech, their ship designs, their language, and it's all something I wouldn't have been surprised to see in a science fiction movie, because it's all very humanlike. And even though they're engineered from sun bears or whatever, they're from Earth and everything about them has an Earth feel to it. That...." I trailed off, shaking my head. "That's not from anything that evolved on Earth."

"Maybe. We'll figure it out later. All I know right now is that we need the damn things. Where's the fucking airlock?"

"Around this curve. Better get the engineer up here to open it."

Several things happened at once and I wouldn't be sure of the order even much later because my brain seemed to register them as one event, a painting I saw from a distance before getting close enough for each section to clarify. The drydock perimeter corridor curved to the right, a function of the position of the construction berths, designed to make enough room for multiple ships as big as the cruisers to be docked at once for service. As it did, I moved outward to get a look around the corner, but something out of the window caught my eye, movement. Annoyance simmered hot on the back of my neck and I was sure it was simply the reflections teasing at the corner of my eye again, until I realized it wasn't a shimmering but a darkness that had caught my eye...the darkness of Tevynian battle armor. Dozens of them, swarming over the construction arm, heading for the tender and the hyperdrives there.

The warning was forming in my mind, pressing against the back of my throat, ready to burst out when it was interrupted by the flash of motion much closer, just sixty or seventy yards ahead and Jambo yelling in my ear.

"Contact, front!"

I don't know who was more surprised, us or the squad of Tevynians standing guard outside the airlock. I do know who fired first.

When you contact enemy unexpectedly, there are three different options. First, obviously, you can retreat, or to put it in the military terminology that doesn't sound quite so cowardly, you can "break contact." This involves laying down suppressive fire and falling back by teams until you reach a point where the enemy doesn't follow. At that point, you try to find a way to maneuver around them to reach your objective if it's still feasible, or to seek extraction. The second thing you could do was find a defensible position and hold the enemy off until *they* break contact or you can call for fire support or reinforcements. Neither of those was an acceptable solution to the problem, or at least Jambo didn't think they were, because he chose what was behind Door Number Three.

He attacked.

Again, at the time, I didn't have a clear idea of what was going on. You don't a lot of the time when you're in combat, particularly when you hit an ambush. Things happen fast and you run on instinct and training and your mind fills in the details later, if you remember them at all. Jambo was running and gunning, charging right into the teeth of the Tevynians, firing his M900 on full auto and I was running after him, screaming a wordless battle cry like an idiot, since the Tevynians couldn't hear me through my helmet.

I wanted to blast on full auto, too, but I'd pre-adjusted my rifle to single-shot and there sure as hell wasn't the time or opportunity to change it now. I threw the M900 to my shoulder and fired a shot before the target lock had time to travel from my optic nerve to my brain, the memory of touching the trigger warring with the recoil of the buttock against my shoulder for primacy in causation. Bad guys were falling and others were retreating, or trying to break contact depending on the feelings of their respective militaries on the virtue of euphemisms, but others were taking cover behind cargo containers and firing back.

Lasers ripped apart the air, filling the thirty-foot-wide corridor with crackling, incandescent streams of plasma, chopping charred, blackened craters into the interior walls, blowing out light panels in showers of sparks and leaving disconcerting scars on the exterior windows that I hoped to God were only cosmetic.

And into Jambo.

He fell.

I don't remember much of the next few seconds at all. I was moving faster than conscious thought could follow, and I seem to recall *punching* something and feeling it crack beneath my armored fist. When thought caught up with me, I was on the other side of the airlock and a Tevynian was crawling away from me, half his left leg severed at the knee, his right hand clutching for a laser rifle just out of reach. I shot him through the helmet and turned away.

Behind me, everything was dead. There'd been thirteen of the Tevynians, which, I noted with a sort of dazed detachment, seemed like a strange number for a squad. Or maybe not. Six members in two teams or four in three teams, with one leader. Maybe it was the most natural thing in the world for them. Between Jambo and I, we'd killed them all. One of them was sprawled on his back, gun forgotten by stilled hands, the visor of his helmet caved in along with the face beneath it, and I thought I knew what I'd punched.

I didn't want to turn around, didn't want to see it, but I had to. I had to see Jambo.

I'd seen shots like this before, in Venezuela, in Syria. They just happened and you didn't know why. We wore all that damned body armor, hot as shit, sweating our asses off, but you couldn't armor everything. You had to be able to raise your arms and move your legs and everywhere that you left the armor thinner to provide for freedom of motion, you left a gap. People got shot in those gaps and we stood around helplessly and watched them die.

The Svalinn armor was thick enough in the chest and back areas and even on the top of the helmet to resist at least one burst from the Tevynian lasers. We knew because DARPA had tested it using the Helta weapons, which were the same thing. But you could only put so much armor around someone's neck before they couldn't turn their head, powered exoskeleton or not. Jambo had taken a fluke shot in the neck, one in a thousand, like catching an AK round in your underarm, or your groin, or just beneath the waistline when you were running. The burn through hadn't quite severed his spine, but it had taken out jugular and half his throat. Maybe if he'd actually been on board the *Truth-seeker*, they could have saved him, but from here...

Jambo's left arm twitched with a whine of servomotors, and I knelt beside him, pushed open his visor, feeling a surge of unreasoning hope. His eyes were wide, hazing over, unseeing even as he gasped at breaths he couldn't take, blood trickling out of his mouth rather than pouring because the rest of his life was pooling into the back of his suit.

Master Sergeant James Bowie, Special Operations Detachment Delta, veteran of a dozen conflicts over two decades all across a troubled world, and last and most importantly, my friend...had died 1,200 light years from home.

"Oh, fuck." That was Pops. He knelt down beside Jambo, hesitant, as if this was something he'd never even considered. "Oh, Jambo, you stupid son of a bitch..."

I wanted to rage, wanted to curse, wanted to cry, but I just knelt by his body for seconds that seemed like hours, numb, trapped by inertia, physical and emotional.

"What do we do, Major?" Ginger asked me.

I blinked at the question, wondering who the hell he was talking to. I was the only major here and I didn't deserve the rank. I'd barely made captain and then got out of the Corps and into the inactive reserves before they could cashier my ass for public intoxication. I hadn't led anything in years except an insincere prayer at an AA meeting.

But Jambo had thought I belonged out here, that I belonged with his team, out front, with a gun in my hand. He'd known about the PTSD and the alcoholism and the divorce and how fucking pitiful I was as a husband and a father, and he'd still believed I was worth bringing along, that I still had something to offer.

Shit.

What would Jambo have done?

I knelt down beside Jambo and pulled the M900 free of his hands, unbuckling it from the harness securing it to his armor, then cradling it against my left hip. This wasn't something we hadn't considered. Jambo and I had discussed the matter with the DARPA researchers, with Olivera, with the supply chain, and come up with a solution. All I had to do was open a comm signal directly to a dedicated receiver in Jambo's backpack and send it the code he and I and Colonel Brooks had in our systems. In ten minutes, the isotope in his backpack power plant would go critical and melt through the shielding, taking most of the armor and all of the body inside it with it.

It would have, but I thought of US Army Special Ops pilots being paraded through the streets of Mogadishu, or American contractors hanging from bridges in Fallujah and I just couldn't do it.

I straightened, holding an M900 in each hand, feeling like a damn fool but not willing to leave the weapon behind.

"We do exactly what we came here to do," I told the hardened Delta operators, as if I was actually worthy to lead them. "We go retrieve those hyperdrives and we get them on board the cruiser before the enemy ships get here." I nodded toward Brannas-Fel and hit the translation circuit. "Get this airlock open, now." I motioned to the Ranger squad leader. "Masterson, get someone to carry Master Sergeant Bowie's body. We're bringing him with us."

"They're gonna know we're coming," Quinn warned, walking beside the Heltan, one hand on his shoulder as if he thought the alien might try to run. Quinn seemed fatalistic about it rather than worried.

"They are," I confirmed. The inner airlock slid aside and I stepped in, waiting for the others to follow. "I'm going to kill them anyway. Hoo-ah?"

"Hoo-ah, sir," Quinn said, the first to join me, but not the last. "Fucking hoo-ah."

23

I'd been in space, but I'd never been *in space*. I'd never walked out into the black, separated from the vacuum only by the thin skin of a space suit. Stepping through the outer airlock door, the black hit me like a physical force, not just the emptiness, not just the sheer depth of the nothing, but how incredibly *full* it was. If the stars had seemed spectacular in the holographic screens of the *Truthseeker*, through the thin polymer of my visor they were a wall of light so unfathomably far away they couldn't breach the darkness. The distance was what squeezed the breath from my lungs, the depth of field as the camera operators on the show had said when I visited the set. The dots in the black weren't just stars, they were galaxies and if they were insignificant specks of light, what the hell were we?

We're fucked is what we are, if they catch us out on this construction spar.

It was twenty yards across, not so narrow that I was afraid of falling off the side, but not nearly wide enough for us to be anything but a massed target. *Could* we fall off the side? The gravity plates extended below the spar, I'd found that out the second I stepped out of the lock and didn't go floating into space, though I'd guessed it by the movement of the Tevynians in the distance. But it didn't extend outward from the end of the structure, or else the tender would be resting on the metal like a helicopter on a pad rather than floating off the edge of it like a boat in the harbor.

"They haven't seen us yet," Pops told me.

He was on my right, Quinn on my left and I don't know why the hell the only officer present was walking point, but there was a lot about all this that didn't make sense. But he was right about the Tevynians. I'd thought sure one of the guards at the lock had gotten a warning off before we'd killed them, but the enemy troops crawling over the tender were oblivious. I hadn't been able to tell what they were doing from inside the drydock, but now, closer and without the thick window between us, I could see they were strapping storage containers to attachment points on the side of the tender. They'd been after the same things we were, the cruiser and the hyperdrives, and I had to guess what was in those storage crates was either weapons or some other valuable technology.

We'll find out when we get it on board.

I wanted to do the same thing here that I had with Jambo back when we were using MILES lasers, the same thing we'd done with the Russians, sit back and pour aimed fire into them from a distance, but I didn't know how well the hyperdrives would tolerate getting hit by stray shots and I didn't want to find out the hard way. This was going to have to be a close-in fight.

"Staggered column," I ordered. "Masterson, keep Brannas-Fel in the rear and don't let him get shot. Move out, double time and don't fire until I give the word."

We ran straight into the teeth of the enemy like this was the charge of the fucking light brigade because what the hell else do you do when there's hundreds of yards of open ground between you and them and no cover? I was praying speed and surprise would substitute for good sense and remembering how much good praying had done me in the past and praying anyway. Running in a vacuum, on a ridge of gravity in a sea of stars, running for the edge of the world, praying to am omniscient being didn't seem so ridiculous anymore.

Distance closed, yards passing under my pounding feet, my footfalls an eerie, echoless thump carried up through the metal of the suit and my own body. And as three hundred yards turned to two hundred, things clarified, not as if there'd been an actual haze, for there couldn't be in the vacuum, and not as if there'd been darkness, for the work lights of the drydock penetrated well beyond the tender. Instead, it was as if my brain hadn't been able to piece the images into a coherent picture until they'd grown large enough to be meaningful.

If thirteen was the number of soldiers in one of their squads, they had two squads out at the tender, most of them running a daisy chain of storage containers off some sort of robot mule they'd taken out there with them. The gravity ceased abruptly at the end of the spar, as I'd deduced, and the Tevynians lacked any sort of self-propelled transport to get the crates out to the tender, so they were doing it the old-fashioned way, by hand. Troops were attached somehow to the tender, either by cables I couldn't see from this distance, or perhaps by something like magnetic boots, and others standing at the edge of the spar would propel a storage container out from the edge toward the ones hooked to the ship.

No one was on watch because they'd left another squad on guard the only place a threat could come from that they couldn't see it, the lock. We'd have to get close, but it looked like we could, like maybe just this once, something would be simple and easy.

"Andy Clanton! Behind you!"

I didn't know who had tuned Brannas-Fel's suit radio to our

tactical frequency, but I recognized the machine-like quality of the computer translator immediately.

I spun around and very nearly didn't see it. I was looking for Tevynians, looking for one of their cruisers coming in, watching for the threat I expected and not the one I should have thought of. Three squat, cylindrical shapes lifted from the roof of the drydock one at a time on puffs of maneuvering thrusters like ICBMs rising from missile silos. The boarding pods. The Tevynian had left flight crews on their boarding pods.

And if they'd seen us, they wouldn't keep it quiet.

The Tevynian soldiers loading the tender scattered like someone had kicked their anthill over, cargo containers crashing to the hard metal surface of the spar or careening off the hull of the tender and spinning helplessly into open space. The loot took a backseat to their weapons and every one of them was trying to reach theirs, pulling them around on slings attached to their harnesses or drawing handguns from chest holsters.

The Tevynians in front of us, the pods launching behind and who knew what weapons they were carrying? They were trying to pin us between them, catch us in a crossfire. I didn't have to ask myself what Jambo would have done, because he'd died doing it.

"Close with the dismounts!" I yelled. "Don't give their air support a clear shot!" Then I threw a hail Mary, because God alone knew how far my transmission would carry out here. "Shuttle Alpha! This is Alpha Two! Bogies inbound to our position! We need air support ASAP!"

"Wait one, Alpha Two." Relief at the message being heard warred with frustration at the uselessness of the reply. I didn't *have* one!

We were a hundred yards from the tender, a hundred yards from two squads of Tevynians, charging across open ground and about to get fried from the air and the ground.

"Aimed fire! Single shots only!"

The lasers were as invisible and nearly undetectable in the vacuum as they'd been spectacular and obvious in an atmosphere, and I only knew we were being fired on because my helmet's optics picked up the thermal blooms coming from the scrambling shapes of the Tevynians around the tender. I used the flares of heat as targets, settling my aiming reticle over the closest, a particularly brave or perhaps just recklessly stupid enemy soldier who seemed to think standing out in the open and firing burst after burst of a high-signature weapon was the key to a long and happy life.

The KE round took him just a touch higher than center mass and he spun away from the impact, the rifle going out of his hands, coming up short on the lanyard of his harness and recoiling back into its resting place across his chest as he collapsed onto his back. Every detail of it was etched into my mind, indelible. I'd been in some fights where I couldn't remember from one second to the next how many times I'd fired or whether I'd been under fire for ten seconds or ten minutes, where my conscious mind took a backseat to instinct.

This wasn't one of them. Maybe I had a certain quota of instinct to draw on and I'd used it all up in the gunfight at the airlock, or maybe the adrenaline had finally stopped dumping and my mind was wandering out of the fight-or-flight response and back to normal cognition. Or maybe there was just so much of a cushion between sanity and reality and mine had worn away like overused knee cartilage, leaving bone against bone. But every flash of heat, every movement, ever kick of the rifle against my right shoulder was drawn with a vivid clarity beyond the real and into the realm of a bad CGI render. I'd seen that on the show, on the finished product, when the lab had tried to make a special effect seem so detailed and intricate that they'd gone beyond the grit and haze of realism and into images too fractal for real life.

I heard one of the Rangers go down. The radio calls were a

background noise to the fight, the only one the vacuum allowed, but you could tell the flow of the battle from the timbre of the chatter, and you could always tell when someone was hit. I didn't know who it had been, their name lost in the cross-talk, but I knew it wasn't the Delta team because none of their IFF transponders flickered. Was the Ranger dead? Wounded? Had he or she been the one carrying Jambo's body? Had they been killed because of my stupid insistence on bringing him along? I couldn't even take the time to find out.

I shot another Tevynian. It was scary how easy it was to kill another human when they were wearing a faceless helmet. I remembered the first time I'd killed a man. He'd been twenty yards away, aiming an RPG down the street at a Striker armored vehicle. I hadn't had the time to hesitate, but it had seemed like the trigger pull on my rifle had somehow increased by ten pounds and the echo of the shot off the boarded-up buildings on the street front had hung inside my head for minutes. I should have been watching my platoon but all I could do was sit there in the doorway and watch the man bleed out.

This time, I didn't even glance at the aftermath of the shot, trusting the depleted uranium slug to do its job and risking a look over my shoulder at the boarding pods. They weren't fast and they weren't agile, built like tubby water bugs and only carrying enough engine to get them from the Tevynian cruiser that had dropped them off to the drydock and then back again. The three ships were maneuvering slowly, painfully, swinging their aft ends away from us. Once they did, it would be over fast. They were kilometers away, on the other side of the cruiser, but one short burst from their engines would put them in our laps in seconds.

I kept running, only fifty yards from the tender. The Tevynian soldiers fell one after another and I began to see parallels between them and certain militaries I'd fought or seen fighting back on Earth. The Tevynians used their lasers much the same way some of the militias and insurgencies in the Middle East used their AK47s, spraying and praying and if God wills it, the bullets will hit the target. I wondered if they'd even had gunpowder weapons before the Helta had come along and gave them lasers and starships.

And that mindset would probably be enough against the Helta, who had no military tradition. It might have even worked against regular infantry, but not against highly-trained Rangers and a team of the most elite special operations force in the world. Hypervelocity slugs fired with semiauto precision killed an enemy each time an M900 was fired and what had started out as over two dozen of the enemy had been attrited to four isolated individuals, crouched behind the tender, spraying bursts of laser fire at nothing.

"Ginger, Pops!" I barked. "Take the team and go over the top of the tender! Watch your handholds; there's no gravity once you leave the surface of the spar. Masterson, provide covering fire, keep their heads down!"

I left it to them, keeping an eye on their movements but not trying to micromanage. This wasn't materially different than anything they'd trained for, except the environment, and there was nothing involved that they couldn't do a lot better than I could. But those damned boarding pods...

I stopped in my tracks, staring at one of the storage crates. A Tevynian soldier was laid out beside it, his visor shattered by a KE round, and another of our depleted uranium projectiles had shattered the latch of the crate. It had fallen open on its side when the Tevynian had dropped it, and four fat, meter long cylinders had spilled out onto the metal surface of the construction spar. They were weapons. I knew it instinctively, the way you can look at a chipped rock and know someone used it thousands of years ago as an arrowhead, and it seemed fairly simple to operate. One handle near the rear, one in the front, a ring on the side that could have been a scope.

"Brannas-Fel!" I yelled back to the Heltan, dropping Jambo's KE gun on the deck and picking up one of the cylinders by the front pistol grip. It weighed more than I'd thought, not too much for the suit but enough it would have taken a strong stance to lift it. "What is this thing?"

The Heltan was at the end of the squad of Rangers, sticking out like a turd in a punchbowl with his hot purple spacesuit and he looked at the weapon like a boiler room tech on a Navy ship might have gawked at a Carl Gustav recoilless rifle.

"It's a plasma gun, I think," he told me. "I've never actually shot one, or even seen one except on video. It's an infantry weapon." He pointed at the boarding pods. "But they might bring those down!"

"Goddamn, I was hoping you'd say that." My eyes danced around the battlefield, figuring my choices. The Delta operators were on the other side of the ship, finishing off the Tevynians, which left the Rangers, only a couple dozen yards away, and only three of them actually firing their weapons. I went with the names I knew, because sometimes being quick is better than being precise. "Masterson, Quinn, get over here!"

I could already have picked Quinn out of a lineup of Svalinn-armored Rangers from before. Everyone who puts on the armor has a certain, unique gait to them, a way their natural stride translates to the exoskeleton. Masterson I didn't know, either in or out of the armor. I vaguely remembered him as short and wiry, with a pock-marked face, but I could see none of that now.

"Grab one of those things!" I told them, waving at the cylinders. "They're sort of like Carl Gustavs but with Helta tech, so figure out how to fire them at the bogies. And if you figure out how, for fuck's sake, don't keep it to yourself!"

I let my KE gun fall free of my hands and the harness system pulled it close into my chest automatically

The thing I thought was a scope was on the left side of the tube, so I rested the rear of the weapon on my right shoulder and tried to look through the ring. There was nothing, just the glow of the reflected sunlight off the closest of the boarding pods. No crosshairs, no reticle, not so much as a digital readout. If you had to have some sort of ID chip or key for this, we were fucked. I felt around on both pistol grips and my right thumb touched something, an indent on the interior of the grip. The scope, or aiming ring or optical sight, or whatever it was called, lit up purple, then green, then what looked like an MRI of a nautilus shell appeared in glowing blue.

That had to be some kind of sight. I had no idea where to aim, but it was a sight. If the thumb controlled the sight in back, maybe the trigger was in the front? I searched the same place in the front and when my thumb reached the same spot on the opposite side of the foregrip, the thing fired.

Brannas-Fel had called it a plasma gun and I hadn't given much thought to the words at the time, other than that it had sounded powerful and badass. When it drove me back a step despite the armor, I gave it serious consideration. Firing a plasma in a vacuum would require a serious magnetic field, plus maybe some sort of beam emitter to turn the ammo into a plasma in the first place. But mostly, I realized that plasma wasn't just focused light, it was tiny, superheated bits of matter shooting out the barrel at relativistic speeds and it kicked like a son of a bitch.

The discharge of the gun was very visible. Unlike a laser, which had to interact with an atmosphere to make any sort of visible beam, a plasma gun carried its atmosphere along for the ride. A flare of white energy blasted out of the barrel and off into eternity, coming nowhere within a hundred meters of the boarding pod and I spat a curse.

"To fire it, you have to touch the insets where your thumbs rest on the grips," I told the other two. "But don't touch the front one until you have the damned thing aimed!"

How long did the thing take to recycle? Was it single shot? It would suck if it was single-shot and I wasted time trying to shoot a second round out of it. I threw down the gun I was holding and it landed heavily on the deck without making a sound and rolled a half-revolution before the pistol grips caught it. I bent down and grabbed the last one out of the container, straightening just in time to see Quinn fire his plasma gun.

The shot looked like ball lightning, a coherent packet of ionized gas held together by God knew what, and Corporal Randolph Quinn, Space Ranger, was a more instinctive shot than Major Andy Clanton, Space Marine. The boarding pod was facing right into us now, and Quinn had fired the only place he could, right into the nose of the thing. The ball lightning struck directly in the center of its flat nose and a flash of sublimated metal erupted from it.

I don't know what I expected. Too many science fiction movies, as well as the episodes of my own streaming show, unfortunately, prepared me for an explosion like a fireworks show that would leave nothing but glittering bits of incandescence expanding in space. That obviously wasn't going to happen shooting a single plasma shot from a man-portable weapon at a spaceship. I also wouldn't have been surprised if the shot had spalled off the nose of the ship with no effect at all. It *was* a spaceship, after all.

Instead, the ship stayed exactly where it was, its main drive dark, barely moving relative to us. Maybe he'd killed the crew, or else he'd fried the controls. The other two didn't wait around for our follow-up shots. Sergeant Masterson's blast went wide of the second ship in the line and then the rocket motors flared bright and the two boarding pods surged forward.

I didn't know if the things had weapons, but I wasn't going to wait around for a demonstration.

"Get inside the tender!" I yelled.

It wasn't a perfect idea. They might not care about damaging the tender, in which case we would all be gathered in one convenient place for them to blow up. Or even if their weapons weren't heavy enough to destroy the ship, it might be that hitting one of the hyperdrives would cause some huge blast that would kill us anyway. But any plan is better than no plan and at least it gave the troops something to do.

Ginger and Pops and the other Delta operators were already behind the ship, hanging onto the superstructure for support and firing off full-power shots at the incoming ships. It wasn't a bad idea, but I had to imagine the pods would be armored enough to deal with micrometeorites, which was what our KE gun rounds were when you got down to it.

"Hurry!" I urged Brannas-Fel and the Rangers escorting him, waving at the tender. "Get him in there now! Get that thing flying!"

They didn't reply, saving their breath for running, and I wanted to scream at how slow they had to move to carry the Heltan along with them.

"Can these things fire more than once?" Quinn asked me.

I was about to reply that I didn't know, when we found out the hard way that the pods were, indeed armed. In fact, they were armed with the same damn thing we were shooting at them, the plasma guns. The ball of white-hot star-stuff was much more impressive incoming than it had been outgoing and I jumped instinctively. I couldn't leap tall buildings in a single bound even in the Svalinn armor, but it did add *up* to my game and I was maybe three meters in the air when the plasma blast rammed into the metal of the spar where I'd stood a moment before.

I didn't bother to look at what it had done to the deck, but I assumed it was bad and I wanted to avoid it happening to me. I was aiming the plasma gun before I hit the ground and pushed the triggers about the same time as my boots touched. The extra punch from the discharge put me on my ass, which would have been pretty damned embarrassing if I hadn't hit the target like a boss.

"Yeah!" I blurted reflexively in the glow of the expanding halo of gas.

Metal sublimated from the gun turret in the side of the pod, the source of the shot that had almost got me, and sparks flared from electromagnetic coils shattering under the heat of the plasma. The boarding pod pulled away in a desperate blast of maneuvering jets, their ignition a puff of white smoke at the nose, spinning them upward, facing the main drive bell downward.

Something prickled down the back of my neck as I realized the pod was less than a hundred meters overhead and I remembered something I'd read in another, much more talented writer's books way back when I was a little kid and people read paper books.

A reaction drive's efficiency as a weapon is in direct proportion to its efficiency as a drive.

Corporal Quinn stepped between me and the yawning drive bell and tested whether the plasma gun could indeed be fired multiple times. The answer, we both found out in a brand-new sunrise, was yes.

In the half-second between him bringing the gun to his shoulder and firing, I had the thought to yell at him not to target the drive bell, figuring the interior of a rocket engine might be tough enough to take a hit from the plasma gun without significant damage. I didn't need to worry. Quinn, as Jambo and I had intuited earlier, was pretty smart for a Ranger. His shot went the one place I would have aimed if I'd had ten seconds or so to consider it: the maneuvering jets on the starboard bow of the pod.

Plasmoid was the technical term for what the gun shot, and the plasmoid burned through the thin hull plating over the maneuvering thruster fuel tanks like it wasn't there. I don't know if it ignited the reaction mass, but it definitely blew a hole in the side of the pressurized tank and the result was one, long, unplanned steering jet, pinwheeling the ship around in an uncontrolled spin. I thought it was going to crash into the construction spar and crush us beneath it, and I scrambled to my feet, trying to get out of its way, but there was some backwards thrust to the expelled gas and instead, the pod smashed into the drydock structure.

It was a little like watching a car accident, and even though there was still another threat out there, another armed pod, I couldn't look away. I wasn't sure which would come off worst, but if I'd had to put money down, it would have been on the drydock, since I figured they had to have taken the possibility of ship collisions into account when they designed it.

I would have been wrong. The pod smashed through the window, whatever clear metal or plastic the Helta thought was strong enough to guard against micrometeorites not quite sturdy enough to take the impact of a spinning spacecraft. Ice crystallized on the jagged edges of the window and vapor sprayed out in white puffs as the atmosphere evacuated.

"Sir, the other ship is moving away," Quinn told me.

I was on my feet, the plasma gun still at my shoulder and ready to take a shot at the vessel, but Quinn was right. Maneuvering jets spewed vapor on the side of the remaining pod, pushing it out away from the spar a few hundred meters before the drive bell flared from the main engine.

"Do you think he's out of range?" Masterson asked, fumbling with the gun he'd picked up.

"If he wasn't," I ventured, "he'd probably be shooting at us."

"So, where's he going?" Quinn wondered.

The stubby cylinder rode its boost past the end of the spar, the drive bell going dark after only a couple seconds of burn, and then maneuvering jets began to spin it around.

"Shit!" I yelled. "He's going after the tender!" I waved at Quinn and Masterson. "Come on, follow me and bring those guns!"

Boarding the tender reminded me of the first time I'd set foot on the *Truthseeker* out of the airlock from the *Selene*, except in reverse. It was surreal, walking off the end of an impossible footbridge into empty space and leaving gravity behind with one footstep. Someone in Svalinn armor grabbed my hand and pulled me into place in the open passenger compartment and I sailed past most of the Ranger squad, nearly shooting out the other side before I grabbed at a strut and came up short with a painful jolt in my shoulder. The gun had no weight out in free fall, but it still had a bunch of mass and Isaac Newton wanted the damned thing to keep going.

"Brannas-Fel!" I called. "Twist this thing's tail and get us the hell out of here!"

"Was that supposed to translate as something," the Heltan wondered, "or were you cursing at me?"

I wanted to, right then. Wanted to curse him and the people who'd programmed the translator.

"Turn on the rockets and head for the cruiser," I said. "Did you get *that*?"

"I believe so. Hold onto something."

"Masterson, Quinn, over here with me. Guns out the side."

The two Rangers barely had a chance to find a handhold when the tender's engine ignited and we were all nearly tossed backwards into the metal grating separating the crew compartment from the fuel tanks. Stars moved and so did the Tevynian boarding craft, and I struggled to bring the awkward mass of the plasma gun to bear on the thing. Masterson fired before I could, his shot going wide again. I wanted to bitch him out for missing both times he'd fired, but I bit back the words. It was an unfamiliar weapon with sights and triggers designed by aliens and you can only expect so much from an Army puke.

The boarding pod was side-on to us, slipping back as our drive continued its burn and I took my best guess as to the nature of the animated conch shell of an aiming reticle and fired. I was dead on. The plasmoid took over a second to travel the distance between the tender and the pod and I intuited it was traveling less than a quarter of lightspeed, which wasn't slow for a bullet but was a little on the dawdling side for an energy weapon. The round hit, I was sure of it, but nothing seemed to happen, not an explosion, not a violent maneuver, not so much as a transient glow.

"Out of range," Quinn guessed.

"Oh, damn," Ginger murmured from somewhere. All the armor looked alike. "Sir, I think he's going to get on our tail where you can't take a shot at him and pick us off at his leisure."

"No, he's not."

I didn't recognize the voice until I checked the tiny comms screen on my HUD. It was, I found out, Captain Holden.

"The shuttle!" That was Gus, who I hadn't heard utter two words the whole mission. "It's at our twelve o'clock!"

I couldn't see a damned thing through the cross-beam cage between the crew compartment and the cockpit, so I muttered a curse and leaned as far out the side as I could without losing my grip. And there it was.

It was impressive seen in open space, a hammerhead shark but now in its natural ocean. Its drives were supernovae compared to the low-powered engines of the tender and the boarding pod, and when it fired its chin cannon, there was no doubt at all of the range. The rounds from the coil gun were barely visible, just shooting stars of reflection from the drydock's floodlights, but their effect was much more obvious. The boarding pod ripped in half, riddled by depleted uranium slugs, and I thought I saw a tiny human figure spill out of the opening, maybe just one of the crew who'd neglected to strap in.

"Sorry we took so long," Holden said. The shuttle cut its drive, then began to pull a skew flip for braking burn. "We had to wait for the rear guard at the airlock to re-board. Follow me and I'll lead you to the *Truthseeker.* No room for that thing in the new ship's cargo bay...she comes with a full complement of shuttles and spare parts to make three more."

"Thank God," Quinn said, breaking into the open channel with the comment. I didn't chew him out. It was better than we'd expected.

"Don't be thanking anyone yet...those Tevynian cruisers are coming after us hell bent for leather. I don't think we're getting out of this system without a fight."

24

I WAS BREATHING HARD WHEN I HIT THE BRIDGE OF THE *Truthseeker*, catching myself against the doorframe to stop my headlong sprint. Oliver and Julie looked around at my entrance, their expressions equally grim.

"They said down in the cargo bay that you wanted me up here, sir," I told Olivera, still gasping.

It felt odd being out of the armor after moving and fighting and living in it for most of the day. The breeze from the ventilators was a chill down my back, evaporating some of the sweat staining my uniform jacket. It had felt even odder leaving the Delta team back in the cargo bay with Ginger in command.

"That was good work getting those hyperdrives," Olivera said. His eyes closed for just a beat and he shook his head. "I'm sorry about Master Sergeant Bowie. The man was a legend."

"He was my friend," I said simply. Now that I had time to think, an emptiness had opened up inside my chest and I had to blink at something in my eye. I wasn't the kind of guy who refused to cry, but I wasn't going to do it in front of the whole bridge crew.

Julie gave me a sympathetic look, but said nothing, hands weaving patterns in the haptic hologram of her control station even when she was facing away from it.

"Did you need me for something, sir?" I wondered, stepping closer, leaning against the edge of Olivera's command station, exhaustion wearing at me. I was coming down from a series of adrenaline highs and I was going to collapse soon unless I got either sleep or caffeine. And I never had managed to smuggle any Diet Cokes onto the ship.

"The Tevynian cruisers pulled a micro-jump," he said, his tone grim as if he'd announced all our deaths. "It put them about a light minute from us, and while we could jump out of the system right now, the ship we salvaged can't."

"Why not?" I asked, thinking of the Rangers we'd left on the ship. "Did they not take the bridge?"

"They did—" Oliver began, but Joon-Pah finished the sentence for him.

"But they damaged the helm control station," the Heltan said. I knew him well enough now to translate the expression on his face as worried, tense. "Normally, they could use the auxiliary control room to fly her, but the ship was having work done on the control linkages between those stations and the computer core."

"Oh, shit." *Fucking Army. We kept them out of Engineering and they still managed to find something to break.*

"The Helta engineers you left on board think they can get it fixed," Olivera added. "But they're going to need time. Time we may not have." He gestured at the tactical display where three threat icons were nearly on top of our position.

"Have you thought about evacuating the ship with one of the shuttles and making do with the hyperdrives?"

Olivera glared at me balefully. "The President himself told me this was probably the most important military mission in the history of human civilization. I doubt he'd approve of abandoning the one thing that might give us a fighting chance against the Tevynians."

"And why did you want me here?" I asked again, shaking my head. "And if you say it was for luck, I swear to God, I'm going back to my cabin."

"We've had a grand total of one space battle," Julie reminded me. "And you came up with the idea that helped us win it. I'd say that's more than luck, Andy."

"We want you here," Olivera agreed. "And if you do nothing but bring me luck, well...." He motioned at the screen. "We can use all the luck we can get."

"They're going to be in firing range of their particle beam weapons in two minutes," Major Baldwin announced. She didn't sound any happier than Olivera, and if the Helta crew weren't as tense as Joon-Pah, it was only because they didn't understand the gravity of the situation...or had an unrealistic faith in us humans.

"We're just going to sit here?" I asked. "I mean, I know we can't leave the system, but we aren't going to try to maneuver?"

"We are," Olivera assured me. "Right after we lure them in."

"They know the effective range of the particle cannon as well as we do." And it was, in my opinion, shit. I mean, it was a devastating weapon, but at a range of just a few hundred kilometers, you basically had to close in like old sailing ships and trade fucking broadsides.

"Oh, that's right," Olivera said, smiling thinly. "We never did read you in to the new weapons system we installed."

I was exhausted and depressed and not firing on all cylinders and I stared at him blankly.

"Colonel Nieves," he said, still grinning at me, "slave Helm to Tactical. Major Baldwin, target the lead ship with the impulse gun."

"Helm slaved to Tactical," Julie acknowledged, then shot Baldwin a dirty look. "Don't scratch the car."

"Realigning the ship for the spinal mount," Baldwin reported, and I could see it on the holographic projection.

A simulation of the *Truthseeker* floated at the center of it, only a few hundred kilometers from the spiderweb structure of the shipyard and the Helta cruiser still docked there. The *Truthseeker* rotated counterclockwise about twenty degrees and aimed its nose at one of the Tevynian ships boosting in about a thousand klicks away from us, just outside particle cannon range. And I didn't know why we were bothering.

"What the hell is an impulse gun?" I asked, sounding a bit snarky and disrespectful, but past caring.

"The ship's warp field is a damned useful thing, as it turns out," Julie said, twisting around in her seat to face me now that she'd surrendered control of the ship to Baldwin, temporarily anyway. "It acts as a sublight drive, it rips open the wormhole to hyperspace, serves as the basis for the defense shield...all because it can distort the fabric of spacetime. But we figured out from your little pinball maneuver that if it can launch a ship away from it at relativistic speeds, it can do the same thing to a three-meter long tungsten penetrator."

A light went on inside my head and I nearly staggered backward at the beautiful simplicity of it. "That's brilliant," I admitted.

"It's brilliant *once*," Olivera corrected me. "Once per engagement, anyway, because we can only fire it in a direct line with the cannon's spinal mount, and, after they figure out what it is, all they have to do is keep out of its way. Not to mention that the capacitors take about six minutes to charge between shots."

"Even if it works, it will still be two to one," Joon-Pah lamented. "And I have doubts that your—what did you call it? I doubt that your pinball maneuver will work with two enemy ships."

"Ten seconds until the lead ship hits the point of no return," Baldwin said.

At my curious expression, Julie explained. "That's when they won't have enough time to react before the shot hits them. With the warp field, they could hop right out of the slug's way if we gave them a few minutes warning."

"And if they see it," Baldwin added. "It's not exactly a shining star on thermal, and lidar or radar would have to reflect back, which takes time at these distances."

"Fire at your discretion, Major," Olivera instructed her, interrupting the impromptu lesson.

"Everyone hold onto something," Baldwin advised. "You might actually feel this."

And feel it we did. I'd gripped the back of Olivera's chair tightly at her warning and I was still nearly tossed forward to the deck at what felt very much like a sharp, violent braking boost, except on a ship that didn't use reaction engines. I figured out what had happened easy enough. Using a mass driver for propulsion had never been my favorite concept—it was inelegant and brute force and didn't fit in well with my type of science fiction. But the principle was, if you'll pardon the pun, rock solid. The expulsion of the mass of the impulse gun round at such a high velocity recoiled in the opposite direction, and only the ship's drive field kicking back in a microsecond later kept us from drifting backwards.

It was even more violent for the Tevynian ship. I knew a little about the shields because I'd bugged Joon-Pah about it one day on the bridge, since they were the only thing keeping us from a horrible death and I had wanted some details on how unlikely said horrible death might be. The strength of the shield was proportional to the output of the power source behind them, and you could overload them with enough energy, kinetic or otherwise. Like the kinetic energy of a solid chunk of metal the size of a minivan slamming into them at a good chunk of lightspeed.

The enemy cruiser seemed to flex and distort as its warp field collapsed, just the faintest of impressions, like it might have been an optical illusion, but what happened next was very real. The ship went supernova. I'm being imprecise, but that's what it looked like from the bridge of the *Truthseeker*, like a star had exploded. The globe of white kept expanding, reaching out dozens of kilometers, filling the display and I gritted my teeth, waiting for it to swallow us up even though I knew it had to be just a trick of perspective, that there was no way an explosion that far away could...

"Hold on!" Joon-Pah warned, grabbed the arms of his chair and closing his eyes.

Oh, shit. I'd been in a major earthquake once, in Chile. I'd been there on leave, flew Allie down because it was faster than me trying to get back to the States, and we both thought it would be more fun. And it had been great, right up to the point that our hotel had started shaking.

This feeling was the same, and as hard and violent as the vibration through the ship's hull was, what hit even harder was the claustrophobic realization that there was no outside to escape to. I was on my knees and didn't remember falling, the trembling rising from the deck into the palms of my hands as if the ship itself was just as afraid as I was. There'd been yells and screams and the sort of hooting and honking the Helta made when they got excited, and it died down into gasps and nervous muttering as the nebula of gas on the screen began to fade, leaving nothing at all at its heart.

"That was the hyperdrive," Joon-Pah explained, calmer than I would have expected. "They must have had their capacitors charged in case they needed to jump. When the round hit, the energy went into the hyperdrive and caused an unstable wormhole."

"Good to know," Olivera said, just the slightest quaver in his voice, the hint of sweat on his forehead the only sign he was as scared as the rest of us.

"She's just gone," Baldwin said, as if the power of the weapon scared her. "I'm not picking up anything at all, nothing but hot gas." She shook herself and her eyes seemed to refocus. "The other two cruisers are moving away. A thousand...no, four thousand kilometers now and still withdrawing."

"Colonel Olivera, we have a message from Colonel Brooks on the other ship."

That was a Space Force First Lieutenant, a baby-faced puppy who probably couldn't have rented a car without his parents being listed as the primary driver. I couldn't remember his name, but he'd been attached to the Helta Communications officer at some point during the trip when Olivera realized trying to get Baldwin to double down on Tactical and Comms wasn't working.

"It's text-only," the young man clarified. "She says they've got the controls fixed, or at least fixed enough to get them moving. They're separating from the docks and should be ready for the jump to hyperspace in less than half an hour."

Half an hour seemed like forever on the ground with a gun in your hand. Out here, where everything moved with glacial slowness, it was as good as immediate and the tension went out of the bridge crew like the air hissing out of a balloon.

"We can stand them off for half an hour," Baldwin assured Olivera. "All we have to do is keep them maneuvering out of the way of our line of fire. They don't know long it takes the weapon to recycle, so they won't take the chance." She shrugged. "Or at least I wouldn't."

The Helta Communications officer began gabbling, still not good enough with English to try to use it in an emergency situation. *We really should have set up a translation circuit on the bridge.*

But no, that wouldn't have worked either. In an emergency, when everyone is already talking over everyone else, having a time-delayed computer voice yapping at them wouldn't have worked very well.

"One of the Tevynian vessels is sending a video signal," Joon-Pah said, translating for the other Heltan. "He wants to talk to the ship's captain."

"Let me see it," Olivera said. "But don't let him see us, yet."

The Heltan Comms officer touched a control and a section of the central display shimmered briefly before manifesting the view from the bridge of one of the Tevynian ships. It was nearly identical to our own, stolen from the Helta, but the Tevynians had added their own touches here and there.

"Are those...*skulls*?" Captain Cochrane asked, his face going pale.

"Quiet," Olivera snapped, but the same awed horror was in his eyes. And maybe in mine.

The bleached white skulls were mounted along the bulkhead beneath the line of system monitors, not in a gaudy fashion, not as if they were there to inspire fear in us or any of the Tevynians' enemies, but rather in a casual, matter-of-fact manner like the deer heads in a hunting cabin. Which made it so much worse. It took me a second to realize that not all the skulls were Helta. A few were clearly from some other species we hadn't encountered yet, and more than one was human.

It was hard to pry my attention away from the skulls and back to the Tevynians. I didn't *want* to call them humans, but they obviously were. Even with the strange, checkered patterns of their clothes, the odd hairstyles, the facial tattoos that would have seemed over the top at a heavy metal concert, and the golden torques most of them wore around their necks, they were human. Not so much as a bumpy forehead or a brow ridge to be seen.

The captain looked just like the owner of the tattoo parlor in Tampa where I got my only ink over twenty years ago, right after I made it through boot camp. The eagle, globe and anchor rested over my heart and they always would, but I had no desire to turn my skin into a canvas. This guy had different ideas, and the whorls and waves outlined in blue across his face told a story of his culture and his place in it, a story he believed was more important than the face he'd been born with.

His was a good face for a canvas, broad and flat with a high brow and cruel eyes. I'd seen eyes like his before, usually on the wrong end of an AK47. When he spoke, the computer translated it into English a second or two behind the words, but the words themselves seemed somehow familiar, though I couldn't have told you what Earth language they reminded me of.

"Helta ship, this is Captain Thanylaxia Ranalixia of the Confederation warship *Sword Dancer*. I have claimed this system in the name of the Tevynian Confederation and you will surrender your vessel to me immediately. You may think this weapon you have used to kill my brothers and sisters of the *Longspear* will save you, but we will stay out of its range and once you have left this system, we will have our vengeance on the citizens of the world you call Fairhome. We will execute ten of your people for every one of ours you've killed!"

Julie spat a curse and I agreed with the sentiment.

"You will respond immediately," the Tevynian went on. "If there is any delay, I will signal my ground commander in your city to begin the executions with your civil administrators and shoot one of them every five minutes until you surrender."

The image froze just after the last word and the wind went out of me like I'd been kicked in the gut. And not just me. Michael Olivera was a fighter pilot, the dictionary definition of decisive because hesitation could get him killed. Now, he hesitated, and I could see the indecision in his steely eyes.

"Joon-Pah..." He clearly didn't know what to say. He couldn't give up this ship, but these were Joon-Pah's people and his ship and he couldn't bring himself to give an order that would lead to the deaths of thousands of them. For once, he didn't know what to do.

But I did.

"Get all the Helta off the bridge," I said. It wasn't a request. It was an order I had no right to give, but I gave it anyway. "Then put me on with this asshole."

Olivera's face went from doubt of his own judgment to doubt of mine, which, I suppose, was something of an improvement.

"You sure you know what you're doing, Andy?" Julie asked, though not with the skepticism I'd expected.

"We can't let him blame this on the Helta," I said, shaking my head. "We can't let them die for us."

"I'm taking a hell of a lot on myself making this decision," Olivera pointed out.

"That's part of being the captain," I said, then grinned lopsidedly. "Even if you Space Force yahoos call it a colonel."

"Joon-Pah," Olivera said, eyes still fixed on mine, as if making the decision while he spoke the words, "if you could please have your people leave the bridge, and tell Lt. Collins here...." He nodded toward the human Comms officer. "...how to get a live feed with the Tevynians."

It took nearly a minute to get the Helta off the bridge, and I gritted my teeth at the delay, imagining Captain Inky giving the order to kill the first Heltan while we dragged our feet. But finally, Collins nodded to me and touched the control the Heltan had shown him.

It was the same bridge, the same man, but the image shifted to the left as if I was watching an old film roll and there'd been a spliced break in the reel. Captain Thanos...Thanos Anal Licker? I couldn't remember the fucker's name. Captain Inky would have to do. Captain Inky's eyes went wide when he saw me, saw the other humans on the bridge.

"By the gods..." he breathed. "Who the hell are you?"

When I answered, the words came automatically, the way they did when I was writing a novel, dancing freely out of my thoughts as if laid there by the muse.

"I am Captain Andrew Clanton of the United Stars Space Fleet. This is my ship, the *Wayfarer*, seized from the weaklings you call the Helta and refitted with the mighty weapons of the Empire of the United Stars. We are taking the other ship and if you attempt to stop us, you will meet the same fate as your comrades on the *Longspear*." I made a slashing gesture across my chest, something dramatic and theatrical that I'm not sure anyone has ever made in real life. "If you value your lives and your pitiful Confederation, do not seek us out. We have our own enemies and our own battles to fight. Be wise and do not become one of them."

I made a slashing gesture across my throat to Collins, then remembered my science fiction movies and made myself clearer. "Cut the transmission."

Collins signaled all clear and it seemed as if the whole bridge was holding its breath.

"They're still moving away," Baldwin said. "It doesn't look like they're going for the other ship. I think they're standing down."

"The TV show?" Olivera exploded, face red, eyes wide. "You used the United Stars Empire from your TV show?"

Julie was laughing and pretty soon, the rest of them were, as well. Joon-Pah and the other Helta stared at them as they reentered the bridge, though I couldn't tell if they thought we were stupid or just crazy.

"It's as good a name as any," I said, feeling a bit defensive. "The key is whether he buys it."

"I believe he will," Joon-Pah said, putting a hand on my arm and squeezing firmly. I wasn't sure whether it was a Helta gesture or if he was imitating a human one. "He may or may not accept your declaration of a far-away empire, but he will know it wasn't us, and that's enough. Thank you, Andy Clanton."

I offered him a hand and he shook it, knowing what the gesture meant from his time on Earth.

"I hope he's right," I said softly to Olivera.

"We did all we could." He gave me a sidelong look. "Shit, I think we did more than we should have. I hope we aren't both court-martialed when we get back."

"Let 'em." Now that the crisis was over, I felt as if the air was going out of me, leaving me hollow and shrunken in on myself. "Either way," I told him, "when we get back, I'm done with this. I've had enough."

25

I TRIED TO IGNORE THE KNOCKING. I WASN'T ASLEEP, WASN'T even sure if I *should* have been. I didn't know what time it was, or rather what the local day-night cycle was on the ship, and I didn't much care. I hadn't left my compartment since we'd jumped out of the Fairhome system and I fully intended to see just how long I could stay in here before hunger or thirst drove me out.

The knocking persisted, and I remembered Jambo waking me up for the jump to Alpha Centauri and my guts knotted yet again, trying to see his face and only managing a memory of blackened, seared flesh inside a broken helmet.

"Go away," I murmured, not caring if whoever was on the other side of the door heard it.

"Major." The voice was muffled through the door, but I recognized Pop's voice. "Andy. Please let me in."

I propped my head up and looked down at myself. I'd laid down in the bunk dressed in a T-shirt and shorts and I briefly considered pulling my fatigues back on, but rejected the notion. If it was that damned important, he'd have to take me as I was, hairy white legs and all.

I towered over Pops and outweighed the man by a good thirty pounds, but I felt small compared to him when I opened the hatch. I felt like an outsider.

"What is it, Pops?" I hung on the inside of the door as if I was using it as a shield against him, against the guilt he made me feel.

His eyes flickered down as if he were embarrassed to be here, or maybe embarrassed for me.

"Andy, I'm really sorry to bother you. But I know you and Jambo were pretty close and...well, that is," he dithered, "the boys and I are having a little memoriam for him in one of the conference rooms in a few minutes and they all wanted me to ask and see if you'd come." His lean, sharp-edged face brightened a bit. "We managed to scrounge up a couple bottles of tequila."

I tried to smile, but it felt as if my face was frozen. I didn't want to move, didn't want to speak, and certainly didn't want to sit around and bullshit with Delta operators after I'd let their leader get killed. But I wasn't going to say that, so I played the alcoholic card.

"I don't think I'd fit in, Pops," I admitted. "I'm three years sober. I kind of lost it for a while after Venezuela."

"Hey, didn't we all?" Pops' smile was tinged with bitterness. "Come on." He jerked his head toward the passageway outside. "I swear on a stack of Bibles, I'll make sure you don't drink anything except Diet Coke."

I laughed softly.

"Oh, God, I wish. I'm jonesing for one. But I didn't have time to get any shipped up here before the Russians hit our base and we had to haul ass."

"Jambo smuggled a 12-pack on board," Pops told me. His smile broadened, the bitterness gone, replaced by a fond memory. "He swore us to secrecy. Said he was going to give 'em to you on the way back in, once we'd pulled it off."

"That son of a bitch," I said, shaking my head. I tried to laugh, I *wanted* to laugh, because it was such a Jambo thing to do.

And somehow, instead, I was crying. Not the stoic, single tear thing you see in movies when men cry, but the blubbering, sniffling, wailing that happens when real people deal with real death. It wasn't the first time, but I had thought, I had hoped, I had dared to *dream* I'd never have to do it again. I was nearly bent over, sobs racking my shoulders, and I realized Pops was holding me, patting me on the back and murmuring comforting words until I'd let it out.

"Oh, Jesus," I said, wiping my arm across my face, sucking in a labored breath. I couldn't meet his eyes. I tried to joke my way out of it. "A few years as a civilian and I've turned into a little bitch."

"Andy," Pops said, a knowing tilt to his head, "you know better than that. You ain't hardly the first operator I've had to watch cry. Why, you know we had this dog, sweet little mutt that hung around our FOB in downtown Caracas. We called him Pedro, gave him bits of our MREs. Jambo was always giving us shit about feeding him. Then one day after a mortar attack, someone found Pedro's body and we buried him out behind the bunker. And that night, I found Jambo by the grave, bawling like a fucking baby."

"No shit? I guess he always was a big softy..."

Pops laughed long and hard, and I soon, I was laughing as well.

"Come on, Andy," he said. "Throw some clothes on. Trust me...you'll fit right in."

I wasn't officially invited to the bridge for the jump back to Earth, but I showed up anyway, and no one told me to leave.

"Hey Andy," Julie called to me, turning in her seat as I came up the ramp from the hatchway. "Looking forward to getting home?"

I wanted to say yes, just for conversational politeness, but the word caught in my throat. What the hell did I have to go home to?

"I'm just looking forward to being a civilian again," I said, and that was a lie, too. I wondered if she knew it. I hadn't felt as complete or alive in years as I had wearing the uniform again.

"I doubt there'll be any problem with you getting out after this," she said, and her tone was cheerful, if maybe a bit wistful. "I mean, it's not like there'll be any secrets that need keeping after this. You can go back to being a famous science fiction writer."

"I'll be famous, but not for being a science fiction writer." I sighed. "I'll just be one of those assholes I always despised who uses being a celebrity to make millions of dollars."

"Oh, that sounds like a fate worse than death," she said, putting a hand to her chest in mock sympathy. "I'm sure you'll donate all the money to charity."

"Let's not get carried away!" I laughed sharply. "I full intend to become as big of an asshole as any other millionaire celebrity!"

"Well, you're going to have to wait until we get back to our own dimension, Major Clanton," Olivera said. "Which will be in one minute and thirty-six seconds."

"I'm just glad we didn't run into any Tevynians at Alpha Centauri." Julie laughed, the sound rough but somehow also sweet. "And there's a sentence I didn't think I'd ever find myself saying."

"I wonder what's been going on since we left?" Cochrane said. The Engineering officer hadn't spoken more than two words to me the whole time I'd been on the ship and I wasn't sure if he was talking to me now, but I answered anyway.

"I'm sure it's been a bit tense, considering Russia sent troops onto US soil. But they probably used officially retired Spetsnaz who were already on record as mercenaries. They bought their shit surplus on the black market, so it can't be traced back. That means plausible deniability." I shrugged. "Popov will probably claim it was 'hardliners' in his government or some such bullshit. And then there'll be yelling and investigations and sanctions and I'm sure the UN will have some very entertaining debates." I barked a laugh. "And that's not even considering the three-ring clown circus going on in Congress. I can't wait to scroll through the videos."

"Jumping in twenty," Julie reminded us. "Clench your stomachs, folks. No puking on the deck."

Joon-Pah had been silent while we bantered, which wasn't entirely unlike him, but I thought I noticed a difference in his demeanor, something in the eyes. I expected Olivera to say something to him, since they were theoretically equal in rank, but the Space Force Colonel was busy having a conversation with the Comms officer.

"You okay, Joon-Pah?" I asked, going over to his command station. "Sorry your Fairhome system got taken, but this'll be the first step to getting them all back, right?"

"The mission was successful, to a degree," the Heltan agreed. "But I have a strange feeling, that no matter who wins this war, nothing will ever be the same for us. And if we Helta wish to survive, we shall have to become less what we have been and more what you are."

Well, *that* was depressing, if not vaguely insulting. But he sounded like he needed encouragement, and I tried to remember how to do that.

"Ever hear the term gestalt?" I asked, shrugging. "Maybe when we put our heads together, the whole will add up to more than the sum of the parts."

"Jumping now," Julie said.

I hadn't prepared for it, which was fine because it didn't seem to get any better when I did. Someone made retching noises on the other side of the bridge, but I didn't look around to see who it was. No use embarrassing them.

"We are in the Earth-Moon system," Julie announced, waving at the image in the main display, a very familiar one, but one I hadn't been sure I'd see again.

"Where's the other ship?" Olivera asked her. "Is she out yet?"

"I hope they don't name her something stupid," I murmured, thinking of the conversation I'd had with Jambo.

"There she is!" Julie fairly whooped. "A thousand kilometers off our port bow."

"Port bow?" Olivera repeated, frowning at her. "Have you been picking up bad habits from Clanton?"

"Just surrender to the inevitable, sir," I warned him. "You're gonna be the Space Navy, eventually."

"Colonel Brooks and Captain Adams report everything is green on their end," Collins said. He paused, putting a finger to his ear to shut out the cheering and chatter from the rest of the bridge crew, listening to something over his ear bud. I saw his fingers working the haptic controls and small video screens popped up in the larger display at his station. After a few seconds, he looked up sharply, frowning. "Sir, I'm picking up some transmissions from the news networks on Earth. Things aren't looking so good."

"Put it on the main display, Collins," Olivera ordered.

Collins looked doubtful, as if he didn't think we should see it, but he did it anyway, casting the videos he'd been reviewing over to the central holographic projection.

He hadn't been kidding. The video streams were flat screens floating in the midst of the projection, the sound off, but I didn't need to hear it. Riots were still raging in cities around the world, and the list of cities and casualties scrolled down one side of a screen as images of carnage showed burning shops, cars overturned, Molotov cocktails being thrown at riot police. None were happening in the US, Russia or China, for differing reasons, but Europe was awash in sectarian clashes, and a lot of it was being blamed on infiltration from radical groups based in the Middle East.

Iran, Iraq and Syria were in the middle of an attempted invasion of the Golan Heights, but Israel had held them off so far, though according to the scrawl, there were fears nuclear weapons would inevitably be used. The main reason the US hadn't gotten involved was Mexico. The Mexican Revolutionary Government had launched attacks all along the border with Texas and managed to get mixed into the local population before the new defense satellites could be brought to bear. There were reports of Russian involvement and Russian troops had been killed alongside their Mexican allies, but Popov insisted it was mercenaries not under his control.

Terrorist attacks were happening every day, and the consensus among those polled was that this was the end of the world.

I tried to add up casualties being reported on the various screens and stopped when I reached half a million. The President's coalition was hanging on by a thread and there was talk of impeachment in Congress. Again.

"Holy shit," Cochrane said, his earlier question answered.

"The whole world's gone insane," Julie hissed, her face screwed up in disbelief. I wondered if she was worried about her daughter. I knew her girl was a young teenager, living with her ex-husband. We'd commiserated about the heartaches of absentee parenthood a few times over lunch in the ship's mess.

I thought of Zack living in Austin and felt the same sort of worry. But Paul wasn't a complete idiot. He wouldn't leave them in a war zone. Would he?

"Have you contacted Space Command?" Olivera asked Collins, face grim but no hint of emotion betrayed in his voice.

"They've told me to wait one, sir." Collins' hand went to his ear again. "Sir, they just said the President wants to speak to you personally."

"Did he request a secure line, Collins?"

"No, sir."

"Then put it on the main screen."

Damn. I was beginning to respect Olivera as well as like him, neither of which I'd expected. He wasn't afraid to let his staff see the sausage being made.

The Presidential seal appeared in the projection, occupying more than half the screen, and when Crenshaw's face replaced it, he was outsized, bigger than life. I could see every crease that tension had added to his face, every line the lack of sleep and stress had given him.

"I'm glad to see you back, Colonel," the President said. "I'm afraid things have been a bit rough since you've been gone. I might have to keep you in orbit a bit longer than we expected. We're worried about threats to the landing facilities for the shuttles." He shook his head. "I'm about to give an address to the networks to try to calm things down, but I don't know if it'll do much good."

"Whatever you need us to do, sir," Olivera said, the good soldier—or spaceman, rather—as always.

But I remembered something Joon-Pah had said and decided to do what I did best: talk out of turn.

"Mr. President," I said, stepping up beside Olivera. "Could I make a suggestion?"

26

"I can't believe I let you talk me into this, Clanton," Olivera had to shout to be heard over the roar of the engine and the vibration of the hull. "This is a fucking starship! It was not meant to be flown in a fucking atmosphere!"

"Actually," Joon-Pah corrected him, "the cruisers are quite capable of atmospheric entry, they are simply not equipped to land. The plasma drives should be quite adequate to keep us aloft. As long as we don't drop below a thousand meters in altitude, we should be fine."

"Roger that," Julie said, her lips skinned back in a fierce grin, as if the air buffeting the ship and the vibration threatening to rip the hull apart were the ultimate experience of her career. "No nap-of-the-Earth runs in the starship."

I couldn't even concentrate enough to make a smart remark. We'd made atmospheric entry in a starship—no, in *two* starships. The ship with Brooks and her Rangers aboard was five kilometers behind us, dipping slightly below our altitude of 9000 feet. Below us, the ocean glittered in the late afternoon sun, giving way in seconds to the arid sands of the Arabian Peninsula.

"All right then," Olivera said, sighing his resignation to the inevitable. "Colonel Nieves, take us down to 3000 feet. I want them all to get a good look at what they're going up against."

"At that altitude," she warned, "we're going to be blowing out windows and setting off car alarms. These ships displace a lot of air and we're going pretty damned fast." She laughed sharply. "I can't believe I get to fly the biggest aircraft ever. I'm going to be in so many record books..."

"Broken windows are fine," Olivera assured her. "I could even live with a bit of moderate structural damage. There are some people down there who need to get slapped in the face with a dose of reality."

Now, I had to laugh, and I finally found my voice.

"And nothing screams reality like a pair of starships the size of city block flying over your city."

I couldn't see a damned thing, of course. I was strapped into one of the spare acceleration couches on the other side of Engineering and it didn't have a very good view of the one screen showing the view from the ship's belly cameras, so I was counting on Baldwin to do the play-by-play.

"We are passing over the Golan Heights now," she narrated. "Heading inland over the Iranian and Syrian battle lines. Oooh, the people down there are loving this. Lots of lookie-loos. And there goes the first SAM. Should I shoot it down, sir?"

"Why bother?" Olivera said with a snort of bemusement. "Unless it's a nuke, it won't even scratch the paint."

"Yes, sir, ignoring it." She laughed. "There are actually Iranian troops firing rifles at us."

"That would have to be a hell of a golden BB," Julie said, eyes still locked on her controls.

"And we got our first fighter jet! A MIG, I think. It's not even launching air-to-air—" Baldwin looked up from her screen with a broad smile. "I think he's going to try to kamikaze us! What the hell does he think this is, a movie?" I didn't hear anything, didn't feel so much as a speed bump, but the minute flare of an explosion winked on the edge of the camera view. "Ouch. That's not going to buff out."

"Give the Iranians a nice, good look at both ships," Olivera said. "Collins, pass it on to Captain Adams. As soon as we're past the main body of their force, give it some gas and take us over Tehran."

"Reports are they have nuclear-tipped SRBMs, sir," Baldwin warned him, sounding concerned for the first time.

"Then don't let them shoot at us. There's nothing they have that can touch this ship if we don't want it to."

"I feel I should apologize," Joon-Pah cut in. "I sought your help out of desperation, but it seems our very presence has caused great violence on your world."

I barked a laugh at that, louder than I should have.

"The violence has always been there," I assured him. "All you did was give the usual suspects an excuse to kill each other."

"The President is giving his speech," Collins said. "It's going out on every network, every service, even in Russia and China."

"Put it on," Olivera told him. "Audio, too."

I twisted around in my seat, which was more difficult now than usual. Olivera had instructed everyone to strap in tight during our foray into the atmosphere since the ship's artificial gravity wouldn't be working under the influence of the Earth's all-natural, organic, gluten-free gravity, and he didn't want anyone getting tossed around like an old episode of Star Trek.

"Why the hell didn't they have seat belts?" had been his comment on the matter, and I couldn't disagree.

I was just able to turn enough against my seat restraints to see Crenshaw's face appear next to the video feed from our external cameras, his comments seeming to run in counterpoint to the missiles flying at us from below. Baldwin had decided not to take any chances, I suppose, and had switched on the ship's ECM dampening field, because whenever one of the SAMs got within a few hundred yards of the hull, it swerved away and self-destructed in mid-air.

"My fellow Americans, my fellow *humans*," he began, laying the earnest statesman act on thick, "today we are faced with an opportunity unlike any given to us in all of this world's history. When the Helta visited us and offered us a chance to enter not just a larger world but a larger galaxy, when they gave us the chance to reach the stars and join them in fighting against an aggressive enemy that threatens all peace-loving people, it frightened many of you. And I don't blame you for being frightened. These are frightening times. Great opportunity always comes with great risk."

I'd never been to Tehran, although I'd fantasized about it when I'd been a young Marine infantry platoon leader, eager for battle and not knowing any better. The Alborz mountains outside the city seemed terrifyingly close, and I worried more about running into them than I did the surface-to-air missiles streaking upward at us from all around the downtown area. I had my first sight of the other Helta cruiser since we'd arrived in-system and my breath caught just a bit in awe of the image of the massive starship floating as if by magic only a thousand yards above the downtown buildings of the city. None of the weapons came within two hundred yards of the *Truthseeker* or her sister ship, though a few tumbled back into the city and exploded in sheets of flame from the rocket propellant tanks.

"And as always, in times of fear, the frightened have struck out at their neighbors, blaming them for problems far beyond their control. To these people, to the rioters, to the terrorists, to the rogue governments trying to seize control of contested lands or get revenge for old wrongs, I would ask them simply to do this. Go out in the street and look up. What you see is not a threat from the United States and her allies, it's a promise of a better world. Look up and see the evidence of the size of our universe, the scale of the threats we face and the steps we are ready to take."

"Get us some altitude," Olivera directed. "Get us over those mountains and into Russian airspace."

Julie snorted a brief, harsh laugh as she complied, probably at the idea of flying the ships over Moscow, letting them see first-hand just what they were up against.

"The promise of the marvels you will see in the air above you this day, from the Middle East to Europe and across the rest of the world is quite literally a brand-new day for our species. Even now, new medical wonders are being shared with governments around the world, the means of curing cancers, repairing spinal cord injuries, of lengthening the human lifespan and ameliorating the ravages of old age. If your government tries to withhold these medical miracles from you, find a way to contact the nearest American embassy and we will make sure you are treated. This is a gift given to the whole human race and it's one we intend to share with anyone who wants it."

The image of the President was replaced by a drone shot of a fusion plant, the one I'd heard about the government building with Helta help out in the Nevada desert.

"And the medical miracles are only a part of the gifts we've been given. This is the first commercial fusion energy plant in history and it will be online in less than three months. The United States will offer its expertise and the aid of our Helta allies to any nation who wishes to build their own fusion reactor. You provide the raw materials, we build it for you and after that, it's yours, no strings attached. Safe, cheap energy to power your homes, your cars, desalinization plants to provide fresh water, to make sure no one has to do without electricity. Again, if your government won't agree to this out of fear or jealousy or an attempt to control its people through artificial scarcity, ask us for help. We have the ability and the luxury of being able to aid everyone who needs it, who wants it. Don't let tired old men living in the past keep you from having enough to eat and proper medical care. In addition, we are developing cheap and easy to maintain fabrication plants that take 3D printing to new levels and can build basically anything, given the right raw materials and patterns."

Crenshaw smiled, and I saw just a hint of the cynical combat operator in that smile.

"And now you're all asking, what's the catch? And there is one. These aren't Christmas presents from Santa, after all. There's a war going on out there. The Helta and their allies are peaceful people who have helped their neighbors and asked for nothing in return, but there are always those who take what you give them and begin coming up with ways to take everything you have. The Tevynians are such a people. They took the technological gifts the Helta offered and used them to build a military and try to seize control of every star system they could reach. They've overrun their neighbors and unless they're stopped, they'll get around to us. We have to provide aid, provide soldiers for this war. The United States and her allies have volunteered to do this. We do not wish to force anyone else to make this decision, but if any of you wish to help, wish, as individuals, to enlist and be trained, we will make the opportunity available to you, and you'll be among the first to take advantage of the new technologies we're developing."

The smile thinned out, became something less pleasant. Below us, the mountains and the Caspian Sea had been left behind for the western steppes of Russia.

"And for those who still believe they can wrest control of the power the Helta offer and use it to oppress their own citizens and threaten our own, then yes, the promise of those ships you're going to see passing over you today *is* a threat. If you don't wish to participate in the defense of this world, no one will force you to do it. You'll still receive the medical advances, still be given the chance to build fusion reactors and fabricators. We won't ask for troops or support in return. But if you try to attack us, try to sabotage our effort to keep this world safe, then we can and most certainly will put you down. If you had a military, you won't have one anymore. If you had a government, you'll have a different one. Because this isn't an American war, and it's not a European war, it's not even just a human war. This is a war between those who believe in peace and autonomy and those who think the universe belongs to them.

"And we're not going to lose without one hell of a fight."

27

The medal around my neck dragged at my shoulders, but the one in my hands seemed to weigh more than worlds. I stared at the case, at the words inscribed on the brass plaque. "Command Master Sergeant James Edward Bowie Jr."

"Why the fuck did they give it to me?" I said under my breath. But not softly enough.

"Because he didn't have anyone else," Pops told me.

Pops, whose real name turned out to be Chief Warrant Officer Mark Tremonti, looked like a different man in his dress blues, but then so did we all. The awards ceremony had ended only minutes ago and the crew of what was officially referred to as Operation Bridgehead was milling about the East Room of the White House while carefully-chosen reporters interviewed President Crenshaw and Colonels Olivera and Brooks.

"I know he was married once," I said, not quite an argument but more of a question.

"He was." Pops' eyes flickered downward. "She died. Cancer. Fifteen years ago. His mother and father both passed away when he was a teenager. No siblings. Us, you...." He waved a hand around at the rest of the Delta team. "We're the closest thing he had to family."

"Then you should have it," I said, trying to hand the case off to him. "You guys worked together."

"We did. But we also kept a professional separation. You have to when you do the shit we do. He didn't keep that separation with you, sir. I think he would have wanted you to have it." He shrugged. "At least that's what I told Colonel Olivera when he asked me."

I blew out a breath, squeezing my eyes shut for a second against another surge of unwelcome emotion. I hadn't been able to stop myself when the President read the citation.

"All right," I conceded. "It'll take good care of it." I fiddled with the blue ribbon around my neck. It felt as if it was about to choke me to death. "I don't know how I ended up with one of these instead of you, or Quinn, or Colonel Brooks."

"We'll get ours," Pops told me. "Silver stars, bronze stars, enough for everyone on the mission most likely, from Colonel Olivera down to the lowliest maintenance tech. It was one of those sorts of operations, you know? But being honest, sir, not a one of us would be alive if you hadn't figured out how to use those big-ass guns against the enemy ship. And we wouldn't have the hyperdrives to build three starships if you hadn't made the call to go for them after Jambo died. That could be the difference between winning and losing this war." He laughed softly, eyeing Crenshaw and the gaggle of Defense Department suits clustered together in a protective formation against the press. "Besides, I think the need for a positive press spin on everything helped. They needed heroes, dead and alive. And the hero the press loves the most is an unlikely one. You're about as unlikely as they come."

"Clanton." I nearly spun around at the voice behind my right shoulder before I recognized it as Olivera. The look on his face told me this was business, not pleasure. "Find someone to take care of the medal for you. The President wants you in the Situation Room in ten."

"Shit." It wasn't quite "yes, sir," but I was already trying to transition back to civilian life. I had moved back to my house in Vegas three weeks ago, just after Jambo's funeral and I'd had to get a haircut before the ceremony so I wouldn't look like a shitbag in my dress blues.

I handed the case off to Pops and followed Olivera. At least I wouldn't have to wait around for the reporters to take their turns at me. Julie and Colonel Brooks fell into formation with us as we strode down the hallways, and I had to force myself not to march in step with them.

"How's Vegas?" Julie asked me.

She looked younger, I realized with a start. Not that she'd ever seemed old or unattractive, but she was a woman who'd lived an active life in a stressful career and you don't get to your early forties as a Navy pilot and not look it. She no longer looked it. She could have been thirty or even twenty-five again, and I wondered if it was the same for me and I just hadn't noticed because the change had been so gradual.

"It's hot," I said, trying to sound coherent, and I wasn't sure if I was speaking of the early fall weather in Nevada or her. "Taking a bit of getting used to after so long in Idaho. Have you had time to visit your daughter?"

She laughed and even the laugh sounded younger.

"Yeah, she couldn't shut up about how much I'd changed." Her smile smoothed into something more thoughtful. "You know, hers may be the last generation to remember old people. Blows my fucking mind."

Daniel Gatling was waiting for us, though it took me nearly three seconds to recognize him. He'd apparently taken advantage of the retelomerization process as well, and his beard was free of grey, his skin smoothing out at the neck and forehead. Joon-Pah sat beside him, quietly conversing, and I was surprised the Heltan was down here. I hadn't seen hide nor hair of him on the news for weeks and figured he'd be busy upstairs helping refit the new ship. Of course, there were so many shuttle flights up and down every single day now, it wouldn't be too hard for him to sneak back down for the meeting.

We'd been told ten minutes so I expected to wait at least a half an hour for the President, but I'd underestimated either Crenshaw or the gravity of the situation, because he showed up almost immediately, before I could even finish greeting Gatling and Joon-Pah, without as much as an announcement or a Secret Service escort.

"Attention!" Olivera barked, coming to his feet, but Crenshaw waved it away impatiently and signaled for his National Security Advisor to close the door behind us.

I looked around the room. The President, Gatling, Joon-Pah, Thomas Caldwell, and us. No generals, no admirals, no Secretaries of State or Defense, no CIA. The hackles raised on the back of my neck. Something was up.

Crenshaw sat at the head of the table, fingers steepled together, tired and thoughtful.

"Ladies and gentlemen," he began, "I'm not going to bother telling you all what an incredible job you did, because we just spent a few weeks doing that." He eyed my medal. "Quite visibly and earnestly. You brought us hope and your timely arrival quashed what had the very real potential to be World War Three. What I am here to discuss is what comes next. And I can see in all your eyes, you're wondering why the people in this room are here and not someone higher-ranking or some Secretary or department head. You're here because you've been out there and seen it. I know I can trust you because you've proven it. Nothing said in here goes further than this room."

We all nodded. Again though, I thought he might have been looking at me a bit longer than the others.

"Before we begin, I need to ask you a question, Major Clanton. Are you in or out?"

"Sir?" I said, feeling inane but unprepared for the question.

"I understand you want to be a civilian again. If that's the case, I can arrange your separation immediately. I'd still like to keep you around as an advisor, but I'm certainly not going to force you to remain active duty military. I've been where you are." He tapped a finger beside his eye. "But I look at you, look at your record, and I can't help but think you'd be better utilized in the field."

"In the field as what, sir?" I asked. "I'm not a Ranger, I'm not a pilot or a Space Force tech. I was barely a company commander for a few months before I got out of the Marines, and now, I'm at a staff rank without a staff. This...." I pointed at the Medal of Honor around my neck. "...which I don't deserve, was awarded for actions I took leading a squad-sized element, and any one of those Delta operators is a better tactical commander than I am at any level. My only virtue was in being more familiar with the technology involved than they were at the time."

"What you are, Major," Crenshaw told me, "is mentally flexible, and you'd be surprised what a rare quality that is. Which is another reason you're all here and the Joint Chiefs are not. Colonel Olivera...." He smiled thinly. "Sorry, soon-to-be *General* Olivera wants you with him out there. He's made that very clear."

I looked at Olivera, my eyebrows shooting up.

"You're a pain in the ass jarhead," Olivera said, shrugging, "always calling shit port and starboard and bow and stern, but I like having you hanging at my shoulder on the bridge. You're like an oversized Jiminy Cricket."

"Not to mention," Crenshaw went on, "that Chief Warrant Officer Tremonti told me you're the only officer he'd want to follow into battle. You asked me what you'd be doing, and here's the idea I've kicked around, Andy. The Rangers are going to be our strike force, a hammer to any of our problems that look like nails, but I need someone there who can handle the problems that don't need a hammer, that need a scalpel. The Delta team is going back out and no, you aren't near qualified to lead a Delta team. But they're not going out there as hostage rescue specialists, or to retrieve high-value targets, they're out there to be our utility outfielders, people we plug in where we need them. And I want you to be their commander. So, are you in or out?"

Well shit. What could I say? The President of the United States wanted me in, Olivera wanted me in, Pops wanted me in. And even though I'd tried to tell myself I was done, I wanted me in. How the hell did I ever think I could go back to writing science fiction and making a living off of being a celebrity when the greatest challenge in human history was staring me in the face? It wasn't as if I had anything worth staying here for.

"I'm in, sir."

"Glad to hear it. Because our next operation isn't going to be with the Helta looking over our shoulder. It's going to be on our own ship, the USS *James Bowie*."

I looked up, my focus sharpening on him. He nodded, the corner of his mouth turning up.

"Congress approved it this morning. Hard for them to say no, given the Master Sergeant was the first American to die fighting aliens in another star system."

"She'll be ready within three months," Daniel Gatling added. "My people are modifying the crew quarters, controls, even the acceleration couches. And installing the new Impulse Gun and a few other surprises we thought up after reading your mission briefs."

"As to where you'll be going," the President went on, "well,

Joon-Pah has been busy while we've been refurbishing the ship." He nodded to the Heltan.

"I took the *Truthseeker* clear of your system and used the warp field to send a message to Helta Prime, our homeworld and the center of our Alliance. I told them what occurred at Fairhome, and how you were able to retrieve something positive out of yet another Tevynian incursion, how valuable you would be as allies." He looked around the table at us. "You must understand, not everyone feels as I do, as my faction does. Some think it is madness to seek aid from you, who are so like the Tevynians in appearance and temperament. But I believe the time is right to bring you to the Alliance leadership and see you and your people incorporated into our struggle. When you're ready, your ship will follow ours to Helta Prime."

"And hope they don't shoot us down," Olivera added.

"I'll drink to that," I said. "Figuratively, of course."

"Delia Strawbridge will be handling the diplomatic contingent," Baldwin put in, speaking for the first time since we'd entered, "and your team, Major Clanton, will be her personal bodyguard."

"You're going to be representing the whole of the human race," Crenshaw added. "Don't fuck it up."

I stood in my doorway, staring at the emptiness of a house full of expensive furniture and feeling a strange sense of gratitude that I didn't have any pets. I got the feeling I wasn't going to be back to Las Vegas much in the next few years and I would have hated to foist any wayward cats, dogs or fish off on the various acquaintances I had once called my friends.

The sun was setting across Sin City, gleaming off the buildings and setting the mountains on fire. I'd miss the sunsets here, but maybe I'd get to see other stars set on other planets, which seemed a worthwhile tradeoff. I'd turned on the air conditioning via my phone app on the drive from the airport, and I closed the door rather than continue, as my father had used to say, to refrigerate all the great outdoors.

I had a luxury this time, not like the last starflight I took. I had time to pack, to spend a few days back at my house and decide what I wanted to bring with me for however long we were gone.

What do you take when you might never come back?

My books and music and movies were all on my phone and tablet. I mean, I still had cases full of physical books, as every author does, but I wasn't about to try to pack them in the two duffle bags I was allowed.

Clothes? I'd pack maybe two sets of casual civilian clothes, but I'd be wearing a uniform almost all the time. What the hell else did I even have in the house? My gun safe? I was pretty confident the military would provide the weapons I'd need on the trip. My camping gear wouldn't be of much use. I suppose I could roll up some of the movie posters hanging on my walls if I wanted to decorate my compartment on the ship. I just wasn't a collector, wasn't someone who carried a lot of things around with me.

I walked into the kitchen and opened a cupboard, pulled out three family-sized bags of Sour Patch Kids and a case of Diet Coke. There. Finally, something I'd really need for the trip.

The doorbell rang. I frowned, thinking of all the people who might show up here unannounced, which included solicitors, religious proselytizers and the press and deciding none of them were welcome. It rang again. I cursed softly and pulled out my phone to check the camera.

Staring into the video pickup was a face I'd dreamed about and seen in nightmares, at once warm and heart-shaped, with blond hair as soft as the clouds and yet carrying the chill of a mountain pass in winter in her blue eyes and the stubborn set of a stone statue in her jaw.

It was Allie, my ex-wife.

I hesitated, still unsure whether to answer. Why would she come here? I hadn't seen her outside of a courtroom for four years.

Oh, fuck it. What's the worst thing she can do? Sue me? Where I'm going, I won't need the money anyway.

I pulled the door open. Allie stood there, still looking damned good in her designer blouse and $500 jeans and $900 shoes.

Beside her was Zack. I almost didn't recognize him. He'd shot up until he was nearly as tall as me, the once chubby and childish face thinned out now to a teenager's sharp edges, his brown hair shaggy and shoulder length.

"Hi," I said, helpless and nearly incoherent. "I, uh..."

"I was going to call," Allie said, "but I didn't know if you'd pick up."

"Hey Dad," Zack said, his voice deeper than I'd ever expected it to be. He seemed as awkward as I was. "I missed you."

And that was all I could take. I pulled him into a hug, barely able to keep myself from breaking down, thinking of all the missed time, how much of our life I'd pissed away.

"I saw you on the news," Allie explained. She smiled, an expression so full of sadness and pain and regret, I wondered how it could even qualify. "And I talked it over with Paul and...well, if you can keep your shit together long enough to save the world, we both thought we could trust you enough to be part of his life." She laughed. "We tried to reach you through the military and the family liaison told us you were going on two week's leave before you were going to have to take off again. So, I kind of...." She put a hand over her face, embarrassed. "I grabbed Zack and drove here from Austin and kind of, well...parked across the street and waited for you."

I let Zack go reluctantly, as if he might vanish into dust once he was free of my embrace. Allie handed him a bag.

"Mom and Paul said I could take a few days out of school," he said, sounding excited, whether about seeing me again or getting out of school, I wasn't sure. "If it's okay with you."

"It's more than okay," I assured him. "It's perfect." I turned to his mother and guilt warred with gratitude. "Allie, I've thought and said some pretty nasty things the last three years, and most of them were probably unfair to you. I was a mess, and I don't blame you for wanting out."

"We were both a mess. And I guess I wanted to blame it all on you because I didn't like what I was feeling about myself." Allie shook her head as if she were shaking the memories away. She waved back across the street, where a new model Tesla was parked by the sidewalk. "I'll be back to pick him up Friday."

I watched her go before I closed the door, looking at my son in amazement.

"What are we gonna do?" he asked me. "I've never been to Las Vegas before. Do I get to go to the casinos?"

I barked a laugh.

"Not for another seven years. But I have a garage full of camping equipment I haven't been able to use in months and I've been cooped up on a starship full of recycled air. What do you say we go head up to the mountains and do some hiking?"

"I don't know," he said, looking at me with skepticism in his dark eyes. "What's the cell phone reception like up there?"

"It's wonderful," I assured him. "There is none. Not a single bar."

As he tried to convince me how horrible that was going to be and how he'd told some girl named Kelley that he'd video chat with her every day, I couldn't help but grin like an idiot. There was one thing I could take with me on the *James Bowie*, luggage allowance be damned. A reason to come home again.

RESCUE MISSION

Next comes a bonus novel from Rick Partlow, *Rescue Mission.*

You'll discover what happened to Andy in Venezuela...and the outcome of an attempt to rescue a crew of Helta technicians from the Tevynians' clutches.

1

THE MID-MORNING SUN VAPORIZED MY SWEAT BEFORE IT had a chance to gain purchase on my skin. I was in a convection oven and I fought an urge to pull out my phone and check the date again, sure I'd lost track of time and it was actually mid-July instead of well into the fall months. The flap at the back of my fishing cap covered my neck, but any exposed skin sizzled, eating away at the sunscreen I'd applied only an hour ago.

"I can't believe how hot it is down here," Zack said, as if he were reading my thoughts. He paused on the sandstone-red trail to tighten the shoulder straps of his backpack. "Can we hike back up into the mountains again where it's cooler?"

I laughed softly.

"Just this morning, you were saying how you wanted to get back down to the campground so you could get cell coverage," I reminded him, "so you could video chat with that girl again."

"Yeah," he admitted, tilting his head down so the brim of his cap hid his eyes. "I dunno though, I think I'd rather take a chance of getting Kelley mad at me than hiking any more in this fu—" He broke the word off, looking up at me like a prairie dog at a circling hawk. "...this *freaking* heat," he finished.

"Glad you caught yourself," I told him, wiping off a fake drop of sweat. "I am unused to that sort of rough language and might have fainted dead away."

A snorting laugh from him sounded almost as if it struggled free against his will.

"Mom doesn't like me swearing," he confessed. "She makes me put money in a jar every time she hears me. She says it makes me sound dumb."

"It does." I shrugged, more a tilt of my head than anything with my shoulders because the pack was weighing them down. "It's easier than thinking of a more intelligent, creative thing to say. But it also frees your mind up for other things. That's why Marines are always swearing, because we've usually got more important things on our mind than coming up with creative things to say, like trying not to get shot."

"So, you don't mind if I cuss?" he asked, a sly, teenager-trying-to-slide-by smile on his face.

"I do not mind," I said, giving him my dad-isn't-as-stupid-as-you-think smirk, "as long as you're in a situation where your life is in danger and you're trying to free up brain cells. Other than that, I'm going to have to support your mother on this."

He sighed and seemed to sink under the weight of his pack again and I forced myself to appreciate the magnificent view of the sandstone hills giving way as we left the highlands behind and headed back toward the car. Though it wouldn't be the western Nevada scenery I'd remember from this trip so much as the first opportunity I'd been given to spend time with my son in years.

"I hope you had a good time," I said, wincing at the inanity of the statement even as it left my mouth. It was one of those things you said when you had no idea what else to say. "Despite the heat and the lack of signal."

"Yeah, it was fun. I haven't been backpacking since last year. Paul took me to Yosemite, but he was too busy this year."

For nearly a minute the only sound was the crunching of footsteps and the rustle of a welcome breeze, but I could sense words forming, pushing against a reticence born of the years we'd spent apart.

"Dad."

"Yeah?" I kept the reply casual, though I knew the question wasn't going to be a comfortable one.

"Mom and Paul said Venezuela messed you up. What happened there? Why were we in Venezuela, anyway?"

"Didn't they teach you that in school?" I wondered.

He rolled his eyes, somehow using his whole head in that way only a teenager can.

"Yeah," he said, "but you know how teachers are. Especially my AP US History teacher, Ms. Sorrentino. Paul says she's a huge bleeding-heart liberal."

I barked a laugh.

"She probably is. What did your mom think of Paul saying that?"

"Oh, he would never say that in front of Mom! He knows she'd argue politics with him for hours if he did."

Yeah, that sounded like the Allie I had known.

"Maybe it messed me up," I said, changing tack back to the subject, not wanting to criticize my ex-wife to our child. "Or maybe I was already messed up and the war just brought it to the surface. People tend to want to blame war for falling apart, but I've known a lot of guys who went through the same shit and didn't let it get to them."

"You said 'shit,' Dad," he pointed out.

"I did. Maybe because my brain was busy working on something else."

"Like what?"

"Like how to answer your question honestly." I tried to organize fifteen years of thoughts into something coherent. "Let me try to explain why we were there first. That's the easier part. Venezuela is an oil-rich country, which meant it was a *rich* country for a long time. And at one point, a socialist government took over. And at first, everyone was happy because having all that oil money meant the government could pretty much take care of everyone and have a lot left over. But then the government decided it wanted a bigger slice of the pie and nationalized the oil industry." I glanced at him, gauging his expression. "Do you know what that means?"

"I think?" he frowned.

"It means before, international oil companies owned the facilities and ran them with their own people and just paid taxes to the government. But afterward, the Venezuelan government took ownership of the drilling and the refining and put their own people in charge. And they found out there was a *reason* the people who ran the oil fields made lots and lots of money." Another shrug. "There were a lot of other factors, but the bottom line was, the economy started to go downhill. And then a lot of people who'd been okay with the president getting reelected with no opposition for all those years decided that wasn't okay anymore and they wanted the chance to vote for someone else."

"And I bet the guys in charge didn't want *that*."

"No, they did not. And they began to crack down on the opposition, and at the same time, the economy collapsed and the whole place was in chaos. The regime held on as long as it could, but eventually, they couldn't pay the army and at that point, there *was* no real government, just warring factions. And when you don't have a government, you have a big honking vacuum, and all kinds of stuff flows in to fill that. In this case, what came to fill it was terrorist groups of all shapes and sizes. The biggest and baddest was the People's Army of Venezuela, or the EPV."

"EPV sounds like a venereal disease."

"Doesn't it?" I agreed. "It's for *Ejercito Popular de Venezuela*."

"Do you speak Spanish, Dad?"

"Pretty much. I took it in high school and all four years of college, but I didn't *really* speak it fluently until after a few months in Venezuela. You gotta hear it every day, all day to really get it down. Anyway, the EPV pretty much took over Caracas and began killing everyone who tried to stand up against them, except for the Citizen's Militia."

"What's that in Spanish?"

"It wasn't anything, because the Citizen's Militia was a fictional creation of General Carlos Martijena, a former Air Force officer who had tried to overthrow the socialists and been forced into exile. The CM was designed by the CIA for consumption by the American press and public because we wanted a local face on the opposition. And maybe that's how we would have left it, funding the CM, running some covert ops off the books, maybe a few drone strikes...until Bayamon."

"You mean that bombing in Puerto Rico?" He had the excitement a kid gets when you mention something that they're familiar with. "I watched a video series about that in history."

"Yeah. Three hundred dead, a thousand wounded. After that, we weren't going to let the CM handle things for us anymore. And that's when we started putting boots on the ground. Including my boots. I was a Marine infantry platoon leader with about a year under my belt in the position and I should have been promoted to first lieutenant and slipped into a company XO slot in a few weeks, which was what your mom wanted because company XO's generally aren't leading rifle platoons on patrols in the middle of the worst parts of Caracas... but I wasn't going to be, because we didn't *need* any company XO's, we needed infantry platoon leaders."

"So, tell me what happened," he prompted, sounding like my first therapist. "What did you see there that fuck—" He bit off the end of the word, wincing. "that *messed* you up so much? Mom said you had nightmares and wouldn't stop drinking the times you came home on leave."

"She said that, did she?" I asked, trying to tamp down the festering anger. Allie had made the first move toward peace by letting me be part of Zack's life again, and getting pissed at her for past sins wouldn't help anything. "Well, I did have nightmares. Sometimes I still do. But you know, I don't think I have ever since the *Selenium*, when I met the aliens."

"Why's that?"

"Someone once told me the secret to not getting *messed* up by the things you see in war. I didn't listen to him back then, but now I think he was right." I chuckled. "Come to think of it, the day he told me that might have been the worst day I had in the whole damned war."

"Tell me the story."

I regarded him with a doubtful frown.

"I'm not sure that's a good idea, son."

"Why? You think I haven't heard worse?" His chin jutted out, red with a nascent sunburn, in a challenge to my adult reticence. "There's videos of that shit, dad. I've seen kids getting killed and dead bodies with their legs blown off and their guts hanging out."

"I know you have, Zack." And the knowledge dragged my shoulders down with a weight heavier than the pack. "I had, too, when I was your age." He squinted at me doubtfully and I shook my head. "Yeah, we had the internet back then, too. It's actually older than I am. But seeing a video doesn't tell you everything. It doesn't tell you what a rotting body smells like. It doesn't tell you about the cold that runs up your spine when you just know someone is aiming a gun at you but you can't see them. It doesn't tell you what it's like when a kid barely four or five years older than you are now, who trusts you to keep him safe and get him home dies ten feet from you and there's nothing you can do about it."

I hadn't meant to get so intense...or so defensive. Zack seemed a bit cowed and I sighed, closing my eyes for a second.

"I'm sorry," I told him. "I'll tell you what. One story. I'll tell you one story about Venezuela. Just one, but I won't hold anything back."

"Okay." He started walking again and I hurried to catch up. "One story. I want to hear the story about your worst day."

"Okay." I took a sip of water from the hose attached to my shoulder strap, running back to the bladder in my backpack, buying myself some time. "But to tell that story, I have to go back to the day before." I laughed. "Which wasn't that wonderful of a day either."

2

"Shouldn't we have them new ARV's by now?" Chamberlain whined.

The man whined incessantly. I wasn't sure he'd stopped since we'd landed in Caracas two months ago and I was beginning to wonder if he'd try to keep the streak alive for the whole nine-month deployment. I could have ditched him, could have asked Gunny Moore to find me another RTO. Hell, it wasn't as if the position was as vital as it used to be, anyway. The Radio Telephone Operator was an anachronism that the Marines had yet to shed. I had a satellite radio on my belt and I could contact anyone hands-free without using the Chamberlain or his bigger, bulkier backpack rig.

But theoretically, every platoon leader was supposed to have an RTO to put through calls for fire support, air support, dust-off, and all that other good stuff you have to radio for under fire, so he or she could direct fires and movement and basically do platoon leader stuff without being stuck on the radio. The position wasn't that important and that wasn't a bad thing because Chamberlain wasn't very good at it.

The downside was, I was stuck with him in my Stryker. And, as he said, it wasn't an ARV. I was about to tell him to stop whining, as futile as that might have been, when our corpsman saved me the trouble.

"The Armed Reconnaissance Vehicle," Hospitalman-3 Peterson droned, sounding like a tour operator at a theme park, "is being deployed in phases. We are not in phase one. The Marine Corps already divested itself of the LAV and the only alternative for our brigade would have been up-armored Humvees." Peterson speared Chamberlain with a glare. "Would you rather be patrolling the streets of Caracas in a fucking up-armored Humvee or a Stryker infantry carrier, Lance Corporal Chamberlain? Because I value my pale, hairy ass and I don't want to place the responsibility for its continued existence with a forty-year-old SUV that someone welded iron plates to and called it all good."

"But they're *Army*," Chamberlain moaned, and maybe I sympathized with that argument just a bit more.

I didn't want to argue with Chamberlain, not least because I had more important things I should have been concentrating on, but looking through the periscope at the streets of Caracas was too much like playing a video game, especially with the thermal filters on and everything glowing in fluorescent reds and yellows. I sighed, confident no one could hear it over the rumble of the giant tires on the rutted roads, and slapped the leg of the nominal vehicle commander, Sgt. Alvarez. He ducked down through the gunner's hatch and pulled up his goggles, a question in his dark eyes.

"Let me ride the gun for a few minutes," I shouted to him.

Alvarez seemed annoyed but he nodded because what else was he going to do? He could probably get away with telling a butterbar like me to go to hell if I told him to do something stupid or unreasonable, but this was neither, and it wasn't like I hadn't played vehicle commander in a Stryker before. We'd been stuck in the hand-me-down Army vehicles for a couple of months and we usually had more of the things than we had qualified vehicle commanders.

I took the comm cord from Alvarez and plugged it into the connection of my headset, mounted the platform and grabbed the gun mount for support. The wind slapped me across the face like a scorned lover, and I cursed myself for forgetting to pull my goggles on first. The ENVG-22 night vision goggles were awesome pieces of gear, like something out of science fiction, except for the big, awkward battery pack you had to wear strapped to the side of your helmet to power them. Still, barring some big breakthrough in battery life, it wasn't likely to get any better and we were lucky to have them. They'd been in development for three years and we were one of the first regular infantry units to field them, which I think had more to do with the fact that we were on rotation to run combat patrols in Caracas and the brass wanted some feedback from the line troops.

The 22's had thermal imaging built into them like the older 8's, but they also had some shit-hot computer software that even the periscopes on the Strykers lacked. Standing in the open hatch, the warm breeze of a summer night in Caracas not doing a damned thing to cool me down, I could have been looking out at the city at high noon. The thermal and infrared filters didn't turn everything to a pale green or light it up with the colors of its internal heat. Instead, the 22s meshed it all together with a state-of-the-art computer animation program that painted everything in perfect, shadowless detail.

It was unnatural, not the sense of a video game cut scene like with the periscope, but instead as if I had stepped into a Japanese animation version of hell. Think of the worst slum in the worst part of the worst city you've ever had the displeasure to visit, then multiply it by a hundred and you'd still be shy of the horror that was Caracas. Row houses slouched glumly, shoved together like refugees in a train car, some collapsing with the pressure. Blackened ruins interrupted the regular spacing, bad teeth in a rotting smile, and the people who lived in them were the lucky ones. They had a roof over their heads.

The streets were crowded with the others who lacked even a cracked and collapsing roof to call their own, the ones who huddled beneath the cover of whatever overhang they could find and tried to last the night. The beggars who would have thrown themselves in front of our short column of Strykers if they hadn't found out the hard way that we wouldn't stop for them. The prostitutes who would sell themselves for a half of an MRE and weren't worth that much, their dresses little more than rags hanging off skeletons. And worst of all were the children. They had hollow eyes and hollow faces, like they were already dead and didn't know it yet. If there'd been shadows, if there'd been darkness, it would have been bad enough, would have seemed like a nightmare. But it was as brightly lit as a carnival midway, every detail of every pockmarked cheek and tangled hair jumping out at me.

Cars lined the streets, ten or twenty or sometimes forty years old, patched together in multicolored quilts of metal, some rusted out in spots, covered in Bondo in others, yet none would move again. In a nation awash in oil, gasoline was impossible to get. The only ones driving were us, the Citizens' Militia and the EPV. Well, and the nominal Venezuelan Provisional Government that we'd supposedly put in charge of the country. *They* got whatever they wanted as long as they made the right noises to the press.

And yes, I *am* that cynical at twenty-five years old after just two months in Caracas, why do you ask?

"Bravo Four-One Actual, this is Bravo Six-Three, do you copy? Over."

Sgt. Alvin Gregory, First squad leader. He was in the lead

Stryker, just ahead of mine, and most of what I could see to our front was the ass-end of his vehicle. It was a very impressive ass-end, for all that I didn't like using Army hand-me-downs. As for Gregory's ass-end, I hadn't honestly noticed, but I assumed his wife liked it.

"This is Four-One Actual," I replied, touching the send button on my shoulder. "Good copy. Over."

"We got a roadblock ahead about a kilometer. Looks like a bunch of wrecked vehicles dragged into the middle of an intersection and we got some tires burning in the gaps between them. Over."

"Shit," I murmured but didn't transmit.

I scanned the street around us. No turn-offs, no alleyways. The last intersection had been a klick behind us and there was barely room for our column to fit through the disabled vehicles on either side, much less turn around. And suddenly, no people. The beggars, the wanderers, the prostitutes, even the kids had disappeared. Only vacant, boarded storefronts. This wasn't some random roadblock set up by the locals to shake down some money or food.

"Hold up here, Six-Three, over."

"Copy that. Out."

The end of his Stryker got a lot closer until my driver hit the brakes and I came against the trigger housing of the ancient M2 fifty-cal on the turret mount. I didn't let go of it, swiveling the barrel off to the left of the lead vehicle with one hand, then touching a control on my radio to switch frequencies.

"Bravo Four-Two, this is Bravo Four-One Actual, you copy?"

"Yeah, I copy like a son of a bitch," Moore growled. "This is a fucking ambush, L-T. Fucking over."

Moore wasn't just *a* Marine, he was what I imagined a Marine was when I'd been a fourteen-year-old.

"It is," I agreed. I agreed with Gunny Moore a lot, which was why he'd kept me around. "And they expect us to get bogged down in it right here, which means they have forces getting ready to cut us off from behind. Over."

"And unless these fuckers are different than any of the rest of these EPV assholes we've run into, that barricade is rigged with an IED. You got any ideas on how to avoid that? Over?"

"I have just one," I said, "and I don't know if the Captain would like it. Over."

"Then I'll probably be tickled pink. Don't let me stop you. Over."

"Hold your position then. And hold your ears. Out." I switched over to the driver. "Gomez, take us forward twenty meters. We're going to be driving through that shit in a second."

"Sir, there ain't no way we can drive through that. Even if the cars wasn't there, those tires would bog us down."

"Just get ready." Back to Gregory. "Six-Three, there's likely an IED in that shit ahead and an ambush waiting, and I'd like to spoil their timing. How'd you like to finally use that TOW missile launcher? Over."

"You serious, sir?" Gregory was a hardened veteran, one of the few NCOs in my platoon with prior combat experience, but he sounded like a kid in a candy store. None of us had gotten to live-fire a TOW missile out of the Strykers since we'd gotten them. "Over."

"Serious as a court-martial."

Using the magnification built into the scope mounted on the machine gun, I scanned the blockade. It seemed deserted, but that was an illusion. A pair of twenty-year-old Ford pickups formed the center hold of the thing, parked nose to nose, their tires flattened. Purposefully easy to clear. A temptation to just send a squad over to it and put the things in gear and push them out of the way by hand. But was the bomb in the pickups or in the tires? They were stacked four high, flames licking around them, black smoke pouring up into the night sky. Again, the barrier was small enough to make me want to send Marines to move them. And again, why I shouldn't.

I couldn't see anything to either side of the intersection, couldn't tell if there were a thousand troops on either of the connecting streets, or no one at all. And of course, I could be totally wrong about this. I could be about to waste thousands of dollars of Marine ordnance. I could and probably should launch a drone, but doing that would probably force their hand. I wanted this done on my schedule, not theirs.

"Aim for the engine compartment of the vehicle on your right," I told Gregory. We were still about three hundred meters from the intersection, which should be plenty far enough. I hoped. "When I give the word, fire that missile and hit the gas at my word. If you see a way through the roadblock, take it and don't stop unless I tell you to. We're charging through this and through whatever's on the other side of it. Target the thing and get ready. Out."

One more frequency switch, this one to the COP, Combat Outpost Morton, at the edge of town, ten klicks away.

"November One-Four, this is Bravo Four-One, do you copy? Over."

"I got you, Bravo Four-One. This is One-Four Bravo. What's up? Over." Not Captain Glenn, who would have been One-Four Alpha. This was First Lieutenant Fielding, the XO, the guy whose job I should have already had.

"I just hit a roadblock at Checkpoint Alpha on Route Fairbanks. Suspect IED and am about to attempt to circumvent. Over."

"Circumvent?" Fielding repeated. "Circumvent how? Over?"

"Loudly. Out." Back to Gregory. "Fire."

I wanted to see it, wanted to keep my head stuck out there like some tourist watching Old Faithful erupt, but training and common sense told me to duck down behind the shield of the machine gun. I ignored common sense. The Tube-launched, Optically-tracked, Wire-guided BGM-71 TOW missile has been around since the 1970s and, like the Browning M2 fifty-cal, it stays around because no one has designed anything as cheap, simple and effective, and because the US keeps fighting enemies who it works against. Plus, it was just really cool.

The missile was kicked out of the tube by an initial charge, a punch to the chest, then it seemed to hang there for a beat, just long enough to see it for a split second with your naked eye but you could really catch it if you watched a slow motion video. The main rocket engine ignited just as the back of the missile began to sag downward, whipping it forward, guided by a wire I could *almost* see in the enhanced optics of the night vision goggles.

I wondered if any of the EPV were watching nearby. I hoped they were. I hoped they were huddled right by the damned rear bumper of the truck and got to watch the big, black dot backlit by the rocket engine for just a single second before it hit the engine compartment.

One of two things could have happened when it hit. If I was wrong about there being an IED, or if I'd misjudged where it was hidden, the warhead would blow the shit out of the trashed Ford pickup and we'd have to go move the damned thing anyway.

The other thing happened.

Most IEDs are made from artillery shells, and how big of a bang they make is usually determined by how many shells the assholes managed to stuff into them. Looking back, I figured what they must have done was remove the engines of both pickups and just stuffed artillery shells under the hood, because when that missile hit, not only did it blow both of those trucks about thirty feet into the air, it also blew out the front walls of the stores on all four sides of the intersection and pushed Gregory's Stryker back three feet before the driver could hit the brakes.

The concussion hit me like a fist in the face and knocked off my goggles—would have ripped off my helmet if it hadn't been for the chin strap. I grabbed at the fifty for purchase, trying not to fall back into the vehicle like an idiot after claiming the gunner's position from the vehicle commander, which would have done more damage to my pride than to my body, given the amount of body armor and padding I was wearing.

I might have done some permanent damage to my hearing, though. A maddening, tinny whine drowned out the crackling of fires, the patter of debris and what was likely a chorus of interrogatives in my headphones, and I wondered if maybe I should have had the column back up just a *little* more before Gregory fired that TOW.

Black clouds drifted through the intersection, blinding us more effectively than any smoke grenade, glimpses of hellish red glinting through the haze from the small fires burning fiercely and bits of flaming debris, though the larger ones that would likely rage for hours in the surrounding buildings weren't yet visible. And I had to take a chance whether the blast had cleared the intersection, because sitting here in a line with buildings all around us, I might as well have hung a target on my neck.

"Six-Three," I yelled into my mic, barely hearing my own voice and hoping like hell he would. As an NCO and therefore, by definition, having more sense than me, he had likely been inside the vehicle when he fired the TOW. "Six-Three, this is Four-One. Advance. I say again, advance through the intersection and do *not* stop until the last vehicle is through. Do you copy? Over."

I *thought* heard him say that he copied, but whether he heard me or not, his Stryker started moving forward, trailing wisps of smoke where the heat of the blast had seared off a layer of paint. He disappeared into the roiling cloud and we rumbled after him while I tried to keep an eye on our surroundings, hoping if there were any EPV fighters inside the smoke, I would still spot them on thermal.

Since they were evil rather than stupid, there hadn't been any of them close enough to get killed in their own explosion, but they had to be watching. And they would have a backup plan to use, once they figured out that they hadn't taken us out with the bombs. I tried to radio the trail vehicles to make sure they were following, but Moore beat me to it.

"Sir, we got multiple vehicles coming up on our six about a half a klick back and closing. Technicals, three of them."

That meant commercial pickup trucks with crew-served weapons bolted to the beds, sometimes heavy machine guns, sometimes missile launchers, either of which could cause us some serious problems. We could take three of them. I could have the trailing vehicles traverse their turrets and take them out, but they knew that, too. Evil, not stupid.

"Forward, pedal to the floor," I said over the platoon frequency. "All Bravo drivers, full speed. Over."

We surged forward and I traversed the fifty to the left, following what felt like a gut instinct but was more likely a fifty-fifty guess.

"Contact left!" Gregory yelled, letting me know I had guessed correctly. "Technicals! Lots of technicals!"

3

Staff Sergeant Jim Gregory wasn't using proper radio etiquette, but I didn't think even Gunny Moore would give him shit for it at the moment. His warning came about two seconds ahead of the pickup trucks sliding into view, piercing the veil of smoke and catching sight of us about the same time I saw them on thermal. It was an Old West showdown at high noon except it was closer to midnight, and we were trying to outdraw each other with heavy machine guns.

The four pickups were all Toyotas. They were *always* Toyotas, no matter whether the terrorists were in Libya or Iraq or Venezuela, and I wondered if there was some sort of word-of-mouth advertising going on, like some big terror trade show held in a secret location every year talking about tips and tricks. The drivers and the gunners wore the universal trademark of the EPV, black balaclavas. I'd seen some of them sporting older-generation night vision, but not these guys. Their eyes were right out in the open, so I could see them get really wide when they saw the barrel of my M2 pointing their way.

There were few things in life I enjoyed more than firing a

fifty-cal at pop-up targets at the range, but I had not shot one at what Gunny Moore acerbically referred to as "reactive targets"—humans. Until now. The weapon shuddered in my hands, its cyclic rate so slow I thought I could have fired a semiauto faster, but we didn't use the thing for its rate of fire, we used it because a 360-grain tungsten penetrator did really nasty things to vehicles, equipment and the human body, sometimes all with the same shot.

We were at about two hundred meters and at that range, with the optical sights mounted to the gun, it was almost impossible to miss. I walked the burst up from the driver's seat to the gunner, coating the interior of the cab with a red mist before the next two rounds smacked into the receiver of the DShK heavy machine gun, an old, heavy piece of Russian metal that saved the little shit's life, for the moment. The truck fishtailed, driverless, and the gunner honored the miraculous intervention of Saint Dushka by leaping out of the bed of the pickup and hitting the pavement at about twenty miles an hour.

I hoped he at least got a nasty case of road rash from the fall, but I had more important things on my mind, like the 12.7mm slugs smacking into the armored Stryker only a few feet from my head. I didn't try to find the one who was shooting at me, because all of them were shooting now and getting rid of the next one was the most important thing in the world at the moment.

Brass cases as long as my hand whipped sideways through the air out of the receiver of the Browning, black metal links spinning off them to bounce off the surface of the Stryker's roof and skitter into a pile near the edge. Some of the casings would gather there as well. I'd seen them rolling across the roof after the gunner had cut loose with a few bursts at enemy positions, though we usually never saw whether we'd actually hit anything.

This time, I hit something. Three bullets right through the engine compartment of the next truck in line and it drifted forward, black smoke pouring from under the hood. I slewed the barrel upward, knowing the DShK was still dangerous even if the truck was disabled. Its muzzle flared and I swore as a slug sparked off the ring mount of the M2, but I didn't let go, clinging to the handles like they were the last life preserver on the *Titanic* and thumbing the butterfly triggers. This time, I didn't settle for Russian metal, putting three rounds into flesh.

The fifty-cal does nasty, nasty things to a person and I tried not to look too close, satisfied that what remained of the man tumbled out of the truck. I hunted for another target, but Gregory hadn't been sitting on his ass. The other two trucks were still rolling forward, guided by momentum, but no living hand was at the wheel and no one was shooting at us.

I swiveled the turret around to the right, my heart thumping like a snare drum inside my chest, the beat of my pulse in my ears drowning out the hollow whine. Nothing. Nothing to the front either. But there were those trucks in the rear.

"Four-One, this is Four-Two," Moore growled into my headset. "The technicals behind us are bugging out, pulling a suicide U-turn and heading back south. Over."

I should let them go. I knew it. It would be the safe thing, the thing that would get me in the least trouble with the captain, the colonel and everyone else in between. But they'd been specifically trying to kill me and my platoon and while I knew it was nothing personal, it sure *felt* personal.

"Six-Three," I said to Gregory. "Use the intersection. Pull a U-turn and head back the way we came. Out." Back to Moore. "We're turning around. We're going to chase these motherfuckers down. Over."

"You sure that's a good idea, sir? Over."

"No," I admitted. "But it's what we're going to do. Out."

I let go of the gun, suddenly conscious of the reality that I'd killed three people. Not dwelling on it, not panicking about it, just aware, the way I was aware it was night time and eighty degrees and humid as hell. I was tired. I was hot. I was sweating. I had killed three people. I wasn't sure if they were my first because we usually didn't even see what we were shooting at, but they were the first I'd seen die.

The Stryker began to turn, coming close enough to the burning buildings at the corners of the intersection for waves of heat to wash against my bare face, and we were turned around, heading back the way we'd come. The sorry bastards would run, and I had a feeling they'd run home. Unfortunately, they'd reach it a lot faster in the pickups than we could.

"Six-Three," I transmitted to Gregory, "launch a camera drone and follow these assholes." My lips peeled back from what might have been a smile but felt more like a rictus. "They wanted us and now they're going to get us."

"There they are," Chamberlain said, tapping the screen on his tablet with a stylus.

"Thanks Mr. RTO," Gunny Moore murmured, grabbing the display and holding it between the two of us. "I never would have recognized those Toyota pickup trucks with Russian Dushkas on their back if you hadn't pointed them out for me."

"It's my job, Gunny," the kid said, his tone plaintive, a sour expression on his face. "You'd get mad if I didn't do it."

"I would," Moore told him, arching an eyebrow in a way I knew could be dangerous, even if Chamberlain hadn't experienced it yet. "And I'm annoyed now, and neither is a good thing, so perhaps you should do your best to stay off *my* radar, Lance."

"Yes, Gunny." The kid was at least smart enough to slink off and go back to our Stryker. I would rather he have taken his M27 and gone out to guard the perimeter like the rest of the platoon, but away was good enough for now.

We'd pulled the Strykers into what I thought had once been a parking garage, though it was hard to tell with one wall down and the roof gone. The platoon was guarding the entrances except for me, Gunny Moore and the vehicle crews, and I kept glancing around at the inky blackness pouring into the place from outside, chasing phantom movement.

"This building is two klicks south of here," Moore said, reading the mapping overlay on the drone transmission. "Right in the heart of what our briefings all say is an EVP hotbed. The trucks parked at this side and the tangoes went into the northeast entrance here." He tapped at what looked like a side door to the crumbling apartment building. It was L-shaped, with a long alley between it and the one next door. "That was about five minutes ago, so they should still be inside."

He eyed me sidelong.

"Have you talked to higher about this?"

"I tried." I tapped the radio control at my shoulder. "It's not getting through. Chamberlain's rig couldn't, either. And you know what that means."

"Broad-spectrum jamming," he said, shaking his head, lip curled in disgust. "And there's only one place they could have gotten that kind of tech. Fucking Chinese."

"Every time Chamberlain tries to take the drone closer in, the control signal fritzes out." I gestured at the view, which was from an oblique angle. "This is a klick away and that's about as close as we can get. The camera is zoomed in pretty far." Which was obvious from the way the image shook violently with every gust of wind.

"What the fuck is that?" Moore demanded, pointing at movement in the alley between the buildings. It was a vehicle, about the same size as the Toyota pickups.

"Is it another technical?" I wondered, trying to zoom the view in more but only succeeding in making it fuzzier.

"No, it's an SUV. *Two* SUVs. See, the second one is parking behind the first."

Tiny figures swarmed out of the vehicles, what looked like six from each, and the computer recognition algorithms flashed red indicators, telling us they were carrying what it had decided were rifles.

"Great," I sighed. "More tangoes. We're going to have to pull back somewhere on the far side of this jamming and call in air support."

"I don't think so, sir," the Gunny mused, tapping a knuckle against the screen. "Look at the way they're moving. They're not coming home, they're moving tactically."

I frowned. He was right. The figures were spreading out from the vehicle, taking up watch positions around it, up and down the alley.

"Oh, shit," I murmured. "That's one of ours."

"Who the fuck would be way out here alone?" Moore snorted a humorless laugh. "Except our crazy asses, I mean."

"SEALs?" I shrugged. "MarSoc? Someone who thinks their shit don't stink. Problem is, they're heading into that same fucking building, Gunny, with one team and nothing heavier than a few suppressed rifles. They think everyone's going to be asleep, that no one is going to be ready for them. And we just chased, what? Six or seven armed tangoes? Right into their line of advance. And we can't even warn them because of the jamming."

"Oh, shit," he spat, realizing what I was saying.

"Get everyone mounted up," I told him. "We're rolling hot."

Was I scared? Hell yes, I was scared. The Strykers were good vehicles, for all that they'd originated with the damned Army, but the streets were narrow and if there likely wouldn't be IED's here in their home territory, there would be lookouts who might have spotted us already. They would have RPG's at a minimum, maybe even Russian Kornet crew-served anti-armor missiles. Hell, maybe even our own stuff from back when Venezuela had been an ally.

But when I tromped back up the ramp, I popped the hatch behind the gunner position and stuck my head out the top, resting my M27 across the roof. Alvarez grinned as he took back his fifty and I returned it, keeping the fear out of my expression. I *wanted* the gun. It was a totem, a shield, and a magic sword all rolled into one, and if it did nothing but make me a bigger target, well, it *felt* like it did something. I pulled the stock of my Heckler and Koch carbine into my shoulder and whispered a prayer of thanks to the military procurement gods that we weren't still using M4's like when I'd enlisted out of high school. Two years with the direct impingement weapon was enough to convince me I hated it, and when I'd come back to active duty after four years of college and the reserves, they'd handed me the piston-driven HK M27 and I'd fallen in love.

Now if they'd just get around to issuing us the 6.8mm versions instead of this wussy 5.56, I might actually feel adequately armed with just a carbine.

"Six-Three, this is Four-One. Take point. We're heading southwest into the alley where the SUV's are parked. It's marked on your mapping software. And haul ass. The only thing slow and cautious will get us is more time for one of these assholes to call out all his buddies and their rocket launchers. Over."

"Ooh-rah, Four-One! Over."

The engines of the Strykers were obscenely loud in the quiet night, and I knew someone was going to hear us. The ancient, battered apartment buildings and rowhouses stared down at us in forlorn silence, lightless and lifeless, but not unoccupied. They held eyes, maybe electronic, definitely human, kids charged with being the lookouts for the EPV, paid in food or drugs they could sell to get food. They'd have AK's and maybe be stupid enough to try to use them, but the most dangerous weapons they'd have would be hardline comms, impossible to jam, run underground so we couldn't find them and cut them.

A mile and change, maybe four minutes if we didn't hit a snag. One minute in, someone shot at me.

The crack of the rifle was high and spiteful, the whine of bullets off metal petulant, the attack more a teenage temper tantrum than any real threat, but Gregory took it as one. The full-throated roar of his M2 was an adult yelling at those damned kids to get off his lawn, the slugs turning mortar and cement into powder and fragments on either side of the window where his weapon sights had seen the muzzle flash, their software showing him where to shoot. That was new, barely beating us into service in Venezuela and it didn't always work. When there were a lot of lights and very little contrast, it couldn't pick out a target. But in a situation like this, it was gold, and if whoever had taken the potshot wasn't dead or wounded, they were in no mood to stick their head out of what was left of that window.

The downside, of course, was that everyone *else's* heads were sticking out of their windows.

"Faster, Six-Three," I snapped, sweeping the muzzle of my M27 from one window to the next, searching for weapons. "Go fucking faster. Over."

He didn't reply, likely because he couldn't hear me. We were well into the jamming now. I switched to the wired intercom and yelled at my own driver instead.

"Get up on Six-Three's ass, Gomez. Maybe honk your horn and flash your brights at the son of a bitch until he speeds up or pulls over."

"Phillips can't drive for shit," Gomez commented, his words punctuated by the engine revving, closing the distance between us and Gregory's vehicle to less than twenty feet.

I don't know if Phillips, the driver, saw us in his rearview camera or Sgt. Gregory did, but the lead Stryker sped up and opened another twenty yards, just in time to hit the brakes again and cut a sharp, right turn into the alley between our target and the abandoned, burned-out building next door.

They fucking saw us now. Heads popped out of windows and dark-clothed figures ran out of doors. They carried AK-103's, the most prolific weapon among the EPV's, twenty years old and imported from Russia by the old regime, the one that had run the country into the ground and then had the poor grace to not stick around for the inevitable civil war. The weapons were basically the same AK-47's that had been around since just after World War Two, copies of the German StG-44, polished and made cheaper and easier to produce and used for the last fifty years by just about every evil son of a bitch who ever thought that they were doing what God would have done if only He'd been aware of the facts of the matter. It was the one thing they all had in common, the Avtomat Kalashnikov, the peasant's weapon, reliable and durable and if it wasn't accurate, well, to quote Joseph Stalin, quantity has a quality all its own.

I'd gotten very accustomed to the bark of the 7.62x39 cartridge in the last two months, though I'd first heard it as a PFC on a deployment at the border when the cartels had gotten frisky. It had been distant then, a defiant spit at our feet from across the border and across the desert. This was a knife in the dark instead, way too up close and personal. I put the red reticle of my M27's optical sight over the sunken chest of a slender young man firing an AK from the hip and pressed, not pulled, with the pad, not the joint, just the way they'd taught me in Boot Camp seven years and a lifetime ago. There was next to no recoil, not with 5.56. I'd shot the 6.8 and that thing had a kick to it.

The skinny kid didn't fly backwards the way people did in the movies when they got shot. He lowered his rifle and stumbled a step, like he'd realized something had happened, something hurt, but he wasn't quite sure how bad it was. Then the fifty from the lead Stryker turned him and everyone standing with him into hamburger, their blood neon red in the artificial, computer-enhanced light of my goggles. Anime hell.

I tried not to stare at the sight as we drove by, but I did anyway. It had caught my attention and wouldn't let go and a tinge of nausea tugged at the bile in my throat.

M2 machine guns slammed a sledgehammer into the concrete behind me while M27s barked around the edges, like a yappy little Chihuahua standing behind a Rottweiler and pretending to be tough. I wish I could have heard what they were targeting, but we had no comms and we had no time. In seconds, we were even with the SUVs, a pair of pristine, late-model Range Rovers and a handlebar mustache stepped out from behind one to meet us, attached to a deadly scowl and the red eyes of night vision goggles.

The man was tall and lean and wearing tactical gear over a beat-up tiger-stripe BDU top and blue jeans and I knew immediately what he was. Not that I was some seasoned expert on all aspects of the military, but everyone had seen these guys around, usually from a distance. When General Baldwin stopped by to visit the troops, you'd see these guys, dressed in odd combinations of military gear and civilian clothes, their hair shaggy, bearded or mustached, wearing shades and carrying chopped-down SIG M68's in 6.8mm with suppressors at the end. Or sometimes when we drove by the CIA compound in the FOB, they were there, talking to the field officers.

I knew SEALs, and these guys weren't SEALs. Not even DevGru looked like these guys. These dudes were older, more chill, less tightly wound. They were Delta. Delta Force, Combat Applications Group, •First Special Forces Operations Detachment Delta, whatever you wanted to call it, they were the OG doorkickers. And this one looked like he wanted to kick me in the teeth.

"Who's in charge?" he asked, a slight twang in his voice that could have been Texas or thereabouts. "Who the fuck is in charge of this clusterfuck?"

Yikes. I was almost level with him, looking down from the rear hatch, my M27 trained back the way we'd come, off to the side so I wasn't sweeping my own vehicles.

"I am." My voice did *not* break. I was very proud of that. "Listen..."

"Do you know how many weeks we've been planning this shit?" he snapped, waving at the others in his team, who were blending in with shadows I couldn't see through my enhanced optics. "We had an HVT in there! *Had*! He's probably halfway to Maracaibo by now thanks to you fucking Marines! What the fuck do you—"

"Shut up," I snapped, slamming my palm against the roof of the Stryker.

His eyes went wide, the corner of his mouth twisting into the beginnings of a snarl. Where I got the balls to say that to a Delta operator, I have no idea, but this guy was reminding me of every asshole who'd ever dressed me down and the annoyance together with the gathering fear of standing around here worked a testicular miracle. Which wasn't going to save me from getting my ass kicked, so I talked fast.

"These fuckers tried to ambush us on Route Fairbanks five klicks northeast of here. We trashed their IED and chased them back here. Everyone inside was going to be awake and waiting for you, so your op is fucked. I saw you on a long-range drone feed, which is the only view we had because they have a shitload of broad-spectrum jamming coming out of those fucking dishes." I pointed at the roof, where transmission dishes sprouted like flowers off a vine. "And I could have just left your ass to deal with all those fuckers by yourselves and un-assed the area to call for help outside the jamming." I waved a hand at my platoon convoy. "I can still do that if you like. Or you can get in those pretty Land Rovers and use us for cover to get the hell out of here. You're the snake-eater, you tell me."

The man squinted up at me, not shaken by the gunfire echoing off the walls around us, seemingly not offended by my tirade, just smiling crookedly. He obviously found the whole thing funny as hell.

"Are you fucking sure you're a second lieutenant?" he asked, nodding at the rank on the Velcro tab on my tactical vest.

"Lt. Andrew Clanton, Fourth Battalion, First Platoon," I rattled off automatically. "My friends call me Andy. We're out of COP Morton. And I'd dearly love to get back there ASAP."

A round spanged off the side of the Stryker, a fragment of the bullet smacking me in the shoulder, embedding itself in my vest. I cursed and fired at a side door across the street in the supposedly abandoned building. A squad full of EPV were charging out of it and I caught the first one with a burst to the chest, but the next one out was carrying an RPG and the guy in front just wasn't falling out of the way fast enough.

The round flew so close by my head that the heat from the rocket exhaust singed my neck, travelling about two feet over the Delta team and slamming into a staircase. The explosion dumped me back down the hatch and I held myself up with a hand against the bulkhead, my ears ringing again, head swimming from the concussion. I looked down at myself, expecting to see blood, but I didn't see any frag wounds.

Alvarez had ridden the storm out and the vibration from his fifty firing vibrated through the skin of the Stryker, in chorus with Sgt. Gregory's gun. I climbed back up and wondered if the guy I'd been talking to would be dead.

He was still standing there, the suppressor at the end of his

6.8mm carbine glowing red from the burst he'd just fired. Smoke poured from the doorway into the back corridor. The door had been blown inward by the explosion and I suppose most of the fragmentation had been contained inside. The Delta operator cocked his head toward me.

"All right, Andy," he said as if our conversation hadn't been interrupted by an RPG. "I think I'll take you up on that offer. He whistled sharply and spun his finger in a circle, looking back over his shoulder at the others.

"Mount up boys, show's over."

The rest of them moved smoothly, with rehearsed precision, eeling out of the shadows back into the seats of the SUV's. The big man with the mustache turned to join them, but paused.

"By the way," he told me, "I'm James Bowie. But my friends call me Jambo."

Of course they did.

4

"Wait," Zack said, stopping in his tracks, despite the fact that we were in sight of the parking lot and my Bronco was in view, full of shade and air conditioning and a cooler with iced Diet Cokes. "That was *the* James Bowie? The guy who died out in space, your friend? The guy who got the Medal of Honor?"

"He was my friend," I confirmed, smiling despite the sudden stab of pain in my gut. It hadn't been that long. "And there was only one James Bowie."

"So what happened then?" he prompted. "Was that it? Did you see him again? I mean before the *Selenium*?"

"Well..." I began but a persistent beeping interrupted my continuation of the tale. I scowled, ripping at the Velcro fastenings of a pouch on the belt of my backpack. "Damn it."

"I thought there was no cell signal up here," he said, frowning deeply, no doubt suspecting I'd lied to him about the cell reception.

"There isn't," I promised. "This isn't a cell phone."

It wasn't. It picked up cell signals, too, but also laser-line-of-sight, satellite, shortwave, just about everything. And it was partially based on Helta technology. We called them comm units and while I had felt pretty confident leaving my cell phone in the car, I'd been obliged to bring the comm unit along.

I pulled the earpiece out of its niche in the side of the device and wiggled it into place before I pushed the button on the side of the device.

"Clanton," I answered. It was not how I usually answered the phone. I knew guys who answered the phone like that and I always thought they were douchebags. But there was a protocol to answering the comm unit.

"Sorry to interrupt your leave, Andy." It was General Olivera. I didn't have to look at the caller ID to know his voice. "There's a situation. We need you back at Alpha."

Shit. I wanted to be annoyed, but I knew exactly how useless that would be.

"Yes, sir," I said. "But I'm with my son and I'll have to drop him back in Austin first."

Zack looked at me open-mouthed, as if I was betraying him and I winced.

"Understood." Well, he might have understood, but he didn't sound too happy about it. "Can he travel alone?"

Now I *did* get annoyed.

"Not if I ever want his mother to let me see him again," I growled. This might have been life or death, end of the world and all that shit, but Zack was my son.

Olivera sighed, as if all this human connection shit was such a burden for him.

"Fine. We'll send a Gulfstream out to McCarran. It can take you to Austin, then back to the Alpha Site in maybe three or four hours."

"Copy that," I said. "We're heading back to Vegas now."

I glanced over at Zack, who still looked hurt.

"I have to go?" he asked. "I thought we had a couple more days!"

"It's apparently an emergency." I gestured with the comm unit before I put it back in its pouch. "That was General Olivera and they need me back at our base in Idaho ASAP." I grinned. "But I did get us both a ride in a private Gulfstream. Paul ever get you guys a ride on a private jet?"

"Yeah, one time," he said, then he seemed to understand he was one-upping me. "But we had to share it with this friend of his and his whole family," he went on hurriedly, "so it wasn't just the three of us."

"Nice save," I told him, nudging his arm. "Come on, we'll stop and get some lunch on the way."

"But what if it's urgent?" he asked, quickening his pace toward the car.

"If it was really urgent," I assured him, "they'd have sent a shuttle."

Now, *that* would have impressed him.

Staging Base Alpha was, for once, beautiful.

In the summer, it was sweltering, in the winter, frostbite-cold. But there was a brief period in spring and again in the fall when the weather was perfect. And in the fall, just after the leaves turned, I could convince myself that this part of Idaho was the most beautiful place in the world.

Until I saw the base. Military bases are never beautiful, at least not since they closed down the Presidio, well before I was born. They share a utilitarian ugliness, built by the lowest bidder on the public dollar by a bureaucracy that cares a lot more about funneling money back to the constituencies of the congresscritters who vote for overly complicated weapons systems than they do about providing comfort to the men and women who have to use them.

"Need any help with your luggage, sir?" the corporal who'd driven me from the airfield down to the base asked, the look on his face bright and hopeful, like a man waiting for a tip. Since I knew he didn't actually expect me to slip him a few bucks, I had to think he was actually hoping I'd say no.

"Naw, I got it, thanks."

The two duffel bags had been mostly packed before I'd left with Zack to go camping and I'd taken the time to swing by my place and pick them up before heading to the airport because I didn't know how long this "emergency" was going to keep me tied up and I couldn't see going weeks without a stash of Diet Cokes and Sour Patch kids. I slung them over opposite shoulders and waddled into the admin building, flashing my ID at the clerk manning the front desk. He barely looked up, with the universal assumption that if I'd made it this far, I must belong here, as if he'd already forgotten the Russian mercenaries who had invaded the base not that long ago. Or maybe he just knew me. It wasn't as if I was anonymous, not after the *Selenium* and the Medal of Honor ceremony, which had been internationally televised.

The conference room was straight down the main hallway, and I didn't need to ask to know that was where the general was waiting for me. He'd messaged me about twenty times while I was in flight from Austin, telling me where I should go once I landed and asking repeatedly why I was taking so long. He *could* have just told me what the whole thing was about via message and skipped the meeting, but that wasn't something generals did, because then people wouldn't get to see how important they were and how vital their jobs were.

Olivera was standing at the center of the room, arms folded when I entered as if he knew exactly when I would get there. Which he probably did, thanks to the tracker in my comm unit. I'd expected him, and I guess I should have expected Dani Brooks. The Ranger colonel was sitting, relaxed, not caring about making me feel like I was a shitbag for being late, which was remarkably chill for both a Ranger and a colonel.

I had *not* expected Joon-Pah. As far as I knew, he was on his way back to Helta space to bring back some technicians to help out our modernization process and the last I heard, he was supposed to be gone for weeks. He was dressed in the typical Helta Napoleonic artillery officer uniform and Brooks and Olivera were in combat utilities and I was acutely aware that I was the only in the room wearing civilian clothes.

"Greetings, Andy Clanton," he said, offering me a hand in the human way. He was technically a Helta ship captain, a military officer, but at times, I thought he was more a diplomat than anything else. "I grieve to be the cause of you losing time with your child."

"That's okay," I told him, even though it wasn't. I let the duffle bags slide off my shoulders and dropped them inside the door before I shook his hand. "But I didn't think you'd be back this soon. What's wrong?"

"Murphy strikes again," Dani Brooks explained, still sprawled in her seat. From her tone and her body language, I had the impression she'd been on base for hours, maybe even days, and wasn't feeling particularly patient about waiting to fill me in.

"Captain Joon-Pah," General Olivera cut in, probably not pleased at the conversation beginning without him, "was supposed to travel to Helta Prime to procure a crew of shipwrights to aid us in building cruisers around the hyperdrives you and Master Sergeant Bowie retrieved from the Helta shipyards."

"Shipwrights?" I repeated, raising an eyebrow. "That's what they call them?"

"It's the nearest translation to English," Joon-Pah said, settling into what I'd come to understand was a resting stance for the Helta, feet canted outward, hands clasped in front of him. "If I called them engineers or technicians, it would not adequately convey the intricacy and complexity of their vocation. To craft a starship requires years of education in hyperdimensional physics, years more of technical training and nearly twice those years as an apprentice. Even then, the shipwrights are constantly experimenting, refining their techniques. A master shipwright is rare and invaluable, and the Tevynians know this. Whenever they capture one of our colonies or shipyards, the first thing they do is check every prisoner to see if they have found a master shipwright."

"But you had one who would work with us?" I assumed. "One who wouldn't blab to your government until you got the chance to bring us in and let us meet with them?"

"He *did*," Olivera snapped, thumping his fist against the hardwood tabletop. "Until, as Colonel Brooks put it, Murphy stepped in."

"We translated out of hyperspace at the last outpost world from Helta Prime," Joon-Pah related, "and I received a coded transmission left at what you would call a dead drop from Master Shipwright Shaylon-Kao. He was reassigned by the Prime Facilitator to the great shipyards in our asteroid belt. Trying to move him out now would raise too many questions."

"Well, shit," I sighed, leaning against the table.

We needed those ships. The Tevynians had a whole fleet and if they came after us before the Helta decided to accept us into their alliance, just the one cruiser wasn't going to save us.

"There is, however, another possibility," Joon-Pah went on. He knew by now how to inflect his English for the desired emotional effect, and the impression I got from him was of someone who was trying to tell a good news/bad news joke. "There is a well-respected Senior Journeyman Shipwright named Fen-Sooyan who was travelling with his crew to his final assignment before attaining the rank of Master. The final assignment was to be at Waypoint."

"Well, that was a bust." I didn't quite laugh, though God knows I've laughed at darker things. Waypoint's shipyards were where we had acquired the *James Bowie*, our one complete cruiser, as well as the three hyperdrives. The Tevynians had been defeated there, but I was pretty sure that shipyard wouldn't be building anything for a while. "Where did they send him instead?"

"That's just it," Olivera broke in, constitutionally unable to remain silent despite his Miranda rights. "They sent him to Waypoint and his ship made a stop at the planet first before they headed to the drydocks. And then the fucking Tevynians invaded."

"Did he get out with the civilians who evacuated before the invasion?" I asked. It might be tricky to extract him from the middle of a bunch of refugees on some outpost without revealing who we were, but not impossible.

"Unfortunately, no," Joon-Pah shot the idea down. "We have scoured the list of evacuees who managed to escape before the invasion and his name was not among them."

"Then what's the point of talking about him?" I wondered. "The Tevynians control that world."

"They do," Brooks said, turning her hand over in counterpoint, "and yet they don't. Not *really*."

I pulled a chair out from the table and dropped into it.

"Obviously, you all know something I don't. Has there been a group decision made to punish me for actually having a life or is someone going to tell me why I'm here?"

And yeah, they were both my superior officers, and no, I didn't care.

Joon-Pah saved the day by actually answering my question.

"We have been monitoring the situation at Waypoint since the battle there," he explained. "We launched sensor-shielded drones toward the planet and had them send back burst transmissions before they self-destructed. Once the shipyards were damaged and all the usable hyperdrives taken along with your cruiser, the Tevynians repurposed their forces there, sent most of them to support other missions. They still occupy the planet, of course. They constructed a military base outside the city, and they've left behind fighters and orbital weapons platforms, but their cruisers are gone."

"If we hit them now," Olivera said, his smile feral, like a stalking wolf, "with the *Jambo* and the *Truthseeker*, before they reinforce what they have, we could get in there and rescue this Fen-Sooyan and his crew, get them out before the Tevynians know what's happening."

"And by now," I said, leaning forward, hands flat on the table, "you mean like *now*, don't you?"

"Your briefing package has been messaged to your comm unit and your team is waiting in their arming bay." He motioned at the door. "Shuttles launch in three hours."

Those damned duffle bags got heavier every minute I carried them, and despite the relatively cool autumn temperatures, I was sweating two minutes into the walk from the admin building to the barracks the Delta team occupied when we were at the staging base. I skipped the front door since I wouldn't be using either my barracks room or my office, and jogged around to the rear of the building, to a heavy, metal double door usually secured with a biometric lock.

At the moment, it was wide open, with equipment scattered on the pavement outside and crates of ammo and batteries already loaded onto pallets, waiting for a forklift to come and take them to the shuttle. The team was half in and half out of the arming bay, helping each other strap into their Svalinn powered armor. We'd wear it onto the shuttle, because previous experience had shown us that it was too big of a pain in the ass to ship it up separately and then try to yank it out of the cargo bay after it had been offloaded. It took useless, futile hours and since I was in charge and I wasn't an idiot, I'd changed the policy, which had been implemented without asking me so I didn't ask if I could change it.

Colonel Brooks had changed the procedure for her Ranger company as well, though I think she had gone through the trouble of getting permission, which was ever so much more complicated than just begging forgiveness.

"Hey, sir," Pops said, nodding. He had his suit on and squared away, except for the helmet, which he carried tucked under his left arm. "They catch you on your vacation?"

Chief Warrant Officer Mark Tremonti was older than me, which was quite an accomplishment for a man who'd called Delta Force his home for over a decade and had hardly lived a staid, sedate life before that. Deep lines were etched into a face the color of old teak, though perhaps not as deep as they once were. Like the rest of us, Pops had taken part in the retelomerization treatment the Helta had developed in conjunction with our medical researchers, and I'd been told it would begin to make us all look younger as the changes in our DNA had time to make their way outward as cells died and were replaced.

Would he still be "Pops" when he looked twenty-five years old again? Would people take colonels and generals seriously when they looked the same age as captains and first lieutenants? Those were questions I doubted anyone else had bothered to ask before they'd foisted longevity and restored youth upon us, but I was a science fiction writer by trade, or I had been before reality had caught up with science fiction a few months ago.

"Yeah," I said, dumping my bags on the ground beside the door and stepping into the bay, intent on grabbing my own armor and weapons. "Bastards couldn't even let me go the full two weeks before they snatched me back up."

I did a quick headcount.

"We got everybody?"

"Now that you're here. You know the op?"

"I got a three minute summary and probably know as much about the op as you do from the briefing package. We're going back to the place we just came from to do a snatch-and-grab on some assets we could have gotten while we were there last time, and we're hoping the enemy has the good grace to not fight us too hard."

"Damn," Pops said, nodding in appreciation. "That may be the most succinct summary of an op I've ever heard."

"Well, I am a writer," I said, shrugging. I waved at my Svalinn suit, resting in a cradle marked with my name in magic marker on a strip of masking tape. Very high tech. "Wanna help me get this shit on?"

I nodded to some of the other team members. I couldn't always remember their real names, but their nicknames, I knew. Dog, Ginger, Gus, Rodent, Cowboy, Quaker, Bubba, Chuck, Swag, Frank—which was short for Frankenstein because the guy was nearly seven feet tall and looked as if he should have bolts sticking out of his neck, and Pops. There'd been a twelfth, Jambo, and I was the thirteenth warrior, the outsider pulled in because they needed somewhere to stick me. Now, I was one of the twelve. Maybe.

Pops was behind me, checking the gaskets on the torso plates of the Svalinn and everyone else had moved on outside.

"I'm a bit nervous about this shit," I admitted.

"Can't be any worse than what we saw on the shipyards," he said, shrugging. He adjusted my neck yoke. "Is that too tight?"

"No. And that's not what I mean. This is going to be my first time leading the team without Jambo."

I couldn't see his face, just felt him yanking at the straps holding the hard-plates onto the exoskeleton around my left arm.

"It's our first time without him, too, don't forget that. We'll all have to adjust," he said.

"I know that. But every one of you has been through Ranger School, SFAS, Q School, Delta Selection and Assessment and all the training that comes after that, and I was just a fucking Marine rifle platoon leader."

He stepped out from behind me, the corner of his lip curled up in amusement.

"Andy," he said, "in all those fucking training courses and schools, exactly how much do you think the curriculum included aliens, powered armor, starships, fighting in a vacuum in zero gee..."

"It's more accurately called free-fall if you're in orbit," I corrected him automatically, remembering a bad review from my fist book, "or microgravity if you're not."

"Ex-fucking-zactly." He slapped my shoulder hard enough to push me back a step. "You think any of us would have known that unless you and Jambo taught us? Hell, the two of you are the ones who created most of the training we've done. All that shit you were talking about, you know what it's for? It's to weed out the pretenders, the wannabes, the ones who aren't qualified. It's to give us an excuse to keep them out of Delta, the ones who just don't belong, to make them prove themselves. You...." He tapped a finger against my chest, metal clicking against metal. "...have already proven yourself. They don't give The Medal to wannabes or pretenders. Every one of us saw what you did at the shipyards at Waypoint. And we all know what you did against the Russian mercs who tried to infiltrate this base. No one here has any doubts about how you'll do in combat. Trust me."

"Thanks, Pops." I nodded. "I guess I just wish Jambo was here."

"We all do. We were his family." Pops shrugged. "Even if you did know him longer than any of us."

I'd never had the time to finish that story for Zack.

5

The TOC—Tactical Operations Center—at Combat Outpost Morton wasn't high tech or high speed or pretty much high anything. It was a laminated map tacked up to the wall, a sand table and a bank of radios, along with an overworked, overtired RTO manning them. *Crewing* them, I should say, because in this case, the RTO was Lance Corporal Clarice Molina.

Molina smiled wanly at me when I entered through the blackout curtains.

"Morning, sir," she said. "I hear you had some fun last night."

"Only if you consider ordering a TOW missile fired at an IED and watching a whole city block explode, Molina," I said, trying to appear stern and by the book. It didn't work. A snicker busted through and spoiled the whole thing. "Hell yes, I had fun. The skipper around?"

"He's in his office," she said, jerking a thumb behind her at another curtain.

I knocked on the wooden frame.

"Come."

I pushed aside the curtain and found Captain Glenn sitting

behind his desk, which is what he insisted on calling the plastic table where he set his laptop. He squatted on a folding, three-legged stool behind it, his boot soles flat on the ground, making sure his oversized bulk didn't tip over. Brian Glenn was a big man, six-three, 220. He had played defensive end at the Naval Academy and still looked it. He could have been drafted into the pros, he had assured me more than once, if he hadn't blown out his ACL in the first game of his senior year.

"You sent for me, sir?" It wasn't a question, really. He *had* sent for me. But it sounded politer than what the hell do you want.

"Come in," he waved at me. "Close the door."

I didn't sigh in exasperation, but it was a battle. The "office" was about the size of a linen closet, which meant there was barely room for Glenn, much less me. And I wasn't a small man. And the door was a fucking curtain that wouldn't hold in or keep out any sound, so if privacy was a concern, the whole thing was pointless.

But then, so was Captain Glenn in many ways. Oh, he wasn't a coward or a martinet or a micromanager, so I considered myself lucky in those respects. And he wasn't *stupid*, not really. He was just...dull. In every sense of the word.

"Yes, sir?" I asked, after I'd gone through the motions of pulling the curtain shut.

Inside the windowless alcove, the only light came from a battery-powered lantern sitting on the upturned base of a spent 155mm artillery shell, and the shadows it threw cast a false malevolence over Glenn's squared off features. In reality, he wasn't interesting enough to be evil.

"What do you know about that special operations team you encountered last night?"

Again, I resisted a sigh. We'd gone through all this last night. Or should I say, early this morning.

"They have shitty taste in sport utility vehicles," I said, unable to resist at least one smart remark. "Aside from that, the guy in charge said his name was James Bowie and they were wearing civvie clothes and carrying M68's, among other things. The SIG's probably mean they're Army, and the clothes and facial hair tells me they're probably Delta."

Glenn grunted, eyes focused on the black curtain that served as a door as if he were watching a slide show projected on it. When he looked back at me, his face was twisted into a deep frown.

"Is something wrong, sir?" I wondered, slipping unconsciously into parade rest in case a dressing down was coming. "Did he complain about us blowing his op? Because there was no way we could have known he was running one in that area."

"He's here," Glenn said, cutting me off.

"Sir?"

"Your James Bowie character," he amended. "He's here. He drove up an hour ago, while you were racked out. He wants to see you." Glenn shrugged. "He wouldn't tell me anything else until you showed up, so I made him wait outside the wire."

I laughed. Glenn might have been uninteresting and unimaginative, but he was as stubborn as a case of the clap. He didn't share the laugh.

"I don't like this, Andy," he said. "Guys like this showing up, it's never a good thing. Like those SEAL pricks who dragged Third Platoon out on that interdiction."

I nodded agreement. Lt. Campos had been a good guy. And the SEALs hadn't even bothered to come back to the COP after to tell us they were sorry he'd bought it.

"I think I've kept him waiting about as long as I can." He stood, the folding stool tipping over backward without his weight to hold it in place on the uneven plank floor. "I'll have Top bring him in."

Jambo looked different in the light of day. Well, in the light of the interior lamps. The TOC didn't have windows or a skylight or any break in its concrete and sandbags that would let fragments and bullets through. Without the helmet and the night vision goggles, I could see that his hair was shaggy beyond regulation, and the combination of the hair, the mustache and the clothes was about to give Master Gunnery Sgt. Lopez an apoplectic fit. He left the man with us, not saying a word, but the deep scowl on his face telling his story.

Molina was watching Jambo intently, as if she expected him to break into song and dance or a stand-up routine. Maybe she was just bored.

"Nice to see you in your native environment, Andy." Jambo said, nodding to me. "Hope you fellas made it home all right last night. Those old Strykers looked like they'd seen better days. Like in Iraq or Afghanistan, maybe."

"Our Strykers aren't as likely to break down as those Land Rovers," I returned the jab. "You guys have a Triple-A membership to go with them?"

"You take what you can get." He shrugged. "Which brings me to why I'm here." He met Glenn's eyes, the good-natured amusement fading away. "I'm going to need to borrow your boy here for a couple days. And his platoon."

"Absolutely not," Glenn snapped. "This COP runs more patrols and takes more incoming fire than any other in the city." He said that as if he was proud of it. "There's no way we can spare a whole platoon. Not for two days, not for two *hours*."

Well, he might have been exaggerating there, but he was standing up for us, so I didn't correct him.

"Sorry to insist, Captain," Jambo said, "but I think if you'll have your RTO there call battalion, you'll find the decision has already been made."

Glenn's jaw clenched, shoulders hunching like he was about to blitz the quarterback.

"Molina," he said, emphasizing each syllable, "get me Battalion. Now."

"Who at Battalion, sir?" she asked, retrieving a handset, preparing to punch in a code.

"Battalion *Actual*, Lance Corporal."

Molina's eyebrow went up. That meant that Glenn wanted to speak to Lt. Colonel Masterson personally.

"Yes, sir."

"This is a nice little place you guys have here," Jambo said as Molina put through the call. "Good location, good sightlines, well-defended."

"Two-car garage," I elaborated, "screened-in pool. Our realtor is having an open house next Tuesday."

"I have Uniform One-One Actual, sir," Molina reported, holding the handset out to Glenn.

"Sir, this is Captain Glenn," he said. It was a secure line, so there wasn't any need for call-signs or oblique references. "I have a man named James Bowie here who's asking...."

Glenn trailed off, eyes narrowing at the reply buzzing in the handset.

"Yes, sir, but—" he tried to break in, but snapped his mouth shut sharply. "Yes, sir. Yes, sir."

Yessir, yessir, three bags full.

Glenn handed the handset back to Molina, his mouth pursed like he'd tasted something sour.

"I have been instructed by Colonel Masterson to give full cooperation and support to *Master Sergeant* Bowie and his team." He bit down on the man's rank, as if it were a special insult to be ordered around by an NCO, particularly an Army NCO. "So, Andy, I guess you're going with him, whoever and whatever he is."

"I'm with Combat Application Group," Jambo told him, his expression deadly serious, as if he'd shared some dreaded state secret with Glenn that could get them both killed.

"You mean Delta Force," Glenn said.

Jambo laughed. "No one calls it that anymore. Except bad movies. First Special Forces Operational Detachment Delta, if you're feeling long winded."

"Tell me something, Master Sergeant. Bowie, why the hell are you picking on us?" Glenn waved around demonstratively. "Don't you and your boys usually grab a handful of Rangers when you decide you need backup?"

"We do." Jambo leaned against the sand table with casual disrespect. "But the Ranger battalion rotated out and you Marines rotated in and this is time-sensitive. And just plain sensitive. I don't have time to fly in a couple platoons of Rangers from the states, so you're it."

Glenn sighed, as if unsatisfied with the explanation but knowing it was the best he was going to get.

"And as for why I picked Lt. Andy here," Jambo went on, "well, he demonstrated qualities last night that I appreciate in a soldier...or a Marine. And I'd rather have someone I can count on to have my back, whether they eat crayons in their off time or not."

"What's the op?" Glenn demanded.

"Compartmentalized." Jambo shook his head. "Need to know."

"Well, I fucking need to know, since it's my platoon going on it!"

Jambo stood, arms folded across his chest.

"Do we need to get Colonel Masterson back on the horn so he can repeat his orders, Captain?"

I'd been silent the whole time, letting Glenn do his thing because

I had the gut feeling this was going to happen and I didn't want to fuck things up with either the captain or this guy Jambo. Because I found it all intriguing for some reason I couldn't have put into words. Yeah, it could be dangerous as hell, but this was fucking *Delta Force*, and if it wasn't Chuck Norris and motorcycles with rear-firing rocket launchers, it was still Shughart and Gordon laying their lives down and hunting HVTs in Afghanistan and Iraq, and a whole bunch of other shit that I would have given my left nut to have been a part of.

But now it seemed like Glenn needed rescuing and the whole thing was academic. I was going and there was nothing he could do about it, nothing I *wanted* him to do about it.

"Should we load up the Strykers?" I asked Jambo. Glenn offered me a glare but said nothing.

"No Strykers, no Humvees, no MRAPs. Prepare for dismounted operations, though we will have vehicles available."

"Be fucking careful, Andy," Glenn advised me, grabbing my tactical vest to get my attention. "Just because these cowboys think they can pull off any mission doesn't mean they won't leave you and your men hanging out to dry."

Jambo smiled thinly at him.

"Sorry, you must be thinking of the SEALs." He motioned toward me. "Come on."

I shifted my 27 around from back to front, pulled my helmet back on and followed him out of the TOC and into the glare of the mid-morning sun. I'd showered not that long ago, but sweat trickled down my back and beaded on my forehead just a few steps into the brisk walk across the outpost. Dirt-filled HESCO barriers formed the walls and sandbags were packed against every interior surface, adding layers of cheap armor against mortars and rockets.

"Where are we going?" I asked Jambo, struggling to keep up. The man had long, quick strides like some of the avid back-country hikers I'd gone backpacking with during my summer breaks from college.

"Your platoon bay." His arms were resting on his M68, hanging off his neck and chest by a patrol sling. "Gonna get your Marines geared up for this operation. Make sure they bring enough food and extra batteries for three days." He shrugged. "It's your call, but I might tell them four, just to be sure everyone actually brings enough and doesn't try to get by with the lightest weight they have to carry."

"Yeah," I agreed. "There are a few who try to pull that shit, but Gunny Moore straightens their shit out. I have him check the loadout whenever we go on patrol."

He squinted at me from under the brim of his black boonie hat. "What's your normal ammo loadout?"

"Minimum is 310 rounds per," I said. "Seven loaded mags, five boxes of ammo in stripper clips."

"Leave the boxes, load up another five mags each. More if they can find a place to stick it. Don't worry about humping it, we'll have motorized transport."

I stopped, and I thought for a second he would keep going without me, but he only took another two steps before he turned, hands raised in a "what?" gesture.

"Can you tell me where we're going?" I asked. "Now that we're out of the TOC, can you tell me what the mission is?"

He chuckled, and I didn't know the man, but I thought I detected embarrassment behind it.

"The truth is, Andy," he said, leaning in as if it was our secret, "I don't even know yet. But I know who we're going to see who's going to give us the details of this mission, and the who and the where make it need to know. And fucking dangerous." He grinned and slapped me on the arm, heading back off to the other end of the COP, where my platoon barracks were. "That's why

I'm bringing you along. Come on," he urged. "We have to be at the airfield in two hours."

I tried to smile back, tried to act like the badass I wanted him to think I was, but something tightened in my gut. That was the problem with being a badass and doing badass things, of course. They had the very real possibility of getting you killed.

6

If there was one aphorism which summed up the total of military existence from the first armies thousands of years ago right up through to the first half of the Twenty-First Century, it was "hurry up and wait."

The shuttles, I'd been told, were to leave in three hours. We'd shown up at the landing field with an hour to spare and found Brooks and her Rangers already lined up at their shuttles, waiting on the small, robot forklifts to finish loading ammo and supplies in through the belly ramp before they could board, and the flight crews nowhere to be found. We walked past them and I tried to hide the "told you so" smirk wanting to fight its way out. The rest of the team didn't bother, some of them actually laughing and pointing.

We'd been standing around a half an hour by the time the Space Force passengers showed up, just life's little way of reinforcing its inherent irony.

"Hey Andy," Julie Nieves said, stepping around the rest of the security team to trace a line across the shoulder of my armor. "Almost didn't see you in that robot-man suit."

Something electric crackled across my skin even though I couldn't feel her finger. I hadn't seen her in a few weeks and until that very instant, I hadn't realized that I'd missed being around her. Julie and I were of an age, though she wore it better than I did. I wasn't sure if the Helta anti-aging treatments had already done their work with her or if it was natural.

"Hey," I replied, never sure whether or not to call her by her name or her rank, since she was my superior officer by a rank, a Space Force light colonel. "You get any time off before they dragged you back into this?"

"Oh, yeah," she said, her smile a bit wistful. "I spent five whole days with Traci on the beach at Kauai before the call came through. God*damn* that girl has gotten big."

"Tell me about it," I commiserated. "Zack is going to be taller than me soon. He's already two shoe sizes past me. Kid can barely walk without tripping over those flippers." I gestured at the shuttle. "I don't suppose you're part of the flight crew for this thing, are you?"

"Sadly, no," she sighed, her shoulders sagging. "I've had to resign myself to being the Helm officer of the *Jambo* and leaving flying shuttles and other fun stuff like that to Captain Lee and the rest of the flight crews."

"Is that a comedown for a former Navy fighter jock?" I wondered. The tone was teasing, but the question was serious. Most fighter pilots I'd known considered it the end of their career if they got slipped over to flying transport planes.

"At first, maybe," Julie admitted. "But then someone pointed out that I was the first ever human to pilot a starship, which was pretty damned cool."

"And a woman," I added. She smiled.

"Thank you for noticing."

"It's so weird being the first to do everything," I mused, trying to ignore the remark, afraid I was misinterpreting it. She could have just been trying to be snarky. "First humans to meet aliens, first humans to travel to another star system, first humans to pilot a starship, first humans to fight an interstellar war...."

Julie had a look like the cat that ate the canary, like I'd delivered her the perfect straight line.

"What, Andy?" she asked. "You're telling me you've never been the first to do...anything before?"

It was warm in the armor out in the sun, but not warm enough for my face to be this hot.

"Umm, not since high school," I said, trying to sound as if the humor didn't bother me. And normally, it wouldn't have. I was a Marine and bawdy didn't begin to describe the sort of joking around we usually did. Hell, *disgusting* didn't do it justice. But for some reason, when I was with Julie, I felt...intimidated? Maybe?

"I see nothing's changed even in this new space age," Pops said from behind me, unexpected enough that I nearly jumped, which might have taken me a few yards off the ground in my armor. "The Marines are still trying to get a ride from the Navy."

Now my face wasn't warm, it was on fire and I turned on Pops with my eyebrows so far up, they drove my hairline back into my scalp.

"You know, I think I might be interested in trying an experiment on this mission," I said with a growl that was only half-joking. "I'm curious how high a rank an officer has to be in order to tell a Delta CWO to drop to the front leaning rest position and push Idaho into Montana."

"Sir," Pops said, frowning as if deep in thought, "I would say the result of the experiment would probably be that whatever you rank you have, it would require the one just above that."

"Yeah?" I tried to stay mad at Pops, but it was a waste of time, not to mention impossible. "Well, what if it was the President? Who's the next rank up from him?"

"My mother," he answered, not missing a beat. "If you can get her to order me to do pushups, I will pound my face against the ground all damned day."

Julie was laughing now, which gave me no choice but to join in.

Put the fucking armor on, take the fucking armor off. It was the story of my life. The racks in the ship's armory were basically dressing dummies, each bit of the Svalinn stored on the corresponding part of the metal-reinforced plastic in human form. Its arms were outstretched like a crucifix, the Catholic kind with Jesus still on it. I resisted an urge to cross myself when I settled the helmet down on the thing's head.

"How the hell is it you guys always get into the armory first?" Dani Brooks asked, pulling her helmet off and shaking out her neck-length blond hair to free a stray strand from her neck yoke.

Her headquarters platoon was filing into the compartment behind her, chattering like little kids. And some of them weren't that much older than my son. I was suddenly glad the Delta team was made up of older men, senior NCOs and warrants who wouldn't look to me like I was God handing down tactical truth from on high. I remembered what that was like, and what it was like when one of them died.

"There's only twelve of us," I reminded Brooks, waving at the number of Rangers just in her headquarters platoon. "We don't have to drag around four platoons' worth of troops everywhere we go. And that's when you're travelling light."

Theoretically, Brooks commanded a battalion, but in practice, there weren't yet enough Svalinn suits or M900 KE rifles to outfit a whole battalion and have spares for breakage. She had two companies, and this time, we'd had to leave most of one of them behind because of injuries and suit damage during the last mission.

"What do you think about this operation?" I asked her, pulling the security cage down over the team's suits and weapons.

"I think it's a half-assed, spur-of-the-moment idea that only a Zoomie would have come up with." She was referring to Olivera, though she was careful not to say it. "We have very little intelligence, despite the drone recordings Joon-Pah seems so proud of." She snorted, working loose the connections of her torso armor. "The Helta think that remembering to do some basic recon makes them fucking ursine versions of James Bond. All we know is that they built a military base outside the city. We have no idea how many soldiers they're housing in it. Waypoint has a single city and a few outposts, but they evacuated a lot of the population when it became clear the Tevynians were invading. How many soldiers do the Tevynians think they need to control a few thousand Helta? A hundred? A thousand? One for every one of them? Or are they treating the planet like a staging area, bringing troops in to store them and their weapons and gear where they can pick them up along the way to somewhere else?"

"Good questions," I admitted.

"That we don't have the answer to, and won't until we get boots on the ground at Waypoint." She shook her head. "It's nebulous bullshit like this that got so many Rangers killed during the joint campaigns against the Sinaloa Cartel. We moved on incomplete and sometimes just downright wrong intelligence from the Mexican government and walked into one ambush after another." Her voice was calm, even, but when she lowered her torso armor onto the rack, she slammed it down hard enough to shake the mounts and drew stares from the other soldiers in the compartment.

"Sorry," I said, keeping my voice low. "Didn't mean to hit a nerve."

She shrugged, as if it hadn't meant anything. I didn't know her that well, hadn't spent any time with her off duty, but I didn't believe that for a second.

"Mexico has been a clusterfuck for most of the last forty years. I guess I shouldn't have been surprised that the cartels had their hooks that deep into the military, but I was younger and more naïve." Brooks held her helmet in front of her like Yorick's skull for a beat before she set it down on the frame. "Mind you," she went on, meeting my eyes, her expression still calm, "I don't blame anyone in particular. We were in a no-win situation. If we'd done nothing, the cartel would have kept up their terrorist attacks until law enforcement was too busy dealing with them to worry about interdicting drug shipments. If we'd done it without cooperating with the Mexican government, we'd have had to go to war with Mexico on top of going to war with the cartel."

"Now we're almost doing the opposite," I mused. "We've gone to war with the Tevynians for the benefit of the Helta, and we don't even have the Helta government's official help yet."

She laughed, short and sharp and humorless.

"And again, what else could we do? Turn down star travel and fusion and the cure to cancer and old age?"

"You think we're in another no-win situation?" I wasn't sure I wanted to hear the answer to that, given how entangled my fate had become with all of this.

"Like Mexico? No. If Joon-Pah isn't exactly Clausewitz, he's not actively working against us the way the Mexican Marines were."

"What about this mission? You and I are going to have to come up with an op order en route. Any ideas?"

She rubbed a hand across the back of her neck, looking as tired as I felt. "I'd rather wait to come up with something definite until we get some real time intelligence, but I think it's going to be pretty straightforward. We drop down there and kick their asses, knock them back long enough to get this Fen-Sooyan and his group out. It shouldn't be too hard."

"You just said we don't have any idea how many soldiers they have," I reminded her.

"We don't. But one thing we do know is that none of these fuckers, not Helta nor Tevynian, could lead a dozen sailors into a whorehouse. If we hit hard and get out quick, they'll never know what hit them."

Famous last words.

It wasn't the first time I'd heard their like. Some things never changed.

7

"If they ever straighten this hellhole out," Gunny Moore judged, nodding at the verdant mountains surrounding the base camp, "I might have to come back here on vacation."

I had to agree. The plateau we'd landed on loomed over Caracas, close enough that I could see the sunlight twinkling off the glass of the buildings, but far enough away that we could have been on another planet. This far away, I couldn't see the destruction, the violence, the ever-present smoke from burning tires. In the other direction, there was nothing but the slopes of the Cordillera de la Costa Central mountain range climbing into the azure sky.

The unmarked, dull-green Blackhawks spoiled the illusion, their blades still winding down, great scythes swooping with deliberate menace. The platoon had exploded out of the side doors, prodded by well-trained squad leaders, and fell into a security perimeter around the aircraft, their rucksacks like curved turtle shells sticking out of the tall grass. The Delta team was standing, clumped together at the center, watching their textbook reaction with amusement.

"Where's our welcoming committee?" I asked Jambo.

He breathed in the mountain air and smiled.

"They'll be here presently," he assured me. "You ever been here before, Andy?"

"Can't say as I have. But I've probably seen it a hundred times from down there." I pointed toward Caracas. "If I didn't know better, I'd say we were in Hawaii."

"El Avila National Park," he informed me, sounding like a tour guide as he swept a hand at the lush growth closing in around the clearing. "The lungs of Caracas, they call it." He shrugged. "Used to call it. I don't know that anyone here thinks much about it anymore."

"Vehicle," Moore said, his whole touristy vibe going out the window, his M27 going to his shoulder as he went down on a knee. I heard the engine noise a moment after his announcement, a growling diesel.

"Steady, Gunnery Sergeant," Jambo told him, leaving his weapon dangling from his neck. The rest of the team took their cue from him, but I noted they spread out behind the lines of my platoon's defenses, just in case. "Let's not have an incident. We're all friends here." He sniffed. "Theoretically."

The Ford F250 could have rumbled straight out of a showroom and onto the dirt path to the clearing. Its metallic blue finished glittered in the sun, its spotless windshield still beaded with the droplets of a fresh hand-wash, and I wondered if that had been done for our benefit, to impress the Americans with how well the locals treated their equipment. I couldn't see the driver through the reflection from the windshield, and I let my finger slip out beside the trigger of my weapon despite Jambo's reassurance, noting that the vehicle had yet to slow down.

The driver hit the brakes at the last second, sending the pickup into a fishtail, spraying loose dirt in an arc that came just shy of our perimeter.

Fucking show-off.

Cowboy boots as highly polished as the pickup hit the ground first, the blue jeans tucked into them as crisp and sharp as if they'd just come off the shelf at the Wal-Mart. The belt buckle completed the refractory trifecta, large and gaudy enough to serve as the championship trophy for any professional wrestling tournament. His shirt was checked white and red, fastened with pearl buttons, and the leather ends of a bolo tie dangled across his chest. I could have predicted the white Stetson cowboy hat before I actually saw it, but the face between the hat and the bolo was younger than I would have guessed, younger than me, his black mustache spotty, with no attempt at a beard to accompany it, likely because the result would have been embarrassing.

A leather holster rode high on his hip, the cocobolo grips of a stainless 1911 .45 sticking out at an angle as if he fancied himself a gunfighter.

"Is one of you Jambo?" the kid asked, his English unaccented. He had, I was sure, either been born in the States or spent much of his youth there.

"That'd be me," the Delta operator volunteered.

The kid looked him up and down, the corner of his lip curling in what I interpreted as skepticism.

"You come with me," he said, jerking a thumb at the truck. "The others stay here."

"Andy comes with me." Jambo said flatly, hooking a thumb at me.

The kid frowned.

"He said just you."

"Andy comes with me, or I don't come." Jambo folded his arms and waited in stubborn silence.

Why was he insisting on this? I would have been happy to stay right here, where the helos could provide a quick getaway.

Jambo added a coda, perhaps sensing the kid was going to dig in his heels.

"He's the commanding officer for these Marines. He has to go with us, or we get back in the birds and your boss can try again with someone else."

The kid looked as if he wanted to argue the point, but finally, he threw up his hands and turned back to the truck.

"Fine. Just get in. He's waiting."

Jambo motioned for me to come with him and I turned back to Gunny Moore.

"Keep the platoon in one hundred percent security," I told him. "I'll call if there's any problem."

"Copy that, sir." He cast a leery look at the pickup truck and the kid driving it. "Be careful with these yahoos."

I let Jambo have the front seat while I climbed into the passenger's side rear, pushing aside a pile of MRE wrappers. The interior of the Ford smelled like cigarettes and stale beer cut with freon. The kid spun a tight U-turn and headed back up the dirt road, the path tinted green by the lush overhang of branches. I couldn't have named the trees that grew in this park if I'd had a gun to my head, but they were pretty, a nice change from the desolation in the city. I was still wary, because I wasn't stupid, but Jambo seemed fairly relaxed, his carbine propped up on the seat beside him, and I figured he would know if things were going to go bad, so I allowed myself the luxury of staring out the window at the trees passing by on the mountain road.

The seatbelt alarm started chiming thirty seconds into the drive and the kid glared at Jambo balefully. He snorted and pulled the strap across his body, but I left mine off, safety regs be damned.

"You're Ricky, aren't you?" Jambo asked the kid. It almost sounded like an accusation. "His nephew?"

"Yeah. What about it?" Ricky, the kid, scowled.

"You grew up in Miami, right?"

The kid's jaw worked as if he were chewing on something distasteful. "Weston."

"Close enough. Why'd you come back here? You had it pretty good in South Florida. No one would have looked down on you if you'd stayed there."

"I would have," he said, his lips pressing together in mulish stubbornness. "My dad died fighting for this place, for our home, when I was just a kid. Now it's my turn."

Jambo grunted noncommittally, then twisted around to shoot me a look.

"This here is Ricky Martijena, Andy. Nephew of *Generalissimo* Carlos Martijena."

"No shit," I blurted. I knew the name, of course. Maybe not every Marine in Venezuela would, but I would have wagered every officer would.

"Just 'general,' not *generalissimo*," Ricky insisted. "He doesn't like being called that."

"I'll refrain," Jambo allowed, "but I doubt the US press will."

"They should be fucking grateful." The kid's eyes flashed with anger when he finally looked away from the narrow dirt road. "He kept the Communists under control while you and your people sat on their asses. Now your president won't even allow him to fight beside you."

"Policies come and go, kid," Jambo said, sounding unmoved. "Presidents, too. Your uncle has a power base and he knows we're going to have to deal with him on an official level sooner or later. And until then, well...we're dealing with him *un*officially."

We are? It was news to me. But now I thought I had a good idea as to why this whole thing was so top secret.

The first sign I had that we were getting close to our destination was the guards. They tried to blend in with the trees, and if they'd just been setting up an ambush for a few minutes, they might have managed it. But they'd been sitting in their overwatch positions for a while, maybe since dawn, and they'd gotten sloppy. A boot sticking out between tree limbs here, a flash of reflected light off the face of a watch there. Still, it was a good try.

Past the supposedly concealed positions were the overt ones, sandbagged fortifications by the road, protected by M240B 7.62x51mm general purpose machine guns. Men in a mixture of civilian clothes and camouflage uniforms sat behind the guns while others stood out in the open, M16's slung over their shoulders. The choice of weapons was significant, more a political statement than a tactical choice. Those were US weapons, *our* weapons, if older and no longer issued. These people were choosing to visibly align themselves with us rather than the old regime or the EPV.

Then we reached the actual camp.

"Damn," I said. "How'd all this shit get here?"

I'd expected a few tents, maybe some rickety buildings nailed together out of plywood. What I got instead was a small town. The buildings were small and simple, built from brick, brightly colored and cheerful in sharp contrast with the men and women filing in and out and around them, who wore serious expressions and even more serious hardware, all of it made in the USA.

"It's called Galipan Village," Jambo said. "It's been here for over two hundred years." He shrugged. "Well, it *used* to be a village, before everything went to shit. The original inhabitants got their asses out of the area back three or four years ago and the Citizens' Militia moved in."

"No use letting a perfectly good setup like this go to waste," Ricky said, shrugging. "If we can free this place, if we can make our country whole and stable once again, the villagers might come back. Someday."

"Let's keep the good thought."

The Ford crept between the houses and what had once been

shops, pulling up in front of a structure bigger than the rest, what might have been a visitor's center or an administrative office. The soldiers guarding the entrance were better equipped than the rest, dressed in full ACU's, which were complete, if obsolete, and carrying M4 carbines with under-barrel grenade launchers.

They eyed us with something between doubt and resentment when we exited the truck with weapons in hand, and one of them stepped in Ricky's way, speaking quietly enough that I didn't catch the words even though I spoke the language.

"*Tio dice que eso asi*," Ricky replied sharply, loud enough that I could make it out. *Uncle says it is to be so.*

The big man with the M4 clearly didn't want to hear that, but he moved out of the way just the same, and we stepped past. Jambo threw the soldier the ghost of a smile, just a twitch of his mustache as we passed, and the big man's shoulders tensed as if he wanted to punch the operator.

Whatever touristy posters and wall art had once adorned the interior walls of the admin building were gone now, replaced by propaganda posters with the face of an older man with stern eyes and a hard expression, wisps of grey hair sticking out from beneath a beret.

Viva Tio Carlito, they read. Long live Uncle Charlie.

He was waiting for us in what had probably been the office of the director of this place, which was spacious as minor bureaucratic offices went but a bit on the cramped side for the leader of the second-largest organized army in Venezuela. Still, he had somehow managed to acquire several OLED wall monitors and a treadmill desk, so I guess there were some perks to being the CIA's golden boy.

"Gentlemen!" he exclaimed as he stepped off the treadmill, his voice an operatic baritone. "I welcome you to the headquarters of the Citizens' Militia."

The propaganda posters, I had to admit, were fairly accurate.

He was perhaps a shade older now, with a few more lines in his hard-edged face, but the eyes were the same laser-sight sharp, the jawline just as firm. His hair had gone grey, but time hit us all, eventually. And his shoulders still filled out the ACU's, broad and powerful enough for me to believe the man could be dangerous with or without the SIG 9mm holstered at his waist.

"General Martijena," Jambo said, nodding respectfully. "Please allow me to introduce Lt. Clanton. He's leading the Marine platoon we brought along for support on this operation. I have experience serving beside him under fire and I can vouch for his steady nerves and decisiveness."

"A pleasure to meet you, Lieutenant," Martijena said, oozing sincerity in that way only a politician can manage. And generals, I had found, definitely qualified as politicians.

I shook his proffered hand, his grip firm and dry.

"I've heard a lot about you, sir," I said, crafting the words like a fragile, intricate statue that could collapse with a single ounce of pressure on the wrong spot.

Martijena saw right through it, though, and laughed deep in his chest, jabbing a finger toward me.

"This one is crafty, Jambo," he said, grinning. "He knows better than to lie, yet he has the sense to couch his real feelings in a compliment. What you mean to say, Lt. Clanton, is that I am infamous in your country, portrayed by your press as a radical reactionary, the modern incarnation of Augusto Pinochet, ready to throw the Communists out of a helicopter and rule Venezuela with an iron hand."

He shrugged, striding around to the office door. He gave a nod to the guards outside, then pushed the door shut, leaving only the two of us, the general and his nephew.

"And perhaps Venezuela needs an iron hand at the moment, for she is falling apart at the seams and it may be that a firm grip is required to pull her back together. But the truth is, I have no wish to be the dictator of this land. My only desire is to see her united and stable enough for her citizens to again choose their own leader in a fair election." His lip twisted into a sneer. "Which is why I risked my career, my family and my life to try to overthrow the dictator Chavez so many years ago. Why I gave up my home and went into exile in your country for so long, without hope that the time would ever come when I could once again step foot in my homeland. But now my beloved country calls and I must answer, whether or not your current administration wishes to acknowledge my place here."

"What the government is willing to acknowledge publicly," I suggested, again very carefully, "and what they support covertly are often far different things."

"Which is why you're here." His mouth thinned into a grim line and he stalked to a cabinet in the far corner of the room, throwing it open to reveal a collection of liquors and a small refrigerator. He grabbed a bottle of what looked like Grey Goose and poured himself a shot, then stopped with it halfway to his mouth. "Forgive my manners, gentlemen. Would either of you care for a drink?"

"I wouldn't turn down a beer, if you have one," Jambo said.

"And you, Mr. Clanton?"

I badly wanted a shot of that vodka. All we could get even in the FOB was local moonshine, and it was harsh enough to take off paint. I felt like I hadn't had a decent drink in months. But I was on duty, and I wasn't confident enough in my ability to think clearly after a shot or two of vodka to take a drink this early in the day and on a mission.

"I'd kill for a Diet Coke, sir," I said. Which was also true.

"Is Pepsi all right?" he asked, and I immediately decided I hated him.

"Yes, sir, thank you, sir."

Because what was I going to say? *No, you asshole, if I'd*

wanted Pepsi, I'd have asked for it! I *wanted* to say that, but I wasn't going to.

"I have," Martijena went on once beverages had been distributed and tops popped, "a personal issue which I find I cannot trust any of my own people to handle. Something embarrassing that would lessen my status in their eyes. My ex-wife Laura has been living here in Galipan for the last few months, since it became too dangerous for her in her old neighborhood. She had a house where she was raising our son, Paulo. He's only eight and I thought it best he remain with his mother, so long as it was safe. Here, I could visit him at my leisure, see to his needs." He set his shot glass down on top of the cabinet loud enough I half-expected it to shatter. "Until last week, when she fled in the night." He licked his lips, cleaning off the remnants of the vodka. "I interrogated her servants and determined she intended to go to her parents' house with our son. She'd often asked about this before, but they live in an area that is far too violent. I offered many times to bring them to live here, but she insisted they would never agree to it." He sighed, the muscles in his neck loosening as if he were forcing himself to calm down. "Still, I sent my people after her, to retrieve her and Paulo, and if need be to bring her parents with them. But her parents had not seen her. They had never shown up."

I think he would have sat down had there been any chairs in the office, but there weren't and instead, he leaned against the wall.

"I spread money and food and gasoline and threats everywhere I could reach in the city, and I finally found them. She had been intercepted on her journey by the EPV and her and Paulo had been taken to the Catia barrio, the poorest section of the city and a hotbed of support for the Communists." His hands clenched into fists and he closed his eyes, as if gathering his resolve. "I want her back safely, of course, but above all else, gentlemen, I *must* have Paulo back. My cooperation and above all, my discretion in not spreading the word that the US is working with me under the table depend on this. Are we clear?"

"Crystal," Jambo assured him, taking a swig of Pabst Blue Ribbon. And God alone knew how Martijena had gotten ahold of PBR down here. "We'll get it done."

And how the hell, I wondered, were we going to do *that*?

8

"How the hell are we going to do this?" Rodent asked, arms folded across the small table as a rest for his chin. "I mean, do we have a plan yet?"

Rodent had shaved his beard. The whole team had shaved them off and it was still throwing me. What threw me for even more of a loop was that I hadn't *realized* it until a full day after the *Jambo* hadn't gotten underway. Well, some, like Pops, had never had a beard. The beards were affectations from a time when most of their warfighting was done in the Middle East, where the locals wouldn't respect a man who lacked a beard, and thank God I hadn't been around for that, because I couldn't grow one for shit. But Jambo had reveled in his facial hair and the freedom to grow it in defiance of all military regulations, and the attitude had spread through the team. It sort of felt as if the mass shaving was a break from the past, but I didn't ask. It felt like an intrusion on their private grieving to ask.

Honestly, though, some of them should have kept the beards, because Rodent and Ginger and especially Dog looked goofy as hell without them. Standing at the center of the team in the small conference room we'd commandeered aboard the *Jambo*, I felt like I was talking to a bunch of fresh-faced privates. And I didn't need that, because I was already as nervous as a whore in church. I had never briefed the team alone before. Hell, I hadn't briefed *anyone* in years and now I was about to lead a bunch of hardened Delta operators into combat.

"What we have right now," I tried to answer his question, "is that we're going to jump into the system pretty far out, hopefully far enough that they won't detect us, and get a feel for the current disposition of enemy forces. The Helta left some inactive spy drones behind, so we're hoping the Tevynians didn't find and eliminate them already. If they're still around, we'll transmit the activation codes and get a SIGINT report before we make the final translation into the battlespace."

"The battlespace?" Ginger repeated, looking at me askance.

"We'll come out of the jump as close to the planet as we can, then launch shuttles immediately to try to get inside their OODA loop before they can respond. The known unknowns here are where they're containing the civilians and how secure their holding facilities are...." I was blathering and I knew it, and I wondered if they'd say anything or just let me try to swim out of it. Being Delta, they threw me an anchor.

"Question, sir," Ginger said, raising his hand as if he was in a classroom, a shit-eating grin on his ruddy face. "I'm not sure I'm tracking you. How does the timing of our entry into the battlespace interoperate with their C-Cubed-I?"

"Yeah," Rodent added, scratching where his beard used to be. "And does the Command, Control, Communications and Intelligence have an upward trending glidepath showing synergistic nesting effort towards partnered interoperability?"

And that was it, of course. They *tried* to keep straight faces, but Bubba cracked first, his babyface unable to keep a serious expression for more than a few seconds, and once he started sniggering, the rest couldn't stop themselves and neither could I. The little compartment filled with raucous laughter.

"Sorry, guys," I said, raising my hands in surrender. "I know, I know. I guess I'm a little intimidated since you all know more about small unit tactics than I ever will."

"It's just us, boss," Pops said, sitting on the edge of the table beside me. "Tell us what we need to know."

"What you need to know is how much we don't know," I said, relaxing from the parade rest I'd automatically fallen into when I began the briefing. "We don't know how much they've built the place up since we've been gone, we don't know if they've brought back any of the cruisers they stripped away from the system, we don't know how many troops they have on the ground." I sighed, leaning against the table. "Hell, we don't even know how many Helta civilians are left on the damned planet after the evacuations. We're hoping we can get some of that from the sleeper drones, but you know the old saying. Hope in one hand and shit in the other and see which one fills up faster."

An idea struck me, something that would acknowledge their superior experience and still make it clear who was in charge without being a dick about it.

"I tell you what. We have a lot of possibilities here. Ginger, give me an example of a scenario we might be facing when we drop."

"The Tevynians might be mixed with the Helta population," he said without hesitation. "They might be doing it to better defend against any attempt to take back the colony or just because it'd be easier to control them that way."

"Good. What I want you to do is come up with a deployment plan for us and the Rangers based on that scenario. Include a plan for air and orbital support and contingencies for if either or both are unavailable. Throw anything else in that you think is important, don't feel constrained by op order format, what's important is that we don't leave anything out. Copy?"

"Good copy, sir," he said, nodding. He grinned at the others as he pulled out his tablet and began tapping notes into it. "I guess that's what I get for being the first to answer, huh?"

"Not at all, Ginger," I assured him. "Bubba, give me another likely scenario. Not just what you think *will* happen, but what's within the realm of reasonable expectation."

I could see the looks of realization in their eyes, and, more importantly, expressions of approval. This was what I should have been doing instead of parroting the lecturing style of the officers I'd hated when I'd been a platoon leader.

"All right," Bubba said, his Texas accent turning the words into "aw raht." You'd think the guy from Texas would be "Cowboy," but he was "Bubba" and "Cowboy," Staff Sergeant Andrew Foster, was from Oklahoma. "I getcha. We know these Tevynians ain't the brightest fuckers when it comes to the technology they steal. From what I understand, they never went through a gunpowder period, so they got no concept of mines even using explosives at all, so I wouldn't be expecting anything like that, but they been pretty good at finding new uses for the shit the Helta let them get ahold of. I wouldn't be surprised if they take those plasma guns and put them in vehicles down there on the surface. They might not have had to use them much tactically against the Helta, because the fur-faces ain't shit for tactics, but they'll do it just because grunts are lazy and ain't nobody gonna be wanting to haul those things around on a hand-pulled cart."

"A high tech technical," Pops murmured and I snorted a not-entirely-pleasant laugh. I had too many bad memories of technicals to feel any real humor.

"Bubba," I said, pointing at him with a knife hand, "I need you to write up possible mounts and uses for the Helta weapons systems, what you think we might run into and hell, just whatever you think some dumbass Tevynian redneck with too much time on his hands, stuck on some dead-end outpost like this might come up with in a 'hold-my-beer' moment."

"Sounds like the perfect assignment for you, Bubba," Dog told him, braying a laugh.

"Your turn, Dog," I said, and the rest of the team chuckled at his discomfort. "You're the Tevynians. What are you going to do with this world?"

"They know we're around," Dog mused, tilting his head to the side, deep in thought. "I mean, they don't know we're from Earth, and they don't know we're allied with the Helta yet, but they know *someone* else is around, right?" He grinned crookedly at me. "Your United Stars Empire, maybe. So, they might be digging in harder than usual, maybe expecting some trouble. I wouldn't be surprised if that military base has some serious fortifications. That might work to our advantage, though. Maybe when they see us jump into the system, they'll pull everything back inside the walls and count on their air defenses to keep us from just strafing the shit out of them. If that happens and assuming we *can't* just strafe the shit out of them, our best bet would be to set the Rangers on them and pin them in there while we go extract the assets."

"That sounds like a plan," I admitted. "Write it up." I gestured around to the others. "All of you come up with a different scenario and write up your recommendations. We're meeting back here in twenty-four hours and we'll go over all of it." I chuckled. "I'd expect that session to last a lot longer than this one."

"But it won't *seem* as long," Rodent murmured.

"Take off," I told them, nodding at the door.

They filed out, except for Pops, who hung back, waiting for the last of them to head out into the passage before pushing the hatch shut.

"That wasn't so bad," he said. "Told you it would be okay."

"I acted like an idiot," I said, rubbing a hand over my face, my stomach roiling with the memory of it. "I couldn't think of anything intelligent to say, so I just spouted buzzwords."

"No one expects you to be perfect from minute one," he insisted, waving my embarrassment away. "You pulled out of the dive and did something useful." He arched an eyebrow. "You know what you have to do now, though, right?"

I racked my brain for possibilities and came up lemons.

"What?" I asked, surrendering to the inevitability of revealing my ignorance.

"Now you have to go back to your room."

"Compartment," I corrected him absently, earning a grin.

"Crayon-eater," he murmured. "You have to go back to your *compartment* and be one step ahead of those boys. You'll need to come up with all the possibilities *they'll* come up with and more, and what you'd do in all those scenarios, so you know what to say when they come up with theirs."

"Oh." I moaned and closed my eyes. "Oh, shit."

"Yeah," he said, pulling open the hatch and grinning as he left. "Have fun with that."

Sleep dragged at my eyelids, grabbing on and jumping with its full weight, trying to pull them down. I blinked and rubbed at them, wondering if I should turn on the light. I didn't need it for the notes I was taking. The Space Force had finally achieved what the military had always bragged was its ultimate goal, the paperless workplace. Helta tech shuttles might be a hell of a lot cheaper to launch than chemical rockets, but space was limited and we weren't devoting any of it to fucking paper.

The tablets were everywhere and, amazingly enough for a

piece of military hardware, easy to use. But the screen was giving me eyestrain and after four straight hours of typing in one scenario after another and giving my assessment of our plan of attack for each of them. I was about ready to call it a night.

There was a knock on the hatch. I looked up, surprised. The ship ran round the clock, of course, this being space, but the Rangers and the Security Team were all on the same work schedule and I didn't know who the hell would be coming around my compartment this time of my personal night. I switched the light on and pushed myself to my feet, stumbling a little, perhaps because I was groggy or perhaps because I'd been sitting in the same position for hours now.

I was wearing shorts and a T-shirt, my typical shipboard sleepwear, and I thought about throwing on my utilities before opening the hatch, but I shrugged, figuring whoever it was would know what my schedule was and what to expect. I opened the hatch and discovered it was me who didn't know what to expect.

Julie Nieves leaned against the hatchway, one fist against her hip, the corner of her mouth turned up.

"Umm, hi," I said, unable to come up with anything more intelligent.

"Hey, Andy." She looked me up and down in frank assessment. "I guess I got you out of bed?"

"No, not exactly," I admitted. "I was working on some stuff for tomorrow." I waved at the tablet on my desk top. If you can call a tiny ledge that folded down out of the bulkhead a "desk."

She nodded, not seeming that interested in what I'd been doing.

"I just got off shift," she said. "I thought I might go down to the mess and get something to eat. You hungry?"

I blinked. My only excuse was that I was exhausted and fuzzy in the head, and even then, I had a feeling I was missing something. But I was forty-something now and pretty far from the age when I would have followed a girl around all night just on the off-chance she might let me kiss her. Plus, to be honest, I was scared shitless what would happen if I was reading the signals wrong.

"I ate a few hours ago," I said. "And I really have to finish this work up before I go to sleep, but maybe tomorrow I could meet you in the mess...."

She rolled her eyes, regarding me the same way a teacher might look at a student who kept asking the same, stupid question.

'God*damn*, Andy," she sighed. "Have you always been this clueless around women?"

She closed the distance between us in a step, her heel shoving the hatch shut behind her, and then she was kissing me before I understood what was happening. Her lips were softer than I'd imagined, and to quote my favorite smuggler, I can imagine quite a bit. Her arms went around my neck and my hands went to her waist, and then lower.

"The answer's yes," I said breathlessly as we undressed each other. "I *have* always been this clueless about women."

"Jesus, Andy," she hissed into my ear, following it with her tongue. "You're lucky you aren't still a virgin."

"I'm very lucky," I told her, "that it didn't get me killed."

Because it almost had.

9

"This feels wrong, sir," Chamberlain said, speaking up so I could hear him above the rattle of the ancient box truck. I'd never imagined how loud one of the things could be from the inside of the cargo compartment, and I wished to hell I hadn't picked tonight to find out the hard way.

"We'll be all right, lance corporal," I assured him.

As if God had been listening, we hit a bump and a suspension that had needed repairing since I was in high school nearly sent me pitching off to the side into Chamberlain's lap. The stack of boxes blocking us off from the rear doors to the truck didn't move, though. They were held in place by cargo straps, a visual barrier for anyone who might stop the truck and check the load. They weren't much a barrier against gunfire, though, if someone didn't buy the *maskirovka*.

First and Second squad were cheek by jowl, sitting on the bare metal and wood of the floor, weapons propped between their knees.

"I didn't mean that, sir," Chamberlain insisted, scowling. I could barely see his expression behind his night vision goggles. "I mean, these are Red Cross trucks."

I searched for Gunny Moore and remembered, to my chagrin, that he was in the other truck, and I'd have to deal with Chamberlain myself.

"It's technically against the rules," I acknowledged. "But this is a covert operation, and the less said about this, the better." The less he said, the better, *period*, as far as I was concerned.

"It's against the laws of war, sir. We could get charged with a war crime for doing this."

He didn't, I noted, sound righteously indignant, a tone that would have gone well alongside his words. Instead, his voice was sullen, stubborn, more as if he was annoyed at the added risk than offended by the moral breach.

"It's a war crime if you're fighting an actual nation," I told him. "The EPV is a terrorist organization. They don't represent the people of Venezuela. They're the war criminals."

Which they were, but I honestly had no idea if that made what we were doing all right. The Blackhawks had dropped us off further down the mountain and the trucks had been waiting with their big, red crosses on the side and Jambo told us to get in, so we got in, and I tried not to think about it. And it was way too late to back out now.

"If we get charged," I assured Chamberlain, "I'll tell the JAG that I ordered you in. It'll all come down on me."

That seemed to cheer him up. It didn't do much for me except give me something else to worry about. Not that I expected to be scooped up by UN peacekeepers and taken to the Hague upon completion of the operation. Hell, the UN couldn't find two rocks to rub together these days, much less a military force that could counter the US in Venezuela. They were like one of the ubiquitous monkeys in the forests here, chattering loudly and angrily and occasionally throwing their own feces around, but unable to accomplish anything other than making a mess. No one had paid them serious attention since the Gulf War way back in 1991.

But that was today. There were politics behind the scenes of all this, politics I tried not to think about because there was nothing I could do to change them. One US president had gotten us involved in this war, and then the next had wanted badly to end it but couldn't and had, instead, committed more ground forces while cutting ties with the Citizens' Militia and other right-wing groups opposed to the EPV. Except we *hadn't* actually done that, and everyone knew it, despite the official denials. The CIA still worked with them, Delta still worked with them, obviously, and now I was working with them.

Did that mean that a few months from now, some JAG prosecutor would bring me up on charges for what I was doing today? Or just as bad, that some Senate subcommittee would call me to testify?

I tried not to think about that, tried to think about something more pleasant. Allie. Dark-haired and slender, poured into those tight jeans she'd been wearing the first night we'd met, her eyes smoldering with the fire that could lead to some incredible sex as well as some knock-down, drag-out arguments. Like the one we'd had before I left. Allie had been royally pissed that I was being deployed so soon after she'd had Zack. As if it was my idea or I had any say in the matter. What the hell had she expected when she married a Marine rifle platoon leader? I hadn't started the damned war....

That wasn't working. Thinking about Allie was just making me mad, which was more distracting than being worried. I tried to think about baby Zack, but I could only see him in Allie's arms and that made me think about her again, which pissed me off again. Maybe it was just better to worry.

The truck braked again, but this time slow and gradual, not

like some asshole had pulled in front of us, but more like the drivers had come upon our destination. The drivers worried the hell out of me, too. They worked for Martijena. They worked for the International Red Cross *too,* but they worked mostly for *Tio Carlito*, and he had insisted that the EPV wouldn't let them through the checkpoints without drivers they knew at the wheel. Jambo hadn't been too happy about that and I figured if he wasn't happy, I probably shouldn't be happy, either. But Martijena had insisted and apparently, our orders were to make the man happy so he wouldn't make waves.

Voices filtered back through the steel and wood and aluminum of the cargo box, speaking what I called "machine gun Spanish," too fast for me to make sense of it with no context and the tones muffled. I didn't know the voices of the drivers well enough to tell them apart from whoever was talking to them, but from the tones, I assumed this was one of the checkpoints we'd been warned about.

"What do we do if things go south, sir?" Sgt. Gregory whispered, eyes flickering back and forth between me and the front of the truck.

I put a finger to my lips, giving him the stinkeye. What the hell were we, teenagers?

I leaned over across the cab and hissed the answer into his ear.

"If things go wrong, we shoot every single fucking bullet we have to get out of the back of this truck, Gregory. Until then, shut up, okay?"

"Yes, sir," he said. I couldn't see his face, but he sounded abashed.

The conversation outside had ceased while I'd been busy dealing with my nervous squad leader and I strained my ears trying to make out any sign of someone approaching the back of the truck. I had my doubts as to whether the fake wall of boxes was going to work in practice and I was hoping we wouldn't have to find out. I kept the muzzle of my carbine trained on the center of them, but the truck's engine revved and we were moving again...and I was breathing again.

A low mumble from the two squads squeezed into the truck undercut the rumble of the diesel engine, the inevitable chatter of relieved conversation. I didn't try to stop it, just let it run as long as the engine did. We slowed, turned left, sped up, turned right and I gave up trying to map in my head where we were in the city. If we'd been outside, or if the city had reliable cell coverage, I could have used the mapping software in my issue GPS or my personal cell phone, but we were stuck inside this dark cage in a dark-age city and I knew nothing.

We stopped again, and this time the rumble of the engine ceased with a shudder and the truck was still. I didn't have to tell the others to keep quiet now. They shifted their positions, bringing up their weapons, some in the prone, some on one knee, some standing so they would all have clear fields of fire. Marinelli was at the center with his M240B, held at hip level, and several of them checked over their shoulder just to be sure they were well clear of the barrel of the machine gun.

We waited. And waited. And waited some more until my calf started to cramp up from the position I'd worked myself into and I had to shift my weight. I'd just let the barrel of my M27 sag when a metallic clunk vibrated through the cargo box as someone opened the rear doors of the truck. I pulled the stock of my weapon into my shoulder and brought the reticle of the optical sight over the center of the boxes, the pad of my trigger finger resting against the front of the trigger guard.

"It's me," Jambo said. "Move these damned boxes."

That took some doing. Theoretically, there was supposed to be a quick release for the straps holding the wall of boxes in place, but it didn't seem to want to work, and finally, Gregory came over to help me yank on the lever of the thing until it came loose. I tried not to imagine what would have happened to us if we'd had to get out in a hurry.

"Took you long enough," Jambo said when we moved the boxes out of the way. "Hurry up, everyone out."

We were parked in an alley barely wide enough for the box trucks to pass, and there was a chorus of muted curses as Gunny Moore led the rest of the platoon from the first truck in, squeezing through a gap of less than two feet between the bodies of the truck and the unfinished brick of the rowhouse on that side.

"Where the fuck are we?" Moore grumbled, coming up beside me and Jambo.

Jambo's men were kneeling on either side of the mouth of the alley, where it opened onto a back street that had once been packed with shops. Their entrances were boarded up now, though some of the boards had been ripped away and I could see fires guttering where squatters had claimed a dry place for the night. I didn't worry they'd see us. Fires indoors claimed their night vision, while ours was as sharp as noonday. It was the ones who'd be on the rooftops with Chinese or Russian NVG's that I was concerned about.

"We're deep in the heart of Catia," Jambo told my platoon sergeant. "Which ain't nearly as pleasant as being deep in the heart of Texas, believe you me."

And believe him I did. The Catia barrio had been one of the poorest, most dangerous sections of Caracas even before the collapse of the economy and the subsequent collapse of the government. Now, it was a nightmare hellscape of gutted buildings, some empty from the Virus, some from the violence, and what was left strong enough to survive both, or simply desperate enough to risk anything for a chance at a place to stay.

"Get Third Squad down at the other end of the alley," I told Moore. "Take the machine gun crew with them."

Technically, Marinelli and his A-gunner, Pulaski, were attached to the company, but Captain Glenn had quite generously loaned them out to me, probably with the notion that I'd need them more than he would. I certainly hadn't been about to turn him down.

"Jambo," one of the Delta operators said, his words low but heavy with import. "We got someone comin' in from the west."

"Yeah, I see 'em." Jambo had his M68 slung across his chest and while he didn't have to move it to be prepared for a threat, there was a subtle shifting of his hands. "I'm hoping it's our contact."

It didn't take long before I saw him too. The man wasn't trying to hide from us or anyone else, simply walking down the remains of what had once been a sidewalk, hands stuffed in his pockets. He might have been old, or he might have just been poor and starved enough to look old before his time. His clothes were worn but well-kept, store-bought blue jeans, a cheap copy of a Stetson and a Miley Cyrus concert T-shirt from ten years ago.

"You are from *Tio Carlito*?" the man asked, seemingly unconcerned with the odd collection of armed Americans.

"That'd be us, *senor*," Jambo said with a nod. "Would you mind terribly keeping your hands out where I can see them?"

The older man laughed softly and pulled his hands out of his pockets, wiggling his fingers demonstratively.

"Thank you kindly," Jambo told him. "You got a name?"

"Call me Jose."

"Maybe you should have just called yourself 'Juan Smith,'" I suggested. The blank look on his face suggested he didn't get it. Jambo shot me a quelling look.

"What's the situation here, Jose?"

"The woman and child are in an apartment building two

blocks that way," Jose said, pointing off to our left, further into Catia. "But you won't just be able to walk up and grab them." He shook his head, then spat a stream of chewing tobacco to the side.

"You got a chew, brother?" Jambo asked. "I ran out yesterday."

Jose seemed as if he resented the imposition, but he handed a rolled-up bag from his back pocket to the Delta operator. Jambo nodded gratitude and stuck a wad of the vile stuff in his mouth.

"So, what's so bad that's waiting for us up the street?"

"Major Stevie."

"Major Stevie?" Jambo repeated, snorting amusement. "Is that a cartoon character?"

"It's what we call him." Jose shrugged. "You might know him better as Esteban Villanueva."

I whistled softly. Yeah, I *had* heard of Esteban Villanueva. He was the Ace of Spades in a deck of cards with the high-value targets in this city printed on them, one of the most senior leaders of the EPV.

"How the hell did Villanueva know about Martijena's ex-wife and kid?" I blurted, looking at Jambo.

"There's a leak," he admitted readily. "You surprised? This ain't exactly the Pentagon we're talking about out here, and you know how much *that* place leaks."

"The building I saw the woman and child enter," Jose went on, "is one of Major Stevie's safehouses. He spends a night in one, two nights in another and so on, to make sure you Americans never have the chance to launch a Hellfire missile from one of your Predator drones at him while he sleeps. I have not seen him, but I did spot Orestes Cazador, his lieutenant, and wherever Cazador is, Stevie is close by. And there are a dozen trucks parked outside the building along the east side."

I couldn't see Jambo's eyes, but his mouth was set in a hard line.

"Any more good news?"

"You use those spy drones," Jose told him, making a whirling motion with his finger. "Stevie knows this. The building is ringed with those dishes he bought from the Chinese."

"Jammers," I supplied. "Just like the ones on that building last night. Which means we won't be able to call in air support or artillery if shit goes south."

"Tell me about the building," Jambo said to Jose, his voice flat, his accent gone, subsumed in a professional tone.

"Four main entrances," Jose said, "but the east and south are blocked off, unusable. The north and west are open, but guarded inside and out. Good observation on every side from the roof and upper stories, but there's a covered pathway that will get you across the street from the west entrance. Not *all* of you, but some. Ten or twelve. If I take you. There are EPV soldiers patrolling the streets, at least twenty or thirty. Maybe as many again inside with Major Stevie."

Jambo didn't speak for a moment, his jaw working the tobacco. Finally, he spat and began speaking, as if he'd been working the words loose.

"All right, then. Here's what we're gonna do, Andy. My team is going up the street with Jose here. He's gonna guide us into position as close to the west entrance as we can get without being seen. We ain't gonna be able to radio you, so we're gonna have to do this by timing. How long's it gonna take to get into that position, Jose?"

"Ten minutes. No more than fifteen."

"Give us twenty, Andy, then assume we're in position. At that point, I want you to push down the street across from the north entrance and find the first defensible position you come to, start laying down fire at that doorway with your machine gun team. Get everything they have headed that way, draw 'em away from us. That'll give us an opportunity to get inside and grab the woman and the kid."

"Right." I nodded, trying to envision the setup. "We don't have a shitload of ammo, though. Even keeping it to controlled bursts, I doubt we can keep them occupied for more than five minutes, tops."

"That'll have to be enough. One more thing. Leave your platoon sergeant in charge of the main force. I want you to take a team or a squad or whatever you think is sufficient and go disable those trucks on the east side. If they squirt out before we can get to them, I want them left with no option but shoe leather to get out of there."

"Why me?" I wondered. Not because I had a problem with doing it, just because I was curious why he wanted me to see to the task personally instead of handing it off to one of my NCOs.

"Because it's important and could be complicated," he explained, not seeming to take offense at the question. "And you're smart. Which is why I brought you along."

"What about extraction?" I asked, deciding to push my luck since he'd just acknowledged that I was smart.

"We're gonna jump right back in these trucks," Jambo said, nodding toward the vehicles. "Haul ass out of here but with our people in the cabs this time. There's an intersection about two and a half klicks south of here where there's a big parking lot, no cars on it. The Blackhawks are going to be waiting for our signal to come in and dust us off."

"And what happens," I asked, "if Uncle Charlie's helicopters don't show up?"

Jambo grinned and spat again, the stream coming dangerously close to my boots.

"Possibilities like that," he told me, "are what make this line of work so fuckin' interesting."

10

"This is way too fucking interesting," I said through clenched teeth.

The Svalinn armor was strapped tight into its frame in the cockpit of the shuttle, and since both the frame and the straps would take a lot more gees than I would, I knew on an intellectual level that breaking loose and flying across the cockpit into the fuselage wasn't a real danger. But the sheer mass of the powered exoskeleton seemed to magnify every maneuver Captain Lee threw the shuttle into, adding momentum to the violent wrenching jolts, the creak of the stressed metal audible even through my closed helmet.

"We got three fighters on our tail," Lee informed me—and in theory, the other shuttles and the *Jambo* and the *Truthseeker*, just in case anyone else could hear through the ECM jamming and the cross-chatter.

Not that they could do anything about it even if they could.

Things had started to go south right about the time we'd jumped into the outer edge of the system, past the orbit of the outer ice giant. The signal had gone out to the drones and they had, predictably, not responded. Olivera had made the decision to jump in anyway, despite the fact that we couldn't see a damned thing, and I suppose I understood. It wasn't as if we had a backup plan. Hell, this *was* our backup plan.

When I'd explained the situation to the team, we'd all shared a knowing look, one I didn't need to have been a special forces operator to understand. Every soldier or Marine who'd ever heard a shot fired in anger knew that look. It meant, "we're fucked."

And we were, indeed, fucked.

I'd been securely ensconced in the shuttle with the rest of my team and two squads of Rangers when we jumped in towards Waypoint, but I'd also been tied into the ship's tactical net. The data feed into the tiny HUD of my helmet was overwhelming, a wash of images, computer simulated animated graphics and raw numbers I couldn't even hope to interpret, but the important thing was the announcements from the Tactical station.

I couldn't even recall the guy's name, though I had a vague sense that he was OG Space Force rather than any of the Navy officers they'd pulled into service to fill out the *Jambo*'s roster. They all sounded the same during combat, anyway, droning on in an affected attempt at stoic professionalism, trying to pretend they weren't as terrified as the rest of us.

He'd started in a few seconds after we jumped out of hyperspace, recovering quicker than I could hope to, quickly enough that my consciousness began registering his report *en media res*, halfway through a sentence.

"...three enemy cruisers between lunar orbit and two AU's out from Waypoint."

The words had slapped me in the face, shaking me free of the haze I felt coming out of hyperspace. Three *cruisers*? Hadn't the whole idea behind this venture been that there'd be *no* cruisers?

"Communications, signal the *Truthseeker*," Olivera had interrupted the report. "Tell her to concentrate fire on the bogie in lunar orbit, buy us some time. Tactical, what's the orbital situation?"

"I'm picking up enemy dual-environment fighters entering the upper atmosphere. Three squadrons, minimum."

"Alert the shuttles. Helm, once we're in high orbit for shuttle launch, turn maneuvering controls over to Tactical. We're likely to be too far away for point defense turrets to do any good, but try to get us into position for a particle cannon shot that's worth taking."

"I assume you all heard that," Captain Lee had said, his tone dry as tinder. "I'd advise holding onto your lunch, because I doubt this is going to be pleasant."

Captain Lee was a man of his word.

We'd launched into the middle of a gunfight between titans and while none of the glittering blue antiproton beams were aimed at our shuttle, that would be small comfort if we were caught in the subatomic fury of one of the backhanded swipes. If the tactical feed from the *Jambo* had been hard to follow, then the view through Gunfighter One's sensors was nearly unreadable, a jumble of images spinning in the firmament with the barrel roll Lee had sent us into with the steering jets to keep enemy lasers from focusing on one spot for too long.

But I knew there were three of the enemy fighters on us, so I decided to look for them because I had nothing better to do until we entered the atmosphere. The blackness of cislunar space alternated in the view with the blue-green arc of Waypoint in the camera views, not spinning quite fast enough to make me want to puke, but plenty fast enough to make it hard to focus, so I concentrated on the lidar and radar readings instead. They were color-coded for simplicity, and there were way too many red ones as compared to the measly four blue triangles representing our shuttles.

Three of the red diamonds were heading straight for us, skimming the upper atmosphere, unwilling just yet to give up the advantage their air-breathing jets and control surfaces gave them. The shuttles were a hundred yards long and half that wide, with plenty of space for a compact pebble-bed reactor and enough metallic hydrogen fuel for a flight from Earth to the Moon. The Tevynian fighters were more like what you'd get if you took an F22, shifted the jets outward and stuck a rocket engine between them. It was enough to get them to orbit and back, but they weren't going to be taking on a shuttle in open space.

And they knew they didn't have to, because we'd be coming to them. They just fired their lasers at extreme range and kept moving, the same as they did with Helta landers, and assumed we'd be just as easy prey as the fur-faces.

"Mayfield," Lee bit the words off, "see if you can kill me some of those fuckers."

"Launching missiles," the gunner announced.

I couldn't see what he did with his controls because I was pressed back into my suit, which was pressed back into its frame by the three gravities of thrust rocketing us toward the atmosphere, but the missiles shunting loose of the weapons bay smacked against the fuselage like a hammer blow. Their solid-fuel rockets were fireflies against the blue of Waypoint's oceans, corkscrewing down and disappearing and I couldn't find them in the cubist painting that was the bird's sensor, but Mayfield's fervent cursing told the story.

"No joy, Cap," he told Lee. "Their ECM is too good for our targeting systems."

Which made sense since they'd gotten it from the Helta. The fur-faces might not be much for making war, but they were hellacious at jamming signals and cracking codes, which involved no risk to life and limb. But missiles weren't all we had.

"Transitioning to guns," Mayfield announced.

"Can't hand over control during reentry," Lee reminded him, "not unless you'd like to bounce off the atmosphere or burn in."

"Just line me up a shot then, Cap."

The targeting reticle was easy to see on the screen even if nothing else was. It was big and red and hanging over a random point on the surface of Waypoint that our nose happened to be lined up with at the moment and if Mayfield had fired the coil gun right then, it would have likely kept on going right to the surface and a good way underneath it. But Lee was already nudging the nose up, moving it in line with one of the red diamonds.

"Sure be nice if this thing could fire independently of the spinal mount," Mayfield grumbled.

"The coil is nearly as long as the shuttle," Lee reminded him. "If you can figure out a way to fit an electromagnetic coil independent of the belly of this bird that we can still put armor over and land this thing, I'll write up the recommendation. Now fire that thing."

"Firing."

The whole fuselage shuddered with the expulsion of a tungsten slug the size of my fist. It wasn't quite as instantaneous as the lasers from the fighters, but the results were more satisfying. One of the red diamonds disappeared in a white globe, and I wasn't sure if that was all computer animation or if the explosion was actually visible from where we were, but the fighter was gone. The other two peeled away, not forever, but long enough to get us into the atmosphere.

"We going to get any support from the *Jambo*?" I asked Lee.

"Unfortunately, no. Enemy cruisers are closing in and they had to bail. We're on our own for the time being."

"What about the orbital defense platforms?" I asked, squeezing the words out through the pressure on my chest. "I distinctly recall something about orbital defense platforms. We're not going to be shot down by one of them, are we?"

Lee chuckled and I hated him for it. How the hell did these Airedales act like this acceleration was nothing? I was a Marine, for Christ's sake! It was embarrassing.

"Naw, the *Jambo* took those out before we even launched, sir," he told me.

Damn. How had I missed that?

"All we gotta worry about are these fighters...and their surface to air defenses of course. And however many ground troops they got, but that's more your problem."

The atmosphere buffeted the shuttle and the exterior cameras began picking up the flames from the friction, and Lee ignored that just as easily as he ignored the g-forces, guiding the ship down through the upper atmosphere in a broad spiral.

"How are the other birds?" I asked, reluctant to admit that I couldn't figure it out myself but short on time.

"They took some fire, but they're still in the air. We've taken down five fighters, but they've wised up and they're staying out of our forward arc of fire, coming in from the sides. Hold on."

God*damn*it, I hated when pilots told me to "hold on," as if I had some other choice, like I was just going to let go, take off my seat restraints and fling myself across the cabin if they didn't warn me things were going to get rough. And it also meant they were going to do their best to make the rest of us puke.

I didn't, but it was a close thing, and I knew the rest of the team was hit even worse than I was for the simple reason that they weren't talking. Delta has a reputation as quiet professionals, and maybe they are when they're around civilians or regular grunts, but good God, can they talk when they're among their own. But not even Pops was drawling in my ear, and I figured it was because he, like me, was holding his jaws together for dear life.

I don't even know what Lee did with the bird because I had to shut my eyes and not look at the HUD, but it felt as if they turned the damned thing inside out and spun it end for end like a frisbee. All I could tell for sure was that, by the time we leveled off and I could finally breathe again, we were on the night side of the planet and threading the needle of a narrow pass through snowcapped mountains, lit up ghostly white by the planet's single moon.

"We're five minutes out from the settlement," Lee told me. "They call it a city, but it's damned small for a city in my opinion. We still going with the LZ at the front of the city?"

I tried to stare down at the ground moving below us, using the view from the belly cameras in my HUD overlaid with the maps the Helta had given us from before the invasion. No, I didn't want to just set down in that LZ, not when the original plan had been predicated on us getting detailed info from the spy drones that we didn't have.

"No," I said. "I want you to send the other birds into a holding pattern while you run us a low pass over the city and the military base."

"Are you fucking nuts?" Lee asked, turning in his chair to look at me despite the press of the boost and the fact we were both wearing helmets. "Sir?" he added belatedly. "There's a shit-load of ground fire gonna be coming up from the air defense turrets. We make a low pass, we may as well hang a target around our necks!"

"Do it, Lee," I said. "It's an order."

Which I didn't give too often to the shuttle crews because we were in separate commands and they knew their jobs. But I was in tactical command until we were boots on the ground and this was one of those times. Doubt gnawed at my guts, but I punched it in the face and told it to get back to the rear with the gear. Doubt could get you killed quicker than making the wrong decision.

"Aye, aye, sir," he replied sourly.

"We know what we're doing?" Pops asked me over our private net.

"We do." We hoped.

The bottom dropped out beneath me as the shuttle went into a steep dive, made worse by the fact that I had to watch through the camera view because otherwise, this was just meaningless aerobatics. It was early morning on the eastern end of the northernmost continent on Waypoint, the only one with a settlement because the southern continent was a morass of swamp and desert. The northern continent was beautiful, the whole stretch of it reminiscent of western Europe if the Europeans hadn't ruined the whole thing. The Helta hadn't strip-mined the place or overbuilt it with one city after another because that wasn't who they were, but they'd come here for a reason, and not just so the workers at the shipyards would have a planet to visit on R&R, and that reason was the biological treasures the place had to offer.

So, there were algae farms off the coast, soy farms on the plains, huge citrus orchards because apparently, bears loved them some oranges, as well as groves full of some sort of plants they called clearflower that I didn't know and hadn't bothered to follow up with the science staff to see if they knew because I really didn't care. The algae and soy farms were automated and would still be running unless the Tevynians had destroyed them out of spite, but the orchards and groves were tended by hand because, according to Joon-Pah, the fruit and whatever clearflower was reacted better to a gentle touch.

The groves and orchards were organized in clean rows, but not straight and square like in Florida and South America, but instead, sweeping curves and circles and all sorts of geometric shapes. The Helta believed agriculture was an art rather than a science. I tried to imagine what they would look like at the break of dawn, but the cartoonish enhancement of the shuttle's computer systems to make up for the low light made them look too fake. The important thing was, there were no enemy troops or air defense turrets in the groves or among the machinery of the farms, which were only a few miles out of the city.

"Let's designate the flats out in front of the soy fields as LZ Alpha," I said, bringing the other shuttles into the net. "If we need an emergency dust-off, Alpha will be the primary LZ. How copy?"

"Good copy, Gunfighter One," a static-filled voice replied. It was weak, barely penetrating the jamming coming from the Tevynian military encampment, but I still recognized Dani Brooks. I didn't get anything else and I suppose I was lucky that much came through.

"I'm picking up thermal signature from the settlement," Mayfield warned. "Smells like an air defense turret to the targeting computer."

"We're going in anyway," Lee said, and I couldn't see his dirty look but I could feel it. "Launch a spread of heatseekers and see if we get lucky."

I couldn't even feel the missile launch because I was too busy being tossed from side to side by Lee's juking and deking, and I didn't know if he was doing it because we were actually being targeted or if he was just getting even with me.

"Yes!" Mayfield exulted, raising a fist. "We have positive impact! Thermal bloom! We took out the laser turret!"

"And we have visual on the settlement."

We did, and this one was easier to follow than the sensor readings. It was a city. Or it had been. Now, it looked more like a prison.

Helta cities are a different animal than any human town,

having more in common with the Swiss Family Robinson tree-house than an urban area. They tried to live in harmony with nature in ways the most ardent tree-huggers in the history of tree-hugging had never managed. I'd seen pictures and video from the *Truthseeker's* database and usually, they built in and around existing redwood and sequoia forests. But here was different. The farms and the groves were in a very temperate valley, filled with oaks and other trees that wouldn't have looked too out of place in the woods of Georgia or South Carolina, not quite thick or sturdy enough for that sort of structure.

Instead, they'd built their homes out of local clay, which was, I suppose, as eco-friendly as they could manage. They reminded me of the adobe houses I'd seen in New Mexico, except more curved, rounded at the top instead of squared off, and arranged in the same sort of odd geometries as the groves. They had a certain charm to them...or I imagine they had before the Tevynian occupiers had made their additions.

They'd used the quickest, easiest material they could find to confine the Helta, which just happened to be those trees. They'd lasered them down and left the stumps, and hadn't even bothered to strip the bark off before they'd laid them into a wall surrounding a section of the settlement about a quarter mile on a side. It was the ultimate fuck-you to a culture that prided itself on being close to nature.

Our little fuck-you back was evident from the column of black smoke rising from the laser turret at the east corner of the barricaded city, and it was gratifying that there was at least one enemy target our US-built missiles could take down, because they didn't seem to do much to their aerospace fighters.

We were going fairly low and slow for the shuttle, which could burn up the sky with the engines the Helta had helped us build, but we still zipped by the city in seconds, coming out over the line of stumps that had once been a stand of trees. Beyond them was the landing field, the only sin against nature the Helta allowed themselves, cleared of grass, the dirt burned to volcanic glass by the takeoff jets of their shuttles. It was where the Tevynians had kept their fighter squadrons, and where they'd left the cargo haulers they'd used to bring in the construction equipment for their military base.

It was impressive, given the limited time they'd had to build it, about two hundred yards square, the walls sloped and thick and ten yards high, more than enough to absorb the crew-served plasma guns that were the most powerful infantry weapons either the Helta or the Tevynians possessed, maybe even enough to take a couple shots from the laser on one of their shuttles. And before the shuttles got that close, they'd have to deal with the laser turrets.

"Fuck!" Lee blurted and I lost track of the fortress along with my breakfast in a barrel roll. "Laser fire!"

"Launching," Mayfield said, and I finally caught a hint of the strain from the maneuver in his voice, which was satisfying, but not as satisfying as not dying. "Oh, damn! Those fighters are back, Cap!"

"They never fucking went away, Mayfield," Lee snapped. "Gunfighter Three, can you pull back to cover for us?"

We were running low, maybe twenty yards up from eyeballing it, though I couldn't have sworn to it since I couldn't focus on the numbers of the readout with everything screaming by and my vision narrowing into a black-rimmed tunnel.

"Coming, Gunfighter One," came the reply. "Give me ten seconds to break off."

"Oh, we may not have ten fucking seconds, Three...."

We didn't.

"It's on our six!" Mayfield screeched and I knew that tone. It was the tone of a man who knew things were about to go bad.

"I hope you got a good Goddamned look, Andy," Lee said. "Hold on!"

"Oh, Jesus." I snapped, the servo-assisted fingers of my gloves gripping the armrests of the frame so hard I could hear the metal creak at the pressure. "What the hell *else* am I gonna do?"

And then we crashed.

11

"How much longer, sir?" Chamberlain asked me, hissing the words in my ear.

I closed my eyes and counted to ten, and would have kept them closed the whole time if I hadn't been trying to keep track of the Delta team moving up the street. They were black shapes now, barely visible even with the enhancement of the goggles, moving beneath a covered walkway around the edge of the apartment building, barely wide enough for them to walk single file, led by Jose. And then they were gone and I pulled off the nylon cover to check my watch.

"Ten minutes, Chamberlain," I said. "Don't breathe in my ear unless you're buying me dinner."

The RTO withdrew, grimacing in embarrassment. I edged back into the alley and motioned to Gunny Moore, who was crouched down beside Marinelli, speaking to him in low, quiet tones that didn't travel far enough for me to pick up more than a murmur. The platoon sergeant waddled over to me, still crouched down, taking a knee beside me.

"They're out of sight," I told him. "I been checking out the street up ahead and there's an alcove up to the corner with a trash bin." I shrugged. "It looks like it hasn't been emptied in about a year, but it should be big enough for you to get two squads in there. I want you to head down now and stage in the alcove until it's go time, then have Marinelli initiate suppressive fire on enemy positions on that side of the building."

"And you're going to disable their vehicles?" he asked, mouth twisted into a scowl.

"I am. Why? You think it's a bad idea?"

"No, I just don't like spooks. These Delta boys are too much like spooks for my tastes."

"They are," I agreed. "And the whole thing smells dirty to me. But this Jambo guy seems to actually care if we get out of this in one piece, so we're going to do it his way. Copy?"

"Good copy, sir. Good luck."

The noise they made moving out of the alley set my teeth on edge, but there was nothing to do be done about it. Boots on concrete made sounds, equipment rustled and there was no getting around it. There was a certain background hum to the streets, something you tuned out after a while, and I just had to hope it would drown out their maneuver.

With their absence, Gregory moved up with his squad to take their place. The young E-5 came up beside me, moving smooth and casual, like we did shit like this every day.

"We moving out, sir?" he asked me, just a little breathless, eager to get into a fight. His M27 had an M320 grenade launcher mounted beneath the barrel and his left forefinger was tapping against it like he wanted to load up a round right now.

"Yeah. You see that alley about a hundred meters up this road?" I pointed ahead of us, the way the Delta team had gone. They had turned at the front of the next building across from us, cutting down the covered sidewalk, but the route I indicated was past that and would bring us out on the other side of the target building, where our HUMINT asset Jose had told us the cars were parked.

"Got it."

"We're taking that left and moving up the next street over. Get across this street fast and get us down that alley, but hold up midway through. I don't want anyone near the target spotting us before the Delta team gets into place."

"Copy that, sir. I'll put Napier on point."

It was his call, but it was a good one. Lance Corporal Napier was a steady point man who wouldn't get spooked and shoot at every stray cat.

"One minute," I told him. "Double-check ammo loads and NVG batteries."

While he did that, I turned back to my "platoon headquarters," which consisted, at the moment, of Chamberlain and the corpsman, Peterson. I was tempted to bring Peterson along, but we were split up into two units, and it made more sense to keep him at a central location where we could bring the wounded back to him. And Chamberlain was just about useless since the radio wouldn't work worth a damn here with the jamming equipment.

"Both of you stay with the trucks," I told them. "If we get back here and those fuckers—" I motioned at Uncle Charlie's drivers, who were leaning against the front fender of one of the trucks, smoking and speaking softly to each other. "—have taken the trucks and un-assed the area, we're pretty much dead. Keep your eyes on them and keep this alleyway secure. Shoot whoever you have to who isn't one of us. Clear?"

"Clear, sir," Peterson said. He was a Navy corpsman, but I trusted him to take down any threats more than I did Chamberlain, who was theoretically a rifleman in the way all Marines are supposed to be riflemen first.

"Stay here," I repeated, this time jabbing a blade hand at Chamberlain. "Don't fucking leave this position unless you're overrun. Don't come help us, don't go looking for trouble, don't follow any Goddamned stray dogs, just stay here and keep these trucks secure. Do you copy, Chamberlain?"

"Five by five, sir."

I wished I could see his eyes, because I didn't trust his words. If anyone could fuck up a wet dream, it was Chamberlain. But the alternative was leaving the trucks unguarded, and even though Jambo hadn't specifically told me to guard them, I figured it was important enough to take the initiative.

"Come on, Gregory," I said, slapping the bottom of my magazine to seat the rounds. "Load up some frag and let's go."

There was a quality to the streets in Catia, something I hadn't noticed before, driving in a Stryker, seeing the world through its periscope or targeting screen. The Strykers scraped the edge of the walls in places, yet somehow it seemed more claustrophobic on foot, as if the walls leaned inward, each empty window a possible sniper hide. The place beat down misery, dripping with it like the ever-present humidity, like every single poor son of a bitch who'd already been born with next to nothing to live here in the first place and then lost everything three times over had finally been forced out of even this place, the last place anyone else would ever want. The men went first, either drafted for the government's army back when there'd been a government, or later by the EPV when they'd stepped in and told the poor that they could either join with them or be the enemy. Then the women, because war is an equal-opportunity employer, and finally, the kids. Anyone old enough to hold an AK.

And when all that was left was the ghosts and the few old people who'd survived the starvation and the unrest and the Virus and the war, the EPV had moved in and made use of what was left, wearing the skin of a corpse. And we were walking through it, through the cemetery of a country.

The alley was so dark, even the NVG's could barely penetrate it, the computer's simulation little better than a 16-bit video game from before I was born, and I wanted to rip them off. I didn't, because I was an officer and had to set an example, and because I'd need them. The end of the alley was lit up day-bright by comparison, even though the only lights were what could leak through the blackout curtains from the apartment building.

I snorted dark amusement. The EPV had Chinese jamming equipment mounted on their roofs, but they couldn't even manage light discipline, as if radioing for air support was the only fucking thing American troops could do to kill them. Well, to be fair, we *did* have a history of using a shitload of air support, but that was just because we could.

Okay, I'll be frank, the lack of air support worried the shit out of me, but if the Delta team thought we could pull this off, then I believed it, too. Not because they were supermen or anything, although there was a part of me that couldn't help but believe that, but because they weren't known to throw their lives away pulling jobs they couldn't complete.

Napier held up about twenty yards from the end of the alley, crouched down behind a rusted-out burn barrel—what had once been a 55-gallon oil drum back when this place had produced oil —the rest of the squad taking alternating positions along the walls with as close to tactical separation as we could manage in the narrow alley. One RPG could still have killed three or four of us, but concealment was key for the moment.

"I can see the cars from here," Gregory told me when I moved up beside him and Napier.

And of course, I could see them just as well. They were mostly European and mostly over a decade old and looked it.

"You know what the difference between a BMW and a porcupine is, Gregory?" I asked him quietly, staring at the late-model SUV's.

"Negative, sir."

"Porcupines carry their pricks on the *outside.* Napier, MacMurray, you got the tools?"

"I got the Benchmade," Napier said, holding up the oddly-shaped tool in one gloved hand. It was called a Safety Cutter and could slice through seatbelts with one end and punch out window glass with the other.

"I just got my knife," MacMurray admitted. He had an orange lock-blade with a ridged metal stub on the butt end, which should be enough for side windows.

"Start at opposite ends," I told them, motioning at the cars. "Break the driver's side windows, pop the hoods." I waved behind me, catching the attention of Benitez and Williams. "You two come in behind them and cut the battery cables, the radiator hoses, anything you can get your hands on."

"What if they got car alarms, sir?" Napier asked. He was a skinny kid with a gaunt face and with the helmet and NVG's, he looked like a praying mantis.

"By the time you start busting windows, things'll be too loud for anyone to hear them." *I hope.* "Get going. The rest of you, cover the windows and the ends of the street, if you see anyone who's armed who isn't one of ours, take them down."

I took a final glance at my watch. Thirty seconds. Napier and the others jogged out of the end of the alley and the rest of us moved up in their wake, taking up overwatch positions, Gregory at the front, his Bravo team covering his Alpha team. I scanned the streets, but the only thermal signatures I saw that weren't from our guys were rats scurrying around in the trash-strewn gutters.

Napier's arm was cocked back to crack through the driver's side window of a 2019 X5 when the 240B opened up from the other side of the building. There was no mistaking the sound. Nothing else sounded quite like it, nothing the EPV had anyway. The lighter chatter of M27's took the soprano notes of the song and as I'd promised, when the car alarm of the X5 sounded at the shattering of the window, it was background music to the main event.

Return fire rattled high, echoing around the streets and off the walls of the ancient brick buildings, twisted by crumbling stucco and my guts twisted despite the fact I'd known it would happen. Those were my guys under fire, and I should have been with them. Instead, I was stuck watching the four Marines from Alpha team yanking open the hoods of German utility vehicles and speeding what the lack of maintenance and spare parts was already doing its best to accomplish.

I waited for EPV soldiers to run around the corner at any second, waited for someone to recognize that the gunfire was a diversion and come to check out the car alarm, but the corners remained clear and the crack of the AK's stayed on the opposite side of the building and, for an instant, I thought maybe everything would go exactly as planned.

I just happened to be looking at the side of the building when something from the barricaded doorway that had used to be the east entrance to the apartment building caught my attention. They'd nailed plywood across the door and I'd assumed they piled furniture or oil drums filled with sand or some such thing on the other side to make the whole thing protection against attack from this side. I might have been wrong, or maybe they'd just had a way to remove it quickly, because something was pounding against the plywood from the other side and the right end was already beginning to give.

I had about ten seconds to make a decision, I figured, before the barricade gave way and that closed exit became an open escape point. The easiest way to deal with it was probably to have my guys put a hundred rounds or so through the plywood to dissuade whoever was on the other side from trying to come out this way, but that was problematic. It might have been innocent civilians who'd been stuck in the building, though I doubted it. It might have been the Delta team looking for a safe exit. And I couldn't ignore that we were here to extract Uncle Charlie's ex-wife and kid and firing blind through a door might be contraindicated.

The second possibility was just to have Napier and the others withdraw to the cover of the alley and concentrate our forces from a defensible position to see what came through the door. The problem with that was, I wasn't sure I could get their attention above all the gunfire and if even one of them was late getting back, they'd be in our firing arc and we might shoot them or the bad guys might shoot them, but either way, there was a damned good chance of them getting shot.

And then there was what I'd already decided I was going to do and was just going through the motions of arguing the point.

"Follow me!" I yelled at Gregory, then I ran out into the street just like Captain Glenn and Gunny Moore would have yelled at me not to do.

Napier and the others had worked their way through four of the vehicles, leaving their hoods propped open and leaving them near the middle of the street, only a few yards to either side of the entrance. It would have been just too damned convenient if one of them had managed to look up and see the plywood flapping in the wind like the ensign on a British yacht, or been able to hear me yelling at them over the thunder of full-auto fire, but they were too buried in their work, counting on us to watch their backs.

I was maybe forty yards from the door when the plywood gave way and two of the biggest fucking Venezuelans I'd ever seen came through it shoulder first. Behind them was a machine gunner gone full Hollywood, carrying his PKM at the hip, with ammo belts draped over his shoulders and a black bandana tied around his head, and behind *all* of them, being pushed by another pair of EPV soldiers, were Laura and Paulo Martijena.

The image smacked me in the face, that moment in a dream when you realize it's actually a nightmare, that moment on a battalion run when you think you're a mile away from the finish and then the Sergeant-Major goes left instead of right and takes you up Heartbreak Hill again and you know it's going to be another four miles instead and you have to run faster than anyone else and not show how badly you think it sucks, because you're an officer.

The best thing to do would be to have Gregory put a grenade into the middle of them, but that would have killed our hostages, which would have been, as Captain Glenn liked to say, suboptimal. The next best thing would have been to put everyone behind cover and hunker down, maybe lay down fire at the edges to keep them penned inside, but the downside to that would have been the EPV assholes taking the hostages back into the building and time was a huge factor. And none of them had taken the time to put on night vision goggles. The big assholes who'd broken down the door hadn't seen us, hadn't noticed the hoods up on the cars, hadn't had nearly enough time to let their eyes adjust to the dark outside, and any delay would give them time to react.

So, I did something stupid. Because if you can't do something smart, do something quick, that's what I always say. Well, I'd recently started saying it. Like right then.

I was running pretty damn fast, and shooting accurately on the run was difficult, but I was about fifteen yards away from the door and if you can't hit a man-sized target at fifteen yards with an M27, you're not much of a Marine. The red targeting reticle in the carbine's optical sight danced with every pounding step of my boots on the cobblestone, but the mooks in the door had very big torsos and I pulled the trigger.

5.56x45mm has next to no recoil, and my adrenaline was

pumping, rocking that auditory exclusion and I for a single, fleeting instant, I thought I'd forgotten to take off my safety. But the big man stumbled, still off balance from running through the door, his AK slipping out of his hand as he went down. I transitioned to the other doorkicker, this one sporting a bushy beard and a mop of curly black hair sticking out beneath an olive-drab military cap. His eyes went wide and white at the muzzle flash, finally seeing that there were armed men rushing straight at him, and he tried to dig in his heels and stop and bring around his AK all at the same time.

I shot him through the face.

I wasn't some badass commando, and this wasn't some highly-trained, intricately-practiced move, though later on, looking back, it might have seemed that way. But the truth was, I was just rushing headlong into them and shooting as I went and the only reason I didn't get killed immediately was technological—I could see them and they couldn't see me.

That said, the machine gunner would have got me. He had warning and he had my position from my muzzle flash and I had no way to dodge in time to get out of his way, but he also had that big-ass, front-heavy, long-barreled PKM 7.62x54mm GPMG and he was lugging it freehand with the bipod folded. If it had been a lighter weapon, something easier to maneuver, he could have shouldered it and put a magazine through my chest before I could do a damned thing about it. He tried. He squeezed the trigger even before he moved the muzzle, chopping heavy 30-cal Russian rounds through the wall beside him, trying to pan the gun to his right across the lot of us.

Unfortunately for him, the big guy I'd shot through the face hadn't gone down yet, momentum carrying him forward another step, and he was a big guy. Big enough that the rounds lost energy going through him and when they punched into the SAPI plate over my chest, they didn't quite penetrate, though I wasn't immediately aware of that fact.

I'd already pulled the trigger before the baseball bat slammed into the right side of my chest and drove the air out of me, which was a damned good thing, because I sure wouldn't have thought to do it afterward. I didn't go down despite the pain, but I think that was more a function of the headlong sprint than any special fortitude on my part, because the fact I'd shot the machine gunner barely registered in my consciousness. He was going down and I was, too, stumbling forward, tripping over him and right into the woman.

She was, I thought, a bit haggard, rougher around the edges than she had been in the photos we'd been given, wearing threadbare blue jeans and a flannel shirt instead of the yellow sundress of happier times. Her long hair was tied into a ponytail, and her hand was wrapped so tight around the boy's wrist that when I knocked her over, she brought him right down with us.

I barely felt either of them beneath me, because I was wrapped in Kevlar body armor and elbow and knee pads, tactical vest, spare mags, pistol holster, helmet, NVG's and all the other battle rattle we brought with us, not even counting the fact that my entire chest was numb. One thing did penetrate the pain and the fog, though, and that was the thought that the last two guys in line were going to kill me. I couldn't see their faces, just their boots, old, black leather Venezuelan Army boots, laced up haphazardly, as if they'd been pulled on in a panic. But they both had AK's, and if those were also former Venezuelan military from five years ago as well, they'd probably still work for all that.

I heard the shots, penetrating the auditory exclusion and the adrenaline-fueled pounding in my ears, like being on the inside of a drum kit, and yet something sounded wrong about them, too high-pitched to be the ancient Russian weapons. The boots scrambled backwards and then a body fell, AK blasting a dying burst into the ceiling, sending plaster and glass from a long-dead light fixture showering down around us. The other EPV soldier turned and ran, chased by bullet strikes in the walls.

"Get your ass up, sir," Alvin Gregory yelled in my ear, grabbing me by the casualty handle on the back of my vest and hauling me to my feet. "If you get yourself killed, Gunny Moore is going to kick my balls into next Tuesday."

I tried to take a breath to answer him and winced at the pain it caused in my chest. He tugged at my vest and felt around beneath it, then withdrew his hand, seeming satisfied.

"You're not bleeding," he declared. "It didn't penetrate. Don't get shot again, sir."

"Working on it," I wheezed at him. "Secure the hostages."

But it was already being done, because they were a Marine infantry squad and not a bunch of idiots who needed me to tell them to tie their shoes. I couldn't tell who it was because their backs were to me and one armored, helmeted Marine pretty much looks like another when they're wearing NVG's over their face, but they'd pulled Laura Martijena and her son off the floor and were urging them toward the door, but the woman was trying to break away, yelling at them in Spanish. Her son just stared up at me with wide eyes, like I was some sort of alien life form.

I drew on my reserves of Spanish and tried to intervene.

"Mrs. Martijena, don't be scared. We're United States Marines and we're here to rescue you from the EPV. Come with us and we'll get you out of here."

"I don't want to leave!" she yelled at me in nearly unaccented English, still trying to yank her wrist away from the Marine holding onto it. "I wasn't a prisoner! These people are my friends, damn you!"

My chest hurt and it wasn't from the bullet.

"Oh, shit."

12

"Oh, shit."

I don't *think* I lost consciousness. The hit had been pretty hard, but not as hard as it could have been. I hadn't registered the words at the time, but now they echoed in my memory as much as the pained moan I'd just uttered.

"Belly jets!" Lee screamed, and I hadn't been sure if he was giving an order or making an announcement, but at least some of the intense discomfort of the next few seconds had come from the sudden and wrenching boost from the shuttle's landing jets scorching the ground beneath us.

The rest came from hitting the ground a hell of a lot harder than the bird had been designed for. I don't know what hurt more, the actual impact or the emotional pain of hearing the entire, priceless, currently-irreplaceable shuttle that was also my ride to safety creaking and cracking like something big and very important had broken beyond repair.

But I flogged my brain into action, moving past the emotional and physical shock.

"Out!" I yelled, yanking at my quick release. "Everybody out of the damn bird now!"

I nearly fell right out of the seat, because we were down at an angle, about ten degrees or so to the right, close enough to flat that I could get out without climbing, but far enough off level that I knew we didn't have landing gear down.

We couldn't stay here. We were a giant, fucking target for those fighters and the only way to survive was to close with the enemy. Luckily, Pops and the others in the Delta team knew that better than I did, and most of them were already up and heading for the auxiliary airlock, aware just as I was that the belly ramp wouldn't be operational.

"Is anyone hurt?" I asked, grabbing the back of the pilot's seat and pulling myself up behind Captain Lee. "Are you two okay? Chief, any injuries in the crew?"

I didn't even remember the name of the shuttle's crew chief, though I was sure it was something eastern European with a lot of consonants, but I knew there was him and two other Space Force crewmembers, and I couldn't see any of them from up in the cockpit.

"I'm okay," Lee insisted. He was moving at least, working at his restraints, but Mayfield was still sitting back in his seat, hands in his lap.

"Mayfield!" I yelled at him, shaking his shoulder. Which was a damned reckless thing to do if he had a spine injury, but this was the whole burning car scenario and un-assing the vehicle was paramount. "Are you operational, Lieutenant?"

He moaned by way of reply, but his hands moved and he pulled at his helmet. Beneath it, a pressure cut oozed blood down his eyebrow, but his eyes seemed focused, the pupils not dilated, so I pulled the quick release on his seat restraints and dragged him up.

"Get your weapons," I told him and Lee. "If you have a bug

out bag with water and food and medical supplies, grab that too and then get out of this bird before someone pulls a strafing run on us."

The Delta team was already piling out the airlock, the inner and outer doors open at once because, of course, the pressure was the same on both sides. Which meant I was stuck waiting for them to file out one at a time, and then the Ranger squad behind them. I tried not to fidget, tried not to show how badly I wanted to get off the shuttle.

The crew chief was pushing his people ahead of him just behind the Rangers, handing out M27's and Musset bags of magazines and yelling at them to get their asses in gear. Lee and Mayfield were stumbling along behind him, the pilot shouldering a MOLLE pack and both men carrying HK MP-7 submachine guns, compact weapons that fired a tiny 4.6mm bullet that didn't impress me much. Hopefully, they wouldn't have to use them.

"Sir, get out here!" It was Pops, his transmission loud and clear, laser line-of-sight transferred from one suit to another. "We got a shit sandwich out here!"

I wedged myself in front of the squad of Rangers, scrambling through the lock, pushing the last of the Delta team ahead of me. The relief of finally being outside was muted by the urgency of the threat, but I took a moment to scan our surroundings and figure out exactly where the hell we'd landed. It was both better and worse than I thought.

We'd plowed into the dirt less than two hundred yards from the wall across the front of the Helta city and, looking back at the shuttle, it wasn't nearly as bad as it had seemed when we'd hit. The fuselage was intact, the wings still attached, and I didn't see any tears in the metal. What had brought us down was obvious, though. The port air intake was charred black and although I couldn't see it, I figured the hit was from a laser and it had cut off the airflow to the turbojet suddenly and catastrophically.

That was the better part. The worse part was in the other direction. The ground between the city and the military base was flat and open, now that the Tevynians had cut down all the trees, a broad plain interrupted only by a few cargo shuttles at the edge of the landing field, empty and desultory in their isolation. And a little over a mile across that plain was the military base, big as life and twice as ugly. The primary star was rising behind the city and a grey wash of cold, pre-dawn light splashed over the cyclopean walls of the fortress, a grey hill against fields burned brown and glinting off the cargo vehicles heading our way.

"All Gunfighter birds this is Gunfighter One," I transmitted, hoping someone would read. "We are down, repeat, we are down just outside the walls of the settlement."

"Gunfighter One is damaged," Lee put in, limping out of the airlock just behind me, "but she's reparable. We need a team down here to replace the port air intake."

I glared at Lee even though he couldn't see me. There were more important matters to attend to.

"Enemy vehicles are heading our way from the base," I transmitted. "Moving slow. We probably have minutes at most. We could use some air support."

I waited, staring upward into the lightening sky, trying to get a glimpse of our birds, hoping against hope someone was in position to hear my call.

What sounded like a peal of thunder rolled across the cloudless firmament and I knew it was a sonic boom, then another and a third, until it seemed as if the whole world would split apart from the unceasing drumbeat of the gods of war. I couldn't see the discharge of the coil guns or differentiate the missiles from the engines of the aircraft, but there were distant flashes of heat lightning far above us from the laser weapons firing, and my gut clenched at the thought there was no one left to answer my call for help.

"I read you, Gunfighter One." I'd expected one of the pilots, or maybe the gunners, but it was Dani Brooks. "The other shuttles are tied up with the fighters and they can't get clear to set down my people or provide air support. If you can secure the Helta crew, we might be able to free up a shuttle to retrieve them."

"Roger that. Any contact from the *Jambo*?"

"Negative, both ships are fully engaged. We're on our own for now."

Fuck.

"Roger that. We're going into the settlement."

"Be careful. We'll get to you as soon as we can."

I switched off the mic.

"Yeah, I'll hold my fucking breath."

"If you're done praying," Pops told me, "we got troops coming out the front gate."

Of course there were, because God forbid anything should go simply today.

The timber walls looked so much like the frontier forts I'd seen in the old western movies my dad used to love, that when the gates swung open, I expected the US cavalry to charge out on horseback, bugle blaring. Which would have been cooler than what actually came through.

There weren't a lot of them—maybe forty in all. They probably figured they didn't *need* that many to watch over the Helta prisoners, because an aggressive Helta has a lot in common with an honest politician, which is to say, they're scarce to the point of nonexistence. They hadn't mounted heavy weapons on the walls of the town, likely for the same reason, and they came charging out at us like we were Iron-Age warbands going at each other with swords and spears, which was their loss.

"Spread out!" I yelled, falling to a knee and bringing my rifle to my shoulder. "Flight crew, get behind the shuttle and take cover!"

The enemy, I thought, didn't realize who they were dealing with and wouldn't know about the weapons we carried. That wouldn't last much longer, but it would still work this time. They opened fire on the run, their lasers crackling ionized static trails through the morning mist, one of the bursts of energy passing so close that I could feel a brush of heat through the visor of my helmet. Some of them might have hit the shuttle, but I wasn't overly worried about it. It was built to take shots from the laser weapons on a fighter—the rifles the Tevynian soldiers carried wouldn't scratch its paint.

I shook my head at their tactics, a swell of pity in my chest. They wore armor and they had balls big enough to bowl with, the women too, which was as much credit as I was willing to give them. Beyond that, their tactics weren't that different from the ones my Uncle Eddie had seen from the Shia militias in Iraq in 2004. They just fired everything they had as fast as they could and rushed in, trying to overwhelm their enemy. And to be fair, without the Svalinn armor and the KE rifles, it might have worked, since they outnumbered us two to one.

But since we did...

"Fire at will."

A laser blast glanced off the armor over my right bicep and I ended a guttural expletive to the order at the sudden, scalding heat, knowing I'd picked up a second-degree burn, but also knowing I'd have had the arm burned off at the shoulder without the armor. I touched the trigger and the buttstock of the M900 Kinetic Energy rifle thumped into my shoulder hard enough to irritate the burn, but it hurt the Tevynian on the other end of the equation a lot more. At least I assumed I'd shot him. There was a lot of tungsten going downrange and although the Delta team and the Rangers were both well-trained enough to stick to their fields of fire, that didn't mean the ones on either side of me wouldn't be shooting at the same guy. However many people shot him, he pitched forward ass over teakettle and didn't move again, and I only noticed him going down because I'd shifted to the soldier a few yards to his right.

I was too late for that one, then too late for the next one and by then, forty had been winnowed down to twenty, and they weren't running at us anymore. There was a tipping point as there always was, when the lot of them recognized how many of their number had gone down and the headlong charge slowed, then faltered and turned into a shambolic withdrawal. It *had* to be shambolic because they didn't withdraw when they were fighting the Helta, and you didn't practice something you never believed you'd have to do.

Another mistake, and probably not one they'd have made if they'd ever used any of that high tech weaponry they took from the Helta fighting each other. According to Joon-Pah, they hadn't. They'd gone straight from wars between tribes using weapons that wouldn't have seemed out of place at the Battle of Hastings to uniting against the Helta.

We couldn't let them run. If they went back into the city, we'd have to root them out before we began the search for Fen-Sooyan, and with those vehicles coming across the plain, that wasn't an option. No one needed me to give the order to keep firing. The Delta boys knew the score as well as I did, and shooting at the enemy was the natural rest state of a Ranger. The barrage seemed to drag on for interminable minutes, but it was actually only a few more seconds before the last of them fell.

I felt like I should have been horrified. Forty humans, of a sort, had just died at my order. But I wasn't, and maybe that said something dark and twisted about my soul, or maybe it was just the helmets. It was hard to think of the Tevynians as fellow humans when they went into battle dressed in black body armor, reflective visors covering their faces. I didn't have to see the light go out of their eyes when they died, didn't have to see their eyes at all. Another miscalculation on their part, though not one I could blame on them. They'd simply stolen the designs the Helta had used, and the Helta had gone with the look out of practicality. They'd wanted combat armor that could serve as a spacesuit at need.

"Cease fire!" I yelled, waving my hand in front of my face in the universal military signal for the order, mostly out of habit. No one was looking my way and they could all hear my order over their helmet headphones. "Move up! Everyone, get inside those gates now!"

Pops led them, sprinting across the hundred yards in a time that would have made an Olympic athlete go green with envy, the rest of the team arrayed in a wedge behind him. The Rangers went next and I chivvied the flight crew ahead of me, determined to be the last one through. It was hard trying to run slower than the Zoomies, particularly when they were still weighed down by their pressure suits and I had to restrain myself from picking a couple of them up under my arms and carrying them, which I could have.

The vehicles were about half a mile away now, growing from dots against the scorched, black field into white, angular wedges of metal. No plastic. The Helta didn't like to use it, because it could only be made from oil and to get oil, you had to drill into a living planet, while metal could be extracted from asteroids without ever "despoiling nature." But there was something satisfyingly old-fashioned and weighty about a big, metal tractor, something I would have appreciated so much more if they hadn't been bearing down on me with plasma guns and laser weapons.

I backed through the gates, squeezing off a half a dozen shots at the approaching vehicles. I know I hit them. The trajectory of a round from the KE rifle stayed flat for well over a mile, and the stabilization system in the armor made a hit nearly automatic. But the metal on the heavy construction vehicle was thick and worse for me, the electric motors were built into the axles of the wheels, with the isotope power pack in the undercarriage, so putting rounds into the front of the thing might be spitting in the wind.

"Come on, sir!" Pops yelled at me. "Everyone's inside and we want to get this gate closed!"

Oops.

I turned and ran through the gate just ahead of the blast from a crew-served laser, the heavy weapon ripping into the ground where I'd just stood, throwing up a steam explosion as the moisture in the pavement vaporized and spattering the back of my armor with debris. I ducked to the side of the gate and Dog and Ginger pushed it shut, their suits doing work that would have taken four or five men without the exoskeletal assist. Wood creaked and I could see now just how thick the walls were, constructed from twin layers of timber with rocks and dirt packed between them.

An irrational surge of relief at being inside the walls was dispelled by a thundercrack and a gout of flame from the other side of the wall. One of the Rangers had been standing right next to the area and he stumbled away from it, the right shoulder of his armor coated black with soot. It had been a shot from a plasma gun, probably mounted on one of the vehicles and just the one blast had blown right through the thick wall, which meant it was most definitely concealment, but by no means cover.

I had seconds to come up with something and I scanned the area behind us in desperate haste. Buildings, curved and tan and anonymous, nothing in their design to indicate to me whether they were homes or businesses or workshops. They arced around in a pattern that made no sense to my aesthetics, but I suppose they were quite practical to bipedal, talking sun bears. Fur-lined faces peeked from doorways and windows, residents too scared to come out into the street to see what was happening, but too curious not to sneak a look.

We could take refuge in the buildings, but they'd be just as vulnerable to the heavy weapons as the wall, and we'd just be endangering the Helta civilians. In the street, there were no personal vehicles, no building materials, nothing that—

Something just around one of the senseless curves in the street caught my eyes, something white and metallic sticking out from behind one of the adobe structures.

"Pops!" I snapped. "There are a couple of construction vehicles down there. Drive them over in front of the gate, block it off!"

"How the hell do we drive those things?" Ginger demanded.

"There's a step-by-step translation program for every type of Helta machinery in your comm unit," I told him. "And the damned bears make everything so easy to use, even a bunch of Iron-Age morons like the Tevynians can operate it. You telling me you aren't smarter than those spear-chuckers?"

"Come on, Ginger, Dog, Ringo," Pops said, breaking into a loping run. "We'll figure it out when we get there."

We had to give them time. The nearest house to the wall was tall, three stories if it had been a human building. We could get a good shooting platform up there.

"Follow me," I told the others. "We're clearing the civilians out of here and establishing a firing position on the roof."

The door was surprisingly humanlike, and, shockingly, made of wood, although it was oval and didn't have a knob of any kind that I could see. I didn't bother looking for one, just planted the sole of my boot into the center of it. The wood was old and solid, probably taken from a dead tree if I knew the Helta, but it splintered under the impact and I stepped into a room. I couldn't have told you the purpose of the chamber, could barely have described it in human terms. There were things that might have been bean bag chairs, or maybe they weren't and I was totally misinterpreting them. There were chest-high tables running the length of the walls with depressions in them that might have been bowls for food, but I might have been getting that wrong, too. And there was some sort of glass chest with...things in it. They were little bits of twisted glass or crystal in shapes I didn't recognize.

And there were a dozen Helta huddled in a corner of the room, eyes wide, teeth bared like they were trying to look fierce but only succeeding in looking terrified.

I touched the keypad on my left forearm and activated the external speakers and the translator program.

"You need to get out of here," I warned them, "and get away from the walls. The Tevynians are attacking and it's not safe here."

"The Tevynians are attacking?" one of them repeated, pushing himself to his feet. Well, I thought it was a him. I was hardly an expert. He wasn't wearing a military uniform and I barely remembered what their civilian clothes looked like from the files I'd seen. His were loose-fitting trousers with some sort of toga or long tunic over them, his shoes resembling closed-toe sandals. "Who are you if not the Tevynians? You are not of us!"

That was rather forward and bold for a Helta, and I had a sudden hunch. Probably wrong, but worth checking out. I raised the visor of my helmet and the Helta gasped...except the one guy, the talker.

"I'm Major Andy Clanton of the United States Marine Corps," I told him, "from Earth, the world you call 'the Source.' I'm an ally of Joon-Pah, captain of the *Truthseeker*, and he's sent me to find a friend of his named Fen-Sooyan and his crew of shipwrights. We've been sent to take them to safety."

I didn't know Helta well enough to be certain what a shocked expression looked like on their furry, ursine faces, but I was willing to bet this was it.

"I am Fen-Sooyan," he told me and I wanted to pump my fist. *He shoots, he scores!* "But how do I know you are who you say you are?"

"Do the Tevynians have this?" I asked him, waving at my powered armor, then at the door. "Would they be shooting at each other? If nothing else, you can see that we're their enemy and that should be enough. Now, we need to get you into one of our shuttles and off this world before we're overrun."

"You wish us to leave all behind all the rest of the Helta kept as prisoners and hostages here?" Fen-Sooyan asked me. "We can't do that!" He took a step back and this time, I think the shocked faces from the other Helta were aimed at him. He ignored them, his shoulders squaring. "They'll be slaughtered! The Tevynians will assume we helped you, that you are Helta military!"

"That's vaguely insulting," Rodent said from the doorway, covering our backs.

"Look, we don't have time to argue," I insisted, fingers clenching around the grip of my rifle. "It's going to be a close thing whether one of our shuttles can break loose of the Tevynian fighters long enough to pull you and your crew out. There are what? Thousands of you here in this enclosure?"

"Over nine thousand," he told me, and the translator gave his words a grim tone. "All that is left after the evacuation...and the hundreds slaughtered by the Tevynians."

"We have four fucking shuttles," I blurted, "and one of them is damaged. There's no fucking way we can pull all those people out of here!"

"Well, then," he replied, chin tucked down into his chest with a gesture the translator informed me indicated stubborn insistence, "I suppose if you want my crew of shipwrights, you'd best kill every last one of the Tevynians."

13

Something exploded.

I wasn't sure what, couldn't immediately tell what direction the blast had come from, but it rattled the few surviving windows on the block and lit up the sky with a diffuse, yellow glow. Laura Martijena shrank against me, forgetting our positions on opposite sides of the conflict for a moment in sudden shock and fear. I hadn't. I pulled a white, plastic flex cuff out of my thigh pocket and handed it to Gregory.

"Secure her hands," I told him. "Have someone carry the kid. We're getting the fuck out of here."

She started cursing and screaming and tried to fight, but Gregory and one of the others grabbed her wrists and strapped them tight, then whoever the hell it was Gregory had called forward grabbed her wrists by the cuff and pulled them up to keep her off balance. Between the screaming and cursing and the gunfire, I almost didn't hear the crackle of the radio.

"Boneyard Two-One," the call came, faint but audible, "this is Boneyard One-Zero, over."

Jambo. It was Jambo. I'd nearly forgotten the call-signs we'd agreed on, since I'd given up hope of actually being able to communicate with the radios. I touched the key on my shoulder.

"One-Zero, this is Two-One, good copy, though I don't know how. Over."

"That big explosion you heard? That was their expensive Chinese jamming gear going bye-bye. I knew that C-4 would come in handy. What's your sitrep? Over."

"We have the targets," I informed him. I wanted to suggest we use the newly-operational comms to call in air support, but even if there was something on station not tasked with another mission, it would take way too long to get it into position, not to mention the fact that the Delta team was already inside. "We're taking them back to the trucks. If you can get out, we can be Oscar Mike. Over."

No immediate response, which worried me. More chattering sounded, closer this time, upstairs in the apartment building, intensifying into the sort of persistent jackhammer beat you'd expect from a road crew.

"Two-One, we are pinned down." The racket in the background of the transmission was a louder, more obnoxious cousin to the echoing rattle from upstairs. "We're going to try to break contact, but if we are not at the trucks in five minutes, I need you to get the woman and the kid out of here and make the rendezvous with those choppers."

Jambo didn't sound fatalistic. In fact, he sounded supremely confident in his own ability to get out of this or any other bad situation. Me, though, I wasn't so confident. We were beetles trapped in a mound of fire ants.

"I'm bringing up a squad to get you," I told him, less because I was worried about him and more because I wanted to get the hell out of there and didn't have any confidence I could accomplish our exfiltration without Jambo.

"Negative," he snapped. "Do *not* come up here! We will find a—"

Whatever assurance he'd meant to give me, it was washed out in another wave of gunfire. Somewhere above us, a grenade banged petulantly.

Fuck.

"Gregory," I said, grabbing the man by his vest and pulling him close so he could hear me, "take your Bravo team and get the woman and the kid back to the trucks. Keep them there until Gunny Moore reaches you. He's in charge then. I'm keeping your Alpha team with me. The Delta team is pinned down and I'm going to go try to break them out."

Gregory's eyes were concealed behind his goggles, but I had the sense they'd gone wide.

"You sure, sir?" Which was a dumb question.

"Go," I told him, pushing him gently.

Gregory shouted urgent instructions to his people and in seconds, he was jogging across the street, dragging Laura Martijena and her son along. She was still caterwauling, but I'd kind of tuned her out, a background noise just like the gunfire. I touched the key on my shoulder and switched freqs.

"Boneyard Three-One," I called to Gunny Moore, "this is Boneyard Two-One, do you copy? Over."

When the reply came, I thought, at first, it was filled with static, until I realized I was hearing gunfire, probably the 240.

"Two-One, this is Three-Zero. Good copy, over."

"We have the targets," I told him, "and we're heading back to the vehicles. Pull back to the trucks. Over."

"Copy that. We'll break contact here. Over."

"Two-One out."

I found Napier out by the sidewalk, crouched down, watching our approaches.

"Come on," I said, slapping him on the shoulder. "You're with me. Get Alpha team unfucked and follow me."

If he was confused, he didn't let it get in the way of following my orders, and they were up and ready to go in seconds. Edging closer to the doorway, I tried to catch even a flicker of movement, a shadow, but the walls were bare and unresponsive, offering no help. I had a single fireteam and I was about to head inside to take on God knew how many EPV terrorists who had already pinned down a Delta team. This was a brilliant plan and I was sure it was just the sort of thing the promotion boards would look at when they made me a general.

"Napier," I said, "smoke."

The lance corporal pulled a cylindrical grenade off his tactical vest, pulled the pin and whipped it as far down the entrance hall as he could, bouncing it off the wall at the end and sending it careening down to the left. Light flared briefly, followed by billowing clouds of white smoke that filled the hallways. I gave it a few seconds, then ducked inside.

Taking point wasn't the brightest idea, but I wasn't sure where we were going and I didn't want to try to communicate in these narrow confines on top of trying to find the Delta team and not get killed. Plus, I had a run of really bad decisions going and there was no point in jumping off that train at this point in the ride.

I charged through the smoke, hoping to not give whoever might be waiting on the other side the chance to get a bead on me, my stomach twisting with that feeling I got when I was in the lead car of a roller coaster, hanging at the first big drop. It seemed like a certainty, like my fate was etched in stone and the bullets were already fired that would end my life.

But they weren't. The ground floor was unoccupied on the east, which shouldn't have been a surprise. My Marines were shooting at the place from the north and the Delta team was attacking on the upper floors, and since that one guy had escaped when we'd taken the woman and her kid, they knew we had people down at the vehicles. The EPV would be trying to get out the west entrance, and to do that, they'd have to go through the Delta boys.

The apartments were empty shells, their doors hanging open —the ones that still *had* doors. I stopped at the first few, checking them quickly, but then decided I'd have to take my chances and bypass them all. I needed to find the stairs. I hadn't thought it would take so long to find the damned stairs, just had a vague idea that I'd go inside and voila! There would be the stairs. Instead, there was just row after row of cookie-cutter apartments and *where were the goddamned stairs?*

Some buildings in Catia had external stairs, but I'd seen from the outside that this one didn't. It was more modern, probably built during the high times of the Chavez regime before everything had gone to shit, when he tried to spread that oil money to the poor by building new housing. It hadn't worked the way he thought it would, because people who get given shit they didn't work for don't appreciate it, and all those shiny new people-boxes turned to shit within a few years. But he'd accomplished one gigantic blow against the hated Americans: he'd hidden this Goddamned staircase.

More gunfire from the next floor up guided me to those mythical stairs like a signal flare, leading me to the right down a short hallway to the blocked exit to the south. And there they were. I turned back to Napier, pausing to get a head count and make sure everyone had followed us. Yeah, there hadn't been any shooting our way, but privates are like small children sometimes and if you don't hold their hand, they can wander off looking for shiny objects.

I waved Napier over and leaned next to his ear.

"We're going up here and I *think* we're going to be coming

behind the enemy, but I can't be sure." I glanced back at the last Marine in line, Private Rollins. She was fairly new to the platoon, a small woman, looking almost like a child playing at war, but she'd never held us back or showed any weakness. She had hard, angular features that could transform into a fierce mask when she was angry. An M320 rode under her M27. "Tell Rollins to load up buckshot and be ready to fire it behind us if I'm wrong."

"Sir," Napier said, after he passed on the order, "let me go first. It's my job."

His tone was gently chiding and I wanted to argue, but he was right and I knew it. I waved him ahead of me, but fell in right behind him, because he wasn't *that* right. We only had one fireteam and none of them had any more combat experience than me.

Napier tiptoed up the steps, throwing his shoulder against the wall as he came to the landing, his carbine aimed upward. He waved to me that it was clear and continued. The gunfire was louder now, echoing off the walls and rattling through my sinuses, promising death and destruction at the top of the stairs.

Why the fuck am I doing this? Jambo ordered me not to. Or he was about to. I bristled and took a long, double-step upward behind Napier. *He's a fucking master sergeant, he can't tell me what to do.*

Napier stopped at the top of the stairs, signaling to me that he had enemy in sight. Which was good, I supposed, since it meant at least we would see them before they saw us. I turned back to the rest of the fireteam and motioned for Rollins to come forward. She climbed up the stairs, holding her weapon at high port, careful to keep it pointed downrange and not at any of us, which I appreciated.

I held up a palm for them to wait and touched the transmit key on my shoulder.

"Boneyard One-Zero, do you copy?" I yelled the words, not

only so he could hear me but so I could hear myself. "One-Zero, this is Two-One, do you copy?"

The response was broken, crackling with static and nearly drowned out by gunfire both in my ears and in the transmission, but I recognized Jambo's voice.

"Two-One, get out of here!" he bellowed. "Get those trucks going! We're pinned down on both sides and we're not getting out of here!"

"Shut up, Master Sergeant," I told him, grinning with satisfaction at an opportunity I'd probably never have again. "We're on your east side in the stairwell and we're about to open up on the EPV from behind. Take advantage of that and get your ass out of there. On three."

I counted down on my fingers for the benefit of Napier and Rollins and the other two, Carter and Wilson, and when I hit three, Rollins, Napier and I sprinted up to the top of the stairs and opened fire.

I had a split second to register what I was seeing, a flash of data that I probably didn't even fully process until moments later. The EPV was spread out between two apartments, one on either side of the hallway, holding their position and pinning down the Delta team with a pair of drum-fed PKM machine guns, chewing apart the walls. Bodies littered the floor, EPV bodies, taken out by the Delta team before the machine guns had gotten set up, but it was no wonder Jambo and his boys were stuck. The two guns were a meatgrinder.

Rollins, like Han, shot first. There's something viscerally satisfying about a buckshot round. It had gone in and out of favor, and when I'd first enlisted in the Marines, before I'd gone off to college to get a degree and a butterbar, it was no longer issued. But it had become popular again with the city fighting here in Caracas and I liked it. Imagine a shotgun with a barrel twice as large as a twelve gauge and a lot more pellets fired from only about ten yards away.

Rollins had aimed at the gunner in the door on our left, and when the round hit him, he disappeared in a red mist and the gun went silent, but the horror of what the round did to the man was, thankfully, blurred and out of focus. My concentration was straight ahead, to the gun team on the right, on my aiming reticle floating over the machine gunner's chest. He was pudgy, a man who got more than enough to eat, which put him a leg up on most people in Catia, and he was wearing designer clothes, or at least very well-made copies. He was one of Major Stevie's personal guards, kept well and given the best because he was likely going to die.

I didn't disappoint him. He jerked at the impact of the rounds, but they didn't kill him, and I realized the black vest he was wearing over his silk shirt was high-class body armor. He let off the trigger of his PKM and started to turn, but I shifted my aim before he could and put a second burst into his head and neck. It had taken only an extra two seconds, but it was enough for the man beside him to spin around and bring up his AKM assault rifle. I wasn't alone, though, and Napier took the man down.

"Move up!" I yelled, clapping Napier on the shoulder.

He sprinted up to the right-hand room. Rollins took off a half-second later, leading the others into the other apartment. And I went straight, because there was still fire coming from down the hallway, though it was lighter—a handful of men with rifles. At the sudden silence of the machine guns, their fire slacked off and I used the lull to rush down at them, hosing the far end of the hall with one burst after another until I reached the apartment where I assumed Jambo had taken refuge. I guessed that because of all the holes in the wall.

I stopped abruptly at the yawning barrel of an M68 poking

out from behind the ruins of what had once been a couch before it had been chewed to pieces. It took a moment before I recognized Jambo behind it. He'd lost his helmet somewhere and blood was trickling down from a cut over his eyebrow, but what concerned me more was the blood welling up beneath the field dressing wrapped around his left forearm.

"I told you to get out of here," he grumbled.

"If you thought I'd listen to that," I told him, "then you're not as smart as all you operator types think you are. Stop bitching and let's get out of here."

The team dug its way out from behind overturned furniture, bookcases, refrigerators, dishwashers, anything they'd been able to drag out to use for cover. And it hadn't been very good cover. Every single one of them seemed to be at least lightly wounded, though a quick head count told me none had been killed, which was a minor miracle. One man, the one I'd heard them call Cube, was limping badly, his right thigh a bloody mess, and two others had to grab him beneath the shoulders and half-carry him out the door.

I preceded them, swinging around the corner and then ducking back as a burst of rifle fire smacked into the wall just above me, sending a spray of plaster raining down around me like snow. The EPV soldiers down the hall had finally figured out their machine guns were down and instead of doing the rational thing and beating feet out of there to fight another day, they were rushing straight at us, because rational people didn't generally become terrorists.

I was about to lean back out and return fire, but Jambo stopped me by grabbing the back of my vest. He had a grenade in his hand, the pin already pulled, and he whipped it around the corner and down the hallway and withdrawing, hands over his ears. The blast was a Lambeg drumbeat vibrating through the wall, through my shoulders and into my skull, and then there was silence except for the ringing in my ears.

"We're coming out!" I yelled. "Don't shoot!"

"Hopefully," Jambo said, his mouth twisting into a scowl, "they listen better than you do."

I didn't bother to answer. All gunfire had ceased, not just in the hall but outside as well. Gunny Moore and the rest of the platoon were probably on their way back to the trucks. We didn't have any more diversions and we needed to get out of here now.

"Napier," I said, "take point and get us down fast."

Unlike me, the kid knew how to follow orders and it was all the beat-up Delta team could do to keep up with him as he took the stairs two at a time. The ground floor had seemed deserted on the way in, but this time, it had a haunted air to it, fraught with menace lurking in every shadow. But we lacked the time to check those shadows or clear the apartments and all we could do was get past them as quickly as we could. I held my breath the whole way to the exit and even when we came out, I wasn't quite ready to let it go. I couldn't shake the feeling there was someone trailing behind, waiting until we dropped our guard to open up on us.

But no one was, and we rounded the curve heading back to the alley with the trucks unopposed, the streets as silent as a graveyard, our pounding footsteps grinding into broken glass on the pavement obscenely loud.

I'd figured we would be the last to arrive, but Gunny Moore and his two squads were just jogging up the street from the other direction by the time we made it to the alley, some of them panting with exertion.

"Problem?" I asked my platoon sergeant.

"Oh, the fucking A-gunner dropped his fucking sidearm," Moore growled, casting a stinkeye at the assistant to the company machine gunner. The man shrank under the attention and tried to hide behind the side of the lead truck. "We had to go back to our original positions to recover it because I'll be damned if some EPV thug is going to kill one of our people with a gun from my fucking platoon."

"Where're the targets?" Jambo demanded, scanning back and forth, his NVG's making him look like some sort of predatory insect.

"Right here, Master Sergeant," Gregory spoke up, emerging from between the trucks, pulling Laura Martijena out by the arm. The woman had a field bandage tied over her mouth and her face was twisted with fury. Her son was hanging off her belt, as if he was terrified to let go of her, but Chamberlain was just behind him, keeping watch on him.

"What's the deal?" Jambo asked, looking back and forth from Gregory to me. "Why is she cuffed?"

"Martijena was lying," I told him. "She wasn't kidnapped, she's an EPV sympathizer. She was here for Major Stevie." I spared a frown for Gregory. "But what's with the gag?"

"She kept yelling and giving away our position," Gregory explained, shrugging.

"We kept the trucks safe, sir," Chamberlain told me, managing to somehow look both smug and resentful all at once.

"Good fucking job, Chamberlain," I told him. "Where's Peterson? We got wounded."

"Later," Jambo insisted. "When we're on the choppers. For now, we need to get the hell out of here."

Several things happened at once. The first thing was the sound. An RPK light machine gun sounds very much like an AK since it fires the same round, and I didn't immediately know which it was, but I knew it was the enemy and I knew they were shooting at me. Or close enough. I'd been looking at Chamberlain, speaking to him, so I saw when he threw himself in front of Laura Martijena and her son, Paulo. It might have been training, might have been instinctive, or it might have been just who the kid was, but he put himself between the civilians and the threat.

And he died for it. The bullets punched through his throat, just above his SAPI plate and blood sprayed out the other side, splashing Laura Martijena in the face. She screamed through her gag and ran. Gregory had been holding her arm, but he'd taken a bullet as well, the round slapping into the center of his chest. I couldn't know it just then, but it had been stopped by his vest, though it hit him hard enough to make him let go of the woman.

I don't know if she was trying to get away from us and didn't even think about her son or if she just panicked, but she ran. I lunged for her but she was past and the boy was trying to follow. I grabbed him by the leg as I hit the ground and he fell flat, stretched out in front of me with his fingers scrabbling.

The Delta operators reacted first, because of course they did. I had just spotted the EPV soldiers coming out of the alley we had cut over to the apartment building in, three of them, though the one doing the damage was firing a drum-fed RPK from the shoulder. The stutter of the Delta M68's was deeper-throated than either AK's or our carbines because they were firing a heavier round with more powder behind it, the 6.8mm. Most of them had the carbines, but two had the light machine gun versions, drum-fed like the RPK, and they chopped into the EPV troops, spraying back and forth until all three were down.

And so was Laura Martijena.

I let out that breath I'd been holding with a feeling like none would ever replace it.

14

"The fucking Helta," Lance Corporal Ryan Quinn told me earnestly, "build their trucks just too damn sturdy."

As if to punctuate the statement, he fired off another two rounds at the incoming construction vehicle, sparks flashing as the tungsten slugs punched through the cab and down into the undercarriage. There were two dozen holes already through the front of the vehicle and yet it crawled on at about ten miles an hour only a few hundred yards from the wall. But this time, Quinn got lucky and the heavy vehicle ground to a halt, smoke pouring from something below it, either the electric drive motors or the power plant.

I shifted, trying to stay balanced on my perch atop the loading claw of the Helta earthmover, and put another round through the body of the truck, hoping I'd catch one of the Helta soldiers inside. We'd already killed the two who'd been crewing the plasma gun they'd mounted on the roof at the rear of the cargo compartment, but they'd pulled the weapon down inside and they were close enough now that....

"Fuck, they're bugging out!" I yelled to Quinn and the other

Rangers who'd climbed up on the earthmover Pops had used to block off the wall. No one else would care because they had their own targets.

The Tevynians had brought out a dozen of the things and we'd taken out the front rank, four of them, but it had brought them to within a hundred yards of the walls. Close enough for the infantry inside to make a run at us. They weren't tactical geniuses and had precious little discipline, but they understood the concept of cover thanks to the Helta and when they un-assed their vehicle, they headed for the only cover available, a low, sod wall separating the city from the landing field, limiting entry to the paved road.

There had to have been close to twenty of them squeezed into the cargo box of the vehicle and they scattered like cockroaches from the light, making it hard to decide on one target. I took down two and saw three more dropped by the Rangers, but the others threw themselves behind that wall and I cursed, thinking there had to be at least forty of the enemy soldiers hunkered down there now.

Lasers speared from behind the wall, most of them passing yards over our head, but a couple of the steadier shots sent sparks and flares of burning metal off the side of the earthmover. I leaned over the edge of the bucket, raised just high enough for us to clear the wall, and fired down on the trench behind the barrier, sending sprays of dirt flying upward and Tevynians diving for cover.

"Gunfighter One, do you copy?" The signal was distorted and weak, but clear enough to make out the words. "Gunfighter One, this is *Jambo*, do you copy? Over."

It was the communications officer whose name I couldn't ever recall so I wound up calling him Uhuru half the time.

"Good copy, *Jambo*," I replied. "Glad to hear your voice. Over."

"Gunfighter, we have taken out two of the enemy cruisers and we're playing a waiting game with the third, but we may be able to get you some orbital fire support. Over."

"The enemy is right on top of us," I told him, "and with their ECM jamming, I wouldn't want to try missiles. Are you in contact with the other shuttles? Any chance we can get some reinforcements in here? Over."

"Not anytime soon. They are still decisively engaged with the fighters. They're making headway, but no ETA on reinforcements. Anything else we can do? Over."

I scanned the plain, seeing the cyclopean walls of the enemy base rising over it and I smiled.

"Yeah, you think you could drop a low-power impulse gun round right on top of that Tevynian base? Over."

There was silence and I thought maybe I'd lost them, but then I considered that perhaps they were simply boggling at the brilliance of my idea. Or something. When the reply came, it wasn't Uhuru, it was Olivera.

"That's awful damn close, Andy," he told me.

I was distracted by the conversation, so I didn't notice the crew-served plasma gun being pushed up over the wall until it was already pointed our way.

"Look out!" Quinn yelled, opening fire on the gunner just a split second too late.

The plasma blast was a second sunrise, blinding and dazzling, impossibly close and unbearably hot even through the protection of my armor, and if it had hit within two or three yards of me, I would have been crisped, broiled inside the metal Svalinn stewpot. It didn't. Instead, it hit the Rangers on the far end of the earthmover and erased them from existence. The catastrophic conversion of the metal in their suit and the moisture in their body into superheated gas was a concussive thundercrack, a wave of pressure that tossed me off the edge of the bucket and sent me tumbling to the ground fifteen feet below.

I twisted in midair, barely getting my feet beneath me before I hit. The suit's servomotors absorbed most of the shock, but I bit my tongue and tasted blood and my eyes were filled with a fireworks show of stars.

"Yeah, it's fucking close," I snapped at Olivera, looking at what was left of the Ranger, "but if you don't do it, we aren't going to last until the shuttles can land." I stumbled backwards, only the suit's automatic functions keeping me on my feet. "Over."

"Roger that, Gunfighter. Give us a couple minutes."

Another plasma blast barely missed Quinn, but he didn't fall off, one hand gripping the side of the earthmover, the other firing off one burst after another from his rifle.

"I'll give you a couple minutes," I murmured, not bothering to transmit it. "I don't know if the Tevynians will be so accommodating."

"Sir," Pops called from the top of the next construction vehicle, further down the wall, "we're running low on ammo. We ain't Winchester yet, but the whole team is down to its last drum."

"Major Clanton," the Ranger squad leader Sgt. Miller radioed, sounding right on the edge of panic, "we have a KIA, sir! Specialist Nunez is dead, sir!"

He was on the last of the three vehicles, the farthest down the wall, and I suppose Quinn had reported the casualty to him.

"I know, Sergeant," I told him, keeping any impatience I might have felt out of my voice. To me, the Ranger was just another soldier, but to him, he or she was a friend. "I was right there. Any other casualties? How's the ammo situation in your squad?"

I jumped up onto the side of the earthmover, climbing back up to my firing position, as precarious as it had been.

"We got three Rangers with laser burns, sir, but nothing serious. But except for me and Specialist Crowder, everyone is on their last ammo drum."

"Single shot only," I ordered. "Don't fire unless you have a clear target. Don't target the vehicles until they're within three hundred meters, and aim for the wheels."

The view I got when I reached the top again was much more depressing than the one I'd left so abruptly. The vehicles were closer, advancing in a line in what wasn't a blinding tactical revelation for anyone who'd studied armor tactics but seemed downright innovative compared to what I'd seen from the Tevynians so far. They knew we had something that could take out their vehicles, something they hadn't seen before, but they weren't scared of it, or of anything else from what I could tell. Dying didn't bother them, and sending other people to die bothered them even less, but they wanted to win and they'd figured out that they could get closer by spreading out our fire to different targets.

"Sir," Quinn said to me. I glanced over, saw him still firing his rifle, speaking to me on a private frequency without looking away from his targets, "I don't think we're going to be able to hold them here."

Plasma splashed over the next construction vehicle over and one of the Delta team spun backwards, falling to the ground like a sack of shit, not even trying to get his feet beneath him.

"Yeah, I think you're right, Quinn," I admitted. "We're going to have to grab the Helta shipwrights and pull back to the other side of the enclosure, force the enemy to dismount and come meet us."

Which wouldn't change the fact we were low on ammo. But we couldn't just stand around here and get our asses fried. At the very least, I should send the flight crew and the shipwrights back away from the

"Gunfighter One, do you copy?" It was Uhuru again. "Over."

"I copy, *Jambo*. What's your status? Over."

"Gunfighter, you need to hunker down. Thirty seconds to impact."

I didn't bother to respond to the comms officer, instead switching to the command frequency.

"Everyone, get down!" I yelled, less for volume than to get their attention. "Hit the dirt and hold on!"

I led by example, throwing myself down a second time, braced so I didn't repeat the painful and annoying cut in my tongue. I wanted to go down on my belly and cover my head, but I had to keep an eye on the others and make sure no one had been so wrapped up in the battle that they didn't hear my order. And sure enough....

"Miller, get the fuck down!"

Maybe he had been up there trying to make sure he was the last of his squad down, but Jesus, what did he think *now* meant? This time he listened and obeyed, hopping down off the digging machine. I was so busy watching him, I almost missed the impulse gun strike. I'd just turned back to the front. A glowing white line had sprung to life while I looked away, connecting the heavens and the earth for the space of a second, the judgement of a vengeful God, something straight out of one of my father's hell-fire and brimstone sermons.

A dome of light rose into the sky above the wall, and though I couldn't see, I knew it had to be from the Tevynian military base. The light lingered for a moment, as if this truly was some other-worldly vision and not constrained by the laws of physics, but I knew that was an illusion and we were just waiting for the speed of sound to catch up with the speed of light.

And catch up it did. The shockwave slammed into the wall, cutting off the road to the city with a sound like a freight train running into the side of a mountain. Wood cracked and splintered and bits of rock blew outward, raining a vicious, spiteful hail down around us. The construction machines lurched and wobbled and tilted at the impact, and my stomach dropped at the thought of them toppling over sideways and burying us all underneath tons of steel, but they gradually settled back down on their globe-shaped wheels, shifting back and forth fitfully, as if they weren't quite sure it was all over.

"What the *fuck* was that?" Rodent asked, awe mixed with confusion in his voice. "Did we nuke them?"

"Up!" I yelled, jumping to my feet and grabbing the side of the earthmover, clambering up its side. "Over the top! Now! Before they have a chance to recover!"

I didn't hang back to lead from the rear, not just because that wasn't my style, but also because it didn't matter if no one followed, this had to get done now. The Tevynians would be stunned, disbelieving, not understanding what had hit them because they'd never seen the impulse gun in action before. But whatever else they were, they weren't cowards, and they wouldn't stay stunned forever.

It was hard getting over the wall, mostly because there wasn't much left of it, but what was left was leaning against the construction machines we'd parked there, propping it up just the way we'd meant to as a defense against the enemy. It was the third fucking time I'd had to jump off the top of the damned earthmover's bucket and I was getting pretty sick of it. My knees *hurt* despite the shock-absorbing pistons in the hips and knees of the suit, and my teeth clacked together hard enough I thought I tasted bits of enamel ground off of them.

My only consolation was that the Tevynians inside the cargo trucks were worse off. The shockwave had lifted vehicles up and flipped them end for end, scattering the soldiers out the back and sides, tossing them yards away, leaving most broken and twisted. And above where the base had been, rising out of the horizon like a tombstone, was a black mushroom cloud, not a nuke despite what Rodent had thought, but with the sheer kilotonnage of a tactical nuclear weapon just the same. And we were, I thought not without some melancholy, the first to ever use it on a planet.

Regrets later. First, I had some assholes to kill.

The base was gone, the vehicles were trashed, but the Tevynians who'd taken refuge in the ditch behind the turf wall could still be alive and kicking. They'd been buried under a few inches of dirt and debris, but some of them were digging themselves out even as I touched ground, pulling their laser rifles from beneath clods of soil. I switched the selector of my weapon to full-auto, dialing back the muzzle velocity to the minimum needed to penetrate their armor, and swept across the trench directly in front of me.

Thank God for those helmets. The helmets meant I didn't have to watch their eyes when the light went out of them, didn't have to see their faces contort when the electromagnetically-launched slugs chopped through their flesh and bone. I still would have done it. I couldn't have sworn that any of the individual Tevynians were bad people. They might have been kind to children and small animals, devoted to their families and faithful to the tenets of their religion, sterling examples of the best their people had to offer. But they were stuck in the Iron Age, flying starships and wielding lasers but no more advanced ethically than Attila the Hun, and if we didn't kill them, they'd sure as hell kill us.

The others hadn't abandoned me, hadn't given in to the shock of the orbital strike. Pops and Rodent were on either side of me, the rest of the Delta team filling in the line of what amounted to a firing squad. Some of the Ranger squad had joined us as well, though others still hung back behind the wall, slow to move. It was all right. We didn't need them. In seconds, there was no further movement from the trench.

"Cease fire," I ordered, then had to repeat it twice more before the last of us let off the trigger.

Silence descended over the scene, so complete I could hear nothing but the patter of dirt and rock falling out of the sky, out of the debris cloud still rising from the Tevynian base.

"I fucking repeat," Rodent said, staring at me, "what the fuck was that?"

"That's what we call fire support," Pops answered for me. "God help us all."

"Gunfighter One, this is Gunfighter Two," Dani Brooks said into my ear. "We're clear. The fighters made a run for the other side of the planet when they saw the blast. We'll be landing in a half an hour to reinforce your position. Three is headed back to orbit to grab repair parts and a crew to get your bird working again. Over."

"Roger that, Two." I sighed, the energy running out of me, the post-adrenaline shakes already starting. One good thing about the Svalinn, I might get weak in the knees, but it never would. "We'll be ready."

The gate, I saw, was gone. It had been blown inward, then bounced off the earthmover parked against it and tumbled in two pieces on the hard-packed road into the city. There was just enough of a gap between the vehicle and the wall for a man to squeeze through. Or a Helta.

I didn't recognize Fen-Sooyan at first, but I didn't know who else would risk coming out here, so I figured it had to be him. He was staring at the destruction, wide-eyed, his eyes going from the mushroom cloud to the Tevynian dead, then back to us.

"What have we done?" he asked, voice filled with fear.

"What you had to," I told him, too tired to try to be reassuring. "Just like the rest of us."

I hesitated, my hand hovering over the metal hatch before I finally knocked on it. I was exhausted, drained, the recently-treated burns still stinging beneath my fresh clothes and I didn't know what the hell I was doing here. But the Delta boys were having a drink I couldn't share, and I couldn't sit in my compartment and stew and I didn't know where else to go.

Julie Nieves answered. She was dressed in shorts and a tank top, what I recognized by now as her normal sleepwear. The room was dark behind her. Her eyebrow shot up at the sight of me.

"What you doing out and about this late?" she asked me. "You ground-pounders had a rough mission. I thought you'd be asleep by now."

"Couldn't," I said, leaning against the bulkhead just outside her door. The passage was empty, so I wasn't worried about anyone seeing us. And I wouldn't have been anyway. "I thought maybe you might want to go get some food...."

"I already ate," she told me, stepping closer. I could feel the heat coming off her skin, feel the warmth of her breath on my cheek. Her hand went behind my neck and she pulled me into her compartment and into a kiss. "Shut up and take me to bed, Major."

It was an order I was prepared to follow.

15

I STARED INTO THE UNSEEING EYES OF JACOB CHAMBERLAIN. Someone had thumbed them closed before we'd boarded the helicopters, but they'd popped back open on their own. I wanted to look away, but I couldn't. It would have been disrespectful to ignore him.

The only thing that could pull my gaze away from the dead Marine was the kid. His expression was as lifeless as Chamberlain's, and only the subtle rise and fall of his shoulders gave any sign he was more than a second corpse propped up in a seat. Jambo sat beside Paulo Martijena, a hand on the boy's shoulder, as if worried the kid might throw himself out the open door of the chopper. He'd ordered the body of Laura Martijena transported in the other bird, so the kid wouldn't be forced to stare at her the way I was staring at Chamberlain.

I was plugged into the helo's communications system, but no one was talking. There was nothing to say. Later, there would be. There would be a long and awkward explanation to Captain Glenn, reports to fill out, a very painful letter to write to Chamberlain's family, a memorial service on the company level and a smaller, more personal one we'd have on the platoon level where I'd have to run things. And I'd have to pretend that Lance Corporal Jacob Chamberlain was a valuable Marine who had always been an asset to the platoon instead of a constant pain in everyone's ass.

"Two minutes out," the pilot announced.

I looked up, surprised we'd already made it to the base camp. And then I was surprised because it was daytime. The sun had risen between the time we'd lifted off from Caracas and arrived in the mountains outside the city, but it seemed like we'd lost time along the way, as if the trip had taken days instead of just minutes.

There was a welcoming committee at the landing pad this time, Citizens' Militia soldiers arranged on either side of Carlos Martijena, their weapons carried at low port. I met Jambo's eyes as we stepped out of the helo.

"Is there gonna be trouble?" I asked, my voice dull and lifeless, sounding foreign to me, as if it was coming from a stranger.

"No," he assured me, pain from his wound tugging at the corners of his mouth. "It's an honor guard."

Paulo's face was ashen when he saw his father, pure fear.

"Jesus Christ," I hissed to the Delta NCO, reluctantly following him as he stepped down from the Blackhawk to the cracked surface of what had once been a parking lot for the tourist area. "We can't hand this kid over to Martijena. He's terrified of him."

The rest of the Delta team was disembarking on the other side of the bird, keeping it between them and the CM forces despite what Jambo had said about them. My Marines didn't move, waiting on my order, one I wasn't ready to give.

"He won't hurt his son," Jambo insisted, his mouth barely moving. "Just be cool."

"How do you know he won't hurt him?" I demanded, probably too loud since we were only about thirty yards from the general, but I was nearly past caring.

Jambo rounded on me, eyes flaring, for once losing the chill demeanor he'd shown even under fire.

"Because he knows I'd kill him if he did."

I shut up, and just in time.

"Paulo, my son," Martijena said, kneeling down and opening his arms. "I thank Mother Mary and all the saints that you are safe."

The boy didn't run away when Jambo let go of him, which either meant I was overestimating how afraid Paulo was of his father or underestimating how much control Martijena had over his son. The boy stepped forward slowly, fatalistically, and the general swept him into a hug, lifting him up as he stood to face us. His expression over his son's shoulder was one of real gratitude, and a sense of relief took at least a bit of the weight off my shoulders. The general might have been a cynical, manipulative killer, but I did believe he loved the boy.

"I am so sorry about your mother, my son. Believe me when I say I will punish the people responsible for her death. I will not rest until this country is rid of them."

He was staring at us as he said it and I chose to take it as a promise to support the US effort to defeat the EPV instead of the alternative, that he blamed *us* for his wife's death and was going to kick us out of the country.

"I understand you lost one of your own bringing my son back to me," Martijena said, and this time he was speaking directly to me. I wondered how he'd known, but I supposed the helicopter pilots must have radioed ahead to him.

"Yes, sir." I didn't want to talk to him. I was afraid I'd say something stupid and fuck up the whole thing, because I really *wanted* to say something stupid. "His name was Jacob Chamberlain. He was a very young man."

Shit. I wasn't much more than a young man myself.

"He will be remembered," Martijena promised me. "My men will retrieve Laura's body from the aircraft."

He nodded to one of his lieutenants, a short, broad-shouldered man with a scraggly beard unsuccessfully trying to hide nasty pockmarks. The pockmarked man snapped an order in Spanish to the honor guard and they jogged across the pavement, slinging their weapons over their shoulders, circling around to the second Blackhawk. My Marines were watching them, rifles at low ready but hands on their pistol grips, sullen resentment in their eyes.

I said nothing, didn't even bother to watch them unload her body. I was staring at Martijena.

"She wanted to be there," I blurted, unable to hold it in. Jambo glared at me but I ignored it. "She was one of them."

I expected him to rail and rage at me, to be furious, but his face lengthened, his age finally showing.

"I know. I suppose I knew from the beginning." Sadness dripped off of his words and I almost empathized with the old man who'd thought his young wife and young son would be a new start. "We lie to ourselves for love, though, don't we?"

And then they were gone. The whole lot of them, the dead woman, the boy still in the general's arms all loaded into the vehicles at the edge of the landing pad and left us behind. I watched them until the last of the trucks were out of sight, until the I couldn't hear the rumble of the engines anymore.

"That's it, then?" I asked. I wasn't sure if I was asking Jambo or God, but it was Jambo who answered.

"What did you expect?" he wondered. "A hug? We did our job."

"I guess I expected a promise," I told him. "I mean, we did this to secure his help, to make sure he would back us even though we aren't officially backing him. I mean, I won't even be able to tell Chamberlain's parents how he died. I won't be able to put him in for the medal he deserves for saving the kid. I guess I wanted Martijena to say this was enough, that he'd keep his word."

Jambo's laugh was a low rumble, almost a growl, but there was no anger behind his dark eyes, just a naked cynicism.

"That's not how life works, Andy," he told me. "Ain't no guarantees. We do what we have to do and hope it means something in the end."

I wanted to snap back at him, to tell him that was a shitty way of looking at the world, but then I remembered who I was talking to and how many shitholes like this he'd spent his career fighting in.

"Come on," he said, slapping me on the shoulder, then wincing as the motion aggravated the pain in his arm. "Let's get out of here so I can go get this looked at by a professional."

"Don't let Doc Peterson hear you say that," I warned him. "You know how Navy corpsmen are." I shrugged. "Or maybe you don't, since you're army."

The pilots had already restarted the helicopters and the rotors were beginning to spin up as the two of us stepped into the bird.

"Hey," Jambo said, leaning in closer to be heard over the rising whine of the engines, "I'm really sorry about your Marine. I know what it's like. If you need to talk about it, I'm gonna be around. And don't think you can get away with ignoring it and hoping it'll go away, because it don't."

I nodded. I didn't want to think about it, but I was going to have to, eventually.

"Thanks."

"Also..." he trailed off, hesitating for a moment, and when he continued, he had to almost yell to be heard over the engines. "We're gonna need support from time to time on operations here.

Nothing like this again, I'm hoping, but I like having someone around I can count on. You mind if I ask for your platoon again? Or have you had enough of this shit?"

It was a good question. Gregory was sitting beside me, eyes half closed, like he might nod off at any point. I leaned over to him, nudging his arm.

"The Delta guys say they might want to use us again. What do you think about that?"

He shrugged.

"Shit sir, it sucks about Chamberlain and all, but being honest, this was the most fun I've had since we got here. And it sure as hell beats working with the SEALs."

Well, I couldn't argue with that.

16

I HATED FLYING COMMERCIAL.

After riding in shuttles that could break Mach 20 on reentry and starships travelling faster than light, it seemed ludicrous to spend four and a half hours in the air and change planes to get from Boise to Austin. At least I could afford first class, though the money from the TV show wasn't going to last forever and maybe I should think about selling my house in Vegas and renting a place somewhere closer to the Alpha Site.

This was going to be my life now. It hadn't quite sunk in yet. No more arguments with my agent, no more touring the conventions, pimping my book and the show, no more late-night video chat sessions with the Propellers, my author Mastermind group. Three of us had TV or movie deals now, and there'd been a time not so long ago when I'd thought that was the most noteworthy organization I'd ever belong to.

"Hey, excuse me, dude."

I blinked, focusing on my immediate surroundings and the young man sitting across the aisle from me. He was college age, I guessed, a notion confirmed by the evidence of the University of

Texas sweatshirt he was wearing, and had the general lean fitness of an athlete. His family must be at least mildly well-off to spring for the first class ticket. I was guessing baseball or lacrosse, but then I realized I hadn't answered him.

"Yes?" I replied, pulling half of "More Than a Feeling" out of my right ear to hear him better.

"Sorry to bother you," he said, "but you look just like that guy I saw on the news. The writer who met the aliens and got the Medal of Honor."

"I get that a lot," I said, smiling with what I hoped was a deflection.

"Oh, so you're like, not him?" he asked, the air going out of him.

I sighed. I wanted to lie to him, but he seemed so damned disappointed. And he reminded me of someone, someone young and idealistic and annoying who I'd once known.

"No, I get it a lot because I *am* him."

He frowned, started to say something and then visibly stalled and tried again.

"So, you *are* the dude?"

"Jeff Bridges is the Dude, but I'm Andy Clanton."

"Yeah, that's the name!" the kid said, snapping his fingers, as if he'd thought of it instead of me telling him. "Man, I just wanted to tell you...." I braced myself, thinking it would be yet another person thanking me for my service, or maybe saying how much they envied me the chance to fly to the stars, or sometimes complaining about getting us all involved in an interstellar war. "... how much I enjoy your TV show. United Stars is the best, dude!"

"Thanks." I tried hard not to clench my teeth. "Appreciate it. I'm gonna listen to my music now, if you don't mind. Had a rough week."

Boston assaulted my ears once again and I brought up my cell phone, paying attention to its screen so I wouldn't have to listen to anyone else. I brought up the web browser, figuring that I'd paid extra for the Wi-Fi, so I may as well use it.

I had, I discovered, somewhere in the neighborhood of four thousand unread emails and they were going to stay that way for now, even the ones from my agent. *Especially* the ones from my agent. I opened up a search window and considered whether I wanted to check the latest news about international relations. Things had cooled down some from when we'd flown the *Jambo* over every major nation to make it clear we could take any of them down if we wanted to, but only in the sense that no one was shooting at anyone for the time being. There was still a lot of screaming and shouting and finger-pointing. I didn't really want to read about it.

Instead, I typed in a name. I don't know why I hadn't checked on him before. Maybe a guilty conscience, maybe a strong desire to put that night out of my memory forever.

Paulo Martijena. I hit enter.

I don't know what I expected. I know what I feared. I feared I'd find out he'd been killed in the war, or gone over to the Communists insurgents who had taken the place of the EPV after the war.

Instead, I found an article and a picture. He was around the same age as the Longhorn sitting across from me, though slimmer and darker. And he was also a student in an American college. The University of Miami. According to the article, he'd spent the last two years as a member of the Justice for Venezuela Foundation, an organization formed to lobby the US government and the International Criminal Court to prosecute what they considered to be war crimes by the Martijena regime and to protest for free elections in the country. Which still hadn't happened due to frequent "unrest." Good for Paulo.

His relationship with his father, according to the article, was "strained."

Shit. Welcome to the club, Uncle Charlie.

Allie looked good for her age. Even the disapproving glare hadn't changed after all these years.

"I didn't expect to see you back after you dropped Zack off early from your visit," she said, leaning against the door frame of what I could rightly describe as a mansion. My rental car looked incredibly out of place in the long, curved driveway.

"Yeah, I'm really sorry about that," I said. "I was called up by the government to go out of...the Solar System."

It felt weird saying it, weirder still that she didn't even question it.

"I suppose," she allowed, "that's going to be the new normal, huh?"

"I'm afraid so. But I'd like to try to make it up to him if you'd let me." I waved at the car. "I know it's last minute, but it's the weekend and I thought maybe I could at least like go get some dinner with him? Maybe take him to see a Longhorn game?"

Her frown softened and she arched an eyebrow.

"Let's start with the dinner," she conceded. "We'll see about the rest after that." She leaned back into the house and called out. "Zack! It's your father."

He didn't exactly run to the door, but he was smiling, which was a good sign.

"Sorry I had to leave early before, son," I told him.

"That's okay," he said, waving it off. "I mean, you had to go to another solar system." He snorted. "Not a lot of guys can say that about their dad, right?"

"You wanna go grab some food?" I asked him. I glanced

behind me. It was getting dark and my body was telling me I was hungry, though whether it was for dinner or breakfast I wasn't sure. "Wherever you want."

"The Peached Tortilla?" he asked.

"Sure." I was kind of relieved he hadn't asked for sushi. I hated sushi.

"Let me go grab my shoes," he said and jogged back upstairs toward his room.

"You want to come in?" Allie asked, waving a hand invitingly.

"Maybe next time," I begged off. "He'll be back in a second."

She gave me a thin smile.

"Andy, I don't bite. Much. Anymore."

"I know," I admitted. "But like you say, one step at a time, right?"

"Ready!" Zack announced, barreling down the stairs. He'd grabbed a jacket along with his shoes, though it didn't feel cold enough for one to me. "Seeya, Mom!"

"Love you, honey," she called as we headed down the front walk, and an old instinct almost had me saying it back to her before I latched my jaws shut and kept walking.

Zack said nothing as we got into the rental SUV, kept silent until I'd taken us down the driveway and out into the street, and I knew that was a bad sign.

"Dad," he finally spoke up, "you know, you never did finish that story you were telling me about Venezuela."

My gaze flickered from the Audi approaching the four-way stop to my son beside me.

"I will finish it," I told him, "I promise. But do you think I could tell you another story first? About a mission a lot farther way than Venezuela? Because this one has a lot happier ending."

ACKNOWLEDGMENTS

Special thanks to Walt Robillard for help with all the military gear and procedures that have changed since I served back in the Paleolithic era.

ABOUT RICK PARTLOW

Rick Partlow is that rarest of species, a native Floridian. Born in Tampa, he attended Florida Southern College and graduated with a degree in History and a commission in the US Army as an Infantry officer.

His lifelong love of science fiction began with Have Space Suit---Will Travel and the other Heinlein juveniles and traveled through Clifford Simak, Asimov, Clarke and on to William Gibson, Walter Jon Williams and Peter F Hamilton. And somewhere, submerged in the worlds of others, Rick began to create his own worlds.

He has written over 40 books in ten different series, and his short stories have been included in twelve different anthologies.

He is currently writing the best-selling Drop Trooper series for Aethon Books, a mil-SF alien invasion series and the ongoing Interstellar Bounty Hunter series.

He lives in central Florida with his wife, two children and a willful mutt of a dog. Besides writing and reading science fiction and fantasy, he enjoys outdoor photography, hiking and camping.

Made in the USA
Coppell, TX
03 October 2020

39155852R10277